DEADLOCK

ALSO BY IRIS JOHANSEN

Dark Summer
Quicksand
Silent Thunder (with Roy Johansen)
Pandora's Daughter
Stalemate
An Unexpected Song
Killer Dreams
On the Run
Countdown
Blind Alley
Firestorm
Fatal Tide
Dead Aim
No One to Trust
Body of Lies
Final Target
The Search
The Killing Game
The Face of Deception
And Then You Die
Long After Midnight
The Ugly Duckling
Lion's Bride
Dark Rider
Midnight Warrior
The Beloved Scoundrel

The Magnificent Rogue
The Tiger Prince
Last Bridge Home
The Golden Barbarian
Reap the Wind
Storm Winds
Wind Dancer

DEADLOCK

IRIS JOHANSEN

**Doubleday Large Print
Home Library Edition**

ST. MARTIN'S PRESS ✿ NEW YORK

ISBN-13: 978-1-60751-808-2

**This Large Print Book carries the
Seal of Approval of N.A.V.H.**

DEADLOCK

ONE

Darlov, Afghanistan

"That's the end of it." Joel Levy stepped back from the bed of the truck with a sigh of satisfaction. "Now, can we get the hell out of here, Emily? I don't like the look of those clouds. All we need is to get caught in a snowstorm to make this trip a total waste of time."

"It's not been a waste of time," Emily Hudson said as she zipped up her fleece-lined jacket. But Joel was right, the temperature had dropped dramatically in the last hour, and the air had a bite to it. "Just because we didn't find anything that we haven't seen before doesn't mean that those artifacts aren't worth saving. It means something to these people, this country."

"Save the lecture for your class at the university," Joel said. "All I know is that we drove all the way up here into the mountains to this little museum that no one but us seems to give a damn about. And no wonder. Most of those artifacts are less than a hundred years old."

"And you wanted to find Alexander's sword or a new version of the Bible." Emily made a face at him. "And I'm not lecturing you. Do you think I'm nuts? I know it would be hopeless. I don't know how you got your doctorate. You're no scholar, you're an Indiana Jones wannabe."

"You're just jealous." Joel grinned. "You want to be Indiana Jones, too, but you're weighed down by paperwork and responsibility. All that stuff is sapping the joy of life out of you. You should never have taken this job, Emily."

She shrugged. "It needed doing."

"And the U.N. wasn't willing to pay anyone else enough to risk their necks like we do." He corrected himself, "Like you do. After this job, I'm going home to settle down and write my memoirs."

"No publisher would buy it. You're only twenty-seven."

"But I've aged in the last five years I've worked with you. I'll lie a little, embroider a little, and then Spielberg will buy my book for the movies."

"Good luck." Joel was always threatening to quit, but he never did. He had a fine mind, but he was too restless for university work and liked moving from country to country. He'd certainly had enough of that working with Emily. The U.N. sent them to the hot spots and war zones of the world to catalog, verify, and move the contents of museums to special preservation centers until it was considered safe to return the cultural treasures to their home bases. Not only did Joel have a Ph.D. in Archaeology and Antiquities, but he was fluent in Hebrew and several other Middle Eastern languages, making him invaluable to Emily. "But if you stay home, Maggie will make you marry her. No more ships that pass in the night."

He flinched. "Maybe I'll go on one more job with you."

"Is that the last load, Emily?" Al Turner stuck his head out the window from the driver's seat. "We'd better hit it. It looks like snow."

"I'm surrounded by weathermen," Emily said as she turned back to the museum. "That's it, Al. You and Don go on. Joel and I will take one more look around, then follow you in the other truck."

"Don't be too long," Al said. "You don't want to be caught by weather in these hills. I know the U.N. said they'd cleared the area of bandits, but they've been wrong before."

No one knew that better than Emily. She and Joel had almost been blown up in Baghdad when the military had assured them that the area the museum occupied was in a safe zone. Joel swore that the U.N. had pressured the military to make a hasty judgment. The artifacts in that museum had been priceless, and the U.N. had not wanted either theft or damage done as a result of the war effort. It would have been "awkward."

The museum had been booby-trapped, and there had not only been treasures lost, but Emily had ended up in the military hospital in Germany with a concussion.

Like Joel, she was now wary about trusting any reports of peace in any region. "It's been pretty peaceful so far. And I just got a call that our military escort is almost here."

Al scowled. "They should have been here hours ago. They were supposed to meet us before we even entered this zone."

"That's what I told them. They stopped to help remove a land mine at a village near here. You'll probably run into them before you've gone far." She waved. "Get out of here, Al. I'll see you in Kabul."

She watched the truck go down the hill and then lifted her gaze to the mountains of the Hindu Kush to the north. Magnificent mountains whose rough paths had been walked by Alexander the Great, Russian invaders, and local warlords. They always looked austere, but with those storm clouds hovering over the peaks, they were particularly forbidding. She turned to Joel. "Let's go back and check the cellar again. We were working so fast that I didn't get a chance to examine the walls to see if there were any cubbyholes where the curator might have hidden anything."

He followed her into the building. "Why wouldn't he have taken anything valuable with him?"

"He might have done it. The report said he'd been killed by bandits while he was trying to get out of the area. But you know we've found hidden artifacts before." It wasn't that unusual for museum staffs to pilfer artifacts, then blame warring forces. "Come on. Maybe you'll find the Holy Grail."

"Not likely." He glanced around at the empty cases of the first-floor exhibition room. "We didn't find one display case that could have preserved anything ancient. Cheap, very cheap. I can't figure out why they even had a museum out here in the boondocks. There's only a little village in the valley, and that's practically deserted after all the bandit activity in the area."

That had puzzled Emily, too. The area had just been opened to the U.N. after a violent year of bandit and Taliban activity. It was strange that the museum had appeared to be untouched by the violence taking place around it, but perhaps stranger that it existed here at all. "I was told the museum was funded by Aman

Nemid, a member of the National Council who was born in that village. He's very proud of it. He was the one who requested we be sent here to save it."

"Save what? I think that curator would have considered an old print of *Casablanca* an art treasure."

"It was. I liked that movie." She was already on her way downstairs. "I know, I'm a sentimental slob."

"Yep," he said as he followed her. "You need someone to jar you into the real world. I can't understand why you're not a cynical, hard-bitten shrew, considering the job you do."

Her brows rose. "You mean I'm not? What a concession coming from you."

"Well, I have to keep you in line. You'd be impossible to work with if I didn't."

"I am cynical," she said quietly. "I just can't let it poison me. There are scumbags walking this earth, but there are good people too. I figure if I look straight at the goal ahead, maybe I won't see the ugliness." She smiled as she glanced back over her shoulder. "And good company helps the bad medicine go down. You qualify at least seventy percent of the time."

"Ninety percent."

"Eighty-five." She was looking around the dim cellar. It had been used as a storage area as in most museums, and they had packed up everything that qualified as a possible artifact. There were rusting farm tools thrown in the corner, but they couldn't have been over twenty years old and had probably been used in the garden in the back. The few wooden storage boxes piled across the way had already been searched and deemed not worth transporting. "You check that wall. I'll do this one. If you see any cracks, any thickness that might conceal a compartment, give a shout."

"I know the procedure." Joel moved toward the wall and turned on his flashlight. "But we're not going to find anything. Give it up, Emily."

"Your approval rating has just gone down five points. Be quiet and just look." She didn't blame Joel for being reluctant to waste time here. This job had gone wrong from the time they had arrived in Afghanistan. They were supposed to have been sent to Iraq again but had been diverted to Kabul. Then there was the snafu with the military escort, and when they arrived here, the museum had been deserted and the supposedly priceless artifacts as disappointing in value as Joel claimed. Well, all she could do was do the job and hope the next one went better. She turned on her own flashlight. "I want to get out of here, too. But I need to leave knowing that I didn't miss anything."

"Yes, boss," Joel said. "It's only fair to tell you that I'm rethinking the hard-bitten shrew."

"I'll live with it." She started going over the walls, first visually, then with the tips of her fingers. "I'll just watch a DVD of *Casablanca* when I get back to town, and maybe I'll remember that some men are willing to sacrifice what they want now and then."

"That hurt. When you were down with flu, didn't I do your paperwork on that job in Chevnov? I'd say that was a gigantic sacrifice."

"You only did it because you wanted to use it to blackmail me for the rest of my career." It was a lie. Joel had been as caring as a mother with her child when she had been ill. He had found her a decent doctor and finished the job in Chevnov himself. No one could be a better friend than Joel had proved to be. She'd be devastated both personally and professionally if she lost him. "Check those walls."

"Okay. Okay." He shined his beam on the walls. "But I bet Humphrey Bogart wouldn't have wasted his time. There's no drama in this. Boring."

"But Ingrid Bergman would have done it in a heartbeat. She knew about duty."

Joel sighed and repeated, "Boring."

"I'm done," Joel said. "Nary a cache in sight. Do you need any help?"

"No. I'll only be a few more minutes." She moved a few feet, her gaze narrowing on the wall. "You'd just get in my way."

"If you take any longer, I'll build a bonfire of those trunks." He blew on his hands. "We've only been down here ten minutes, and it's like an icebox."

"A few more minutes," she repeated absently, her fingertips probing the rough stone wall.

Joel leaned back against the wall, watching her. She probably didn't even feel the cold, he thought. Once Emily focused on a project, nothing existed but the work at hand. That was the reason she was admired and respected by military and diplomats alike in this part of the world. She was brilliant and dedicated and had credentials out of the stratosphere. She was only thirty, but she had been working for the U.N. since before she had gotten her degree. At first, she worked under Oxford Professor Cordwain, but she had taken over after he opted out eighteen months later.

More power to her. He wouldn't have her job on a bet. He didn't mind being on the team, but he liked his personal life, and Emily had none. Every time she started to have a tentative relationship, she was sent to another part of the world.

Why hadn't he tried to get her into bed? They worked together with a closeness that should have lent itself to a more sexual intimacy. God knows, she was attractive. Maybe not in the usual sense. She was tall and thin, but with a grace and strength that were kind of sexy. Her brown eyes were wide set and slanted, giving her a faintly exotic appeal. She wore little makeup, but her skin was baby soft and clear, and her short blond-brown hair was always clean and shiny.

So why hadn't he hit on her?

Because he'd sensed the fragility beneath the strength. In spite of what she faced every day, she was a dreamer, and dreamers could be hurt. She wanted to believe in a better world that had all the beauty of the past, and ignored the fact that the past had been as violent as the present.

No, she didn't ignore it. But she refused to dwell on it. Maybe that was why he liked her so damn much. She wanted the world to be good and was doing something about it. She was right, he only wanted the adventure, the excitement, and the friendship that Emily gave him.

And occasionally, when he was on leave, a roll in the hay with Maggie Nevowitz, who was cute and bawdy and not at all fragile.

"Nothing." Emily took a step back. "I didn't really expect it."

"Then will you tell me why I'm freezing my balls off down here?"

Her smile lit her face. "Because it could

have been." She started for the stairs. "The most magical words in the language."

He followed her. "No, the most magical words are heat, food, and sex." He turned up his collar as they went outside. "Brrr." His gaze went to the mountains. "It's coming fast. Look at those clouds."

"Then let's get going." She jumped into the passenger seat of the truck. "At the speed you drive, we should be out of the province before the storm catches up to us. And the military escort will meet us long before then. It should be okay."

"Yeah." He didn't move, his eyes on the roiling gray-black clouds. He was feeling a chill that had nothing to do with the temperature. His chest was tight, and he was experiencing a weird panicky sensation. It was as if those threatening clouds were alive and stalking him.

Stupid.

"Sure." He tore his gaze away from the approaching storm. "It'll be okay."

"They're coming." Borg fell down beside Staunton on the side of the hill overlooking the road. "Just a few minutes away." He lifted his rifle. "Shall I blow out the tires to make them stop?"

"No, they'll stop." Staunton lifted his binoculars. "They have a reason. We don't want to damage the artifacts in the back if they skid off the road." He focused his glasses on the front seat of the approaching truck. "Yes, there she is in the passenger seat. Emily Hudson. She's smiling and talking to the man next to her. What's his name? Levy. No sexual relationship, but they're friends of long standing. And her attitude toward him leads me to believe our reports are accurate."

"They're going to see it soon," Borg said. "We should be ready."

"I'm ready." Staunton said. "I'm always ready." He put the binoculars down. "Stop worrying, Borg."

"We can't delay that escort any longer. They're going to be right on top of us within thirty minutes."

"Thirty minutes can be a long time. I've prepared everything. It will all go well."

"Sure." Borg clenched his hand on the stock of the rifle. Staunton had ice water running through his veins. The bastard

was always cool and certain of everything. "Do you think she has it in that
truck?"

"I hope she does." He smiled. "It will be
so much easier for her if it's there."

"For Pete's sake, will you turn off Bruce
Springsteen?" Joel asked. "You played him
all the way here. I need a break."

"You're never satisfied." She started
searching her iPod. "I'd think you'd appreciate the difference between The Boss and
Casablanca. 'Born in the U.S.A.' is definitely not sentimental."

"But he goes both ways. 'Dancing in the
Dark' is a little too—what the shit!" He
jammed on the brakes. "It's Al's truck!"

Emily's eyes widened in horror. "My
God."

The truck was turned over and artifacts
were strewn all over the gravel road and
bordering ditches.

"I don't see Al or Don." Joel opened the
door. "Where the hell are they?"

"No!" Emily grabbed his arm. "Don't get
out of the truck. Get us out of here."

"No way. I have to find—"

"You know what we're supposed to do

when we run into anything unusual. We'll come back as soon as we run into the escort. This could be a trap."

"And it could be a hit-and-run by those son-of-a-bitchin' bandits or Taliban. If our guys are hurt, they could bleed to death before we can get back to them." He grabbed his gun from the glove box and jumped to the ground. "Stay here. I'll check it out." He strode toward the overturned truck. "Call for help."

If he was going to do it, then she couldn't let him go in alone. She grabbed her Glock and got out of the truck. "Be careful, dammit. Don't go barging in and—" She stopped as she saw the blood.

A thin red stream was running toward them from behind the truck.

She forgot about being careful. She was around the truck before Joel got there.

"God in heaven," she whispered.

Al was crumpled near the ditch. His head had been almost torn from his body by a barrage of bullets. Don was half under the truck as if he'd tried to get away from the attack. He hadn't succeeded. Bullet holes peppered his entire torso.

"Butchers," Joel said huskily. "They didn't have a chance."

Emily tore her gaze from the bodies. *Bodies.* So impersonal a word. These had been her friends and companions. "We can't do anything for them. We have to get out of here."

He didn't move. "Sons of bitches."

Emily grabbed him by the arm. "We have to leave. Now. They could still be—"

"And they are." She whirled to see a tall, loose-limbed man with sandy hair coming toward her, an AK-47 cradled casually in the crook of his arm. "Don't lift your guns. This weapon could cut you in two before either of you could press the trigger."

"You killed them?" She stared at him in bewildered horror. "Why? If you wanted anything in the truck, they would have let you have it. Those are our orders. We're not supposed to fight to protect those artifacts."

"But, love, I needed a distraction." He raised his thick sandy brows. "How else could I be sure to engage your attention?"

His voice was smooth, casual, and had a faint Australian accent. In comparison, his words were shockingly ugly and cold. "Now lay your guns down on the ground. Very carefully."

Emily hesitated. "Do it, Joel." She put her gun down.

Joel didn't move for an instant, then reluctantly laid his gun down, too.

"Very smart." The Australian lifted his fingers to his lips and gave a piercing whistle. "Time to check your cargo. Stand very still while we do it, and you may live for a while longer."

"Bastard," Joel said. "You killed them in cold blood."

"Of course. It's always best to keep a cool head when violence is involved." He glanced at the six men who had streamed down from the hill. "Borg, be quick about it. I want to know in the next five minutes." He turned back to Joel. "If you'd been a little cooler, we might have lost you. I saw the lady trying to make you stay in the truck. If you'd been less emotionally involved, you could have—"

"It wasn't his fault," Emily interrupted. "I would probably have done the same thing."

"You're defending him even in these circumstances? You must be very good friends. I can't tell you how happy that makes me."

Emily was watching his men carelessly tossing artifacts out of the back of the truck. She flinched as a three-foot-high vase broke. "Tell me what you're looking for. You don't have to destroy everything."

"How devoted you are to doing your job. Preserve and protect."

"That's right." She had to figure a way to get out of this. The situation was too dangerous to make mistakes. "Let me protect the rest of these artifacts. Tell me what you want."

"I will if we don't find it." He called, "Borg?"

"It's not here, Staunton," A short, burly man with thinning brown hair jumped to the ground and motioned to the other men to leave the truck. "I thought maybe in the vase, but it wasn't there either."

"Look, there wasn't anything valuable in this museum," Emily said. "If anyone told you there was, they lied."

"I was told there was a very valuable item, and my source is very reliable." He shook his head. "Which means that you're lying."

"I have no reason to lie. I told you, our orders are to give up any artifacts if it means risking personnel. What are you looking for?"

He tilted his head and studied her expression. "Zelov's hammer."

"What?"

"Maybe you don't recognize it by its name. But I'm sure you'd recognize the treasure hidden in the handle. You're an expert in Russian artifacts. Was it too tempting for you to give up?"

"We don't know what the hell you're talking about," Joel said. "There weren't any tools on display at the museum. Certainly none with any hidden compartments."

"No tools at all?"

"There were used gardening tools in the cellar of the museum," Emily said. "Go check those out."

"I will," Staunton said. "You're being very cooperative. I'm impressed."

"Then let Joel leave. You don't have to keep both of us as hostages."

Joel began to curse. "No way."

"He doesn't like the idea," Staunton said. "Neither do I." He smiled. "But I do like the idea of getting out of here. We've run out of time." He turned away. "I'll call the helicopter. Bring them."

Borg was coming toward them. Emily tensed. Going anywhere with these murderers might be a death sentence. She had no choice but to make a move.

Her gun that she'd dropped at Staunton's order.

She fell to the ground, reaching for it.

"Oh no, bitch." Borg swung viciously, and the stock of his rifle struck her in the temple.

Darkness.

"Wake up. I'm getting impatient."

Emily tried to open her eyes, but the pain was too great.

"Wake up!" She was lifted by her shoulders and slammed against the wall.

Her eyes flew open.

"That's better." Staunton was standing before her. "I thought you might be playing possum. I've actually been very lenient, but it's time we got down to business. My employer wants answers and isn't at all pleased with me."

Australian accent, deadly words.

Don and Al lying butchered by the side of the road.

The memory jarred her into full consciousness. Her gaze flew to Staunton's face. "You killed them."

"We've already gone into that. You're beginning to bore me. We've already moved on." He shook his head. "And I've already lost time because you were stupid enough to try and go for that gun. I do hate waiting."

She glanced around her. She appeared to be in a hut of some kind. "Where am I?"

"The mountains. Actually quite near the stronghold of my good friends who used to rob and pillage this area."

"Bandits."

"Yes. Though Shafir Ali regards himself as a warlord. Unfortunately, the national government doesn't agree. He's a little too barbaric for them."

"Then I can see why you consider them friends. Why didn't you get them to rob our trucks?"

"I couldn't trust them. But I had them do their part."

"The killings?"

"No, I did that, but of course I'll give them credit."

"Or blame. You don't think the U.N. is going to sit still for this, do you?"

"No, but this country is still barbaric in many ways. The civilized world doesn't always know how to handle barbarians, and the U.N. is nauseatingly civilized. There have been bandits wreaking destruction here for centuries. Very few are brought to justice because they know these mountains." He smiled. "I hate to disappoint you, but there won't be any cavalry coming to your rescue."

"You're the one who will be disappointed. Westerners don't just disappear without a cry being raised."

"I'll take my chances."

"Why? It's crazy that you—" She stopped as fear surged through her. "Where's Joel? What have you done with him?"

"Nothing yet. He's just been placed in the hut next door. I thought it more convenient."

"Convenient for what?"

"Persuasion." He squatted beside her, and his hand wrapped around her throat. "For him. For you."

"Don't touch me." She moistened her lips. "I told you that I don't have what you want. Did you check the basement of the museum?"

"Yes, we went immediately to search it. There was no hammer, though the other tools were of Russian make." His hand tightened on her throat. "A conspicuous absence, wouldn't you say?"

"I thought they were garden tools. They appeared to have been used. They might be. There was nothing of value in that museum. You have to be wrong."

"I could be. But my employer believes it was there before your arrival. He said he was absolutely certain it was. That makes it necessary for me to make very sure. He said to explore every option . . . extensively."

"We don't know anything about any hammer."

"You'll have to convince me." He drew even closer to her, his blue eyes glittering in his long face. "And I'm going to be very hard to convince."

"Use a lie detector. Give me truth drugs."

"There are ways to beat both of them. I'm an old-fashioned man. I believe traditional methods are best." His voice was soft. "Shall I tell you what I'm going to do? I'm going to take your friend Joel Levy and hurt him beyond your ability to imagine. When you think he's had enough, all you have to do is tell me what I want to know."

Panic.

"What big eyes you have," Staunton said. "You're frightened. It's an awesome responsibility to have the power to stop another's pain, isn't it? Tell me now, and we won't start it."

"Why Joel?" she asked hoarsely. "Why not me?"

"Your turn may come. I believe this will be much more effective. Besides, I've always found that torturing women has bad side effects. For some reason, it's regarded as particularly heinous and rouses opinion against you. Seems unfair, doesn't it? Sexist. But if by chance you ever got free, I'd be hunted down without mercy. No, you'll tell me where it is after a few days of our persuading Levy."

"I *can't* tell you," she said, agonized. "I don't know anything about it."

"I almost believe you. But I have to be sure." He rose to his feet. "I'm going into Levy's hut now. Borg is waiting for me. Don't try to leave. There's a guard outside, and my bandit friends are camped a short distance from here in the hills." He drew a machete out of the holster at his hip. "I think I'll start on his fingers first. You'll be able to hear him screaming."

"Don't do it. There's no sense to it. He doesn't know anything. I don't know anything. Please."

"You're begging?"

"Yes," she said unevenly. "Don't hurt him."

He was staring at her. "You feel things with such intensity. What a delight you'd be to break. Begging is always satisfying, but it's not enough." He headed for the door. "If you're stubborn, we'll have to move on to the bigger stuff soon. Then I'll bring you in to watch."

"But we don't *know* anything."

He was gone.

Dear God in heaven. Panic was flooding through her. It was a nightmare. How could she stop it? How could she convince him? Why wouldn't the bastard believe her? Maybe he was bluffing. Maybe he only wanted to scare her.

And then she heard the first scream.

TWO

**Two weeks later
Kabul, Afghanistan**

"The director called again," Ralph Moore said when Ted Ferguson came into the hotel room. "He wanted to know why he couldn't reach your cell phone. I told him there must be satellite interference."

"Good man," Ferguson said. "Not that he'll believe it."

"You should have taken the call."

"And what was I to tell him? That we still can't find Emily Hudson and Joel Levy? I told him that yesterday and the day before. How the hell could he expect the CIA to find them when the military and U.N. are coming up zero? Even if we knew where they were, these damn blizzards would keep us from moving on them." He scowled. "I'll be lucky to have a job when this is over."

Moore shrugged. "The Company is having tremendous pressure put on it by Congress and the media. You know that, Ferguson."

"I know that we're drawing a blank. Why aren't our informants able to give us information? It's as if Hudson and Levy dropped off the face of the earth. If they're not dead, why haven't we had a demand for ransom? All the forensic evidence around the trucks indicated that it was a probable bandit hit."

"They probably are dead."

"Then show me the bodies, dammit. Let me turn the Marines loose on whoever did it."

"And get you off the hook."

He nodded curtly. "I'm as mad as anyone else at the murder and abduction of American citizens, but I won't be made the bad guy. I have to get them out of Afghanistan or show the world they're dead."

"I've called MI6 in London, but they still don't have any leads," Moore said. "None of their Middle East informants have come up with any info. We may be out of luck."

"No way." He dropped down in his chair and reached for his phone. "I can't give up yet. Is John Garrett still living in London?"

Moore straightened in his chair. "Garrett?"

"Is he?"

"As far as I know."

"Then get me reservations there in the next few hours."

"Garrett won't help. He stopped doing jobs for us three years ago. And you can't rely on money. He's got money to burn these days."

"Tell me something I don't know. Smuggling evidently pays exorbitantly well," Ferguson said grimly. "But he'll do this job. I'll find a way to make sure he does. I *need* him. He spent years in Afghanistan when he was a kid and has kept his contacts. And he knows those mountains like the back of his hand."

"I'll bet you don't get him. He was royally pissed at us after Colombia."

And who could blame him, Ferguson

thought. The whole scenario had gone wrong, and the CIA had been forced to leave Garrett to fight his own way out of a very sticky situation. Well, maybe not forced, but he'd regarded Garrett as expendable at the time. "I'll make him an offer he can't refuse."

"What?"

"How the hell do I know? I'll decide that on the way to London." He was dialing as he spoke. He'd had the number on hand for the last week, when it had become obvious what a disaster this case was shaping up to be. And involving Garrett might cause the situation to spiral out of control even more. There was no question that he was efficient and deadly in the field, but he could be volatile. In his late teens, Garrett had been a mercenary; later, he had become involved in smuggling and high-tech embezzlement. He had allowed them to use him occasionally when he'd been low on funds, but he'd always been a loose cannon. He had a sudden memory of Garrett as he'd last seen him in that jungle in Colombia: stripped to the waist, sweating, muscles gleaming with explosive tension, his dark eyes glittering with rage when he'd realized they were leaving him. Hell, he might not even take the call.

Garrett picked up after four rings. "You must be sweating blood, Ferguson."

"Things are . . . difficult. I'd like to come and discuss it with you."

"Such politeness. You used to demand or use blackmail."

"But you always managed to get your own back. May I come?"

Garrett was silent a moment. "You're not my favorite person. Why do you think I'd let you?"

"Because you didn't ignore my call. Because you may be a son of a bitch, but you're not petty." He paused. "And because I thought you might be getting bored. You lived on the edge too long."

Another silence. "Come ahead. But you're probably going to be wasting your time. I'm not inclined to do you any favors."

"I'm not asking for anything but information."

"Bullshit. I've been down that road before." He hung up.

Ferguson let out his breath as he

punched the OFF button. He hadn't realized how tense he'd been until Garrett
had agreed to see him. "It's a go," he told
Moore. "Get me Garrett's file. I want to
read it on the plane. I've got to find a
hook."

"Ferguson is coming," Garrett said as
he turned to Jack Dardon, who had just
come up on deck. "I think I'll go back to
London."

"Good. You've been lousy company."
Dardon sat down in a deck chair. "Is he
going to beg and plead?"

"Not if he can use coercion." Garrett
got up and went to the rail and looked out
at the coast of Greenland. "He thinks
I'm bored."

"You are. So am I. We should go to
Amsterdam and find you a nice talented
whore to spark a little interest."

"You can get whores anywhere."

"But I like the Dutch."

"Then you go to Amsterdam."

"Maybe I will. I'm not like you. I like things
easy." Dardon was silent a moment. "Don't
get involved, Garrett. It could be one big
headache."

He shrugged. "I'm just going to listen to Ferguson."

"Is that why you've been on the phone for the past two days with Karif Barouk?"

"Karif's an old friend. I spent four years with him and his family with his tribe in the mountains when I was a boy."

"So you told me. And the two of you did everything from ambushing Russian troops to raising hell in Kabul. It would be natural to call on him if you needed information, wouldn't it?"

"I'm curious." He turned and walked back to his deck chair and picked up the newspaper that had photos of Emily Hudson and Joel Levy blazoned on the front page. "And I don't like puzzles that have missing pieces. It annoys me."

"And that's all?"

"No." He gazed down at the photo of Emily Hudson. "Sometimes I get pissed off. God knows, I know that nothing about life is fair. Look at me. I've been a selfish son of a bitch since I was a kid and crawled out of the gutter. Yet here I am now, safe and on Easy Street because I fought and clawed and learned every dirty trick in the book." He tapped the picture of Emily Hudson. "She seems to have done everything right. Worked her way through school and still went on youth trips to help third-world countries. She spent most of her adult life risking her neck trying to preserve some kind of cultural heritage for people who would just as soon kill her as look at her." His lips twisted. "As a reward, she's probably going to die, if she's not dead already."

"As you said, life's not fair." Dardon tilted his head. "But why is this particular inequity bothering you so much?"

Garrett had been asking himself that same question. He didn't know either Hudson or Levy, and those sob stories the media had been broadcasting for the last two weeks shouldn't have roused the anger he was feeling. It was just another atrocity in a world filled with them. He'd thought he was hard enough to be totally immune.

He shrugged. "Maybe I've had too much time to think about it. The life of leisure isn't what it's cracked up to be. I'm used to being busy."

"Is that all?"

"No." He tossed the paper back on the chair. "I like her face."

"Your face is getting thin," Staunton said. "You're not eating. I don't like that."

"What does it matter?" Emily said dully. "You don't care whether I live or die."

"Oh, but I do. My employer would be upset if you died before you told me where you hid the hammer."

Emily didn't answer. It did no good to deny it. He wouldn't listen. "Then he's going to be upset. I can't tell you what I don't know. What kind of a monster would pay you to do this? Who is he?"

"I have certain business ethics. It wouldn't be honorable of me to give you his name."

"His name is Satan."

Staunton chuckled. "I won't tell him you're so disrespectful. He might take offense." Then his smile faded. "Yes, I don't like your condition at all." He covered her with her blanket. "You have to keep warm. It's still snowing outside. And you're not sleeping. No more tears, no more screams, no begging me to spare that poor lad. But of course there's not much of him left to spare, is there?"

"No," Emily whispered. "And may God send you straight to hell."

"Not nice, Emily. Now I want you to eat today. If you don't, I'll find a new and more excruciating way to hurt Levy."

"You couldn't hurt him any more than you have."

"You know better than that. You've watched me do it. It's only been two weeks. A few burns, a few body parts . . . Did you enjoy yesterday, Emily?"

"Enjoy?" She repeated the word in disbelief. "You burned out his eyes, you bastard."

"You remember?"

"Of course, I remember."

"Nothing else?"

She stared at him in bewilderment. "What?"

"I've noticed you try to block out certain choice episodes. Like the one yesterday."

"You son of a bitch."

"Now that showed some spirit. Eat your food. I want you fresh and strong when I take you to Levy's hut." He stood up. "Twenty minutes, Emily."

She closed her eyes. She desperately wanted to cry. But he was right; the tears would no longer come. She had wept too much, drowned in horror and helplessness and guilt.

But it wasn't over. Staunton always kept his word. He would find a way to punish her by tormenting that poor shell of the man who had once been Joel Levy.

She sat up and began to eat.

"Nice place," Ferguson said as he looked around the large living room whose west wall was entirely composed of tall windows overlooking the sea. "But not as palatial as I thought you'd choose, considering your present affluence."

"You mean ill-gotten gains, don't you?" Garrett smiled. "You're being tactful. How amusing. Would you like a drink?"

"No." Ferguson felt a ripple of annoyance as he watched Garrett pour himself a whiskey. This wasn't the sweating, fierce man of the last time they'd met. The bastard was so damn confident and at home in this house that had probably cost as much as Ferguson's entire pension would bring him. Was he jealous? Why not?

Garrett had it all. He was dressed simply in jeans and a white cable-knit sweater, but he wore them with casual elegance. He was in his late thirties, tall and muscular, and he moved with the litheness that Ferguson remembered. His brown-black hair was clipped close, and his dark eyes dominated a face that effortlessly held one's attention. And, dammit, not only was he smart, he was more lethal than any man Ferguson had ever met. He'd even intimidated Ferguson on occasion. "The Company could have stopped you from settling here, you know. All we would have had to do was drop a few words in the right ears. Criminals aren't welcome here in England. After all, you're a smuggler and a mercenary."

"Am I?" He shook his head. "I'm retired, Ferguson. And if you want to try to blacklist me with Her Majesty's government, go ahead. I don't care."

He was telling the truth. "I'm not threatening you."

Garrett smiled. "Not unless it would do you some good. You're not handling this well, Ferguson. I'm getting impatient. Get down to it."

Ferguson pulled a file out of his brief-case. "Emily Hudson, Joel Levy. Kid-napped two weeks ago by bandits in the Hindu Kush. We need to get them back."

"And?"

"I need help."

"Yes, you do. You'll be lucky if they're still alive."

"Damn you, we've done everything we could to—" He stopped. "You know the area, and you have contacts. I wondered if we could talk you into using those con-tacts to get us information about the ban-dits."

"That's better. To the point and almost polite." Garrett took a sip of his whiskey. "They weren't taken by bandits."

Ferguson stiffened. "What?"

"There was some bandit involvement, but they were taken by foreigners."

"The killings were done by AK-47s of Russian make used by the bandits in the area. The footprints by the trucks were made by boots that came from a village in those mountains."

"Red herrings."

"Then who?"

Garrett shook his head. "Not bandits. Not Taliban. Not Al Qaeda. No one from the Middle East. Maybe someone English, Irish, European . . . I don't know."

"Then who does, dammit?"

Garrett shrugged. "I've told you all I could find out. I can continue to try, but it will take time. You don't have time."

"But you could find out more if you were on the ground there?"

"Maybe." He gazed thoughtfully down into his drink. "Yes, probably."

Ferguson wanted to strangle the bastard. "You could find them?"

"Yes, I think so."

"Then go in and get them," Ferguson said through his teeth.

Garrett leaned back in his chair. "Are you ordering me?"

"You're damn right."

"It appears the gloves are off." Garrett's eyes narrowed on Ferguson's face. "And you wouldn't do it unless you thought you could get away with it. You can't blackmail me, and you can't bribe me. I've put myself beyond your reach. What's left?"

"Jack Dardon," Ferguson said. "He's

worked for you for the last six years, and you've been friends since the old days. You don't have many friends, do you?"

"Enough. Where's this leading?"

"We can't touch you, but Dardon has left a few strings that we can unravel. He evidently wanted to be independent and set up his own smuggling operation after you retired. We have information that would cause him a good bit of trouble with the Greek and Russian governments."

"Evidence?"

Ferguson nodded. "Affidavits, photos. Sufficient to put him behind bars for a good many years. Would you like to see the file?"

Garrett slowly shook his head. "I don't think you'd bluff under these circumstances."

"No bluff. Go to Afghanistan and get Hudson and Levy out."

"And you'll turn over Dardon's file and any hard evidence?"

Ferguson nodded. "Dardon isn't important to us."

"Except as a tool. We're all tools to you. I wondered what you'd come up with to tip the balance."

Garrett's tone was without expression, and Ferguson had a sinking feeling that he'd failed. Garrett was going to tell him to go to hell. Maybe Dardon wasn't as good a friend as he'd hoped. There was no anger, no intensity, none of the ferocity that he'd remembered in Garrett.

"Don't doubt I'll do it, Garrett."

"You probably would." Garrett finished his drink and stood up. "So I'll tell you what you're going to do, Ferguson. You call off all those Marines and U.N. forces who might fill me full of bullets. You make sure everyone knows I'm one of the good guys . . . in this particular instance. Your men stay out of the area. I don't want you anywhere near me unless I yell for help. And when I do call, you'd better come. It had better not be another Colombia."

"I had no choice but to leave you there. You made it out okay," he said. "You're going to do it?"

Garrett didn't answer him. "Get out, Ferguson."

Ferguson repeated. "You're going to do it?"

Garrett went over to the desk and scrawled a phone number on a Post-it note. "I'm leaving tonight for Afghanistan. When I arrive there, I want to be told by my banker in Switzerland that they've received that file and any other evidence you have on Dardon."

"Not until the job's finished."

"It won't even begin unless you give over the file." He handed him the Post-it. "And I'll have Dardon at the bank to make sure that you've complied. Be certain you turn over everything."

"And what if I don't?"

Garrett stared him in the eye. "I'll come after you. You know how good I am. You sent me on enough missions."

Ferguson quickly looked away. "You may be getting the best of the deal." He rose to his feet. "I don't even know if you can find them."

"I'll find them. I have a few leads."

Ferguson's eyes widened. "You lied to me. What leads?"

"None I'd turn over to you or the military to botch. One blunder, and you'd get them killed. Hell, *I'll* be lucky if I can get them out in one piece. I have to move fast. I made my reservations for Kabul when I docked this morning."

"You son of a bitch. You let me go through this, and you were going anyway?"

Garrett shrugged. "I wanted to know what you were going to use to force me to go." He headed for the door. "I thought I might as well get something out of this mess besides the possibility of being chopped up and spread over that mountain range."

"We have to talk, Emily."

She opened her eyes to see Staunton kneeling beside her. "It doesn't do me any good to talk to you. You don't listen."

"Then I'll do the talking, questioning actually, and you have only to answer."

"I don't know where it is."

"That wasn't the question." He reached out and gently stroked her cheek. "I've grown very fond of you in these weeks. I don't believe I've ever felt so . . . intimate with anyone. What a brave, lovely woman you are."

She shuddered at his touch but didn't move. For the past few days he'd been touching her, stroking her, almost lovingly. She'd ignored it. She wouldn't be the one to suffer if she fought him.

Staunton sighed. "Yes, it will upset me enormously if I have to hurt you."

"Liar."

"But it will," he said softly. "I've been avoiding it by concentrating on Levy, but you just won't help me."

"I can't help you."

"I'm coming close to believing you, but my employer won't be satisfied unless I tell him what I've done to you to verify that." His forefinger traced the curve of her upper lip. "So we have a choice to make."

"What choice?"

"I'm sure you've noticed that Levy is not responding to . . . stimuli. He's dying, Emily."

"Yes."

"And that means that there will be no possibility that you'll tell me what I need to know to stop his suffering. I'll have no excuse." His fingers moved to stroke her throat. "So I decided to leave the choice to you. I can continue to rouse him to pain for another few days. I might be able to do it. I'm very good."

"Or?"

"Or I can spare him and switch my

efforts to you. You know what that will mean. You or Levy. Decide."

Yes, she knew what that would mean. It was her turn. She had known it would be coming.

She moistened her lips. "Me."

He sighed. "I thought that you'd want to spare him. I want you to know that I'm going to regret what I have to do to you."

She shook her head.

"You don't believe me? I'll prove it. I'll give you twenty-four hours before I start." He bent his head and kissed her lingeringly. "Do you know with women it starts with rape? Sexual violation seems to be the ultimate humiliation. But it also has to be brutal enough to bring pain. It would hurt me to be brutal to you in that particular act, so I'm going to turn you over to Shafir Ali the leader of my bandit friends. He's been very cooperative and needs a reward. He has no problem with brutality. I understand he beat his wife to death for not being sufficiently enthusiastic in the sack. He'll probably want to share you with his friends later, but tomorrow night he's going to devote himself to you. I'll deliver you to his tent at exactly this time tomorrow night." He kissed her again and rose to his feet. "You might spend the next twenty-four hours thinking about what Shafir will be doing to you. I'll go and tell Levy that he won't suffer anymore."

Emily watched him leave the hut. She had thought she was too numb, too calloused by Joel's agony, to be afraid, but she was wrong. Panic was rising within her.

God, let her get away from here. Or let her have the courage not to give Staunton the satisfaction of making her break under the pain.

A shot rang out from Joel's hut next door.

No!

She arched upward as if the bullet had struck her.

I'll tell Levy he won't have to suffer anymore.

She should have guessed.

Dear God, she should have known.

THREE

"It's time." Staunton pulled her to her feet. "He's ready for you. Are you ready for him?"

Emily didn't answer.

"I find I'm reluctant to turn you over to him. I've gotten quite possessive of you. I want even your pain to come from me." Staunton slipped her jacket on her. "Mustn't get cold. There's another blizzard starting." He whirled her to face him. "One more time. Where's Zelov's hammer?"

She shook her head.

"Oh, Emily, I did try." He lowered his head, and his lips brushed hers.

Her teeth bit down savagely on his lower lip.

"Son of a bitch!" His fist lashed out and knocked her to the floor. His lip was torn and bleeding. "You little savage. You'll pay for that."

"At least it will be me who pays, not Joel," she said fiercely. "And it was worth it."

"I'll make very sure it won't be worth it." He jerked her to her feet and pushed her toward the door. "I wish I could start now, but you have an appointment to keep."

The snow was stinging her face, and she couldn't see more than a foot in front of her as Staunton pulled her away from the hut toward the bandit encampment a short distance away.

He pulled up the flap of a tent whose rear was sheltered from the storm by huge rocks. "Here she is, Shafir." He pushed her into the tent. "Don't kill her. Anything else is permissible." He touched his lip. "Even desirable."

"She stung you?" The bandit smiled as he rose to his feet. Shafir Ali was huge, with a full black beard and bushy eyebrows. "I thought better of you, Staunton.

I'll have to teach you how to make her behave. By morning she'll be ready to kiss your feet."

"That would be amusing. I look forward to it." He turned away. "Get to work on her." He pulled the flap closed as he left the tent.

"He's angry with you," Shafir said. "I can understand. Women should not be allowed out of control. If you were mine, I'd keep you naked and chained until you learned submission. Perhaps if I do a good job tonight, he'll let me have you for a while." He started toward her. "Come on, bite me, hit me. I'll show you how a man should treat a whore who doesn't know her place." He put his hands on her shoulders. "Are you afraid of me? You should be."

He stank of sweat and leather, and his grip on her shoulders was excruciating.

Ignore it. Fight him. Try to get away. This might be her last hope. Once Staunton came for her in the morning, her chances of escaping would be nonexistent.

"Tell me you want it," he said. "Tell me you want me to fuck you." When she didn't speak, his grip tightened. "Beg me."

Her knee swung up and connected with his balls. As he grunted with pain, she tore away from him and ran toward the tent entrance. He caught her before she reached it and backhanded her. She fell to the hard dirt that formed the floor of the tent. He hit her again.

Her head was ringing as he flipped her over and she was barely able to see him through the haze of pain.

"You run from me?" He took his knife out of the holster at his waist. "I'll just have to make sure you can't do that again." He plunged the knife into the side of her left calf.

She screamed as the pain tore through her.

"That's right," he said as he pulled the knife out and stabbed it into the earth next to them, burying the point in the dirt. "Staunton will like to hear you scream. I'll just keep this handy in case I want to prick you again." He tore open her jacket and jerked open her shirt. "Maybe your breasts . . ." He bent his head, his face flushed. "You bit Staunton until he bled. Do you think he'd be pleased if I bit this pretty nipple and made you bleed?'

The knife he'd buried in the earth was within her reach.

Wait. He was liking this, wanting to hurt her. Pretend to be helpless and in pain. Distract him.

Pain seared her nipple as his teeth sank savagely into it. The moan she gave was no pretense.

He lifted his head and licked the blood off her breast. His eyes were glazed with pleasure. "Now the other one."

His teeth bit deep.

She cried out. She arched upward.

And her hand closed on the hilt of the knife. She plunged it into his side.

He made a sound like a wounded bull as his head jerked up.

She pushed away from him and scrambled to her knees.

Get out of the tent. Get away from him.

But the knife thrust hadn't stopped him. He was moving, rising to his knees, reaching for the AK-47 leaning against the wall of the tent. "Bitch. I'll fill you full of—"

His head snapped back as an arm encircled his neck from behind. With one twist, the man who had seized him broke his neck.

Emily stared, unable to move, stunned. It had happened too fast. She couldn't take it in. She hadn't seen the man until the moment he had killed. High cheekbones, tight lips, an expression beyond intensity. Dark clothes, dark hair, dark eyes glittering in the lantern light.

Angel of Death.

"Grab the AK-47 and any ammunition you can find." The stanger dragged the huge bulk of Shafir Ali's body toward the pallet and dropped a blanket over it. "I'll be back for you in a minute."

"Wait. Who are you?"

"John Garrett. The CIA sent me to get you and Levy out."

Freedom for her but not for Joel. "You're too late. Joel is dead," she said dully.

"I found that out when I got here and made contact today." He moved toward the back of the tent and started to slip through the slit he'd made in the fabric. "Fasten up your clothes and get that gun."

She hurriedly fastened her shirt and jacket and stood up. She almost fell as agony shot through her calf. She'd been so stunned she'd forgotten the wound. She wouldn't forget it again. It was throbbing with pain. She rolled up her pants. Ugly but not much blood. His knife had gone through the fatty part of her calf. She had no time to bandage it now. She limped across the tent and grabbed the AK-47. There was ammunition in the chest beside the pallet. She grabbed that, too.

"We can go now." Garrett had returned. He was wearing a backpack and carrying a rifle. "Good, you're wearing boots. That will help." He reached into his pocket and pulled out gloves and a wool hat. "Put these on. Be sure to keep the hat on. Heat escapes through your head."

"I know that." She pulled the hat down over her ears. "I practically grew up in the woods."

"Good. But the woods aren't as wild as this terrain. We'll climb over the rocks behind the tent and take the path that leads to the ledge that borders the mountain."

She put on the gloves. "There's a blizzard. Do you have transport?"

"Not anywhere close. If I'd had transport, I wouldn't have been able to get near this place. They would have known it, and you would have been taken away. Let's go."

She started toward him and stopped. "I have to do something first."

He frowned impatiently. "What?"

She lifted her shaking hand to her head. It was hard to think. "There's a man. Staunton. I have to kill him."

"I'm sure you have reason, but there's no time. Let's go."

"You don't understand. He can't be allowed to live. I have to kill him."

He swore. "I'm not going to risk my neck and yours because you want revenge. Get it later."

"There's a blizzard. He thinks I'm being raped and tortured by that scum. He wouldn't expect it. If I don't do it now, he may get away."

"No." Garrett crossed the tent and stood before her. "Listen to me." He stared intently into her eyes, and said softly, "You're not thinking straight. You're hurt and almost in shock. It's not going to happen. Not now. If I have to do it, I'll knock you out and carry you out of here."

He would do it. She could sense the

violence in him. She had watched him murder a man.

Angel of Death.

"You know about killing," she said unevenly. "If I go with you now, will you help me find him again so that I can kill him?"

Garrett gazed at her for a long moment. "You must have had a hell of a time here."

"Will you help me?"

He shrugged. "Why not?" He started toward the slit in the tent. "Now can we put some distance between us and these bastards? I want to get a good head start before the C-4 goes off in six hours."

"Explosives?"

"I set enough charges in the tents and the vehicles to cut down the pursuit."

"The huts, too?"

"No, I couldn't get close enough." His lips twisted. "So you can't count on Staunton's being blown up. Sorry."

"You should be sorry." She limped toward him. "No one deserves it more."

"What's wrong with your leg?"

She nodded at the dead man. "Shafir didn't like me running from him. He stabbed me in the calf as punishment. Didn't you see it happen?"

"No, I came in when you stuck the knife in him. Are you going to be able to walk?"

"It's not bad. I can walk."

He glanced at the bandit. "Son of a bitch."

"Yes." She met Garrett's eyes. "But he's nothing compared to Staunton."

He studied her face before he turned away. "Then maybe it's a good thing Staunton's going to be a dead man soon." He disappeared through the slit in the tent.

Yes, Garrett could help her. Those last words had been quiet and yet the deadliness could not have been more evident.

Angel of Death . . .

Emily and Garrett had only gotten a few yards beyond the boulders when a man appeared out of the driving snow. "You've got her?"

"Yes, I told you to get the hell out of here, Karif. I can handle it from now on."

"Don't be selfish." The man grinned, his dark eyes bright. "This is the first fun I've had since you left my mountains. I've been bored."

"Get out, dammit. Go home and keep your mouth shut."

"As you like. I just wanted to make sure that risking my neck was worthwhile." He nodded at Emily. "He'll get you home. Trust him."

He didn't wait for an answer but turned and a moment later was hidden by the thick veil of snow.

She stared after him. "He's Afghan. Can you trust him?"

"Hell, yes. It was Karif who managed to find out where you were. But I told him to go home and keep his mouth shut, dammit. The tribes don't like anyone dealing with outsiders. That's why the CIA wasn't able to find you." He started forward down the path. "Come on. We're losing time."

"Okay?" Garrett called back to her.

She could barely discern him on the path ahead of her. "Yes." It was a lie. The snow was stinging Emily's cheeks, and she was shaking with cold. They had been walking for hours, and exhaustion was dragging at her every limb. "How much farther?"

"Another ten minutes, and we'll get to

the place where I hid the jeep," Garrett said. "Keep moving."

Keep moving, she thought numbly. Easy to say. She'd be lucky just to stay on her feet. One good thing was that she could no longer feel the pain in her calf. Or maybe that wasn't good. Frostbite?

"Do you need help?" Garrett shouted back at her.

Yes. But if Garrett was forced to help her, it would slow them both down. "No." She lowered her head to keep the snow from blinding her and lurched forward. "Let's just get to that damn jeep."

"Yell if you change your mind. I don't want to have to come back and pick you up out of a drift."

"You won't. Shut up. It's hard to breathe in this wind, much less talk."

He was silent. "Sorry. I'll try to be less verbose." He disappeared beyond the veil of snow. "The next thing you'll hear me say is that we've made it."

If those words were ever spoken, Emily thought. Ten minutes he had said, but it seemed more like ten hours.

Keep moving.

Don't fall.

It would be over soon.

She couldn't see.

Snow. Wind. Ice.

Don't fall.

"Come on." Garrett was suddenly beside her, his arm around her waist. "It's done. Just a few feet more."

She could make out the dim outline of the jeep a short distance away. "Thank God."

He was opening the door of the jeep and half-lifting her into the passenger seat. "You'll be warm as soon as I can rev up the motor and get some heat going." He was running around the vehicle and jumping into the driver's seat. "Hold on."

Heat? The concept seemed totally alien at this moment. Lord, she wished she could stop shaking. "Where are you taking me?"

He turned on the ignition. It sputtered and didn't fire. He tried it again and it roared to life. "Out of these mountains. I have a friend waiting in a helicopter in the foothills."

"How could he fly in this weather?"

"With difficulty. But it's not a blizzard farther south. It won't be this bad once we get out of the mountains. We'll be able to make it to the plains, then we'll go by ground to Kabul." He reached over the backseat and grabbed a blanket. "Wrap up in this. It may help until the heater starts functioning." He frowned. "Stop shaking, dammit."

"Don't be stupid. Don't you think I would if I could?" She nestled beneath the blanket. She could barely feel the woolen cover, and it didn't stop the chills. "Do you think they're after us yet?"

"No, the C-4 hasn't had time to go off, and it's only been a little over four hours. We should have time to make it to the helicopter. It would have to be pure bad luck if someone barged into Shafir's tent, and since his intentions toward you were probably known, I doubt if that would happen."

"Four hours. It seems longer . . ." She leaned back on the headrest. "I'm very . . . tired."

"You can't go to sleep," he said sharply. "I have to drive, and I can't keep checking on you to make sure you're not going into hypothermia."

"I won't go to sleep."

"Damn right you won't. Talk to me. Keep talking."

"What do you want me to say?"

"I don't care. Tell me about your family. Your father was a well-known photographer, wasn't he?"

"How did you know that?"

"You're famous. The media has made you the U.N. poster figure of the decade. When you get back to civilization, the paparazzi are going to be fighting to get at you."

It hadn't occurred to her that she would be facing the nightmare of publicity. "No," she whispered. "I can't deal with that now."

"Don't think about it. I wanted to jar you awake, not cause you to flip out. Tell me about your father."

"You really don't want to know."

"Talk to me."

"He was wonderful. We were best friends. He was fascinated by antiquities and took me along on all his photo shoots around the world."

"You liked it?"

"Yes, but I liked it more when he did the wildlife shoots for *National Geographic*. We were by ourselves then. We'd spend weeks in the woods, tracking and camping out until he got just the right photo."

"Sounds great. Your mother?"

"She divorced him when I was two. She died four years later."

"Is your father still alive?"

"He was killed in a car crash when I was in college." Terrible night. Heartbreaking night.

"You still miss him."

"Of course I do. I loved him. I'll always miss him. You don't forget the people you love just because they're not with you. You must know that."

"Do I?"

She rubbed her temple. "I don't know whether you do or not. I don't know anything about you."

"You don't have to know anything about me. All you have to know is that for this moment, this time, you're safe with me." He shrugged. "The rest can come later. Are you any warmer?"

"Not yet."

"That's not good. We're going to have to work on it. Keep talking. Tell me about your first assignment with the U.N. Where was it?"

"Ethiopia. So sad . . . All that parched earth and those dying children. I don't want to think of that now."

"Then your next assignment.

"I'm tired. I promise I won't go to sleep."

"Keep talking. Your next assignment."

He wouldn't give up, and she was too weary to argue. She tried to focus. "Yugoslavia. The museum had been almost destroyed, but there were still some vases that had been left in the ruins. A few of them were priceless, and we had to . . ."

"There's the helicopter." Garrett stomped on the brakes. "Let's get you on board."

"I don't have to talk anymore?" she asked hazily. She hadn't noticed, but the snow had been gradually lessening. She could clearly see the red-and-white helicopter several yards away. She opened the passenger door. "That's good. I don't see how you stood—Bored. You must have been bored. . . ."

"I wasn't bored." He helped her out of the jeep and called to the man who had just gotten out of the helicopter. "Open that door, Dardon. She's not in good shape." He lifted her in his arms and strode toward the helicopter. "We need to get her to a doctor."

"Hypothermia?"

"Maybe. I'm betting on delayed shock."

They were talking about her, she realized. "I'm just . . . cold."

"Yeah," Garrett said. "And we'll take care of that."

"Where's Levy?" Dardon asked.

"He didn't make it." Garrett carefully placed her on the floor at the back of the helicopter. "He died the day before I got there."

"I should have known," Emily whispered. "Staunton didn't need him any longer. Choice. He gave me a choice. I should have known."

"Shh," Garrett said. "Get us out of here, Dardon."

"Right." Dardon hurried up to the cockpit. "There are some blankets in the storage chest."

"I should have known."

"Emily, I need you to focus," Garrett said quietly. "Forget about Levy. We have to concentrate on making sure you're all right."

Forget about Joel? "I can't forget . . ."

He was unzipping her jacket. "What are you doing?"

"I have to get you out of these damp clothes and get you warm. Okay?"

"I don't care. It doesn't matter." She closed her eyes, but all she could see was Staunton's expression in that moment when he had walked out of her hut. "I didn't want him to hurt anymore. I should have known."

"Whatever." He was quickly stripping her. "But Levy is dead, and you're alive. You're going to stay alive. I didn't go to all this trouble to let you go now."

"I don't want to die. I can't—" She inhaled sharply.

Warm naked flesh against her cool naked flesh.

Her eyes flew open.

"Body heat," he said tersely. "It's the quickest way to warm you." He drew a blanket over both of them. "I'd like to say there's nothing sexual about it, but that wouldn't be true. I'm not capable of that kind of objectivity. All I can promise is that I won't let anything I feel get in the way. Now relax."

Relax? "I can't do that. It's . . . strange."

"I couldn't agree more." His hand stroked her hair back from her temple. "I can't remember when I've been naked with a woman who was as bruised and bloody as you. It should put me off." His lips tightened. "Instead, all it does is make me want to go out and kill whoever did it to you."

His dark hair was tousled, and his eyes glittered in his lean face. She was so close she could see the sensual curve of his lips and felt the wiry hair that thatched his chest. It made her chest feel tight and it was hard to breathe. She looked away. "You did kill one of them."

"Ah, yes, Shafir."

"And you promised you'd help me with Staunton." She glanced back at him. "You're going to keep your word?"

"I don't usually break a promise."

"That's not really an answer. You might have told me anything I wanted to hear to get me away from that place. I need an answer."

"What would you do if I walked away and didn't keep my word?"

"I'd still go after him. It would just take me longer."

"I'm going to call Ferguson with the CIA and tell him where Staunton is located. He may be able to get him for you."

"They weren't able to get him before this. They weren't able to save Joel." She paused. "You said you worked with the CIA only sometimes. Why this time?"

"Ferguson blackmailed me."

"How?"

He smiled. "Then you'd be able to black-mail me, too."

"You don't seem to be the kind of man who could be forced to do anything."

"You'd be surprised. My philosophy has always been to do what you have to do and make sure you're paid in full later."

"And you had to go after me and Joel."

"That's right." His hand was still stroking her hair with a gossamer-light touch. "I had to do it. I had no choice."

"But you have a choice whether you'll help me now."

"Not really. I do keep my word. In my business, it was necessary to inspire trust and make a profit."

"What kind of business?"

"Smuggling and other nefarious enter-prises."

"You're a crook?"

"Retired." He smiled. "But my background made me uniquely qualified to find you and get you out. Are you warmer now?"

She was warmer, she realized with surprise. She didn't know at what point the chill had vanished, but her body, pressed against Garrett's, felt almost flushed with heat. "Yes, you can let me go now."

"For a little while." He sat up and tucked the blanket around her. "The chill will probably come back." He got up and moved over to the storage chest. "But I need to get you fixed up first."

He was totally at ease with his nudity, she thought as she watched him rummage through the storage chest. He was a beautiful specimen of a man—tight, hard buttocks, powerful thighs, calves, and shoulders. He reminded her of a statue of Apollo she had moved from a museum in Sarajevo. But Apollo was the Sun God, and Garrett was all sleek darkness and hidden depths.

Not entirely hidden, she realized as he turned back to her. She looked quickly away from his lower body to the first-aid kit in his hand.

He chuckled. "I told you I couldn't be cool and objective. It's not my nature." He dropped to his knees beside her. "I need to clean and put some antiseptic on those wounds on your breasts. It will just take a minute." He carefully lowered the blanket. His lips tightened grimly as he gazed at her cut and swollen nipples. "The son of a bitch. Bites?"

"Yes."

"Human bites can be dirtier than an animal's. And I'd bet Shafir was as poisonous as a cobra. This may sting." He carefully cleaned and dabbed the antiseptic on the tip of each breast, then put on an antibiotic cream. Then he carefully cleaned and bandaged the wound in her leg. "That's it." He covered her again and sat back on his heels. "Or is it? Do you have any other wounds that Staunton gave you?"

"Only my cut lip."

He was silent a moment. "You weren't raped?"

"No, he was saving that. I wasn't hurt at all." She closed her eyes. "It was all Joel."

"Do you want to talk about it?"

"No."

"It would be better if you did."

"No."

"You're starting to shake again, dammit."

"Just give me time. I can't talk about it now. I won't—"

"Shh." He was suddenly holding her again, pulling the blanket over both of them. "You don't have to talk about anything you don't want to talk about. Just stop shaking."

"He hurt. Joel hurt, and I couldn't—"

"I know." He held her tighter. "It will get better, Emily."

"It's too late. He's dead. It can't get better."

"Not for him, better for you. Like it was with your father. The pain won't be as sharp after a while."

"It wasn't like my father. He died on impact. It wasn't like that."

"Shh. I'm not talking about Levy, and neither are you." His lips brushed her forehead. "We're going to lie here and, if you can, you're going to sleep."

"You didn't want me to go to sleep."

"Who said I have to be consistent? I didn't want you to lose consciousness until I knew what I was facing." He tucked her arm beneath the cover. "I can handle it now."

Gentleness. Strange that the Angel of Death would show tenderness. "You're being kind to me."

"Every now and then I have a lapse. I think it was because the sight of those bites tore me up." He drew closer, and whispered, "And that was the moment I decided to give you a gift."

"Gift? I don't want any gifts."

"You want this one." He held her gaze. They were only inches apart, and she felt as if those eyes were pulling her into him, absorbing her. "I'll keep my promise. I'll give you Staunton. I won't stop until he's dead."

She couldn't look away from him. She could almost see the lethal darkness swirling around him as it had when he'd killed Shafir Ali.

"Yes, that's a gift I want." She closed her eyes. "Thank you."

"I don't believe I've ever been thanked for killing a man before."

"You don't have to kill him, I'll do it. I just have to find him."

"I think I'm better qualified than you to do the job." He laid his head down beside her own and pulled her closer. "Don't you?"

"Yes." She had stopped shaking and was beginning to feel the warmth ease through her again. What a macabre response to an even-more-macabre promise. But it was no more bizarre than this bond that was beginning to form between them. She was lying naked in his arms and felt . . . joined in some manner. "I knew that the moment I saw you." She cuddled closer to him, taking his warmth, taking his strength, embracing the darkness. "Angel of Death . . ."

FOUR

"Shafir is dead," Borg told Staunton. "He had a wound in his side, but he died of a broken neck." He paused. "The woman's gone."

"Son of a bitch." It was what Staunton expected from the moment the explosions had started to rock the encampment. He gazed out at the spiking fires he could see through the driving snow. "The vehicles?"

"All damaged except the van closest to the huts. Six of Shafir's men are dead."

"I don't give a damn about that asshole's men." But he didn't want them to be captured and talk either. "Tell them all to come to the woman's hut, and I'll give them enough money to scatter and head for the Pakistan border."

"Don't we need them to go after her?"

"Do you think she did this herself? C-4 was used. Someone came to get her. But it couldn't have been a large force, or they wouldn't have hit and run. We have time to do damage control."

"Perhaps we'd better cut our losses," Borg suggested tentatively. "You spent weeks, and she didn't break. Maybe she didn't know anything."

"But I didn't get the chance to make sure, dammit." Anger was beginning to surge through him as he remembered those last moments before he had tossed her to Shafir. "I didn't get to work on her."

"You couldn't expect this to happen. The blizzard and the—"

"Excuses? He won't accept excuses." And neither would Staunton. He had never failed before, and he wouldn't fail now. "He's trying to hold up on paying me until I bring him the hammer, but it's not going to work. It's got to be pay as I go. That damn hammer was supposed to be here, and he says she has to know where it is."

He lifted his hand to his lip, where the bitch had bitten him, and he added viciously, "Well, he'll get what he wants. She'll tell me everything she ever knew." He turned away. "Pack up. We'll take the van and see if we can catch up with her. They had to be on foot. We would have known if anyone had approached in a vehicle."

"After you pay off Shafir's men?"

"Yes. Be sure they all come to the hut. I want every one of them in there waiting."

"They'll be there." Borg turned toward the burning tents. "They'll need that money. But there are at least forty. It's going to cost you."

"No, it won't." He smiled. "We don't have C-4 but we still have the explosives we used to stop the truck from the museum. I'll set the charge while you round up Shafir's men."

Borg's eyes widened. "You're going to blow up the hut?"

"Why are you surprised? It's the best solution to the problem. No loose tongues, no witnesses." He turned away. "But get them up here fast. I need to get on the road after that bitch."

Emily had drifted off to sleep.

It was a restless, uneasy slumber, Garrett thought, but he'd take what he could get.

He carefully moved away from Emily and got to his knees. He tucked the blanket closer around her, then rose and started to dress. They should be landing soon, and he needed to talk to Ferguson.

Emily muttered something, and her hand was reaching out from beneath the blanket.

Reaching out for him?

He dropped to his knees again and took her hand. She quieted immediately. He sat there, looking at her, waiting until her sleep deepened again. That unconscious gesture of need and trust had taken him by surprise.

Good God, she was treating him like the father she had lost all those years ago.

No, she had never looked on her father as the Angel of Death. Whatever was going on between them had nothing to do with paternal feelings.

On either side.

He cautiously released her hand and rose to his feet. He waited, gazing down at her. After a moment, he turned and went to the cockpit. "How soon are we going to land?"

"Another ten minutes or so." Dardon glanced at him as he sat down. "How is she?"

"On the edge. Fragile as hell."

"What happened to her?"

"She doesn't want to talk about it." He added roughly, "Hell, I don't want her to talk about it. She nearly fell apart when I pushed a little."

"They're going to push her more than a little when you turn her over to Ferguson. She's caused too much uproar for them to just leave her alone."

"And, of course, that's all her fault. She's a victim, dammit."

"Easy." Dardon held up his hand. "I'm not saying that she's not. Just that everyone from the media to the U.N. is going to want answers, and they're not going to be patient about it."

Garrett knew that was true. It was what he'd been worried about since he'd realized how breakable Emily had become during those weeks of captivity. "The media will be after her like a river of piranhas. And Ferguson and the rest will want her to furnish information so that they can go after Staunton and revenge her." His lips twisted. "Even if it kills her to do it."

"Staunton?"

"He's our main target," Garrett said. "Get on the phone and see what you can find out about him."

"What do we know already?"

"Nothing. I can't talk to her about him yet."

Dardon made a face. "Great. You don't know anything?"

"I know I'm going to kill him."

Dardon gave a low whistle. "Radical. I thought it was going to be an in-and-out job."

"It's not turning out that way."

"You know, violence may be the last thing she needs. She appears very frail."

"Then appearances are deceiving. She's going through a rough patch now, but you should have seen her following me through that blizzard. She was wounded and suffering from shock, but that didn't matter. No complaints. No hesitation. She just kept going."

Dardon's brows rose. "My, my, you sound like a proud papa."

That damn father image again, Garrett thought. "When did you ever know me to feel paternal toward any woman? She's just got guts, and I admire her for it."

"And you're proud of her."

He *was* proud of Emily. He was feeling possessive and protective in ways that he'd never experienced for any woman. Even though lust had been very present when he'd been holding her, it had not been the dominating factor . . . yet. What the hell was happening to him? "Just find out about Staunton."

"Why don't you ask Ferguson?"

"Ferguson always has his own agenda. I may not want him involved."

"How are you going to avoid it if you have to turn Emily Hudson over to him?"

"I'm working it out."

Dardon's gaze narrowed on his face. "That usually means complications. I take it you're not ready to share?"

"There's nothing to share." He repeated,

"I'm working it out." He stood up and took out his phone. "Find out about Staunton." He was dialing Ferguson as he stepped out of the cockpit. He glanced at Emily; she was still sleeping. But she was restless, and that sleep was probably filled with nightmares.

"Garrett?" Ferguson answered on the second ring. "Where the hell are you? What's happening?"

"I got Emily Hudson out." He kept his voice low, his gaze on Emily. "Levy is dead."

Ferguson started to curse. "I guess one is better than none. Bandits?"

"Yes, Shafir Ali. He's dead, too."

"And this Westerner you thought was involved?"

"I didn't see anyone but Shafir."

"Where are you? When can I take Emily Hudson into custody?"

"That's up to her."

"No way," Ferguson said flatly. "It's up to me. I'm the one who's taking the heat. The sooner I can produce the woman, the better for me."

"But not necessarily better for her."

"We made a deal. I gave Dardon the evidence. Now where are you?"

"We made a deal that I'd go in and get Emily Hudson and Levy out if they were still alive. I've fulfilled my part of the bargain."

"Where *is* she?"

"I'll have her call and tell you herself." He hung up the phone. He had almost felt the scorching heat of the fury and frustration Ferguson had radiated. The first thing the CIA man would do would be to mobilize all his forces to try to locate him. Which meant Garrett would have to move fast, whatever he decided to do.

He checked his watch. They should be landing in five minutes, and he couldn't let Emily sleep any longer. He grabbed the clothes that Dardon had brought for Emily and crossed back to her.

She opened her eyes as soon she sensed him kneeling beside her. "Garrett . . ."

"We have to get you dressed. We're going to land. I told Dardon to check your sizes. I hope the clothes fit." He pulled the cover down. "Sit up."

She slowly sat up. "I'm . . . stiff."

"You have a right to be." He slipped the straps of her bra over her arms and went around and fastened it. "Dardon got his research wrong. This is too big for you."

"I lost weight. I had trouble eating."

He was silent. "I should have thought of that. The other clothes will probably be loose, too." He came around and held up the briefs, pants, and shirt. "You're stiff and sore, and that leg is bothering you. I can either let you struggle to do the rest yourself, or I can help you and we'll get it done quick. You decide."

She gazed at the clothes. He was right, it was stupid to try to be independent when it would hinder both of them. "Help me. It's a little late to worry about being embarrassed. I feel . . . comfortable with you."

"That's not really what I wanted to hear." He began to dress her. "Comfortable is boring. I've never aspired to boring."

"Where is this field located?" Emily was gazing down at the flat, barren meadow below them as the helicopter began its descent. "I don't see anyone in sight."

"We're about sixty miles from Kabul. You'd see an army of people during the growing season. It's a poppy field. The farmers harvest their opium and ship it out to the world. They can afford to stay indoors during the bad weather." He shrugged. "And it's convenient for us to have a landing spot where there's no one around to be too curious. I didn't think you'd like to be bombarded right away."

"No." She could feel her muscles tightening in response to that thought. "No, I wouldn't."

"Don't tense up," Garrett said quietly. "And don't start shaking. It's not going to happen. I promise."

"I'm not—" She drew a deep breath. "I'm not that fragile or—I was cold."

"Whatever you say," Garrett said. "But I'm still not going to let you be put in the spotlight. I have a certain pride in my work. I got you out in one piece, and I won't let them tear you apart."

"I wouldn't let them do that."

"We won't put it to the test."

The helicopter landed a few minutes later, and Dardon came out of the cockpit. "Safe and sound. The car should be here any minute." He nodded slowly as he stared at Emily. "Hi, I'm Jack Dardon. We weren't formally introduced, but I'm very glad to see you in such good shape."

"And I was very glad to see that helicopter looming out of the snow."

"I would have come with Garrett to get you, but he said it was safer for me to furnish the transport." He tilted his head. "You have better color than you did when Garrett brought you on board, but you're still a bit puny-looking."

"I'm not puny. I'll be fine."

"Well, don't let Ferguson run you ragged. He's a little too eager to prove to everyone that he can pull the magical rabbits out of the hat."

"Go out and flag down the car when it gets here," Garrett said.

Dardon smiled. "Which translated means Garrett wants to get rid of me." He headed for the door. "I'd be pissed, but I'd rather not be included in Garrett's plans. I prefer to save myself to implement the final project."

Emily watched him cross the field toward the road. The snow had stopped, but Dardon's boots were sinking into the deep slush and snow. "Were you trying to get rid of him?"

He nodded. "I had to talk to you before the car arrived."

"Why?"

"The car is intended to take you to Kabul to Ferguson. Once you get there, all hell will break loose. He's going to try to make everyone forget he didn't act soon enough to save Levy by parading you before the media and every nation and organization that has been searching for you."

Every muscle tensed in rejection. "No!"

"And they'll start by asking you questions. About Levy. About Staunton. About those weeks in the mountains."

Emily could feel the panic rising. "I don't have to answer them. I—can't—do—that."

"I think you can do anything you have to do. But not without a lot of pain and bleeding that will send you into a tailspin. You're not in any shape to take that bullshit right now."

"Don't tell me what I can take," she said fiercely. "I took what Staunton did to me. There's nothing your Ferguson can do that could hurt me."

He shrugged. "Then I'm through talking. You've made your choice."

"Choice? You haven't given me a choice. You've only told me that I'm going to end up a basket case because I survived instead of dying in those mountains." She glared at him. "So give me my choice, Garrett."

He smiled. "Okay. You can go to Ferguson and put up with his grandstanding in exchange for the possibility that he'll find Staunton for you. And the possibility that he'll kill him instead of using him for his own ends. He has contacts and power, and he might be able to give you what you want."

"Or?"

"I made you a promise. You come with me and do what I tell you to do. I didn't tell Ferguson about Staunton because he'll get in my way. I find Staunton. I kill him. Your job is to lie low and stay away from Ferguson."

"And how am I to do that?"

"We record a DVD of you in which you tell Ferguson that you can't face all the hullabaloo, and give it to the driver of the car. You tell the world you need time to go away and recover, and you'll be in touch later."

"Will he believe it?"

"No, but everyone else will. And they'll be sympathetic." He paused. "Because you look like you've been through hell and back."

She had been through hell, and it wasn't over yet. It might be only the beginning.

Garrett glanced out the window. "There's the car. Make your choice."

She didn't speak for a moment. "You can find Staunton?"

"I'll find him. Is there anything you can tell me about him?"

"He has an Australian accent." She moistened her lips. "And if you get me one of those police artists, I can show you what he looks like. I know every line of his face, every expression."

"That's something. Anything else?"

"There was a man who worked for him. Borg. He did everything Staunton told him to do. He . . . liked it." Memories were rushing back to her, and her stomach was beginning to churn. Breathe deep. Don't throw up. "That's all I can remember. I'll try to—"

"Hush." He pulled her into his arms. "That's enough. Don't worry about it." His hand cradled the back of head and pressed her face into his shoulder. "I just needed somewhere to start."

"Maybe I'll be able to separate—Just not now."

He muttered an oath beneath his breath. "I said forget it. I'll work it out." He was rocking her back and forth. "And if you start to shake again, I'll—Just don't do it, okay?"

He was treating her as if she were a child in pain. Why not? She was acting as if she was the basket case of which she'd been so scornful. She pushed away from him. "I'm okay. I'm sorry. I didn't mean—" She drew a deep breath. "It won't happen again."

He stood gazing at her. "Does that mean you've made your choice?"

"Yes. You knew I'd choose you. I don't know this Ferguson."

"It could be argued you don't know me."

"I know enough."

His lips twisted. "That's right. You know John Garrett, the assassin. That's all that's important to you, isn't it?"

"Yes." Then she rushed on, "No. I . . . trust you, Garrett."

"You trust me to get you what you want."

It was more than that, but she couldn't explain it to him any more than she could explain it to herself. It was better not even to try. "How do we make this DVD to send to Ferguson?"

"I use my phone and burn it to a disc on my computer."

"Very efficient." She turned away from the window. "Let's do it."

"I'm going to cut the bastard's throat," Ferguson said through his teeth, his gaze on Emily Hudson's face on the monitor. "What the hell does he think he's doing? I *need* her."

"It seems we're not going to get her." Moore was studying Emily's face. "Maybe it's the truth. Maybe she just needs to get away for a while. She doesn't look well and that—"

"I know how she looks. Let her get well here in Kabul, where I can control the situation. I need answers."

"She told you the approximate location where she was held and Shafir Ali's name. We can start with that."

"That's not enough. I need chapter and verse. I've been roasting over the coals for too long, and it's not going to be over until I can furnish enough information to drown those flames."

"So what are you going to do?"

"I'm going to find her and bring her back here."

Moore nodded at the video. "And this?"

"What do you think? I'm going to take it to the director and the U.N. and tell them that I was the one who went in and rescued her. And that I made the decision to shelter Emily Hudson from the glare of publicity. She'd suffered enough, and I couldn't stand the thought of her being exposed to any more trauma."

"Good idea."

"We can tell everyone Levy's dead and that Hudson is free and recovering nicely in a secured haven. With any luck, the media will forget about her in a week or two."

"Very clever. And what about you?"

"Hell, no," Ferguson said grimly. "I told you, she's my number one priority. You can bet I won't forget Emily Hudson."

FIVE

"You did very well," Garrett said as he left the cockpit after the helicopter was airborne. He sat down beside Emily. "The video was just right. Sincere and fragile as hell. Very convincing."

"I didn't mean to appear fragile. I only meant to be as truthful as I could be under the circumstances. I hate lies."

"You are fragile right now. That was no lie." He held up his hand as she opened her lips. "Think about it. Your instinct is to deny it, but you have to admit your weakness if you're going to overcome it."

"Easy to say. Have you ever admitted weakness, Garrett?"

"Once. That's how I know you have to work through it to get strong again."

But he wasn't going to reveal the nature of that weakness, she realized. Well, she had no right to probe when she had no intention of telling him anything more than he had to know right now. "Where are we going?"

"Pakistan. I have some contacts that will keep us below the radar. From there we'll go to Greece."

She frowned. "Why?"

"Because I told you that you have to lie low for a while. I have a house in a small village on an island in Greece that would be perfect for you."

"How long?"

"A couple weeks."

She shook her head emphatically. "That's too long."

"You made the choice. That's the deal. You do what I say." He paused. "And you lie low as long as I tell you to do it."

"It's not necessary. I made that video for Ferguson. That's enough."

"Tell me that after you watch the TV

coverage and go through all the newspaper stories about your disappearance. You created a stir, and it's going to take time for the ripples to die down." He added, "And it will take time for me to find Staunton. Dardon has only started the preliminary search."

"Someone has to know him. If they met him, they'd remember him. He's a monster."

"And does he look like Frankenstein's monster?"

"No."

"Ugly? Threatening?"

"Not on the surface."

"Then at the moment he's only a monster to you. To a next-door neighbor he might appear perfectly ordinary."

She supposed he was right, but it seemed impossible supreme evil would not be instantly obvious. "How long will it take?"

He shrugged. "I don't know. All I can promise is that I will find him." He paused. "It would help if you could tell me why Staunton hijacked your trucks. Can you talk about it?"

Blood running from under the truck.

Joel screaming in agony.

"It's okay." Garrett's gaze was fastened on her face. "We'll talk about it later."

"No." Try not to think of anything but the question. She moistened her lips. "They were looking for a hammer. Staunton called it Zelov's hammer. He said there was some kind of Russian artifact hidden in the handle. He'd been told it was at that museum. He thought I knew where it was, that I'd hidden it away."

"Did you?"

"God, no. I kept telling him, but he didn't believe me. We didn't see any hammer. I kept telling him. I swore on my father's grave that I didn't know anything about it." Her nails dug into the palms of her hands. "Over and over. I kept telling him. He wouldn't believe me. I kept telling—"

"Emily." He gathered her hands in both of his. "Don't talk. I don't need to know anything more." His voice roughened. "I should have known better than to put you through this. You're nowhere near ready to face it yet."

"I have to face it," she said unevenly. "I can't live with myself if I hide from the truth. I don't have the right. It's just . . .

hard." She drew a shaky breath. "I should have thought of the hammer. God knows, it's always with me. Sometimes I even dream about it. It's the way to catch him, isn't it? He wants Zelov's hammer. He'll be looking for it. If we find it first, then we may be able to set a trap for him. Why didn't I think of that before?"

"I'd say it's understandable that you're not acting with crystal-clear logic at the moment," he said dryly. "You start to shake every time the conversation gets anywhere near Staunton."

"I don't—" But she would be trembling if he wasn't holding her hands, giving her his strength. "It's not because I'm afraid of him."

"I know that. It's because the son of a bitch traumatized you. That's why it's a good idea to let yourself heal for a while, so that you'll be able to function in top form."

"I'd be fine if we could go—"

"No," he said firmly. "I'm not going to chance you shattering either before or after we get rid of Staunton. I told you, I got you away from him, and I have pride in my work. You're going to remain fully intact, mentally and physically, for the next hundred years or so."

Her brows rose. "A hundred years?"

"Why not? The world is changing, evolving every second. I believe in the future. Now, you work on treasures of the past and know that a thousand years is only a blink of the eye. We just look at things in a different way." He released her hands. "I'm going to go up to the cockpit and tell Dardon to dump your info about Zelov's hammer into the mix and try to come up with something. Will you be okay?"

"Yes." She watched him turn and leave her. She would be okay, but she would have been better if he'd kept holding her hands. It was terrible to feel this vulnerable and alone when she'd always been strong and independent. It would go away. She just had to be patient, and she would be herself again.

But was that true? Would she ever be the Emily Hudson she had been before she had met Staunton?

Yes, dammit, she would not let Staunton twist her soul as he had her emotions. That would be a victory for him, and she would not give him any triumph.

So she needed to start learning to compartmentalize, keep the pain away, and use her mind and memory as weapons in the battle. The next time she talked to Garrett, she had to be prepared. She must not lean on him again.

"She's not being held by the CIA," Borg said. "Ferguson just issued a statement that he'd sent her into seclusion to recover from her ordeal."

"Bullshit," Staunton said. "He's trying to save his ass. That bitch wouldn't let anyone send her anywhere. She's flown the coop." He frowned. "Maybe it wasn't the CIA who took her back from me. I was wondering how they suddenly managed to find us after blundering around those mountains for weeks."

"Who else?"

He shrugged. "I've no idea. But someone must know. Whoever raided the camp had to have been given detailed information by someone who lives in these mountains. All we have to do is find that informant and ask him a few questions."

"We may not be welcome in the mountains," Borg said. "It's hard to quiet rumors among the tribes. After what you did to Shafir Ali's men that was—"

"Why, I don't know what you mean." Staunton raised his brows. "It was the CIA who blew up that hut. These mountain tribes stick together. It shouldn't be too hard to fan the flames and make it very uncomfortable for anyone who helped that to happen. We'll get someone to point the finger." Staunton smiled. "That's all I need."

Mykala Island, Greece

"It's beautiful," Emily whispered. "I don't think I've ever seen a place this beautiful or peaceful."

"It's the light," Garrett said as he helped her out of the helicopter. "The light here in Greece is like pure gold, and it seems particularly brilliant here on Mykala."

It could be the light or the intense blue of the sea surrounding the island or the shimmering white sands. Whatever the components, the overall effect was like being enveloped in a golden haze, Emily thought. "It's such a small village."

"Yes." He smiled. "Mercifully. One priest, two teachers, and one magistrate. We all get along just fine."

"Where is your house?"

Garrett nodded at a white stucco house on the hill that they were passing. "That's mine." He gestured to a larger two-story structure on the beach. "But that's where you'll be staying. That's our Sister Irana's domain."

She stiffened. "Sister? A nun?"

"Well, technically she's no longer a sister. She was a nun serving in a small hospital outside Athens when I met her ten years ago. She saved my life when I washed ashore with three bullet holes in my body." He turned to Dardon. "Go and tell Irana we're coming, will you?"

Dardon nodded and took off down the path.

"A nun?" Emily repeated.

"Not any longer. Irana Povak. She's a full-fledged doctor now, but she was just an intern when I first met her. She was having a crisis of faith, and I didn't help. Anyway, after she decided to leave the order, I set her up in a hospital and convalescent home here on the island. She only takes a limited number of patients because she's busy doing research. But each of them is universally considered hopeless or belongs to the unwanted."

"I won't go there," Emily said. "I'm perfectly healthy, and there are no confessions I want to make to anyone. Not a nun or priest or—"

"No one's asking you to bare your soul," Garrett said roughly. "That would be the worst possible thing for you right now. All I'm asking is that you stay with Irana two days and see if it works out. If you don't like it, I'm only four miles away. A tough customer like you could hike that distance in no time."

"I could come right now." She turned to face him. "Why don't you want me?"

"I do want you. But I want you to heal quickly. The longer it takes you to recover, the longer it will be until we can go after Staunton."

"And this Sister Irana is going to bless me and make everything all right?"

"Irana is just neutral ground. There's nothing neutral about me, and it could get in the way. She's not going to ask anything of you. And she's too smart to think she can solve all the problems of the world." He held out his hand. "You said you'd do what I told you. Two days?"

She hesitated, then ignored his hand and passed him to go down the hill. "If she doesn't try to save my soul. Nothing is going to stop me from killing Staunton."

"Irana believes that only God can save a soul. And if you don't mention lethal intentions, she'll have no reason to be upset." He followed her down the path. "And since you have no desire to confide in—There she is." He waved at a woman who had come out of the hospital. "I didn't think she'd be willing to wait until we came to her."

"What are you up to now, Garrett?" Irana Povak called. "Dardon says that I may be in trouble." Irana was a slim, athletic-looking woman in her late thirties whose dark hair was pulled back in a loose chignon. She was dressed casually in jeans and a loose white shirt.

"Would I do that to you?"

"Yes." Irana's glance shifted to Emily, and her eyes widened with recognition.

"Sweet Mary, I *am* in trouble. Are you crazy, Garrett? The island is going to be crawling with reporters."

"No one knows she's here. Your nurses won't talk. How many patients do you have right now?"

"Only seven."

"It shouldn't be too much trouble keeping Emily tucked away and out of their sight."

"I don't want to be tucked away," Emily said. "Let's forget about it."

"I could put her in the cottage where we keep contagious cases," Irana said. "No one goes there."

"Fine." He turned back to Emily. "I'll see you in two days unless you call me."

"I won't be hidden away."

"You were willing for me to keep you incognito."

"That's different."

He met her gaze. "Yes, it is. But you'll have to work it out with Irana."

Emily's fists clenched as she watched him walk away.

"It will be all right," Irana said quietly. "He must think it's best, or he wouldn't have

brought you to me. He's not really aban-
doning you."

Emily turned to face her. "I didn't want
to be dumped on anyone. I can take care
of myself."

"But sometimes it's best just to relax
and not have to worry about it. You must
have been through quite an ordeal." A
sudden smile lit her face. "I promise that
I won't cosset you or ask you questions."

"*Cosset*? That's a rather old-fashioned
word, isn't it?"

"Yes, Garret gave me a library full of old
books when I was trying to learn English.
Everything from Shakespeare to Frances
Hodgson Burnett. I thought everyone used
words like that." She chuckled. "And Garrett never corrected me. Sly devil. It took
me a year to weed out all those antiquated
phrases. Some I kept because I like the
sound of them."

"You speak very good English." It was
true. Irana had only a trace of an accent.

"I like the language. It's both difficult and
deceptive. I enjoy a challenge."

Emily's lips lifted in a sardonic smile.
"Like having me tossed in your lap?"

"I had a choice. Garrett always gives me a choice." She met Emily's eyes. "I chose you, Emily. Now you must decide if you wish to choose me."

"What would you do if I didn't?"

"Take you back to him. I owe him a great debt, but he sometimes makes mistakes." She tilted her head. "Is this one?"

Emily didn't answer for a moment as she stared at the other woman. Irana wasn't what she had expected from the few words Garrett had spoken about her. There was nothing serene or contemplative or nunlike about her. She was full of life and humor and vitality. Yet Emily could not see her imposing on anyone's space. "It may not be a mistake," she said slowly, and smiled. "Since you promise not to cosset me."

Irana laughed. "Instead, I'll let you read my Jane Austen. There's something very comforting about that time period. Some of the rules were nonsensical, but at least there were rules." She took Emily's elbow and nudged her down the path. "I'll visit you once a day at the cottage, but you'll have to be the one to invite me to stay. I won't intrude. And I think that Garrett is wrong about tucking you away entirely.

I'm going to put you to work. Have you ever done any nursing?"

"No."

"Well, then, there are plenty of floors to scrub. It will keep you from brooding, and work is good for the soul."

"Yes, it is." Emily felt a sudden surge of relief. "I've had a job since I was sixteen. I'm not afraid of hard labor."

Irana suddenly frowned. "But you're limping. Can you work?"

"It's only a scratch. I *want* to work."

"Good, you'll get plenty of it. But I think we'll just take a look at any wounds and have you throw down some antibiotics." She stopped on the path, her gaze going to the horizon. "The sun's going down. There's nothing more lovely than this time of day on the island. There's a kind of golden radiance . . ."

And there was a radiance about Irana Povak, too, Emily thought as she gazed at her. The bones of her face were bold and well-defined, her lips were wide but beautifully formed. Her deep-set dark eyes shone with spirit, and the few lines that marked her face appeared to reflect strength and endurance rather than age.

Irana glanced back at her. "And Garrett was right to bring you here. This island can heal you if you let it." She started back down the path. "It healed me."

Garrett waited until the third day before he called Irana.

"How is she?"

"The first day she was uneasy. Then when she realized that no one was going to push her to do something she didn't want to do, she relaxed. I put her to work scrubbing floors."

"I wanted her to rest, dammit."

"It's not what she wanted. I have to stop her after working all day and send her back to the cottage. When she gets there, she's tired enough to go to sleep. She wakes up at dawn and comes back to the hospital." She paused. "But she has nightmares, Garrett."

"It would surprise me if she didn't."

"Are you going to tell me what they did to her?"

"No. I don't know much myself. Her friend was tortured to death, and she feels guilty about it. When she's ready, she'll tell me." He added, "Or you. I'm not high on her list of trustworthy people."

"You're wrong. I think she does trust you. You obviously have a bond."

Garrett had a sudden memory of the blood and death that night in Shafir Ali's tent. "Not one you'd appreciate, Irana."

"I don't appreciate a good many of the things you do. Nor do I understand them. But I believe there's a balance in the universe, and since God created the universe, he must have approved of that balance."

"Your Church would not agree with that philosophy. They would say sin is sin, Irana."

"And the reason I left the order is that I was too willful to accept everything the Church accepts. So that also makes me a sinner, Garrett." She changed the subject. "What do you want me to do about the nightmares? I could give her a sedative to make her sleep deeper. I don't want to do that."

"Neither do I." He thought about it. "Don't do anything. Let's see if they go away naturally."

"Maybe if she'd talk about it."

"No confessional. That would blow your credibility."

"There's a sound reason for the confessional. It's a healing tool." She interrupted him as he started to speak. "But don't worry, I know that I have no right to violate her privacy. How long do you want me to keep her?"

"As long as you can. She's not going to permit it for more than a week or two."

"And then once more into the fray. Poor woman."

"I'll keep her safe."

"I know you will. You're a good man, Garrett."

"Only in your eyes."

"True. But I have to trust my own judgment and believe it's not willfulness and vanity. Otherwise, I'd surely be lost. I've given up too much for that belief." She added brusquely, "I'll let you know if there's any change." She hung up.

She has nightmares.

Irana had gone through a nightmare time herself, Garrett thought as he hung up the phone. Not as violent as Emily's weeks of torment, but torment just the same.

"How is Emily?" Dardon asked from the

chair behind Garrett. "I take it that she's settled in nicely, since she didn't ask you to pick her up yesterday."

"*Settled* isn't quite the word. Irana says Emily is literally working her way through the trauma after she found out that Irana was no threat. Once she's recovered, we'll have a whole new situation to face."

"At least we have a short respite."

"Which isn't going to do us any good unless we have something to tell Emily when she's ready to hear it. No word on Staunton?"

"Not yet. I'm checking with my contact at Interpol now."

"Zelov's hammer?"

"Do you know how many Zelovs there are in Russia alone? I've gone through most of them and cross-referenced them with any carpentry or farm-equipment companies. Nothing."

"It's more likely that Zelov is a smuggler or criminal of some sort if there's an artifact hidden in the handle of the hammer. See what you can find in FSB files."

"Easier said than done. I don't have any contacts since the KGB became the FSB. It could get expensive. Any limits?"

"No."

"I didn't think so." Dardon was silent a moment. "Aren't you getting too involved? You could still turn her over to Ferguson."

"That's not an option. Find the connection with Zelov."

"Okay." Dardon got up and headed toward the door. "Right away. Let's get this show on the road. I'm getting restless. I've never understood why you like to come here. This island is a little too sleepy for me."

Yes, Garrett could understand why Mykala was too boring for Dardon. But for some reason Garrett didn't feel the same restlessness when he was here. He felt at home, as if he belonged. Strange, when he didn't feel at home anywhere else. Was it because of Irana and her hospital? He'd had little to do with it other than financing. And Irana was usually too busy to spend more than an evening or two with him during his visits here.

He crossed to the window and looked down at the hospital on the beach. It appeared chalk white in the moonlight, and he could catch a glimpse of the cottage to the side of the building. The wind was curling the surf as it washed up on the sand.

Peace. Is that what Irana felt as she looked out at the sea? Probably. She had earned that serenity. He hoped that same peace was what Emily was feeling now.

God knows, it couldn't last long.

Emily screamed!

She sat bolt upright in bed, her heart pounding.

Staunton. Blood. Agony.

"It's all right. It's only a dream."

Emily's gaze flew to the chair in the corner of the room.

Irana leaned forward out of the shadows and turned on the lamp. "Don't be afraid. I didn't intend to intrude. I just didn't want you to be alone if you woke."

"How long have you been here?"

"An hour or so." Irana got to her feet. "Would you like a glass of water?"

Emily realized her throat was dry. "I can get it."

"Why? I need to stretch my legs anyway." Irana went to the carafe on the nightstand and poured water into the glass.

"I'm not used to being still. If I'm not asleep, I have to move."

Emily glanced at the clock—2:40 in the morning. "You should be asleep." She took the glass Irana handed her. "I don't need you."

Irana shrugged. "Maybe I was the one in need. I couldn't sleep because I was worried about you. I've found that if I don't do something when I'm fretting about someone, I regret it. So I camped out with you." She sat back down in the chair. "Drink your water. I know you want me to leave. I'll do it when I'm sure you're wide-awake. It's too easy to fall back into a nightmare."

Emily took a sip of water. "I'm awake now." But she found she didn't want Irana to leave yet. The horror of Staunton and Joel was still hovering too close. "You're being very kind, but I'm sure you have other patients who need you. I didn't mean to impose when Garrett brought me here."

"You haven't imposed. You work, you eat, you sleep." She paused. "And sometimes Satan sends you a nightmare to torment you."

"Satan?" Yes, Staunton was as close to the concept of Satan as she'd ever known.

"I guess you could say that. There are all kinds of Satans in this world. I suppose it's natural for you to blame it on Lucifer. Garrett said you were once a nun."

"Yes."

"And that you were having a crisis of faith when he first met you."

"Not of faith. I never had doubt in God or my desire to serve him." She grimaced. "It was how I was to serve him that was the trouble. I was always rebellious, always questioning, always too willing to believe that my conscience alone should dictate my actions. The Church is a strong and wonderful institution. I tried for eleven years to serve God in the way that the Church said that I should." She shook her head. "I failed."

"Garrett said that he was partly to blame."

"Did he? He's wrong, and I've told him so a hundred times." She smiled. "But if guilt makes him keep my hospital running and helps to heal my patients, that's not such a bad thing. Someday the guilt will fade away, and there will only be the goodness and generosity of the deed left behind."

"Why does he think he's to blame?"

"Ask him. He told me no confessionals. Even though I'm the one baring my soul." She got to her feet. "And now I'll let you try to go back to sleep. Though I don't promise I won't drop in on you again."

"It's really not necessary. But I do thank you for the thought."

"It's necessary," Irana said. "For my own peace of mind. I'd like to say it's God's will, but I don't have that kind of arrogance. I suspect it's because the Sisters were right and I'm vain and selfish and I believe far too much in my own instincts." She paused as she opened the door. "If you press the button on the nightstand, it will ring in my room. I'll come if you need me."

Emily shook her head.

Irana smiled. "Have it your own way. But you'll have to put up with me serving your meals from now on. And I'm cutting you down to six hours of work at the hospital. That therapy is over."

"No!"

"Yes, that was as much an escape as if I gave you a sedative. It's time we gradually eased you back into the real world."

The real world. Yes, these last days

have been like being in a dream, Emily thought. Hard work, staring down at the tiles she was scrubbing. Then later, the billowing white curtains, sea breeze, bright sun followed by darkness.

"But not yet." Irana's gaze was reading her expression. "I said gradually, Emily. Garrett wants me to keep you resting as long as I can."

"And do you always do as he orders?"

"Heavens no, but sometimes we actually agree." She waved as she closed the door behind her.

The real world. Staunton and ugly memories and nightmares that might not ever stop. She had to face it all soon.

But not now, not this minute. She lay back on the pillow and gazed out at the moonlight filtering through the window. She felt an odd sense of peace and serenity. She could feel the breeze as it rushed past the sheer curtains to brush her cheeks. Nothing harsh, nothing threatening. Irana would come if she pressed the button on the nightstand. Garrett was in his villa on the hill. Neither of them could be called friends, but she felt safe with them.

And she was not alone.

SIX

"Come on." Irana strode across the tiny patio, reached out, and pulled Emily out of the deck chair and onto her feet. "You look entirely too lazy. We're going for a walk on the beach. I need exercise, and I want company."

"You say that every day." Emily smiled as she fell into step with Irana as they walked out onto the sand. "Poor Irana. All these people on the island who love you, and you have to depend on me for company? I don't think so."

"I don't see why not." Irana grinned. "I'd have to make conversation with anyone else. You don't talk that much." She made a face. "But I may have to find someone else soon. You're almost back to normal. Of course, I don't know what normal is for you. All I know is the Emily you are now."

"I'm not sure I know who I am right now either." She gazed out at the sun-baked beach. It was amazing how she had become accustomed to life on this island in the last ten days. She had lived only in the moment, and Irana had been the center of those moments. Walks on the beach, mornings when she'd helped out at Irana's infirmary, evenings when Irana had occasionally dropped in and had her dinner with Emily. "But I know I'm grateful to you, Irana."

"Why? I've done nothing."

"That's it. You've done nothing. You don't ask me questions; you let me take, without giving." She paused. "And you haven't preached at me."

"I don't have the right. I don't know what you went through in those mountains. I can only do the best I can to live my life according to the Golden Rule and try not to hurt anyone else. I let God handle everything." She picked up a seashell. "Isn't this pretty?"

"Beautiful."

"And if God can make something this beautiful, I imagine he can heal what Satan broke. He doesn't need me." She smiled at Emily. "He's already started. Every time you look out at that surf, don't you feel just a little better? Every time the tide goes out, doesn't it take a tiny bit of the pain with it?"

"Perhaps." She gazed down at the seashell in Irana's hand. "God or nature?"

"God is nature."

"Well, God or nature or Irana. I'm grateful to all of you," Emily said. "I'll be sorry to leave this island."

"For the first few days. Then you'll be caught up in the real world. That's where you belong."

"I'm not so sure. It can be very cruel in the real world."

"Yes, but your instincts are to go to battle against that cruelty; you're one of the soldiers."

Emily's brow wrinkled in puzzlement. "Soldiers?"

"We all have our roles in life. Haven't

you battled your entire career to keep beauty and history alive?"

She nodded slowly. "But I never thought of myself as a soldier. Is Garrett a soldier?"

"Oh, yes. Without doubt. The quintessential soldier. And he knows it. He's not like you. He doesn't have one sole focus. He's been fighting all his life in one way or the other. That's why he decided to go after you. He couldn't resist. You were just one more battle he had to win."

"All his life?"

"Most of it anyway. From what I could gather from Dardon and bits Garrett has dropped. His father was a drunkard and a criminal who moved from country to country from the time Garrett was born. He evidently paid no attention to Garrett, who had to scramble just to eat. He was a street kid, and it's amazing that he managed to survive. But he did survive and managed to acquire an amazing if unconventional education along the way. He knows a little bit about practically everything. Do you know he speaks nine languages? The longest time he was allowed to settle anywhere were the years he spent in Afghanistan. His father ran guns there and sold weapons to the rebels. He was killed two years after he arrived in the mountains, but Garrett stayed on with friends he'd made there."

Emily remembered the man who had appeared out of the darkness as they had left Shafir Ali's camp. "I think I must have met one of them. He helped Garrett get me out."

"Karif? Garrett told me about him. They're good friends. Probably as close as Garrett has ever been to anyone. He stayed in Afghanistan when Garrett took off to make his fortune. But Garrett goes back to visit him every now and then." She shrugged. "Evidently he and Garrett are a lot alike."

"Another soldier?"

She nodded. "Everyone is a soldier in Afghanistan. It goes with the territory. If not by nature, by necessity."

"And what is your nature? Are you a soldier, too, Irana?"

Irana shook her head. "I'm a caretaker. I heal the wounds. I hold and treasure what you soldiers win." She chuckled. "Which means I can stay here on my island and let you all come back to me. Much pleasanter."

"But not necessarily easier. I've never seen anyone work as hard as you."'

"Work is good for the soul. And it keeps me out of trouble."

"Trouble? You?"

"I'm essentially lazy by nature. I just have to overcome." Irana pointed to the lighthouse a mile down the beach. "I'll race you. Whoever gets there first has to cook lunch."

"You always win."

"Of course, why else would I want to do it? You don't even have the excuse of that wound in your leg any longer. It's almost healed." She took off. "Did I tell you I ran track in college?"

Emily was on her heels. "I played soccer. But you're not as young as I am. I'll find a way to—"

"You see?" Irana was laughing. "Instinct. You're going into battle mode. It was only a matter of time." She streaked ahead. "Only a matter of time. . . ."

"I hope you're ready," Irana told Garrett when he picked up the phone that night. "Because Emily is very close."

"I was expecting to hear from you a lot sooner." Garrett said. "You held her off amazingly well. I'm grateful."

"Don't be grateful. I like her. I'll miss her." She paused. "Take care of her. I know you won't be able to stop Emily from doing anything she wants to do, but you can protect her. Do it."

"Yes, ma'am."

"I mean it."

"I know you do. But I may not have as much control of the situation as you might think. You've seen her weak and malleable. That's not the Emily I brought out of the mountains. She was tough, very tough. Once she's back on her feet, she'll be a force to reckon with."

"She's back on her feet." Irana laughed. "In fact, she beat me in a race to the lighthouse today. I was proud of her."

Garrett knew what she meant. He had felt the same way on that trek through the mountains. Protective, admiring, and oddly proud. "Then I'll just have to wait for her to make the next move."

"You won't have to wait long."

"How long?"

"Maybe a day or two at most. I've been

expecting her to make a move at any time. Be ready." Irana hung up.

I'm ready, Garrett thought as he pressed the disconnect. He had been edgy and restless for the last week. It had annoyed the hell out of him to have to step back and let Irana handle Emily's rehabilitation. It was the smart thing to do, but he had felt possessive of Emily since the moment he had taken her out of that tent. Maybe before. Perhaps since the day he had first seen her photo in the paper.

"Irana is turning her loose?" Dardon asked.

Garrett shrugged. "She has no choice. Emily will do what she wants to do. But it would help if I could find out something to give Emily when she decides she's had enough of Mykala."

"Was that a gentle nudge?" Dardon asked. "I've tapped practically everyone I can. It's nuts that I can't find a record on Staunton. I'm trying local police records now in Sydney, Australia, and I may be on the right track. She did say Staunton was Australian. Right?"

"Right."

"I found a Robert Hurker, who once

used the Staunton pseudonym in Sydney. I'm following up on it."

"And what about this Zelov's hammer?"

"Now I may really have something there. Not the hammer, but Zelov." He chuckled. "Or I may not. It's pretty weird."

"What's weird?"

"Let me work on it." He got to his feet. "As a matter of fact, I should have some info being faxed tonight. I'll go to the office and check."

"You don't have to work all night, Dardon."

"Yes, I do. You want to know." He added soberly, "And I owe you big-time for saving my ass with Ferguson. I know you don't want me talking about it, but I won't forget."

Garrett turned back to the window as Dardon left. The moonlight was silvering the sands beside the cottage where Emily was staying. There was lamplight shining from a window in the front of the house. She was awake. Another nightmare?

One or two days, and he'd be beside her to help deal with them. One or two days, and the waiting would be over.

That wasn't good enough, dammit.

He wheeled away from the window and strode toward the door.

Take deep breaths, Emily told herself.

She was still in a cold sweat. She ran a damp cloth over her face and poured herself a glass of water. She took a sip, and her hand tightened on the water glass to keep it from shaking.

She shouldn't let Staunton do this to her. She had thought she was getting stronger. She hadn't had a nightmare for three nights.

She *was* getting stronger. It would just take time. She just had to hold on and keep herself from—

A knock at the door.

Irana? Probably. It was strange how Irana seemed to sense when she needed her.

"I'm fine, Irana," she said as she threw open the door. "Though how you—"

Garrett.

"You don't look fine." Garrett was scowling. "You're shaking, and you look like you've been in a steam bath. Irana's nuts if she thinks you're getting better."

She stiffened. "I am better. I'm having a

few problems tonight, but I'm dealing with them. So go away and leave me alone."

He didn't move. "I know that's what I should do. I should never have come down here."

"Then why did you do it?"

"I saw your light." He stood looking at her. "Come on. Let's walk on the beach."

"I'm going to try to go back to sleep."

"The fresh air will do you good." He took the glass she was still grasping in her hand and set it on the chest by the door. He glanced at the oversized tee shirt she wore. "It's not chilly. You won't have to bother getting dressed."

She hesitated. "What do you really want? Why are you here?"

He shrugged. "I don't know. Maybe because I'm feeling this weird sense of possessiveness about you, and it irritates the hell out of me to have to step back and leave everything to Irana. Maybe because I've never been a patient man, and I've been strained to the limit waiting around for you."

"What are you talking about? You're the one who brought me here."

"So I'm unreasonable." He took a step back. "Will you come?"

She stood looking at him. She could see that restless volatility. He'd always been so assured, so completely certain of his actions, that this change in him disturbed her. But she would rather wrestle with Garrett's complexities than stay here alone to battle memories.

"Yes." She didn't look at him as she went past him onto the beach. "Has Dardon found out anything about Staunton?"

"Not yet. The only thing I know about are the rumors Karif told me when he led me to the camp. A foreigner with big-time funds." He paused. "Almost unlimited funds. Was that your impression?"

"I can do anything I want to do. There's no one I can't buy."

Breathe deep. Don't remember anything but the words themselves. Don't remember what he'd been doing to Joel when he'd said those words. "Yes," she said haltingly. "He said that no one would ever be able to catch him. If you have enough—"

"Stop it." He broke in roughly. He sank to the sand and pulled her down beside him.

"Rest. Go blank. All I needed was a yes or no. I didn't bring you out here to traumatize you so that you go back and have more nightmares. Irana said you were already having more than your share."

"She told you about them? Yes, of course she would. I'm sure you've had lengthy discussions about me."

"Not lengthy. And Irana would tell you every word if you asked her. She'd regard anything else as a personal betrayal."

"I believe you. She's very honest. I like her very much."

"So do I. She's been a good friend to me."

"And you to her. That hospital must have been hugely expensive."

"It only cost me money. She saved my neck. I regarded it as payback. I'd say that I came out way ahead."

"You said she treated you for bullet wounds?"

He nodded. "She found me on the beach near St. Cecelia's, the hospital where she was doing her internship at the time. She wanted to take me to the hospital, but I told her that she'd be signing my death warrant. It was the truth. Banaro was right behind me, and I'd have been a sitting duck if I had let her take me up there and sedate me."

"Banaro?"

"Luis Banaro. You might call him a competitor. I'd trespassed into his territory and acquired a statue that he regarded as his property. He wanted to set an example."

"A smuggler?"

"Among other things."

"And she didn't take you to the hospital?"

"No, she took me to a cottage owned by her friend and treated me herself. Then she went back to the hospital and spoke to the Mother Superior. She told her everything. She was ordered to bring me to the hospital and report the gunshot wounds to the police." His lips twisted. "Which was the honorable and proper thing to do. But it would have meant that I'd have been dead meat. Irana refused and left the order."

"Because of you?"

"I was the catalyst. Irana swears that she'd been searching her soul for answers for years."

"You don't believe her?"

"Sometimes." He made a face. "I guess I just don't like being a catalyst."

"I don't think she'd lie to you. And she's happy here."

"Yes. It would be hard not to be happy here. That's why I brought you to the island."

"Because it's beautiful?"

"And because when you're choking on ugliness, you need to strike a balance."

"Does it strike a balance with you?"

"Most of the time. I thought it was worth a shot." He gazed out at the water. "We'll get started searching for Staunton soon. I know you've probably been thinking about it."

"Yes, I have."

"One more day. I have some preparations I have to make with Dardon and Irana."

She looked at him in surprise. "That's not what I expected you to say when you came to the front door growling at me."

"I didn't expect you to look like that. Irana was full of optimism, and the picture she painted wasn't the woman who met me at the door. I didn't like it. I wanted you totally normal."

"Do you think I don't? That's not realistic. I thought I could bounce back, but it's not happening. I'm taking one step at a time." She gazed directly into his eyes. "And I'm done with your pampering, Garrett. I'm not going to fall apart and get us both killed. I'll take whatever I have to take."

"One more day," he repeated. He stood up and held out his hand to help her to her feet. "I'll talk to Irana tomorrow morning. Okay?"

He didn't release her hand and his grasp was warm and strong. It made her feel safe.

No, not really safe.

Strike a balance he had said. Ugliness and beauty. The feeling of being surrounded by his strength balanced against the tingling awareness of danger she always felt when she was with him. Even now, as she gazed up at him, she was conscious of the dark glitter of his eyes, the slight tension of his body.

And the heat. The same heat that had warmed her, healed her when he'd pressed his naked body to her own that night in the helicopter.

Only it wasn't the same, it was more intense, more . . .

She pulled her hand away and stepped back. "Okay. Not that it would do me any good to object, would it? You do what you like."

"If I did what I liked, you wouldn't be going back into that cottage alone." He smiled faintly. "There's more than one way to fight off nightmares. Want to try a few?" Then he suddenly frowned. "Dammit, I didn't mean to say that."

She stiffened. And she hadn't expected him to say it, to put into words the sexual tension that was vibrating between them. It took her off guard. "Sex?" she blurted. "Is that part of the deal?"

His frown deepened. "I don't recall a deal. I made you a promise." He turned away. "And just now I made a suggestion, not a demand. I buy whores when they're selling. I don't try to make any woman into one." He looked over his shoulder, his lips taut. "But you thought about 'the deal' the minute I mentioned going to bed. Tell me, Emily, what would you have said if I'd said yes?"

She was silent a moment. "I'd do anything to make sure I got Staunton."

"Shit."

He strode off into the darkness.

Emily stood gazing after him. He was moving with an almost electric energy, his strides long and purposeful. Totally male, full of anger, full of power. She couldn't take her eyes off him. He was angry with her, and yet she had only told the truth. You wouldn't think a man as mature and clearly sexual as Garrett would have reacted in that way.

But what did she know about how he would react to anything? They were still strangers, and the bond she felt with him was as bizarre as everything else connected with their relationship. Actually, they had no real relationship. He wasn't tied to her in any way but the tenuous threads of his sympathy, his desire to help. Perhaps that was why she had jumped to that conclusion about sex. Maybe subconsciously she had wanted to tie him closer, make his reasons for helping her stronger.

Lord, she hoped that wasn't the truth. She didn't want to believe that Staunton had twisted her to that extent.

She tore her gaze from Garrett and started toward the cottage.

Garrett was swearing beneath his breath with every step.

Damn, he should never have gone down to the cottage to see Emily. There had been no real reason. He could have been patient and let her come to him.

Except he didn't seem to have any patience where Emily was concerned. He had wanted to see her and had blindly obeyed the impulse. He'd been clumsy from the moment she had opened the door until he'd tried to lure her into bed. Hell, half the time he was aching with sympathy, and the other half his aching had nothing to do with pity. He hadn't even known he was going to proposition her until the words had tumbled from his lips. She was still the walking wounded. It was on par with all the wild mixture of emotions he had felt for Emily from that first moment. Pity, respect, protectiveness, and now lust.

Well, they would have to work their way through it. But, dammit, he should have kept his mouth shut.

He glanced back at the beach as he reached the house.

Emily had already gone into the cottage, and her lamp was turned off. Good. He hoped one of them would get a good night's sleep. He wasn't at all sure that he would be—

His cell phone rang and he glanced at the ID display. Private number. He punched the button. "Garrett."

"How do you do, Mr. Garrett? It's a pleasure to be able to contact you. I've had to go to a good deal of trouble to track you down."

Smooth, mellow, deep voice.

Australian accent.

He stiffened. "Who the hell is this?"

"Just a friend of Emily's. I'm sure she told you about me. It was a short acquaintance but very intimate."

"Staunton?"

"You see, she did tell you about me. How is the sweet bitch? I can't tell you how I've missed her."

"How did you know that she was with me?"

"Well, I knew she wasn't with the CIA,

so I went looking for the man who took her away from me. As I said, it was difficult. I had to sift through all kinds of stories and false trails. But I'm a persistent man. I located Karif Barouk here in the mountains. He's such a good friend to you. It took a long time for me to get him to tell me who he told the location of my camp."

Garrett's hand tightened on his phone. "I understand you can be very persuasive. Is Karif still alive?"

"Yes." Staunton paused. "But he's no longer important. He was just the means to bring us together. I have a proposition for you."

"I can't wait to hear it."

"It's very simple. Turn Emily over to me, and I'll let you live."

"Go to hell."

"Or don't give her to me, and I'll track you down and kill you and everyone you care about. I'll wait two days. Isn't that generous of me?"

"She's no good to you. She can't give you what you want." The call could be a trap. He'd been on the phone too long already, and he should hang up. But

Staunton had Karif, and Garrett had to run the risk if he was to have even a chance of keeping Karif alive. "What's Zelov's hammer?"

"Didn't Emily tell you?"

"She doesn't know anything about it, you bastard."

"I prefer to think that she does and just won't tell me. That will make it far more satisfying. I'm very angry with Emily. Give her to me, Garrett."

"No, you son of a bitch. I believe I'll give you to her."

"Really? No, I have the edge. You and Karif must be very close. He was able to give me a surprising amount of your personal information. I've already found out a good deal about you, Garrett. I'll find out more. Then I'll find Emily."

"No way."

"You're really a shade too cocky for my taste. I think you need taking down a peg. Now, what can I do. . . . Oh, I know. Talk to your friend Karif. Hold on, I'm putting him on."

"Garrett?" Karif's voice was thready. "I'm sorry. I tried to—"

"It's okay, Karif. I understand."

"Run. I didn't want—I didn't think I was—that weak. I never—"

"That's enough." Staunton had taken the phone again. "Talking is difficult for him. Everything is difficult for the poor bastard now."

"You son of a bitch."

"Yes, I am. But I took care of ridding myself of that particular bitch years ago." He spoke in an aside to someone. "Yes, Borg? Excellent. I'm going to hang up now, Garrett."

"The hell you are." Stall. Find a way out for Karif. "I want to talk to Karif again."

"Karif? I told you, he's no longer useful. Let's put him out of his misery. A knife, I think . . ."

"No, dammit, wait. We can—"

A scream.

My God. Garrett's teeth clenched, his hand tightening on the phone.

Staunton came back on the line. "He died for you, Garrett. Not many people can claim that kind of distinction. Does it make you feel important?"

For a moment Garrett couldn't speak. Rage was searing, burning through him. "You wouldn't want to know how I'm feeling right now, Staunton. You've just made a mistake."

"Perhaps. I had to balance the possibility of angering you and the satisfaction of putting Karif down. I didn't think there was much chance of your letting me have my Emily, so I opted for killing Karif."

"You'll never have Emily. But I'll see you soon, Staunton." He hung up the phone.

Bastard.

He had to wait a moment until he could subdue the shock and anger that was tearing at him. Smother the memories of Karif and their boyhood together. Block it all out. Control it.

Yes, Borg? Excellent.

What was excellent? Garrett had an idea and he had to move quickly. There would be a time for rage and regret and revenge later.

He moved toward the door, punching Dardon's number in his phone.

Oh, yes, there would definitely be a time.

SEVEN

Istanbul, Turkey

Staunton whirled on Borg. "Where?"

"Greece." He stared at the computer. "An island called Mykala in the Aegean."

"*Yes.*" Karif had told them about Mykala as well as Garrett's other homes around the world. It was only a matter of elimination.

"It will only take us a couple hours to get there. A jet to Crete, then a helicopter from there. I wasn't sure we'd be able to get that info. It must have cost you a mint to get that satellite hookup."

"Enough. But our kindly employer has

deep pockets, and he won't quarrel about it. I won't let him." Nor about the jet and crew of mercenaries that were waiting to go with them to find Garrett. It was a good thing. Hunting down Emily Hudson might have been relatively inexpensive, but Garrett had both means and experience. Not that Staunton was sorry that Garrett had become involved. He would be a challenge, and it had been a long time since Staunton had been stirred to stretch himself. "And while we're on our way, I want you to delve into everything concerning Garrett on that island. I want to know his friends, his property, any place where he might hide our Emily."

"No problem. I can get the basics by that time." Borg was staring down at the body of Karif Barouk. "What do we do with him?"

"Let's see, Garrett seemed to have some feeling for him. I believe we'll throw him out into the back alley for the rats to eat." He added cheerfully, "Yes, that's the ticket. I'll enjoy letting our little Emily's protector know every bit of what it's costing him." He headed for the door. "One bite at a time."

"Wake up."

Emily sleepily opened her eyes to see Garrett standing above her. Darkness. Tension. Power.

Angel of Death.

All that danger was back and tangible. Yet she wasn't afraid . . .

"Come on," Garrett said impatiently as he pulled back the sheet. "We're out of here."

She was instantly awake. "What's wrong?" She sat upright in bed. "It's still—"

"It's time to move." He turned on the lamp. "I sent Dardon to tell Irana we're leaving, but I'll have to go talk to her. You get dressed and pack."

"Wait." She swung her legs to the floor. "Stop trying to bulldoze me and tell me why you're in such a hurry."

"I don't have time for explanations." He moved toward the door. "Later."

"Now."

He glanced back over his shoulder. "Okay. Have it your way. We have to leave. Staunton may know where we are."

She stiffened. "What? How do you know?"

"The bastard called me. He found out that you were with me and wanted to make a deal. I told him to go to hell. But I think he may have tracked my phone, and I want you off the island before he gets here."

She shook her head. "And I want to stay. Now we won't have to go looking for him."

"I'd agree with you, but we're too vulnerable here. There are too many ways, too many people he can go after. We have to protect our backs before I go after Staunton."

"Then you go, let me stay."

"Get packed." His eyes were glittering with anger, his lips tight. "I'm in no mood to argue. I'm holding on by a thread. You'll go, Irana will go, or I'll—"

"Where am I going?" Irana asked from the doorway. "You shouldn't send Dardon to do your dirty work. You knew I wouldn't listen and obey blindly."

"I was going to talk to you. I just wanted to give you a chance to start making plans. You have responsibilities."

"Yes, I do." Irana came into the room. "And that's why I'll stay. I take it you think

Staunton may come to pounce? I'll help you pack, Emily."

"I'm not going."

"Not smart." She turned back to Garrett. "It's dangerous for her to be here?"

"It's dangerous for anyone I know or care about. According to Staunton." He glanced at Emily. "It wasn't you he used to get what he wanted, remember?"

How could she ever forget? "Then let's get him now. Trap him."

"After I get you and Irana off the island."

"I can't leave the hospital," Irana said. "I have responsibilities. I have patients."

"Not any longer. I told Dardon to warn you, then arrange to get them on a boat and take them to Athens."

Irana's hands clenched. "You had no right."

"Tough. It's better than having them butchered. Your nurses will be with them. You can join them on the boat or come with us."

Emily stared at him with bewilderment and anger. Garrett was taking charge, ignoring anything that Irana and Emily might say. "Maybe Irana should leave. She doesn't have anything to do with this. But I'm not going."

"The hell you're not." His hands clamped down on her shoulders, his eyes glittering down at her. "I'm not giving Staunton anything more that belongs to me. He's taken too much already."

"Let me go," she said through clenched teeth.

"I'll let you go to get dressed and pack a bag."

"Let her go, Garrett," Irana said. "Force isn't going to make her give in to you. You'd know that if you were thinking straight." She paused. "What did this Staunton take from you?"

"It doesn't matter." His hands loosened, then dropped away from Emily. "Let's just say that Staunton has managed to make this into a very personal vendetta."

"How do you know he's on his way?"

"He called me for a reason, and he kept me on the phone until he managed to track my location. I thought he might be doing it, but I couldn't hang up. He wanted me to think he was still in Afghanistan, but it could have been a trick. I'm not taking a chance."

"Why couldn't you hang up?" Emily asked. "Or did you really want to draw him here just as much as I do."

"What do you want me to say? Yes, I want him. But that's not the reason I didn't hang up. Now get dressed."

She stared at him for a moment, then turned on her heel, strode into the bathroom, and slammed the door.

She gazed at her reflection in the mirror over the sink. She didn't look afraid, she thought dully. But the fear was there, and she felt a little sick. She had noticed a difference in Garrett from the moment he woke her. The volatile sensuality she had seen in him earlier in the evening was no longer there. The sharp-edged deadliness she sensed in him had never disturbed her, but she had been aware of a rage that had not been present before. There had been an explosive aura surrounding him that had shocked her.

Something had changed.

Everything had changed. Staunton was coming. It was going to begin again.

No, it wasn't. She wouldn't let it. She had to put an end to it.

She had to put an end to Staunton.

"She may not go with you," Irana said. "You went about it the wrong way."

"I don't have time to be diplomatic."

"Obviously." She searched his face. "You're hurting. How can I help?"

"You can get on that boat and get the hell off the island."

"You think that my patients are in danger?"

"I think that Staunton is a crazy, sadistic bastard and that he likes to set examples. He wants Emily, and he's already proved he'll savage anyone who gets in his way." Garrett checked his watch. "I don't know how much time we have. I know I'm not handling this well, but trust me, will you? Just get down to the dock and get on that boat."

"Maybe I could persuade Emily to go on the boat with me. I could tell her I need her to help with the patients."

He shook his head. "I need her with me. She's the target. The rest of us are just means to an end." He frowned. "And she's taking too long in there." He strode toward the door and knocked on it. "Emily."

No answer.

"Shit!" He threw open the door.

Empty.

A small open window with curtains billowing in the breeze.

"Dammit, I'm an idiot." He turned on his heel. "I should have known that she'd— what does she know about the island? Where could she hide, Irana?"

"Just the beach." Irana frowned, trying to think. "The hospital. The lighthouse. I'll go with you."

"No, I'll find her. You get on that boat."

Irana slowly nodded. "That's my job right now. My patients and my nurses. I'll go check and make sure everyone is out of the hospital."

"Dardon will have seen—" It wasn't any use arguing with her. Irana would do what she thought she should do. "Just get to the dock as soon as you can. I'll call Dardon and tell him you're coming."

He strode out of the cottage and gazed at the moon-dappled beach.

Emily couldn't have more than a few minutes' head start, but she wasn't in sight.

He doubted she would go to the hospital.

She wasn't sure that Irana might not go back there, and she would want no interference.

He started up the beach toward the lighthouse.

"We should be in Athens in thirty minutes," Dardon said, when Garrett picked up more than an hour later. "Any sign of Emily?"

"Hell, no," Garrett said. "She wasn't at the lighthouse, and I searched every vacant cottage along the beach. Then I doubled back and searched the hospital from top to bottom. This place is as twisted as a rabbit warren."

"You sound a bit tense. It could be okay. We don't know for sure that Staunton is on his way there."

"I'm sure enough. I'd better be. Irana will draw and quarter me if we moved all her patients for no reason."

"Well, you may have more time than you think."

"And I may have less. My guess is that Staunton was at a jumping-off place that would let him get to anywhere in the

least amount of time. Look, I can't talk
any longer. I have to find her. I'll call you
when I have her off the island." He hung
up the phone.

Where the hell was she?

He strode out of the hospital and stood
staring in frustration at the beach.

Where next? He doubted if she would
leave this area she knew to seek help
from any strangers who lived on the island.
Emily wasn't hiding from anyone but him,
and she wouldn't want interference. She
was on the attack.

He stiffened as the thought sank home.
Attack.

Then why had he assumed she'd be
here on the beach? She wouldn't be cow-
ering helplessly waiting for Staunton to find
her. She'd go where she'd think Staunton
would go.

His gaze lifted to his own house gleaming ivory in the moonlit hills above him.

The place where Staunton would go.

Yes.

He started at a run up the path toward
the house.

He was halfway up the path when he
heard the sound of a helicopter in the

distance. Large aircraft. Low, over the water, coming from the east.

Shit.

From where she stood on the balcony of Garrett's house Emily could see the blue lights of the helicopter spearing down into the sea as it approached the island.

The muscles of her stomach clenched. Don't be sick. Take a deep breath.

"We have to get out of here. Staunton will here within ten minutes."

She whirled to see Garrett coming toward her. His expression . . .

She instinctively lifted the gun in her hand.

"I see you found my private arsenal. You had plenty of time while I was running all over the beach trying to find you."

"I needed a weapon. You had enough guns in that box in the closet to arm a battalion."

"I like to be prepared. Sometimes one gun isn't enough."

"I thought you would. You're that kind of man."

"The kind of man I am is mad as hell at the moment."

"Too bad." She moistened her lips. "You were trying to stop me."

"You're damn right. I told you, it's not the time. Now give me that gun."

She didn't move.

"Give it to me, Emily. I have to get you out of here."

"No. He'll be here soon."

"That's right, and by the sound of that copter, it's big enough for him to bring fifteen or twenty close friends. I think it's a Superhawk. He's probably hoping for a quick cleanup before he snatches you away." His lips tightened. "He's not going to get it. He's not getting anything he wants." He took a step closer. "Because we're going to be out of here before he touches down."

She stepped back. "You go. I'll wait for him."

He held out his hand. "Give me the gun. You're not going to shoot me."

"I might." She tried to keep her tone cool. "I'd only hope to wound you, but I know how much firepower this gun has. I'd keep your distance."

"It's a Magnum, and a bullet would do

considerable damage. So you won't chance it. I'm not your enemy."

"Then stay and help me.

"That's what I'm trying to do." His gaze searched her face. "But I'm not going to be able to convince you, am I?" He shrugged and turned away. "Have it your own way. I did my best to—" He suddenly whirled and the edge of his hand came down on her wrist, sending the gun flying.

"No!"

She heard him mutter a curse as she dove for the weapon.

An agonizing pain shot through the back of her neck.

Darkness.

The blood was rushing to her head.

She was being carried in a fireman's lift, she realized dazedly.

Garrett . . .

She started to struggle. "Let me down."

"Stop struggling, or I'll drop you on your head. I'm having enough trouble."

"The hell I will." She spaced the words slowly and with precise venom. "Let-Me-Down."

"Fine." He dropped her in a heap on the veranda. "Walk. Hurry. Get moving. And if you try to run away, I'll deck you again."

He would do it. His eyes were blazing in his taut face. "You're angry. Good. Then go away. This is none of your business. I don't need you anymore."

"You're my business." He jerked her to her feet. "And I need you. So shut up and do what I tell you."

"I don't—"

"Listen to me," he said harshly. "I made a choice. I knew I might be serving you up to Staunton, and I still made it. But I'm not going to let him win this round. No way."

"I'm the one who—"

"No more talk." He spun her around to face the beach below. "Take one look and see what we're facing and then we go."

"I have to—" She broke off again as she saw that the helicopter had landed on the beach, and men were pouring out of the belly of the aircraft. Staunton was on the beach and directing his forces. Even from this distance she couldn't mistake his lean frame. She couldn't take her eyes away from him. She whispered. "There he is."

"I gathered that," Garrett said. "Now think, dammit. Do we stand here and let him take us, or get out of here and live to fight again?"

Some of Staunton's men were running toward the hospital. Staunton himself was standing, head lifted, staring up at Garrett's house. She doubted if he could see her standing in the shadows cast by the house, but she was starting to shake. No, don't let him do that to you, she thought.

Staunton was gesturing, pointing, then started up the path.

"Emily."

"You go. I can't run from him."

"And I can't go without you. So whatever threat he is to you, goes for me, too. What happens is going to be your responsibility."

Joel.

She closed her eyes. "Don't say that."

"I'll say anything I have to say. From now on, the gloves are off."

And whether he said it or not, the truth was evident. Responsibility. Guilt. Blame. It was happening again.

But she couldn't let it happen again.

She turned away. "Let's go. Get me out of here."

"At last." He grabbed her hand and pulled her toward the path that led around the house. "Run!"

Five minutes later they were at the concrete pad on the other side of the island.

"Get in." Garrett opened the passenger door. "I won't turn on the lights until we're on our way. Staunton should be right behind us. With any luck, he'll be delayed searching the house."

"It's Staunton who seems to have all the luck." She jumped into the helicopter. "Get out of here. I don't want him shooting you."

"Neither do I." Garrett started the engines and the rotors whirred. "But it may happen. I see lights on the hillside."

So did Emily. Men running toward the helicopter pad, flashlights beaming in the darkness. Was one of them Staunton?

Garrett glanced back at the house. "Here we go." The helicopter lifted off the pad. "We're almost—"

A bullet shattered the glass beside her!

"Shit." He spun the helicopter away from the direction of the house. "Keep low."

But Garrett couldn't keep low, she thought desperately.

Another bullet struck the fuselage of the aircraft.

"We'll be out of range in a minute," Garrett said as they climbed higher. "If they don't get the gas tank."

"Comforting thought."

"I told you, the gloves are off." Garrett gazed down at the men milling below them. "Is that Staunton looking up at us?"

A shock of fair hair, long, lean body.

"Yes."

"Then they won't try for the gas tank. Staunton doesn't want you dead." He veered away from the island. "Though he wouldn't mind me getting deep-sixed. I guess we have to be grateful for small—"

His telephone rang.

"I'd bet Staunton wants to vent his displeasure." He turned up the volume as he punched the button. "Garrett."

"I want to talk to Emily," Staunton said.

"She may not want to talk to you." He gazed inquiringly at Emily.

She slowly reached out her hand and took the phone. "What do you want to say, Staunton?"

"I just wanted to hear your voice. I've

missed you. I've never been as intimate
with anyone as I was with you. But we
never took that final step. You ran away
too soon. Garrett took you away, and I
was very angry about that. But now I've
found you, and everything will work out."

"I'm going to kill you, Staunton."

"Really? But I notice you're the one on
the run."

"And I notice that you failed to get your
hands on me again, even though you seem
to have brought in your own Delta Force."

"But it was very close. And I won't let it
be a complete failure. I can't touch you right
now, but I made Garrett a promise. I've
been told he seems to have some involvement with that hospital on the beach. Thirty
seconds."

"What are you going to—"

Fire stroked upward into the dark sky
as the hospital exploded.

Emily stared in horror down at the
roaring inferno below. "Why?"

"The hospital was empty. I was disappointed. Destroying *things* isn't very satisfying, but I take what I can get. I believe
you're still close enough to see Garrett's
house. It will be much more noticeable

shortly. I've ordered it torched. I'm hanging up now. I look forward to seeing you
soon, Emily."

She was barely aware of hanging up the
phone as she gazed down at the island.
"Did you hear? He's torching your house."

"I heard," Garrett banked the helicopter
to the left. "But we're not sticking around
to watch his fun."

She could already see flames curling
inside the house on the hill. The windows
were glowing balefully as the fire devoured
it. "I'm sorry. I should never have stayed
with you after you got me out of the mountains. He might not have—"

"Shut up. It was my choice." He didn't
look at her. "And you always have to take
responsibility for your choices."

"Irana's hospital . . ."

"I'll build her another one." His lips tightened. "Not here. Not now. Not until I kill
the bastard. He was too disappointed that
he couldn't chalk up any body counts."

"She loves this island."

He was silent a moment. "So do I."

And she had taken this place away
from both of them.

But only while Staunton still lived.

"I want you to take me to Athens and—"

"Let you go after Staunton on your own," he finished for her. "No way."

"You have Irana and your own life to protect. Look what happened here."

"I almost got you killed. Staunton wouldn't even have known you were on this island if I'd done what I should have done when he phoned me."

She frowned in puzzlement. "What you should have done?"

"Hung up. I had a hunch he was tracking me. I took a chance because I wanted a few more minutes to try to negotiate."

"Negotiate what?"

He didn't answer.

"Answer me." She was staring at his closed expression. "I know about Staunton's negotiations." She was thinking, trying to put it together. "How did Staunton find out that you were the one who helped me? How did he get the phone number to call you?" But he didn't have to reply. She was remembering that moment outside the camp. The young man with the warm, comforting smile. "Your friend. The man who helped you to find me. His name is . . . Karif?"

"His name was Karif Barouk."

Past tense. She felt sick. "He's dead?"

"Yes."

"Staunton?"

"Yes."

"Why didn't you tell me?"

"Why should I? I knew you'd react the way you are now. You're feeling guilty as hell about the hospital and my house being destroyed. It was Staunton who should feel guilty, not you. As for Karif . . ." He paused. "I'm the one who asked him to help. I thought if he kept his mouth shut, he'd be safe. Karif was sometimes careless. But a good friend, the best friend."

He was hurting. She could sense the pain behind that tough façade. He and this Karif had been close, and his friend had been taken from him. "Staunton tortured him?"

"Oh, yes. And he wouldn't have broken unless it had gotten—Staunton evidently is exceptionally talented in that direction."

"Yes, he is." She drew a deep, shaky breath. "Joel . . ."

"I don't want to talk about your Joel. I don't want to talk about Karif. I want to talk about Staunton. I've been trying to be considerate, trying to let the memories dull, trying to keep you from going off the deep end. I thought we had time to let you heal." He gazed directly in her eyes. "That's over. Time's up. Start thinking. Start remembering. If it hurts, it hurts. I want details. I want clues. Staunton never expected you to get out of those mountains alive, so he probably wasn't as discreet as he might have been. Did he talk to you?"

"Sometimes. But it was usually . . . He talked about what he was doing to Joel."

"Bastard. But he could have interspersed other information. Sift through it."

Hard. Sharp. Merciless. This was the Garrett she had seen those first moments in that tent, when he had killed Ali. All darkness, all lethal skill.

It shouldn't disturb her like this. It was that darkness and skill that she had wanted, what she had embraced. "I'll try to do what you want me to do."

"If you need help, I'll give it to you. I'll probe, I'll ask questions."

She gazed at him in shock.

"Gloves are off," he repeated. "You help me, I help you. None of it will be pretty."

"But in the end, we'll find Staunton."

"That's not good enough."

"What?"

"We'll find Staunton. We'll find the man who hired Staunton. And I'll kill them both." He added softly. "I'm hungry. I want it all."

Emily had not thought beyond Staunton. He had completely filled her horizon for so long that everything else connected to him was blurred. Yet wicked as Staunton was, that evil had been bought and paid for by someone just as evil.

"And you want it all, too," Garrett said. "You've just been so wounded that you've refused to think about it. I'd bet that within two days of ridding the world of Staunton you'd be going after the man who hired him." He smiled faintly. "But you'd be much better going after the lure that would gather them both in at once."

"Zelov's hammer."

He nodded. "You were ready to go after it to find Staunton. It's still the best game in town."

"It's no game."

His smile faded. "No, it's not. But you'll find sometimes it's better to pretend it is. Too much intensity can cause you to make mistakes." His gaze shifted to the window.

"We'll be in Athens soon. It's not safe to stay there. We'll take care of Irana, then take off."

"Where?"

"That's up to Dardon. He came up with a few answers tonight before I got the call from Staunton. It's pretty weird, but it's all we've got. We'll see if he can pull anything else from his sources."

"About Staunton?"

"No, about Zelov." He shook his head. "Later. I don't know enough myself right now. We'll talk about it after we reach Athens."

Garrett's phone rang three minutes after he set the helicopter down at a small airport just outside of Athens.

"Where are you?" Dardon asked. "Irana's on the rampage. One of her friends on the island called her and asked her if she was all right. An explosion?"

"Staunton blew up the hospital. We're in Athens. Are you still at the dock?"

"No, Irana called the Mother Superior of St. Cecelia's Hospital where she used to work, and the patients are on their way there now. We're in an ambulance." He spoke to someone in the background. "She wants to talk to you."

"We should not have left you," Irana said when she came on the line. "Are you hurt?"

"No, and neither is Emily. You did exactly what you should have done." He paused. "The hospital is gone. I'll build you another one, Irana."

"If God wills. He might have had a reason for taking this one away."

"I don't think God had anything to do with it."

"You don't know. Maybe he wanted you to have a reason to build me another one with a better diagnostic unit. I've been thinking perhaps I needed one." She paused. "There's nothing left?"

"I didn't get a close look. But I'd bet Staunton was very thorough."

"Sad." She was silent. "I want to see Emily. I'm not sure what this will do to her."

"Neither am I. She'll just have to survive it. She seems to be coping."

"I want to see her. I'm going to St. Cecelia. Will you meet me there?"

"Yes, but not for long. It's not going to be safe for you or us, Irana."

"We'll talk when you get there." She hung up.

Garrett looked at Emily as he pressed the disconnect. "She's worried about you. She's regarding the destroying of the hospital as an act of God, but she wants to make sure you're okay."

"Cosset," Emily said. "She wants to cosset me." The words brought back the memory of that day on the beach. The sun on the water, Irana's radiant smile. For the first time that night she felt an easing, a lessening of the darkness. "And she's not forgiven you for giving her those old Jane Austen books."

He smiled. "It was really funny until she caught on. It was like listening to someone out of *Pride and Prejudice*."

"I would have found a way to pay you back."

"Oh, she did. I'll tell you about it sometime." His smile faded. "But in the meantime you can concentrate on convincing Irana she can't stay here with her patients. She wasn't about to commit."

EIGHT

"I'll be with you in a minute," Irana said as she strode down the hospital hall beside an old man on a gurney. She was holding his hand and smiling down at him. "As soon as I get Andros settled. Strange places are always a little scary, aren't they, Andros?"

Not with Irana beside you, Emily thought as she watched Irana disappear into a room at the end of the corridor. The woman's hair was tousled, her clothing rumpled, but she still exuded the energy and confidence that made everyone sure that everything was going to be okay. "She seems to have taken charge."

"Yes, what did you expect?" Dardon asked as he came out of the admittance room. "Irana is a law unto herself. The hospital didn't want to take in her patients, but Irana wouldn't hear of them turning her down. She said she knew they'd get the best care here." He looked at Garrett. "And it may be hard to pry her away from them."

"Hard or easy. She can't stay here. She'd be a weapon in Staunton's hands. I won't tolerate that." His gaze went to the door through which Irana had disappeared. "Find a place that's safe for her. I want her so surrounded by guards that she'll stumble over them if she turns around."

"Anything else?"

"Zelov. Earlier tonight you said you had something on him."

He nodded. "I'll give you the report as soon as I get to a printer." His eyes were shining. "Things have started to escalate, haven't they?"

"You might say that," Garrett said dryly. "That should please you."

Dardon grimaced. "I don't mean to be insensitive. It's just that I have a low boredom threshold."

"I know. So does Ferguson. He almost nailed you because of it. Bored or not, you stay close to Irana until you get her secured."

"Will Emily be with her?"

"No way." Emily shook her head. "I won't be sent away with Irana. No more hiding."

"Moderate hiding," Garrett said. "Unless you want the paparazzi to camp on our doorstep." He watched Irana walking toward them down the hall. "Now let's see how Irana is going to react. The explosion at the hospital might be minor in comparison." He raised his voice as Irana approached. "Everyone all settled?"

"As well as could be expected. The sick don't take well to change," Irana said. "Their bodies are already in turmoil. But the sisters here will take good care of them."

"Really?" Garrett's eyes narrowed. "That sounds . . . permanent."

"What did you expect? I'm not a fool. This Staunton wants to hurt you. He blew up my hospital. I'm much more valuable than brick and mortar. I'm sure he would like to blow me up, too. I will have to go away somewhere safe to keep you safe."

"I'm relieved that you're being reasonable."

"I'm usually reasonable. My patients will receive good care. They aren't in danger. You're the one I have to worry about. I have to make sure you're safe. There must be a reason why God linked us together." She gazed at Emily. "You are well?"

"Yes."

"Would you come with me if I ask you? I'll find good work for you to do."

Emily shook her head.

"I didn't think so." She reached out and gave her a quick hug. "Take care of yourself. If you need me, I'll come to you." She glanced at Garrett. "And take care of Garrett, too. He thinks he doesn't need it, but don't pay any attention to him."

"Like you?" Garrett asked.

She smiled. "Exactly like me." She turned to Dardon. "Garrett will ask you to stash me someplace. Right? I will tell you what I require. I don't care where it is, but I want to be able to work. I was thinking of perhaps a medical facility in Africa or South America for the next month or so. They always need help. I'll look into possibilities, and we'll discuss it."

"You'll have to leave right away," Garrett said. "Discuss it while you're getting away from here."

She nodded. "After I give my notes on the patients to the Sisters." She turned away. "I've already sent my nurses back to their homes and told them to keep a low profile." She smiled back over her shoulder. "I told them I'd put them back to work when you build me a bigger and better hospital. I'll probably have to hire a larger staff for the diagnostic clinic."

"I'm sure you will," Garrett said dryly. "And the clinic will probably rival the one at Johns Hopkins."

"Possibly. It's good for your soul to spend your money on such worthwhile things. It only follows that the more you spend, the better I'm treating you." She strode down the corridor toward the nurses' station.

Dardon chuckled. "What a philosophy. I hope she doesn't better your soul to the point of bankruptcy." He started after Irana. "I'll keep an eye on her and see if I can borrow the nurses' printer for your printout."

"Be quick. We'll wait at the elevator."

Emily frowned as she saw Irana smiling at the Sister behind the desk. That radiant smile that had drawn Emily to her from the moment she had met her. "She *will* be safe?"

"From Staunton," Garrett said as he took her elbow. "I can't promise anything else. Particularly if she decides to go to the wilds of Africa. She'll have to handle AIDS, lions, and tigers herself. She wouldn't have it any other way."

"The patients were taken to St. Cecelia," Borg said to Staunton as he came back to the rental car at the dock. "Do you want to go there?"

"Of course I want to go," Staunton said impatiently. "Though I doubt if Garrett and Emily will be there. He'd know I'd check it out."

"Irana Povak?"

"She's a possibility." And he needed a lead, dammit. He'd hoped that he'd be able to gather Emily up during the raid on the island. The attack had been a bit too public. It had been made clear to him when he was hired that Staunton had to be both thorough and discreet. The explosion at the hospital could not be termed discreet. He'd made sure that he hadn't left any loose ends. The mercenaries he'd hired wouldn't talk, but he might have been seen. It was annoying to have to worry about trivialities like this. Though he hoped Garrett wouldn't regard it as a triviality. He'd wanted to anger and send a challenge. He'd had to strike at him in some way. Garrett had taken Emily from him, and that couldn't be tolerated. "Yes, we'll try for Irana Povak. But there are other ways."

"What?"

"First, you make sure that you remove anyone who might know too much."

"And then?"

He smiled. "Then you throw out a lure and let the fish come to the shark."

"Here it is." Dardon thrust the folder at Garrett. "You'd better get going. The man I left at the dock called and said there was someone asking about the patients. You probably have less than forty-five minutes. I'll get Irana out as soon as I pry her away from those nurses."

"Right." Garrett punched the elevator

button. "We'll go directly to the helicopter, then on to Rome. Call me if there's a problem."

"Not Rome." Dardon said as he hurried back toward Irana. "After you read that report, I think you might decide on the U.S."

"We'll worry about that once we're airborne and far away from here." Garrett handed the folder to Emily as he nudged her into the elevator. "Hold on to this. Skim it while we're in the car on our way to the helicopter."

"Okay." She gazed down at the folder. She was feeling an odd reluctance to look at the information inside when she should be eager. Over and over she had told Staunton she knew nothing about Zelov's hammer. Now she was going to find out about it.

No, it wasn't odd at all. Because she hadn't known it had triggered horror, and that horror refused to leave her.

"Why the U.S.?" she murmured, as they got into the car a few minutes later.

"You tell me." He started the car. "In fact, as soon as we get to somewhere that we can talk with any semblance of quiet, I'll want you to tell me everything you remember connected with Staunton. I can't care if it disturbs you."

"I'm not arguing." She looked away from him. "You're the one who sent me to stay with Irana. I wanted to go after Staunton right away. You should have asked me before this. I would have told you."

"I was being kind." His lips curved in a sardonic smile. "God knows why. I'm not kind. It would have been better for everyone if I'd just stuck to my usual modus operandi."

"Irana thinks you're kind."

"Sometimes." He pulled onto the road. "And that may get her killed, too."

"You tried to protect—"

"I don't want you to defend anything I do," he interrupted. "Just scan those pages and see if we can find out anything we need to know."

"Fine." His sharp abruptness stung her. She didn't know what had possessed her to try to offer Garrett comfort anyway. She didn't know anyone who needed it less. She opened the folder. "This will take some time. I can barely read by these dash lights. Should I turn on the overhead?"

"No. The overhead would light us like a spotlight."

And if Staunton was on his way here, that spotlight would make them targets, she realized

She leaned closer to the dash lights. "I'll do the best I can." She shook her head. "No, the print is too faded. The nurse's printer must have needed a new ink cartridge." She tilted the page. "This is crazy. It must be a mistake. I don't even see Zelov mentioned yet. There's only one name that jumps out at me." She bent nearer. "Crazy . . ."

"What name?"

She frowned. "Rasputin."

Emily was only able to read bits and pieces of the report on the short drive to the helicopter. She finally shook her head and put it aside as she got out of the car. "I'll have to have more time. Maybe when we get airborne, I can concentrate."

Garrett nodded. "It's all Rasputin? No mention of Zelov?"

"There was a reference on the third page. Something about Zelov and an organization called Christalis. Then it goes back to Rasputin. So far it's essentially a biography of the life of Rasputin, the mad monk." She grimaced. "Who was apparently as mad and ugly as that nickname implies. Thief, charlatan, debaucher. I'd read about him in history courses but nothing in depth. Only that he lived back at the turn of the nineteenth century and had enormous influence over the Tsar and Tsarina before the Russian Revolution." She got into the helicopter as he held the door open for her. "So far this report is only concerning his early life. He was of peasant stock, and when he was eighteen, he became involved with a bizarre religious group, the Khlysty sect, where he met Mikhail Zelov." She glanced at him as he got into the helicopter and started the engine. "He evidently looked upon Zelov as a teacher and role model and mentions a *Book of Living* written by the master."

"Considering how Rasputin turned out, it doesn't say much for Zelov's philosophy."

"I'll tell you when I finish reading it." She opened the folder again. "It's not a very big file. It shouldn't take long."

"You might skip to the end and see why Dardon thought we might be heading for the U.S."

"Well, we certainly won't be flying this helicopter there. Just set down somewhere we can change to a plane if we need to do it."

He nodded. "We need some time to talk and make sure Dardon managed to get Irana to safety." He thought about it. "Rome?"

"It works for me," she said absently, already absorbed in the pages.

It was working for her, Garrett thought. She was concentrating, moving, mentally alive, and in gear. She had tasks to do, and that was the best thing for her right now. Just as Irana had given her mindless physical labor to start healing, this mental exercise, the sense of purpose, was right for her now.

He turned toward the west. "Then Rome it is."

After they landed in Rome, Garrett rented a car, and they checked into a small gracious hotel on the edge of the city.

"You've been very quiet," Garrett said

as he handed her a room key. "You've hardly said a word since you finished those pages. Give you something to think about?"

"Yes. But it's not enough. I need to talk to Dardon."

"We'll call him as soon as we get settled. I was going to do it anyway." He closed the door of the antique open elevator and pressed the button. "I'm right next door. Shower. Catch your breath. I'll order room service. I'll call you when it comes." He opened the elevator door and gestured to a room down the hall. "Thirty minutes. Okay?"

She nodded as she headed down the corridor. "Thirty minutes."

She paused for a moment after she closed the door behind her. Catch your breath, he had said, and it was a damn good idea. It seemed as if she had been running nonstop since Garrett had pulled her out of bed. She'd been on not only a physical but an emotional roller coaster. And that report she'd been reading had not helped. Her mind wouldn't stop trying to see beyond the sketchy references to what lay beneath.

Stop thinking. Relax. Catch your breath.

She headed for the bathroom. Shower. Shampoo.

She had nothing to wear afterward, but she could always wrap in a towel or a sheet. She'd see about getting clothes later.

It turned out that she didn't have to resort to the towel sarong. There was a unisex white terry robe in the closet. But it was still closer to forty-five minutes than thirty when she heard her cell phone ring.

"Ready?" Garrett asked. "Dinner is only coffee, a sandwich, and pasta salad. It can wait if you need more time."

"No, I'll be right there." She looked down at her bare feet peeping from the oversized robe and shrugged. No shoes. It was only Garrett, and he had seen more than her feet naked.

Garrett's feet were also bare and he was dressed in the same type of terry robe she was wearing when he answered the door. Only he looked good in it, she thought sourly. Like a Roman god in one of those mythology books. He grimaced. "I forgot about clothes. I called the concierge and asked her to pick up a couple outfits and a suitcase for us. She said she'd try to get it to us tonight. But we could have stopped on the way from the airport. Sorry."

"It doesn't matter. The robe's okay for now. But it fits you better than it does me." She came into the room. "I need to call Dardon."

"I've already called him." He held up his hand as she opened her lips to protest. "We'll call him again after we eat. I just wanted to make sure they were both safe, and I didn't want to wait." He smiled faintly. "I told you I wasn't a patient man."

"And are they safe?"

"Yes. They're on their way to Morocco."

"What?"

"It's a good launching pad for Irana. She can look the situation over and see where she's most needed. Frankly, I'd bet she chooses Ethiopia." He held out the chair at the room-service table. "As I told you, chicken sandwich, pasta salad, and some kind of apple pastry for dessert. It's filling anyway."

And Emily was hungry, she realized with surprise. "That will be fine." She sat down at the table. "But coffee, first."

He filled her cup. "Cream?"

She shook her head. "Black. I used to drink it with cream, but I've been in so many hot spots where I couldn't get my hands on it that I learned to like it without. It's all what you become accustomed to. How do you drink your coffee?"

"Black with a shot of vodka."

Her brows lifted. "Well, that's unusual."

"That's how my father drank his coffee. He used to let me take sips of it from the time I was about seven. I didn't realize anyone drank it differently until I was ten." He smiled as he poured himself a cup of black coffee. "I was very disappointed. You can't get vodka with your coffee just anywhere."

"It's a wonder you didn't turn into an alcoholic yourself."

He shook his head. "I pick and choose my vices, and I always know the consequences."

"Your father knew the consequences and still thought it was funny to let you drink."

"Exactly. Sometimes you learn more from example." He sipped his coffee. "Talk to me. Tell me about the Zelov notes."

"As I said, Zelov was just a thread in

the Rasputin tapestry." She looked down into her cup. "But I have an idea there was more than what's in this report. He seemed to be mentioned at crucial times in Rasputin's life. Whenever something happened, Zelov was in the background."

"Interesting. For instance?"

"I told you that Zelov was supposed to be his idol when Rasputin discovered the Khlysty religion. According to several sources, the sect preached that a person could only be forgiven sins if they indulged in numerous and heavy sexual encounters and could only be close to God if they immersed themselves in sin. It was a doctrine that suited Rasputin to a T, and he made it his own. He studied mysticism with Zelov and included that as part of his religion." She took a sip of coffee. "When Rasputin went on his journey to Greece and Jerusalem as a young man, Zelov was said to be with him. Rasputin was a consummate actor and got the reputation for being a holy man. When he returned to St. Petersburg, he became the rage in Russian society and later the confidant of the Tsarina. He persuaded her to accept Zelov into the royal household as an advisor."

She took a bite of her sandwich. "There's a little more. You can read it yourself."

"I intend to do that."

"And if you read it casually, you might even overlook the inferences of Zelov's place in Rasputin's life. Rasputin seemed the dominating force." She took another sip of coffee. "But what if he wasn't? We know for sure that when they started out together, Zelov was in control. What if he continued to be top gun? Maybe he wanted to remain in the background. It was certainly safer when they were trying to manipulate the Russian church and the royal household. Zelov wasn't the one who was murdered because he became too dangerous. Rasputin could have been his puppet."

"Guesswork."

"I have to guess. I don't have enough information to do anything else." She ate the last of her sandwich. "So let's go to the crux of the matter. Zelov's hammer. What could be hidden in the handle of that hammer?"

"Any number of treasures. You said he held a position at the royal palace. Some priceless bit of jewelry that belonged to the Tsarina or the princesses?"

"Perhaps." She frowned in thought. "But would a piece of jewelry be valuable enough to instigate the hiring of someone like Staunton and give him unlimited funds to retrieve it?"

"Possibly. Sometimes the intrinsic value lies in the history and not in the object itself. You know that as well as I do. Alexander the Great's sword would only be priceless if it belonged to Alexander."

Yes, no one knew that better than she did. "It would probably have to belong to the royal family. Maybe Anastasia?"

He shook his head. "I'm bowing out of the guesswork. I need more leads before I take a leap like that." He sat back in his chair. "Even if we've got the right Zelov. We can't be sure."

"I think we have." She was trying to put it together. "You said Dardon looked for a long time before he came up with this Zelov. The farm tools Staunton was inter-ested in at the museum in Afghanistan came from Russia. Zelov was in a position to acquire treasures of all descriptions at the palace. I think it's Mikhail Zelov. Now we have to find out more about him. This was just a teaser."

He smiled. "And you want to call Dardon."

"Of course, I do." She finished her salad. "And I want you to send that concierge for a laptop for me. I feel naked without mine."

"You didn't have it when you were with Irana."

And she hadn't missed it at all. She hadn't wanted to touch or be touched, and the Internet could be terribly invasive. "It's different now."

He nodded. "Yes, you're different now." He pushed back his chair. "Let's get to work. I'll call the concierge, and you get on the phone to Dardon."

"Zelov?" Dardon repeated. "You think I did good? It's pretty weird, but I thought maybe I'd struck gold."

"Pure gold," Emily said. "But there's not enough information about Zelov in this. Just hints, and there's no way to make judgments from this little. When can you give me more?"

"There's not much more to give you that's public record."

"What about that *Book of Living* Zelov wrote, which Rasputin spoke about?"

"I can't find any record of its actually existing. Hell, I can't find much evidence that Zelov existed. There are all kinds of stories about Rasputin, but I only found this one that made reference to Zelov. If this is true, then Zelov definitely liked to keep to himself. Sort of a shadow figure."

Shadows. Yes, that was the impression Emily was getting of Zelov. A man who lived in shadows, only moving out to grasp power and manipulate the people around him. "There has to be some information. What happened to him after Rasputin was murdered? Was he killed, too?"

"I checked death records for ten years following Rasputin's death, and there was no record of a death of a Mikhail Zelov. Of course Russia was in turmoil at that time. The massacre of the royal family, the revolution. There might not be a record, or it might have been destroyed in the wars and upheaval of the last hundred years."

"That's encouraging."

"I know you're disappointed. I'm still working on it. There are a couple more sites I can check."

"Then check them." She remembered something else. "You said that we might want to go to the U.S. Why?"

"I couldn't find a death record of Mikhail Zelov, so I started checking possible descendants. Now I would have run like hell if I'd thought I might be linked to Rasputin after his murder. So I checked immigration records and found that an Alexander Mikhail Zelov left St. Petersburg for New York City about the time of Rasputin's death. If that's the right Zelov, he lived to prosper and have children of his own. His great-grandson Nicholas Zelov visited Moscow only five months ago."

"Why?"

"He listed tourism as the purpose of his visit."

"Dammit, why didn't you tell us about this before?"

"I wasn't sure that this was the right Zelov. I thought I'd try to verify it."

"What's to verify? Mikhail Zelov panicked and took off when he thought he was next in line to be murdered."

"Reasonable. There's only one hitch. Alexander Mikhail Zelov left St. Petersburg several days before Rasputin was assassinated."

She stiffened. *"Before* he died?"

"Coincidence? Or was he part of the assassination plot and wanted to be sure he didn't take the fall?" He paused. "Or maybe this wasn't our Zelov, and we're on the wrong track. Are you going to go to New York and see this Nicholas Zelov and try to find out?"

She didn't even have to think about it. "Yes. Do you have his address?"

"I'll text it to Garrett's phone. It's an estate in Connecticut, not far from New York City. In the meantime, I'll see if I can find out anything else."

"Good. We need all the help we can get."

"You'll get it." He paused. "You sound much better. Irana will be glad to hear that."

"How is she?"

"Being Irana. That's pretty good."

Yes, that was very good. "Give her my

best. Call me if you find out anything else." Emily hung up.

"So we go to the U.S.?" Garrett asked from his chair across the room. "New York?"

She nodded. "The plot thickens. Zelov may have been involved in the assassination of Rasputin. He left Russia days before it happened." She frowned thoughtfully. "And one of his descendants paid a visit to Moscow five months ago. Nicholas Zelov. But Dardon doesn't know much beyond that."

"Give him a chance. We've all been a little busy lately."

"I know. It's time I stopped relying on you and Dardon and worked this out for myself."

"No, it's not time for you to stop relying on us. But I'm glad to see you rallying to the effort," he said. "I'll call and make reservations for tomorrow morning for New York."

"Why not tonight?"

"My, you are eager." He smiled. "But the concierge still has to send up the clothes and the laptop. I don't believe the airlines would appreciate us going on board barefoot and in robes. The skies aren't that friendly. Besides, a night's rest won't hurt either one of us."

She nodded and got to her feet. "Tomorrow. Early." She headed for the door. "At least, I feel as if we're making some progress. Though it's not enough. We're moving too slow."

"Yes, much too slow."

There was a curious note in his voice that made her turn at the door to look at him. His face was without expression, but there was something . . . She opened the door. "Good night, Garrett."

He didn't answer, and she closed the door behind her. That last interchange had disturbed her. He was evidently as discouraged as she about the lack of information they'd gotten on Zelov. Perhaps even more disappointed. At least she felt as if they'd gotten a tiny insight into Zelov and what might be in the hammer. That insight was clearly not enough to satisfy Garrett. How could she blame him? Today he had learned one of his best friends had been killed, Irana was in danger, and his home on Mykala had been burned to the ground.

And it was all because he had linked

himself to Emily and her search for Staunton. Of course, he was impatient. He wanted it over.

And Emily wanted it over, too. They had barely started, and she was already on edge and frustrated. The information about Zelov had given her a sense of overwhelming darkness and foreboding. Evil seemed to surround both the origin of Zelov's hammer and the horror it had spread down to this day.

But she couldn't be frustrated or impatient. She had to think clearly and without emotion. Tomorrow they would get on the plane, and soon they'd be able to take action, find answers that would lead her to Staunton.

Dear God, she hoped that was true.

Garrett hung up after making their flight reservations and sat looking down at the phone. Everything was moving. Irana was as safe as he could make her. Soon they would be on that plane to New York. Maybe he should just accept the status quo. God knows it was what he wanted to do.

But he couldn't do it. That was one of

the mistakes he had made, and Karif had died.

God, Karif . . .

He blocked the wave of sorrow and regret that thought brought. Memories were the enemy. He had no time to grieve now. He had to be hard as a diamond to cut through the web in which Emily was enfolding him. That shouldn't be such a stretch. When had he been anything else?

Hard as a diamond.

NINE

"I'll be knocking on your door in two minutes," he said, when Emily picked up the
phone over an hour later. "Sorry if I woke
you."

"You didn't wake me. I couldn't sleep.
Is something wrong? Why do you want
to—" But Garrett had already hung up.
Emily had just gotten out of the bed and
turned on the light when Garrett knocked.
"What is it? Why are you—"

"Your clothes." He set the suitcase
beside the door.

She felt a rush of relief. "Oh, is that all?

I thought you—" She stopped as she saw his expression.

"We have to talk." He came into the room and shut the door. "Remember, I warned you when we were on the helicopter that we had to find a place to talk."

She remembered, but realized she had subconsciously tried to push that memory away. Now it was staring in her face. She moistened her lips. "This isn't about Zelov."

"It might be. I don't know. You'll have to tell me." He gazed into her eyes. "You'll have to tell me everything, Emily. Every minute, every detail of that time with Staunton."

She flinched. She had known it was coming, but the shock was still sharp. "I don't remember every detail. Some of it is a blur."

"I'll help you."

Help her go through that hell again? "I told you about the hammer. That's all that's important."

"That's all that you remember that's important. There might be more. We'll dig it all out."

"You sound like a dentist," she said

unevenly. "Only you aren't using anesthesia, are you?"

"No." His lips tightened. "And I won't stop until it's over, no matter how much you're hurting. It has to be done. I've waited too long as it is."

His expression was totally hard, totally without mercy, yet it was not without emotion. But she couldn't read what those feelings were. "Your CIA man, Ferguson, wanted to debrief me, and you stopped him."

"You were too fragile. I didn't want you to break."

"Yet now you're going to do it."

"If you break, I'll find a way to put together the pieces."

Dear heaven, she was afraid. "I could say no."

"Yes, you could."

She closed her eyes, fighting the panic. "No, I can't. Because you're right, dammit. I can't trust myself because I didn't want to do anything but shut it out. I can remember lying there in that hut and dreading going back to Joel. I tried to build a cocoon around myself, but it didn't work." Her eyes were stinging as she opened them. "It never worked. Staunton managed to rip it open every time. Yes, I might know something I don't know I know." She drew a deep breath. "I'm sorry I'm fighting you. I promised you I'd tell you everything, didn't I? And I will. It just came as a—I didn't expect it to be tonight." She turned away. "So let's get on with the debriefing. Or should we call it the confessional? That's what Irana would probably—"

"You have nothing to confess, dammit. You're not guilty of anything."

"I felt guilty. I couldn't help him. There should have been a way I could help him." She tried to keep her voice from shaking. "Shouldn't you have a tape recorder or something? Don't you have to take notes?"

"No, I'll remember everything."

"Of course, you will. You're very clever." She curled up in the easy chair by the window, tucking her legs beneath the terry robe. She was cold, terribly cold. "And you'll see that I remember everything."

"Yes," he said hoarsely. "Everything."

"Stop towering over me. Sit down somewhere. Let's get this over with."

He sat down on the edge of the bed.

She looked away from him and stared blindly at the wall beyond him. She could get through this. She only had to remember that she was doing it for Joel. That living through that horror again was the only way she could help him now. Just one more time.

"Where do you want me to start?"

"When you got off the plane in Kabul."

"That far back?"

"Yes. I want to know every detail."

"I'm not arguing. I'm just surprised." But it was a relief not to have to dive into that day at the museum right away. "We didn't actually go to Afghanistan to go to the museum. We were diverted by some high-up official in the central government, Aman Nemid. He'd grown up in the area and . . ." She kept talking quickly, feverishly, not letting herself see the direction she was going.

Until she was there, riding in the truck with Joel. Laughing with him, being teased about Springsteen, worrying about the weather.

She suddenly froze. It was coming. Just around the bend.

"Bruce Springsteen?" Garrett asked. "'Dancing in the Dark'?"

She wasn't really there on that road from the museum. She was here with Garrett. Keep it separate. "I like Springsteen." But she could go on now. Talk fast. Tell him about the overturned truck. Tell him about the blood running from beneath it.

Staunton standing there cradling the AK-47 in his arm.

Talk.

Go numb.

Don't think.

Just talk.

For God's sake, don't think.

"I bit his lip as hard as I could. He was bleeding." The words were feverishly tumbling out. "It felt good. I wanted to *savage* him. It didn't matter any longer. He couldn't hurt Joel. No one could hurt Joel any longer. He hit me, then he forced me out in the snow to go to Shafir Ali's tent. He was swearing and threatening, but it didn't matter. He couldn't hurt—"

"Stop it." Garrett was suddenly beside her, kneeling on the floor before her. "No more."

"But I haven't finished. You said I had to tell you everything. I've got to finish. He took me to Shafir and told him to—"

"You're finished. It's over." He grasped her shoulders and shook her. "Shut up. Okay?"

She gazed dazedly at him. It was the first time she had looked at him since she had started. His expression was no longer hard; it was twisted with pain, haggard. . . . "Finished?"

"God, yes." He turned out the light. He gathered her up and carried her to the bed. "Never again. You can forget it."

"No, I can't." She tried to keep from slurring. "It's there waiting for me. All you had to do was probe now and then, and it all came back. . . ."

"Yes, that's all I had to do."

He sounded bitter. She should try to think why—No, it was too hard. She had barely been aware of him in the past hours. He had only been a voice guiding her, questioning her, making her pause when she wanted to run ahead. At first she had hated that voice, but then it had become part of her. Strange . . .

He was laying her down on the bed, covering her with the blanket. Then he was lying down beside her and drawing her into his arms. "Go to sleep. I'll stay with you. There won't be any nightmares tonight. I'll guard you. God knows, it's the least I can do."

That bitterness again. Yes, keep the nightmares away. She was too weak to do it herself tonight. "Thank you." She closed her eyes and curled closer to him. "I'm very tired. . . ."

"You're practically shell-shocked." His words were muffled in her hair. "I know while you're hating me you won't believe this, but I'm . . . sorry."

"I believe you." She opened her eyes to look at him. "And I don't hate you. Why should I? It had to be done before we could move on."

"And I was the one to do it." His lips twisted. "I seem to be destined to be a catalyst, don't I? First, Irana, now you."

"I couldn't blame you when all of this is about me."

"No. This is all about Staunton." He stroked her hair away from her face. "And you're telling me you didn't hate me even for a moment while we were going through that hell?"

"At first, I—but then you became part of it."

"What?"

She tried to put her thoughts together. "Part of it. Part of me. I wasn't alone any longer. We were together." She couldn't hold her eyes open any longer. "It was a terrible thing going through that horror alone. But I wasn't alone this time. It was as if you were going through it with me, standing beside me."

"I was. I will be."

"So I couldn't hate you. . . ." She had a sudden thought. "Did I say anything that we can use?"

"Yes, a couple things."

"Then it wasn't for nothing."

"No. I'd cut my throat if I thought it was." He brushed his lips across her forehead. "Go to sleep."

She was already dozing off. "I'm sorry about your friend, Karif. I didn't tell you, did I?" she whispered. "I know how it is to lose—"

"I know you do. Go to sleep."

"I just wanted to tell you. . . ."

Emily's breathing was deep and steady, and she was curled against him like a little girl with a teddy bear.

Only he wasn't a teddy bear, and Garrett had spent the last hour making her go through hell. It was no wonder that she had practically fallen unconscious when it was over.

You were part of it. Part of me.

She was right, he had been there. With every word she spoke, he had been drawn deeper into the ugly morass she had undergone. He had felt her fear and her rage and helplessness.

And her hatred for Staunton.

Only now it was his hatred.

Garrett was still in the bed beside her when Emily woke up the next morning. He was lying on his back, his arm beneath his head, staring absently at the wall across the room.

He glanced sideways at her as she stirred. "Awake?" He rolled over on his side and looked down at her. "Are you okay?"

She had been a moment ago, but she was suddenly uncertain. He was too close. Dark eyes gazing down at her, the sensual curve of his lips, the high cheekbones that made her want to reach out and touch. What was wrong with her? She felt as if she couldn't breathe. She could feel the warmth of his body, and her own body was tingling. She could feel the heat in her cheeks.

"Oh, yes," he said softly. His eyes were narrowed on her face. "You're more than okay." He reached out and lightly touched the hollow of her throat with his fingers.

She felt her pulse leap beneath his touch. "I'm . . . fine."

He stared down at her for an instant. Then he took his hand away and glanced away from her. "Good. It's time we got moving. We have a plane to catch." He sat up in bed and swung his legs to the floor. "We may not have time for breakfast here. We'll catch something at the airport."

His briskness robbed the moment of any hint of the former intimacy, she realized, with a bewildering mixture of relief and disappointment. "You said I had to be as incognito as I was able to be. Getting on a plane and flashing ID is hardly in line with that."

"It is, if the ID is right," he said. "I had Dardon working on getting you a phony passport from the day I took you to Irana. When all hell broke loose, I grabbed it before I went to get you. You're Sandra Martinez. The picture in it vaguely resembles you but the hair is dark, and so is the complexion. Pull your hair back from your face in a knot. We'll stop on the way to the airport at a theatrical supply store and pick up a dark wig and makeup."

"Did you have to get a phony passport, too?"

He smiled and shook his head. "I have a few I keep on hand." He headed for the door. "Even though I'm retired, old habits die hard."

"Garrett."

He stopped to look back at her.

She moistened her lips. "Thank you," she said awkwardly. "I would have been all right. You didn't have to stay with me last night."

"Yes, I did." His lips twisted in a wry smile. "I'd like to say it was my pleasure, but it wasn't. I'm not used to sleeping with women without the usual sexual gratification. It's damn hard for me." He chuckled. "Literally." Then his smile faded. "But it was worth it. I needed to do something positive, to give you something, to make up for last night. So I watched over you and kept the monsters at bay. I didn't slay the dragon, but that will come." He opened the door. "Can you be ready in forty minutes?"

"Yes."

"I'll see you then."

She got out of bed as soon as the door closed behind him. She had thought that she would feel nervous and distraught after last night, but it wasn't happening. The memories had been agonizingly painful, but she had gotten through them and survived. *They* had gotten through them, and she felt stronger for it. She had been telling the truth when she had told Garrett that she had felt as if he had become part of her. It had been strange. First he'd been like a hovering shadow, then closer to her, then merging. Strange and . . . comforting.

Comforting wasn't a word that usually applied to Garrett. He was smart, sophisticated, dangerous, and complex. Yet there had been moments when she had felt safer with him than with anyone she had ever known.

And there were moments like the one when she had first opened her eyes this morning and felt as unsure and wide-eyed as she had been as a young girl. Well, she would have to accept both sides of her feelings for Garrett until she could come to terms with them.

She shrugged and moved toward the bathroom. All this soul-searching about Garrett wasn't doing her any good. It wasn't how she felt about him that was important. It was how he could help her find and kill Staunton.

And the man who hired that son of a bitch. She still had trouble focusing on anyone but Staunton. She needed a name, a face.

But she had another name now. Nicholas Zelov. The descendant of the man who had manipulated Rasputin and the royal family. Nicholas Zelov, who had visited Moscow only five months ago.

Nicholas Zelov, the man who might lead them to Staunton.

"Very exotic," Garrett said, tilting his head to look at her as she came out of the theatrical supply house. "Amazing what a change of hair color can do."

Emily shook her head as she touched the short dark wig. "I don't think I look that much different."

"Enough. Dark complexion, dark hair, different style. Most people don't probe or analyze. They accept what's on the surface." He opened the door of the waiting cab for her. "It's the best we can do without getting a full disguise job. That would be uncomfortable as hell for you." He got into the cab. "Believe me."

"Have you ever had to use a disguise?" she asked curiously.

"Yes." He didn't elaborate. "It should do. I just wish we could avoid commercial transportation entirely. But there's not time to make other arrangements."

"I haven't been back to the U.S. for a long time. Is security that tight?"

"Tight enough, but I'm not worried about

U.S. security. We have to make a stop first."

She looked at him in surprise. "What stop?"

"Kabul."

She stiffened. "We're going back to Afghanistan?"

He nodded. "There's something we have to follow up there before we go to New York. I need to talk to someone in Kabul."

"Who?"

"Aman Nemid. You said that was the name of the government official who diverted you from your assigned mission when you got to Afghanistan. He arranged for you to go up to the mountains and clear that museum. Is that right?"

She nodded. "He used to live in that area and had a special interest."

"I'm curious to know just how special. I want to talk to him."

"You think he may be involved in that raid on our team?"

"Maybe. I'm suspicious of anything out of the ordinary when it has extraordinary results."

"He's on the National Council, and evidently the U.N. respects him, or they wouldn't have given in to his request. He may not be involved."

"Good. We'll just ask a few questions."

"You do believe Nemid set up the trap with Staunton?"

"Or maybe he had his own agenda and sent you up there to bring him back the bacon with no risk to himself, if he knew that there were other parties interested in the contents of that museum."

Emily shook her head. "I can't believe he would have sent our team if he knew what was waiting for us."

He shrugged. "It's something we have to explore. Zelov can wait for a day or two." He grimaced. "As I said, I just wish we didn't have to go into Kabul's airport. That's Ferguson's territory, which makes it a double whammy. I'm calling Dardon and telling him to find a way to get us out of there, but I want to move now."

And he obviously thought the risk of recognition was worth it. "Then let's move."

"No arguments?"

"You didn't really think I'd argue with you." Even though she didn't want to go back to Afghanistan. She was afraid it would bring too many memories to vivid life. "If Aman Nemid's involved, I want to know about it. If he hadn't sent us to the museum, none of this would have happened." She looked out the window of the cab. "I didn't make the connection, but I damned well want to know if there is one. Do you know where he lives?"

"I checked it out this morning. He has a house on the outskirts of the city. Which may prove convenient." He smiled. "I like privacy."

"You won't believe it." Moore turned to Ferguson. "Garrett was spotted at the airport."

Ferguson stiffened. "Here in Kabul? You're sure?"

"Dietrich said he's certain. You made all our guys study that photo of him until they were ready to pitch it. He caught a glimpse of him when they were leaving customs."

"They?"

"A woman. Dietrich didn't get a good look at her. Dark hair."

Ferguson began to swear. "He wouldn't

do it. He wouldn't have the nerve to bring her back here."

"Emily Hudson?"

"Who else? Is Dietrich following them?"

"He wouldn't have risked calling you if he wasn't."

"Damn straight. And he'd better not lose them. Tell Dietrich not to interfere with them until I get there." He got to his feet. "Come on. Let's move."

"We're being followed," Garrett said, his gaze on the rearview mirror. "He's being careful, and he's good."

Emily's gaze flew to the mirror. "How long?"

"I noticed him a few blocks after we left the airport."

They had left the airport twenty minutes ago. "Why didn't you tell me?"

"I'm telling you now. I wanted to see if he was going to be joined by anyone."

"Who do you think—Staunton?"

"I'd bet it's one of Ferguson's men," Garrett said. "He was bound to have someone at the airport."

"And you came here anyway?"

"I told you, I have to check out Nemid."

And nothing was going to stop him, Emily realized, once more aware of the ruthless intensity that drove him. "Well, we may have trouble if Ferguson gets in the way."

"Yes, it's time we lost him." He pressed the accelerator, and the car jumped forward. "Hold on."

She had to hold on. The next ten minutes were a nightmare of twists and turns, sudden stops and swerves.

"Okay, I think we're clear," Garrett glanced at the mirror. "And Nemid's house should be a mile up the road."

"And are we just going to walk up and ring the doorbell?"

"No, I like the idea of surprise and an element of threat. I've found it works. I'll look the place over and see if I can locate where he is, then go in."

"What if the doors are locked?"

"No problem."

No, she imagined he might have experience in handling locked doors. He probably had experience in handling all kinds of dubious practices. "Not too much threat.

After all, we're not certain he's done anything wrong."

"I suppose you'll be there with me to make sure that I don't." He glanced at her as he parked the car near a large house surrounded by a low brick wall. "You wouldn't consider waiting here?"

"No." She got out of the car. "I would not."

"I didn't think so." His glance skimmed the exterior of the house. "There's a light on the far side of the house. Let's start there." He took a small black box out of his pocket. "But we might as well have a head start."

"What's that?"

"An infrared detector. The heat indication will show if there's someone in the house."

"Really? Neat gadget. My father could have used one of those when we were tracking animals for one of his photo shoots." Her gaze was fastened on the light shining from the windows. "Do you see anything?"

"Yes." He frowned as he looked down at the infrared detector. "Two moving blips and two stationary in that room. What the hell?"

"What do you mean you lost him?" Ferguson asked.

"He knew he was being followed," Dietrich said. "And he was damn good."

"And if you were good, he wouldn't have known he was being followed. Where was he when you realized he was trying to lose you?"

"About six blocks south of here."

Six blocks.

That was in one of the nicer sections of Kabul. What was Garrett doing in that area? For that matter, what was he doing in Kabul at all? He took his GPS from his pocket, typed in a city map, then narrowed it down to the particular area. Then he started to scroll up the addresses and names of the people living in that area.

"I'm going to get you, Garrett," he murmured. "I'm going to have your ass."

"I don't like it." Garrett stopped short as they cautiously approached the window with light pouring out into the courtyard.

"Four indications of people in that room. But where is his guard? There should be one in the courtyard."

"Maybe he doesn't have one." Though it was unusual. She knew that the tense political situation in Afghanistan made it necessary that the council members be closely guarded. "Or maybe he's not at home."

"Maybe." Garrett stiffened as he looked down at the detector. "Two of the blips are gone from the room, moving toward the back of the house. "I don't like it," he repeated. I'm going in alone to check things out. Don't argue. You don't have a weapon, and you'd be in my way. If I don't call you in three minutes, get the hell out of here."

"No. I want to—"

But he'd already opened the door and was inside.

She muttered an oath as the door shut in her face.

Should she go after Garrett?

If she went blundering in search of him, it could get clumsy and dangerous. He was right, she had no weapon. That wouldn't happen a second time. But it was sensible to stay out here and wait.

She didn't want to be sensible. She wanted to barge in and—

It didn't matter what she wanted. She wouldn't chance getting Garrett hurt. So she'd stay out here and wait, dammit.

It was quiet here in the courtyard. Just the soft trickle of the fountain and the sound of the night insects. It should have been peaceful, but she didn't feel peaceful. She didn't like—

The door flew open. "Come in," Garrett said. "Quick."

His voice was sharp and his mouth tight. Something was wrong.

She was beside him in an instant. "What is it?" She whispered.

"You don't have to be quiet," Garrett said grimly. "No one can hear you." He threw open the door of the library. "I wouldn't have brought you in if I didn't need your help."

Blood.

A man lay crumpled to the left of the door, blood pouring out of his stomach.

"Dear God," she whispered.

"That's the guard." Garrett strode toward the desk. "Nemid is over here. He has a gun in his hand. He evidently tried to reach for a weapon when his guard was murdered."

Emily slowly crossed the room and stared down at Nemid. Or what remained of Nemid. His head was half blown off his body.

"Staunton."

"That's my guess. Or more than likely someone who worked for him. Those moving heat indications were his men, first in here, then running down the hall toward the back entrance. I took a look and the kitchen door was wide open." Garrett said. "These are fresh kills." He glanced around the library. "And afterward they tore up the room looking for something."

For the first time, Emily was aware of the couch cushions thrown on the floor. A wall safe stood open, with documents scattered on the floor beneath it. Papers in disarray on the desk, books pulled out of the shelves. "Maybe they wanted it to look like a burglary."

"Or maybe they were in a hurry and didn't care. That's why I'd bet on its being one of Staunton's men."

"Borg."

"It doesn't matter. There's a chance he

didn't find what he was looking for. He didn't have much time before we drove up. Someone must have been acting as look-out while the other one searched. That's why I called you into the house. We have to move fast. Let's see if we can find what he didn't."

"We don't even know what we're looking for," Emily said. "A hammer? No, he was looking in those books. Some of them are open as if he'd been leafing through them. It has to be a paper of some sort." Death all around her. Blood all around her. She drew a deep breath. "I'll take the rest of the books in the shelves. You go through the desk again."

"Check the books on the floor that they discarded and feel for thickness. It could be under the cover or the faceplate."

"You don't have to tell me. I know all about thieves and hiding objects." She had a memory of going over the walls in the basement of the museum with Joel. "Check the walls for any hidden hollows or safes." She shook her head. "No, I'll do it." She moved toward the wall beside the book-shelves. "I'll be faster."

He nodded. "I imagine you will." He

went to the desk and knelt. "And that's a top priority. Ferguson is damn good. He'll be on our tail in a heartbeat."

"Find anything?" Moore asked Ferguson.

"Nothing." He skipped to the next quadrant on the map. "Neither Garrett nor Emily Hudson had any connection with anyone in that area."

"That we know about," Moore said.

"That's what I need. Encouragement," Ferguson said sourly. "I'll find them."

"We could call headquarters and get them to use a satellite to home in on—"

"And by the time we get through the red tape, Garrett and Hudson will be out of the city." He studied the quadrant and punched the cross-reference button. "This could be faster if we don't have to go through too many—*Yes.*" An address had been suddenly highlighted in red on the screen. A name and telephone number immediately followed. "Nemid. What connection . . . ?" Then it came to him. It was Nemid who had been responsible for sending Emily Hudson to the museum, and he had been one of the most vocal council members urging her to be found. "We've got them." He started the car. "How long is it going to take us to get there?"

Moore checked the GPS. "Eight point five miles."

Garrett found a secret drawer in the left side of the desk. "Nemid seems to have had a liking for secret cubbyholes. The regular safe wasn't enough."

"A safe is the first place anyone looks," Emily said as she ran her fingers over the upper wall. "Is there anything in it?"

"We'll know soon." He took his pocketknife and jimmied the drawer open. "Papers. Documents of some kind. Could be pay dirt."

"Take them." She continued to run her fingers over the wall, then moved to the wall on the other side of the door. "And keep looking. A secret desk drawer is the second-most-popular place to look. Nemid was a smart man. He would have known that he should throw out some red herrings. He wouldn't have used anything that simple."

"This could be what we're looking for. We don't have much time."

"Just a little longer."

"Look, Emily, we have two murdered men and our fingerprints are all over this room. Who's to say you didn't come here to murder Nemid because he sent you on that mission to the museum? We can't afford to be caught here."

She hesitated. "Just a few minutes more." She crossed to the wall behind the desk, keeping her eyes off the crumpled body of Nemid only a few feet away. Her fingertips were light and sensitive on the wall. "Let me do this. . . ."

"Four minutes," Moore said. "Should we call reinforcements?"

"No, I want to handle this myself."

"That's right; Emily Hudson is still something of a heroine in the media's eyes. We wouldn't want her to cause problems."

"She's already causing problems," Ferguson said curtly. "But I'll find a way to stop it. I'll find a way to stop both of them."

TEN

"Got it." Emily tensed, her fingers moving carefully over the surface. "Circular, and the drywall is thicker in the center."

"Great." Garrett was beside her, his knife out. "Step aside, and I'll see what we have." He started cutting into the drywall. "Did I ever tell you that you're pretty fantastic? My kind of woman . . ."

"Because I know how to burgle a safe?"

"Among other things. Definitely a cavity." He carefully widened the hole and shined his flashlight into it. "Bull's-eye." He reached in and drew out a shallow box. He opened it to reveal a single sheet of paper.

"Nemid evidently wanted it well protected." He grabbed her arm and headed for the front door. "Let's get out of here before it's too late. We've been here too long already."

It was already too late.

As they reached the courtyard, a car screeched to a halt at the curb behind their own.

"Shit. Back way." Garrett took her hand and ran back into the house. "Straight down the hall." He opened the door at the end of the corridor, turned left, and darted down the next corridor.

Kitchen.

They tore toward the door across the room.

"There they are," Ferguson said, exultant, as he caught sight of Garrett and Emily disappearing back into the house. "I knew we'd get them." He jumped out of the car and ran toward the front door. "Moore, you come with me. Dietrich, you go around back."

Ferguson drew his gun as he ran through the front door. "Garrett, come out.

You can't get—" His gaze froze on the two bodies on the library floor. "Holy shit."

"Stay behind me." Garrett ran down the steps, and Emily followed close behind. "Ferguson will have sent someone—" He caught sight of Dietrich as he came around the corner of the house and ran toward him. "Keep going."

Dietrich was drawing his gun.

Emily stopped, then started to follow Garrett.

Garrett braced and went low, tackling Dietrich. He gave the CIA man a karate chop to the neck and leapt to his feet as the agent went limp.

"I told you to go on." He grabbed her hand and half pulled her with him as he ran out of the back courtyard into the street. "Run."

They ran.

Down the block.

Turned right, then turned left.

"Can't we double back to the car?" Emily asked, her breath coming in gasps.

"Too risky. Ferguson might have left someone there in case we did."

"Only one man?"

"Yes, but he'd be good. I might have to kill him. I don't think you want that to happen."

She remembered the vicious violence he'd used on the man in the courtyard. "No. But we're on foot. Ferguson must be after us by now in his car."

"Probably." He saw the gleam of head-lights as a car turned the corner three blocks down. "Definitely." He pulled her into the deep alcove of a shop and pressed her into the shadows against the wall with his body. "Not a word," he whispered. "He's moving slow."

She couldn't speak if she wanted to do it. She was holding her breath. Her heart was racing. Slow? It was taking that car forever to cover those three blocks.

Then out of the corner of her eye she saw a beam of light.

Would they catch sight of them? Would the car stop?

The car was alongside them now, only several feet away.

Lord, they were creeping.

Then the car passed them, and Emily

saw the red taillights as it moved down the street.

Her breath escaped in a rush of relief.

Garrett shook his head and put his finger to his lips.

She nodded.

A moment later he took a step back. "They turned at the next corner. We'll double back and make our way down to the market on the cross street."

"Is it safe?"

"No, Ferguson will be searching the entire city, and if he turns the locals loose, it will be worse. But we need to get to somewhere safe, and I know someone who runs a jewelry shop in the market. That's as close to safe as we're going to get." He started down the street. "Move."

She was already half-running to keep up with him. "Should we be running away? It's Ferguson. He's CIA. He should be able to help us."

"If he chooses to do it," Garrett said. "And if he gets his hands on us, he doesn't have to make a choice. He'll be in charge." They'd reached the corner, and Garrett turned right. "We'll have to make sure that doesn't happen. Ferguson likes control, and he's not above sacrificing a few scruples to get it. Believe me, I know. I've seen him operate, and it's not pretty. He once abandoned me to the mercies of drug runners in the jungle in Colombia when he knew the chances of my getting out were slim to none. He didn't even try to save me."

"So what are we going to do? You said I could be accused of the murders." She still felt the same shock she had when Garrett had said those words in the library. "There has to be some way that—"

"There is a way," Garrett said, his pace increasing. "But not until I get to a place where I can make a safe call. And it has to be fast. Ferguson is going to have to make a decision soon, and we have to get in under the wire."

"We need to make a deal," Garrett said when Ferguson picked up the phone an hour later.

Ferguson felt a swift surge of satisfaction. "I don't have to do a damn thing. I've got you, Garrett." He made a motion to Moore to trace the call.

"You haven't got me, or I wouldn't be calling you. And you may not want to have me if it means that you're going to have to bring Emily into this. So let's talk deal. Providing you still have anything with which to deal. Have you informed the Afghan government about Nemid's death?"

"Not yet."

"I didn't think you'd be in a hurry. First, you'd send a team back to make sure that there isn't anything interesting lying around there that could be of interest to the Company. You didn't find anything, did you?"

"I'll have to get a report. It's early yet. What were you after, Garrett?"

"I was after whatever the person who killed Nemid was after."

"And did you get it?"

"Maybe." He paused. "But I don't know what it is yet. I have to have time to find out."

"You're not going to have time. I'm going to have your ass, Garrett. None of this bullshit about deals. I'm on top now."

Moore was shaking his head. No trace.

Ferguson muttered a curse.

"Irritated?" Garrett said. "That must mean you've found out you're not going to be able to trace me. I took the trouble to relay the call several times around the world. It made me a little nervous taking the time, but I knew it was necessary. Now let's talk deal. You don't want to pull Emily into this."

"I do if she shot Nemid. I figure she was pissed at having been sent up to those mountains by Nemid and decided to blow his head off. She was unstable and took revenge on an innocent man."

"Only he wasn't innocent. He was dirty as hell. He wouldn't have been killed if he hadn't been in on the raid. Staunton killed him to keep his mouth shut and to get something he was holding."

"Staunton?"

"The man who killed Levy."

"Why are you telling me about him now?"

"Because I'm very much afraid we have to be partners. Extremely limited partners." He paused. "You don't want them to go after Emily. We both know how that would look for you. You told everyone she was ill and in seclusion and that it was you who put her there. Any way you look at it, you're going to look bad if she turns out to be a killer. Either she's a victim who should have had treatment and didn't receive it. Or she killed her friend's murderer because she couldn't get any satisfaction from the authorities, namely you, and had to do the job herself. Either way, you're not going to look good."

"I can work around it."

"Even if Emily tells the media that you told her that killing Nemid was the only way she'd get justice? The Afghan council doesn't trust the CIA anyway. They'd just assume you had your own agenda and used her to kill off Nemid because he was causing you problems."

No, Emily Hudson could give him headaches galore if Garrett primed her to cause him trouble, Ferguson thought bitterly. He might have to deal. "You didn't kill Nemid?"

"They were dead when we got there. And Nemid must have known his assailant, or the guard wouldn't have let him into the house."

"He would have known Emily Hudson."

"True. But he would have been on the alert since he'd be afraid she suspected him." He paused. "She didn't kill him,

Ferguson. The son of a bitch deserved it, but she didn't do it. Neither did I. It was Staunton or one of his men."

"Why?"

"I don't know yet. I'll find out. But I need time, and I can't do anything if you or the Afghans come after me."

"So what's the deal?"

"You do a cleanup job at Nemid's house and make sure that there's no evidence linking us."

"That could spark an international incident if they tumble to what I'm doing."

"And you never do anything that's not safe and aboveboard? Come on, Ferguson."

He didn't answer for a moment. "Not unless it's worth my while."

"You want to clean all the mud off your coattails and you want the director and the whole world to think you're a hero. That would make it worth your while."

"And you're going to do that?"

"I'll do it. I'll find Staunton, and I'll make sure that you're involved. I'll make you shine, Ferguson. You'll get the credit for bringing the bad guy to justice."

"Why should I trust you?"

"I give you my word." He added sarcastically, "You'll remember, I keep my word. I've never left *you* in the lurch."

"It was necessary." Ferguson was going over his options. Whatever he decided, he'd have to move fast. Garrett did keep his word. He could count on that either way. He'd either make Ferguson a hero or find a way to sting him big-time. "Maybe I don't need you now that I have a name. I can go after Staunton myself."

"And now we're back to Emily and her ability to cause you an infinite amount of trouble."

Yes, there was that stumbling block. Emily Hudson was a heroine and a martyr, and the media would jump at the chance of crucifying him. He thought about it for another moment. "Okay. Deal. But if you try to screw me, I'll hang you out to dry."

"I won't screw you. Now call off your guys. Tell them it was all a mistake, and Emily and I are pure as a child's first prayer. I'll be in touch." He hung up.

He'd better be in touch, Ferguson thought as he hung up. I'm going to be walking a tightrope, and I'm not going to be on it alone. He turned to Moore. "We need to order a cleanup."

"He took the bait." Garrett turned to Emily. "I think. Unless he wants us to feel safe, then scoops us up."

Emily shook her head. "He's that deceptive?"

"He's that self-serving. But if he believes that he'll be better off playing ball with us, then he'll go along." He looked out the shop window. "But we'll know if he cleans up the Nemid scene. I don't think we'd better try to move until we get word on that." He turned to Fatin ben Lufti, a small, plump man with dark eyes. "I thank you for sheltering us. I don't believe there will be any trouble now. Is it all right if we stay here for a little longer?"

"It is my pleasure. I've been waiting for a long time for you to ask a return," Fatin said. "May I get you food? Drink?"

"Food would be good. But not now. Maybe later." Garrett turned to Emily as the small man left the room. "It may take hours before they discover the bodies. Ferguson will want to make sure it's done by someone who has no connection with him. Try to relax."

"That won't be easy. I feel as if my every nerve is wired." She sat down in a damask-draped chair by the window and looked around the shop. It was like an Aladdin's cave with gold chains and jewelry hanging from display shelves all around the store. "Who is Fatin?"

"I told you, he's a friend. I've known him for years. He used to live in the mountains, but he came to the city to make a better living. He did well."

"He said something about a return. You did him a favor?"

"I did a favor for his sister. I managed to get her out of the country to Switzerland before she could be stoned. She made the mistake of being unfaithful to the man she married. It didn't matter that he beat her and treated her like dung. Fatin couldn't help her himself. He'd have been ostracized by his family."

Emily knew that the situation was not uncommon, but it still sickened her. "I thought the government was making strides to give women more freedom."

"They can't stop what they can't see

behind closed doors. They're taking baby steps."

"So there's a reason why your friend is willing to risk his neck for you."

"I wouldn't ask it if I could help it. He knows that."

"You seem to have a lot of friends who are willing to go to the wall for you."

"Yes."

There was a note in his voice that caused her to glance at him. Then it hit home to her what she had said. "That was thoughtless. Your friend, Karif . . . I didn't mean—" She shook her head. "I didn't intend to hurt you. I guess I'm not thinking about what I'm saying."

"Never apologize for speaking the truth. Karif died because I asked him to help." His lips twisted. "This won't be as dangerous for Fatin. I'll tell them I broke into the shop if we're caught here." He sat down in the chair opposite her. "But I don't believe there's any danger of that. I'm just being careful, Emily."

She nodded. "I guess I'm just . . . shaken." She laughed ruefully at the understatement. "I'm not accustomed to dead bodies and chases and having to make deals to keep from being thrown into jail."

"I'd never know it." He smiled. "You take to it like a duck to water."

"I don't want to take to it." She shivered. "It's terrible. Death and blood and . . ."

"The death of a man who didn't care if you and your whole team died."

"I know that." She tried to think of something besides Nemid with his head half blown off. "I felt too helpless back there. I want you to get me a gun."

He nodded. "I'll make sure that we pick one up for you in New York. It would be a little difficult here. Any preference?"

"I usually like the .40-caliber Glock."

His brows lifted. "Usually?"

"Usually," she repeated emphatically. She hadn't liked the way he had assumed that she was to stay safely in the background at Nemid's. She had to set the record straight before they went any further. "You persist in thinking that I'm helpless and unable to protect myself. That's not true. I traveled with my father to some pretty wild places, and he would never have let me go if he hadn't thought I'd be able to take care of myself. I learned to shoot when I was eight. By the time I was twelve, I was pretty damn good. When I was sixteen, my father and I fought off a truckload of ivory poachers at an elephant reserve in Africa. Since then I've had to deal with thieves and guerrillas who thought museums were only for plundering. I don't need you because I'm helpless. I need you because you're more familiar with this kind of battleground, and I have to be sure I'm going to get Staunton."

He smiled. "The Glock will do very well for Staunton."

"That's what I thought," Emily said. "And why was Nemid killed? What's in the box that was in the wall?"

"Let's see." He drew the box out of his jacket pocket. It was approximately four inches by eight inches and intricately carved. "Beautiful box. Very ornate. It might say that he regarded what was inside to be just as important." He opened the box and carefully took out the folded sheet of paper covering a velvet-wrapped object and studied it. "It's a map of Russia and central Europe. Pretty old but nothing special. It's just the kind of commercial map you'd pick up in any shop or train station." He handed it to her. "But according to the script on the top it was published in St. Petersburg in 1913."

She shook her head. "Russian script? Does it say anything else?"

He nodded. "No. I can read Russian. As I said, it appears to be just an ordinary commercial map." He took back the paper and unfolded the cloth. He gave a low whistle. "Well, what do we have here?"

It was a hand-painted amulet of a man with a full black beard and burning dark eyes. Emily had seen that face in too many history books not to recognize it. "Rasputin."

Garrett nodded. "You can't say that face isn't memorable. Those words under his picture are a prayer and blessings on the wearer. And it's much smaller and more delicate than the usual amulet." With one finger he traced the delicate gold frame and intricate scrollwork surrounding it. "But who was the wearer?"

"There's no inscription?"

Garrett shook his head. "It's pretty generic. I wonder if Rasputin gave them out to his fans like the Pope does rosaries. From what I've read, Rasputin had that kind of ego."

"Rasputin was in power just before the Russian Revolution when Nicholas II and his entire family were assassinated. But even if it belonged to someone in the royal family, it couldn't be that valuable. It has no jewels, and it's not inscribed to anyone. Or maybe it's the map that's important."

"I'll check it out and put it through a few tests, but it looks pretty common."

"I suppose I'm reaching for answers." She shrugged. "I don't know. I guess I was hoping for more."

"You mean Zelov's hammer handed to us tied up in ribbons?"

"It wouldn't hurt." She watched him put the amulet and map carefully back in the box. "Staunton wanted that amulet. He killed Nemid to get it."

"Or he didn't want us to have it. If he knew Nemid had it, why didn't he go after it before? Unless it wasn't that important to him."

Emily frowned. "Why wouldn't it be important? Nemid believed it was important, or he wouldn't have hidden it."

"You're right. Maybe Staunton made a deal with Nemid, and the amulet was a payoff. It could be he was biding his time before he took it back."

"But what did this amulet have to do with anything? It's obvious that this isn't the artifact that was supposed to be in the hammer. Staunton thought the hammer was probably at that museum, or he wouldn't have gotten Nemid to send us there." She rubbed her temple. "It's all crazy. Nothing makes sense."

"It will all come together." He leaned back in his chair. "We'll make it come together. But you can't force it. Close your eyes and rest. Try to sleep. I'll wake you as soon as I know if Ferguson is lying or playing straight."

"I won't be able to sleep." But she closed her eyes anyway. It had been a rough night, and she could still see the bloody bodies of Nemid and his bodyguard. Totally unexpected. Totally shocking. Not only their deaths but the fact that Garrett was right, and Nemid had deliberately sent her into that hell. What could have meant enough to make anyone—?

"He deserved to die," Garrett said as if

reading her thoughts. "If Staunton hadn't killed him, I would have done it myself."

She didn't open her eyes because she didn't want to see the darkness in his expression. She knew it was there. She shouldn't mind. She was accustomed to it now.

She did mind. She didn't want the darkness there because of her. It hurt her in some way. She wanted to push it away, push him away.

No, she only wanted to push away the darkness.

Her eyes were still closed as she reached out her hand to him.

She could sense his sudden stillness.

Then he leaned forward and took her hand. "What's this for?"

She shook her head. What could she answer when she didn't know herself?

"Okay. That's fine. I won't push it." His grasp tightened. His hand was warm and strong holding her own.

And even though her eyes were still closed, she knew the darkness was no longer there.

"She sleeps?" Fatin asked several hours later as he came back into the room. "I brought you food. I thought you might need it before you left me."

Emily opened her eyes. "I'm not sleeping." She looked at Garrett, who was leaning against the wall. "When can we leave?"

Garrett gazed at Fatin. "Yes, when can we leave? Have you heard anything?"

He smiled. "According to the radio, it seems our honorable councilman has been butchered by thieves or the Taliban. His body was discovered by his secretary, who came early to help him with a speech he was to give before the council." He set the tray on the inlaid table in front of Emily. "Such a pity. It's a terrible, brutal world, isn't it?" He turned to Garrett. "But sometimes we can skip away from the brutality with the help of friends." He turned and moved back toward the door. "It is only bread, cheese, and pastry. I will bring tea."

"Thank you."

"No, I repeat, it is my pleasure." He flashed a smile that lit his round, dark face. "Do you need clothes? Transportation?"

Garrett grinned. "We seem to be losing our shirts at every turn. But I imagine Ferguson had the rental car taken away from Nemid's house and our suitcases with it. We're not about to knock on Ferguson's door to get them. That might be entirely too tempting for him. I'll ask that clothes be brought by the pilot Dardon arranges to pick us up, but we still need to get out of the city without Emily being recognized." He nodded. "So yes, if you can get Emily some clothes, I'd appreciate it. Preferably something including a veil. Anything will do for me." He turned to Emily as Fatin left the room, "It will just be until we get outside the city."

"You don't need to give me explanations. I don't like the fact that men keep women veiled and under their heels, but it's a disguise that would work." She took a bite of cheese. "I should probably try to wear it on the plane to the U.S. It's only during security that I'd have to shed the veil."

He nodded. "But we'll arrange a private jet to get us to the New York area. I know a small local airport in Connecticut that's safe."

"Safe? Does that mean under the radar

of Homeland Security? An echo from your
shady past?"

"What else is a shady past good for?"
He sat down across from her and reached
for a piece of bread. "We'll whisk you away
from the airport as soon as we hit the
ground in New York."

"I brought you clothes." Fatin came into
the room carrying an armful of voluminous
black garments. "I hope they're suitable."
He set the clothes down on a stool. "If you
have trouble with the proper way of wearing them, tell me and I will send my wife to
help you."

"Your wife?"

"Yes, they belong to her." He shrugged
as he saw her expression of surprise. "It
is tradition."

"I didn't mean—You've been very kind.
Thank you."

Her gaze went back to the smothering
black veils of the *burqua* as he left the
room before looking at Garrett.

"You take what you can get." He
repeated as he started to eat, "Baby steps."

It was Dardon who got out of the helicopter when they arrived at the same poppy

field where they had landed the day Garrett had gotten her out of the mountains.

"I told you to stay with Irana," Garrett said as he opened the car door for Emily. "What the hell are you doing here?"

"Irana didn't need me. She decided to stay in Morocco and work with another doctor who was developing a new vaccine for malaria."

"And Morocco is supposed to be safe?"

"She has an army around her." He lifted his hand to his forehead in a mocking salute. "As commanded. She told me to get out of her way and go somewhere that I could do some good." He gave a low whistle as Emily got out of the car. "Quite an outfit. I don't even recognize you beneath all that drapery."

"I can't *breathe*." She took off the veil. "I don't know how they stand it." She started to strip off as many layers as she could. "That's better."

"I brought you more clothes and a computer."

"Good," Emily said. "I want to check and see if I can find out anything more about Nicholas Zelov and his place in Connecticut."

"I dug a little deeper and found out a few things about him while I was with Irana," Dardon said. "When he was on the verge of bankruptcy, he hired an accounting lawyer, Donald Warwick, to go through the family's affairs and see where they'd gone wrong in the corporation and how to correct it. It took a little of your money, Garrett, but I managed to get Warwick to talk to me. Evidently he was pretty thorough because he went way back to the start of the corporation in 1925."

"And?"

"He found sizeable amounts deposited in Mikhail Zelov's corporate accounts every six months on the same dates until 1943. Then they stopped."

"Where did they come from?"

Dardon shook his head. "First mail, then electronic transfers from somewhere in Belgium. Untraceable."

"Belgium?" Emily asked.

"Don't take any stock in that," Garrett said. "If you don't want someone to know where a deposit is coming from, you can reroute halfway around the world."

"But Warwick said that Nicholas Zelov was very interested in those deposits.

Nicholas said that old bastard, Mikhail, must have had something on someone, and it was too bad that the money had stopped."

"Blackmail?"

"Or payment for services rendered," Garrett said. "But Nicholas might have decided to do some searching on his own and come up with something that he thought might still be of interest. Hence the trip to Moscow."

"And his sudden reversal of fortune," Dardon said.

Garrett nodded. "It does seem a probable connection."

"I'm tired of probable," Emily said. "I want to find out. Where do we go from here?"

"Pakistan," Garrett said. "We'll change to a jet and head for New York."

"That's what you said in Rome." To Emily it seemed a hundred years ago that she'd found out that they were going to Kabul instead of New York. Murder and pursuit and the discovery of that amulet that meant absolutely nothing to them right now.

"This time it's a promise." Garrett lifted

her into the helicopter. "I just had to check Nemid out after what you told me."

She braced herself. "You said that I'd said other things that you thought might help. What were they?"

He was silent a moment. "At one point Staunton was asked to come and talk to someone who had driven up to the camp to see him. He left you and Levy for a few moments."

She gazed at him blankly. "I don't remember. . . ." But now she vaguely recalled muttering something last night in that fever of memories. "Why would I blank that out? Why couldn't I remember he—"

"You were sort of—" He shrugged, then said, "You couldn't focus on anything but Levy. That was the night that Staunton had given Borg the order to burn out Levy's eyes."

Her back went stiff as if he'd struck her. The memory of that night was right before her. "And Borg didn't stop," she whispered. "Staunton left the hut, but Borg didn't stop. And then he came back and said to Borg. 'Let me help. You're not doing it right.'"

"Stop it." Garret shook her gently. "I told

you that I'd never ask you to remember again. But I had to answer when you asked."

She nodded jerkily. "I know." She remembered something else. "That next day Staunton was probing, digging at me, saying something about my blanking out things. It might be that he was trying to find out if I'd paid any attention to his leaving. Why . . . do you think that visitor was important?"

"Because Staunton cursed, and said, 'Damn Babin. He's always nosing around, checking up on me.'"

"Babin?"

"Yes." He climbed into the helicopter. "It's important, but it was going to take too much time to make the connection right away so I called Dardon and told him to start checking for a Babin. But I could see the link with Nemid that had possibilities, and we acted on that lead." He turned to Dardon. "Take off."

"In a minute. I have something more. I want to reveal my supersleuthing and get praise heaped upon me."

"You found out something more about Zelov?" Emily asked.

"No, more important. Staunton."

"What?" Garrett asked.

"Do you remember I told you that Staunton might be a pseudonym for a Robert Hurker?"

"And is it?"

"Yes, it's only one of many. I had time when I was with Irana to buckle down and dig deeper. He doesn't use Staunton very often. He seems to save it for the times when there's no danger of him being booked. That's why I wasn't able to trace the name."

"Tell me about Hurker."

"Born in Melbourne, Australia. His father was a fisherman, his mother a whore until his father took her off the streets. He grew up in Sydney. He was booked for burglary and assault with a deadly weapon when he was ten. After that it was straight downhill. He almost beat a shopkeeper to death when he was fifteen and got off because he was a minor." He paused. "His mother and baby sister fell overboard off his father's fishing boat and drowned when he was sixteen. He pretended to be heartbroken. The social worker who had his case said that there was a possibility he did it himself. It got too hot in Sydney, and he disappeared for a while. He was going to the university and when he came back, the only thing he'd learned was how to be smarter and more vicious. He took off for France, and has been hopping about the world and doing what he does best."

"Murder," Emily said. It was strange thinking of Staunton as a child, even the vicious child painted by Dardon. It was as an adult that he had dominated her life and imagination.

"Evidently he does it well enough to earn a sizeable income," Dardon said. "And attract very affluent clients."

"Where does he live?"

Dardon shook his head. "No address. He moves around a lot."

"Can we contact any of those clients and see if they know anything more about Staunton than we do."

"If we have the time," Garrett said. "I'm not sure we will. We'd do better to concentrate on having him come to us."

"I'm still checking." Dardon started the engine, and the rotors began to spin. "I'll let you know if I come up with anything."

But they knew more than they had

moments before. They could see the pattern, where he had come from. Staunton had been a monster who had dominated her thoughts and emotions since the first moment she had seen him. Now he was being made into a human being.

"He did kill his mother," Garrett said. "He told me that he'd taken care of the bitch. He didn't mention the baby."

"It probably wasn't important to him." Emily said. "What difference does the life of a little baby make?" Her lips tightened. "I want to show him how much of a difference it makes. I want to—" She stopped. Control. Keep cool and calm. "How long before we'll reach that airport in Connecticut?"

ELEVEN

"Your gun." Garrett handed her a box when he came out of the tall brick building at which they'd stopped after they'd landed at the small private airport in Connecticut. "A .40-caliber Glock as you requested. I'd like to see you shoot sometime."

She shook her head. "After my father taught me, he said I should never pick up a gun unless I meant to use it. He was in Special Services before he became a photographer. He never wanted to kill anything or anyone again, but he knew there was always a threat out there." She smiled reminiscently. "I got pretty good. He used to tell me that he'd put me up against any of the guys in his unit. It was bullshit, but it gave me confidence later when I had to deal with the scum who were trashing the museums." She opened the box. "Nice. Is that all you bought here?"

"No, Dardon is picking up some long-range electronic equipment. He'll be out in a minute."

"Electronic equipment?"

"We're going to see if we can trigger a response from Mr. Zelov."

"Got it." Dardon opened the car door and got into the backseat. "Pretty sophisticated. It may be good enough."

"Providing this is the right Zelov, and he has a guilty conscience." Garrett started the car. "We'll have to see. Or rather Emily will have to see."

Emily looked at him in surprise. "What?"

"I think you should be the one to do the Q and A on Nicholas Zelov. He might be less defensive."

"Why?"

"What did you tell me about the private life of Nicholas Zelov?"

She glanced down at the computer she'd been studying since she'd gotten on the jet in Pakistan. "He's divorced, no children, parents dead, was in drug rehab eight years ago. Likes women, loves gambling, hates work." She looked up. "Evidently not like his rather bizarre ancestor."

"Likes women." Garrett said. "And I phoned his house while I was buying your gun. He's not at home, but the housekeeper said that he was at Foxworth, a very plush casino near here." He quoted. "'Loves gambling.' Put the two together and we might hit a home run."

"What am I supposed to do?"

"That's up to you." He got on the freeway. "It should take us about ten minutes to get there. Tell me about what else you found out about Nicholas Zelov and his great-great-grandfather, Mikhail."

She pointed at the photo on the monitor of a palatial-looking mansion on the hill beyond the wrought-iron gates. The ground lights shining up at the onion-shaped towers of the building gave it a Disney-like magic. "That's the Zelov family home. It definitely has a Russian flair. It's said to look like St. Basil's in Moscow. It was built by Mikhail Zelov in 1922." Emily looked up from the laptop. "He kept a low profile and lived in a tenement in east New York when he first arrived, then he took a trip to Canada, stayed there two years, and when he came back, he said he'd struck it rich in the Klondike gold mines."

"Maybe he did," Dardon said.

"And maybe he didn't," Garrett said. "Evidently anything was possible with Zelov."

"At any rate, he lived the high life and left an enormous fortune to his two children. He died in 1943, and his heirs promptly started to run through his money," Emily said. "The present head of the family, Nicholas Zelov, was on the verge of bankruptcy five months ago but managed to pull himself out of it." She glanced at Dardon in the backseat. "That's about the time Warwick told him about Mikhail's private influx of money. Nicholas is still not doing well, but he can live marginally in the style to which he's accustomed." She closed the computer. "I'd like to know if Nicholas is getting any electronic transfers as old Mikhail did."

"That's one question you could ask

him," Garrett said. "But I doubt if you'll get an answer." He nodded. "There's Foxworth. Quite the little Indian reservation, isn't it?"

"Indian reservation?"

"The casinos are Indian-owned."

The neon-lit hotel-casino glowed in the darkness like a magnificent beacon in its setting of lush green terrain. "It's almost as palatial as Zelov's castle."

"Then he should feel right at home." He pulled in front of the casino. "We'll park over there." He handed her a tiny black nodule. "Plant it somewhere on Nicholas Zelov before you leave him."

"I feel like some kind of spy. Anyplace in particular?"

He shook his head. "It's powerful and should broadcast from ten feet away. Just touch him anywhere, and the nodule will attach. I just like to be sure."

She got out of the car and looked at the brilliantly lit lobby. "I'm not dressed for this." She looked down at her black slacks and white long-sleeved shirt. "I'll duck into the washroom and at least wash my face and touch up this wig."

"You look great."

"Bullshit." She strode toward the glass doors, which were immediately opened for her by a uniformed doorman. Clean up. Make discreet inquiries and have Zelov pointed out to her. Then see what she could do about finding out what she had come to find out.

Nicholas Zelov was sitting at the long, granite bar, and Emily had watched him drink two whiskeys in the space of the time she had been studying him. He was a big man in his late forties, with ruddy complexion and black hair. Zelov was barely upright on the stool, and his voice was slurred when he'd ordered that last whiskey. Evidently his alcohol rehab hadn't worked out, Emily thought.

Sad, but that might be better for her purpose.

She slipped onto the stool next to him. "My name is Emily Hudson, Mr. Zelov. I wonder if you'd answer a few questions for me?"

"No, go away." He took another drink. "No whores tonight. A few more drinks, then back to the tables."

"I'm not a prostitute, Mr. Zelov. I work

for the U.N. I was interested in your family history."

"U.N.? What the hell?" He suddenly stiffened and turned to look at her. "You're that woman who was kidnapped. I saw your picture in the newspaper." He reached out and touched her hair. "But the color is different."

She leaned back away from his touch. "People recognize me. This helps a little."

"I don't know why you want to talk to me anyway. I read that you were in seclusion somewhere. Why don't you go back there?" He took another swallow of the whiskey. "Ten minutes. That's all I'll give you."

"Thank you. I'll try to be brief."

"You'd better." He was gazing at her critically again. "You look better than you did in that video they released after the CIA got you away from those bandits. You need some meat on your bones, but you're not half bad looking. Would you like a drink?"

"No, thank you."

He signaled the bartender for another drink for himself. "When I was reading about you, I was wondering what those bandits did to you. Rape?"

She didn't answer the question. "I'd like to talk to you about Mikhail Zelov."

An undecipherable expression flitted across his face. "You came to me to ask about old Guru Mikhail?"

"Guru?"

"That's what my grandfather called him. Stingy, spooky bastard. He tied up all his money in trust funds that couldn't be touched. My father only managed to finally break the will after wasting years in court."

"Why spooky?"

"He claimed he was a holy man and could heal the sick and send his enemies to their deaths." He smirked with satisfaction. "That's what we used to break the trusts. Insanity. All those documents and letters were what cooked his goose."

"That must have made you very happy," Emily said. "But I understand you went through many of his records again just several months ago. Why?"

He stiffened. "How did you know that?"

She ignored the question. "Did you find something then that you didn't find before?"

"Hell, no."

He'd mentioned only documents and letters, Emily thought. She made a leap. "I was actually interested in a book he wrote before he left Russia. It was a kind of a guide to living."

His expression became shuttered. "Oh, that book." He shrugged. "He talked about it." He took a swallow of his whiskey. "I think my grandfather tossed it out with a lot of his father's other effects after the old man died." He looked at Emily. "Why are you prying into the old Guru's stuff? What's it to you?"

She was ready for that question she knew would come. "My profession is preserving artifacts. The book may be historically important. It had a connection with Rasputin I understand."

"Yeah. I think it did. But he didn't think shit about Rasputin." He suddenly frowned. "I told you. The book was tossed. If that's all you wanted to know, you can hit the road."

"That's not quite all I wanted to know," Emily said. "Why did you go to Moscow five months ago, Mr. Zelov?"

"That's all." He pushed away from the bar. "Now you're sticking your nose into my business. I wanted to see my family's home, asshole. I wanted to search for my roots."

"Could we see Mikhail Zelov's letters and journals you spoke about?" Emily asked.

"I don't give a shit. They're all on record with the court as testimony when we broke the will." He was struggling to get off the stool. "I've had enough of you. You're bad news. I'm going to go back to the tables before you bring me bad luck."

She was losing him. In another minute he'd be leaving her.

She reached out her palm that held the black nodule Garrett had given her and grasped the arm of Zelov's jacket. "One more question. Was there a hammer in Mikhail Zelov's effects?"

"What?" Zelov's cheeks became even ruddier. "That's a stupid question. Why would—Get out. I'm a good customer here. I'll have them toss you out on your ear. I've been patient enough because you looked—Out."

"I'm going, Mr. Zelov. Thanks for your time." She slipped off the stool and headed for the exit.

She glanced back over her shoulder as she opened the heavy glass door. Zelov wasn't going back to the tables. He was heading for the French doors leading to the terrace.

And he was reaching for his cell phone.

"He's heard about the hammer," Emily said as soon as she reached the car. Excitement was tingling through her. "I know it."

"From what I heard, I think he has, too." Garrett held the car door open for her. "And we were lucky he was drunk and transparent as glass." He got back into the car and looked at Dardon. "Ready? It should be coming any time now."

Dardon lifted the headset to his ear. "He's already dialing. He probably had to get somewhere he'd get a clear signal. There's too much electronic interference in casinos."

"He was heading for the terrace," Emily said. "You're recording him? You can do that from out here?"

"With the help of that little bug you

planted." Garrett nodded. "Piece of cake with the right equipment. I didn't think we'd get much out of him, but I hoped your asking the questions would send him running."

Dardon nodded. "But we're not getting much. Zelov is in a panic, but the man he's talking to is only impatient, not informative." He listened a moment, then turned the switch. "That's it. He hung up." He looked at Garrett. "Do you want to stick around and see if he makes any other calls?"

"No." He started the car and drove down the driveway. "But I want to hear that call, and I want you to start trying to trace it. We'll check into a motel and go over it. Do you have a general location?"

Dardon nodded. "I think it was somewhere in Russia."

"That's pinning it down. "

"Best I can do right now." He looked back down at his board. "That may be the best I can do, period, if the line is as protected as I think. We may have to call in an expert to tap a phone-company database."

Zelov had called Russia, Emily thought. Who in Russia had reached out tentacles to touch her, touch Zelov, touch Garrett? Deadly tentacles. Even drunk, Zelov had been afraid when she'd mentioned the hammer.

"Okay?" Garrett asked, glancing at her.

She nodded. "He was nervous when I was talking about the *Book of Living,* too. He was lying then."

Garrett nodded. "I'd be very curious to read what's in that *Book of Living.* It might just lead us where we want to go." He glanced back at Dardon. "Providing Dardon can't point the way."

"I'm working on it," Dardon muttered. "But I'm no expert. I think we may have to call in Pauley to do his wizardry."

"Then we'll do it," Garrett said. "But first I want to hear that call. I saw a Holiday Inn about a mile off the freeway. . . ."

"Here's the disc." Dardon handed Garrett the black case at the door of his room at the Holiday Inn. "Suppose I work on the location a little more before I give it up to Pauley."

"No, get him now." Garrett unlocked the door and let Emily precede him into the room. "Tell him I want him here tomorrow morning."

"It will cost you."

"Everything does," Garrett said. "But it may cost me more to delay."

"Whatever you say." He turned and strolled down the hall toward his room. "I'm glad to give it up to Pauley. Though you know he's going to be condescending as hell."

"Who's Pauley?" Emily asked, as Garrett came in and shut the door.

"Mark Pauley. He's sort of a techno-wizard in computers and all things elec-tronic. If anyone can pin down the location of Zelov's call, he'll be able to do it. He's the best hacker I've ever known." He glanced around the room. "Set up your computer and we'll play that CD. There's usually a coffeemaker in these rooms, and I could use some coffee. Maybe it's on the bathroom vanity." He went into the bath-room. "Yeah, here it is."

Emily heard the sound of running water as she opened the laptop and set it on the desk. "It's up. Hurry, dammit."

"We've got time." He came out of the bathroom a few minutes later and handed her a cup of coffee. "And the call was very short, Dardon said."

"That doesn't mean we won't learn

something from it." She took the disc he handed her and slipped it into the computer. "I want to know now."

He sat down in the chair at the desk and leaned back. "Then play it."

She pressed the button.

A sound of dialing and Zelov's heavy breathing. Then the call was picked up on the other end.

Russian. She realized they were both speaking in Russian. Disappointment surged through her. "Dammit."

"You don't speak Russian?"

"No. You do, don't you?"

He nodded. "Pretty well."

He speaks nine languages, Irana had told her.

She opened the desk drawer and pulled out stationery and a pen. She set it in front of him and stopped the disc. "Write it down. I want every word, every intonation, every pause."

He smiled. "I'll try to oblige."

"Don't try. Do it." She started the disc again.

His smile disappeared, and he frowned with concentration, his pen flying over the paper.

She sat on the edge of the bed, watching him. She was once again aware of the intensity, the intelligence in that face. She slowly sipped her coffee and waited for him to finish.

The conversation took only a few minutes. Garrett pushed the sheet of paper away from him and looked at her. "Done. The man Zelov called was definitely not Staunton. You agree?"

Emily nodded. The voice on the tape was smoother, deeper. "It never occurred to me that Nicholas Zelov would speak Russian," she said ruefully. "He seemed so dyed-in-the-wool American."

"I imagine the first Zelov clung very closely to his Russian roots. It seems to have carried down through his progeny." He stood up. "Sit here at the desk. The light is better, and my handwriting isn't wonderful." He smiled slightly. "Though I did try to obey instructions and convey intonations and pauses."

She sat down in the chair and picked up the sheet of paper. Garrett's handwriting was bold, dominant, and incisive. Like his character, she thought absently, but there were many more shadings to his personality. "You're right, your handwriting isn't wonderful, but it's clear. That's all that's important."

"I'm glad you can make it work." He lay back on the bed and propped himself up against the headboard. He lifted his cup to his lips. "Read. We'll talk later."

She was already reading.

"It's Zelov. Dammit, you promised me you'd protect me. You said no one would know."

"I have no idea what you're talking about, Zelov. Are you drunk again?"

"I'm not drunk. Well, maybe I've had a little, but that doesn't change anything. I have a right to do whatever I want. You can't tell me what to do."

"I can tell you whatever I wish, Zelov. And you will listen respectfully, then obey."

"Bullshit. You told me no one would know. You lied."

"Stop sputtering and tell me clearly and slowly what you mean."

"She asked about the book. She asked about Mikhail Zelov. She asked about my trip to Moscow."

"Who asked you?"

"That U.N. bitch."

Pause. "Emily Hudson?"

"Yeah. It was her, but her hair was different. . . ."

"Did she mention the amulets? What did you tell her, Zelov?"

"Nothing. I didn't tell her anything. I told her to go chase herself. She didn't say a word about the amulets. But you've got to protect me. You've got to get her off me."

"How long ago did she leave?"

"Five minutes maybe."

"You fool. You incredible fool to take a chance like this. I'm hanging up."

"You can't do that. Talk to me. Tell me how you're going to—"

"I'm hanging up. Listen carefully. My promise will not be broken. But if you talk to Emily Hudson or anyone else again, you will be punished. Do you understand?"

"I'm not stupid. Of course, I understand. You can't threaten me. You can't do—"

The connection was broken.

Emily finished reading the last words, then went back and started to read the conversation again. Then she played the disc trying to memorize the sound, the intonations, of the man Zelov had called. She wanted to remember that voice if she heard it again. But they had no name. Why hadn't Zelov mentioned his name just one time, she wondered in frustration.

"Finished?" Garrett asked.

She nodded and leaned back in the chair. "But we haven't got a name, dammit."

"We'll get it." He finished his coffee and set the cup on the nightstand. "But not much more."

"We know Zelov is definitely involved in something crooked. And that he did something for this man and was paid off. Did he give him that *Book of Living*? Or did he give him the hammer?" She thought of something else. "Or the amulets. Plural. That meant there had to be more than the one we found in Nemid's wall."

"It would seem so." He paused. "But the man who paid Zelov off promised to protect him, and that may mean he'll try to rid him of us. So I believe that we should get out of here and head for Moscow as soon as possible."

She shook her head. "Not until I get a transcript of Mikhail Zelov's letters and journals, the ones that were used at that trial."

He nodded. "I was going to send Dardon to Hartford to get copies as soon as the records office opened, but I have a lot for him to do. We'll go ourselves. I want to be there before Zelov gets sober enough to request that the documents be kept confidential. Though they can't be that revealing if they've been public for years."

"There could be something that will give us a lead. We've got to try."

"Easy, "Garrett said. "We are trying. I'm just saying that I don't want you to build up your hopes, then be disappointed."

"I don't care if I'm disappointed. I'll just go down another road." She stood up. "I'm going to my room. I'll see you in the morning. What time?"

"Six. I'll order room service for the three of us and we'll get moving." He swung his legs to the floor. "I'll walk you to your room."

"That's not necessary."

"Yes, it is. And it's necessary for you

to keep your door locked and not open it to anyone but me." He opened the hall door for her and followed her out into the corridor.

"You think that man Zelov called will send Staunton after us."

"Perhaps. It's an open game. We're not even sure Staunton is connected to Nicholas Zelov yet."

"They're connected. I feel it." She stopped at her door. "And maybe we should stay here and let Staunton come to us."

"Not when we're ready to widen the circle."

"We can widen the circle later. I want Staunton now."

"What a bloodthirsty woman you are, Emily." He smiled down at her. He reached out and touched her lower lip with a forefinger. "And you look so wholesome and all-American."

Her lip was suddenly tingling beneath his finger. An instant before, she had been only thinking of Staunton and how to trap him. Yet the moment he had touched her she had become acutely, physically aware of everything about Garrett. The spicy, male scent of him, the warmth of his body, his eyes looking down at her. How did he do that to her? She moved her head to avoid his touch. "I don't feel wholesome. And I do want Staunton's blood."

"You'll get it." His hand dropped away from her. "We'll get them all." He turned away. "But don't answer your door no matter whether you want it to be Staunton or not. Not without me beside you, and right now you're obviously not ready to let me occupy that position all night. We don't know how soon or in what manner that promise is going to be kept to Zelov."

Staunton cursed as he saw the name on his phone ID. Dammit, it was Babin. He didn't need this. He was pissed off enough that Borg had told him that Garrett had probably managed to get his hands on the amulet in Nemid's study. Borg had bribed one of the Afghani officials who had been crawling all over the library to describe the condition of the crime scene, and that hole in the drywall had not been Borg's work. Staunton didn't want to have to admit that to Babin before he got it back. The bastard hadn't wanted him to use the amulet to strike the deal with Nemid.

Staunton started talking the moment he picked up. "I was just going to call you. We plugged the leak in Kabul, but Garrett managed to get his hands on the amulet. Not that it will do him any good. No one can tell anything from it, and we'll take care of Garrett before he makes a connection."

"He's already made a connection," Babin said coldly. "I just received a call from Nicholas Zelov squealing like a pig. Emily Hudson paid him a visit tonight. And if she was there, then Garrett must have been there, too."

Oh, shit.

"I didn't think Garrett would track him down quite so soon. As I said, I got rid of Nemid. He was the immediate threat."

"I didn't tell you to kill Nemid. I could have handled it. And I told you that you shouldn't use one of the amulets with him."

"I had to offer him a bargain he couldn't refuse. We needed him. It's my job to keep you from worrying about details. And we'll do damage control." He changed the subject. "Did Zelov tell her anything?"

"He said he didn't, but the idiot called me immediately after she left him. The drunken fool didn't even realize the risk."

"I told you that you should get rid of him."

"I couldn't, dammit."

"I'll jump on the next plane for New York. Do you know where they are?"

"No. Figure it out for yourself. Prove your worth. But you'll arrange for someone else to find and dispose of Garrett and retrieve Emily Hudson in the safest and least public of ways. It's clear you haven't been able to keep a low profile. You know of such a person?"

"Yes, but I'd rather do it myself."

"I don't care what you'd rather do. You'll come here in case I need you." He hung up,

Cold, arrogant bastard, Staunton thought, as he hung up. He was tempted to ignore Babin and go to New York himself. He didn't want anything to happen to Emily before he could get his hands on her. He'd waited too long.

But Babin was a force he had to reckon with. Staunton wasn't quite ready to make a move yet. Everything and everyone had to be in place. This was his big chance, the bonanza he'd searched for all his life. He had to be calm and patient. It would be better to do as Babin ordered, find someone else to do the job, and trust that his orders would be obeyed. He had to have Emily Hudson.

But if he couldn't do what he wanted to do at the moment, then he would find another way to sting Emily. She had to realize that he was still in control.

He reached for his phone and dialed Borg. "Are you still in Kabul?"

"Yes. I thought I'd call you and ask—"

"Get a plane to Morocco. Isn't that where you said we followed Irana Povak?"

"Yes, Tangiers. She's working with some doctor there." He paused. "But I don't know if I can get to her. Dardon has her surrounded with security."

"We'll get to her. One of those security men will make a slip, and we'll find a way to take her. Find someone to bribe. Find someone to kill. Until then we just have to be patient. Watch and wait, Borg. Watch and wait." He hung up the phone and leaned back in his chair. Good advice, but he wasn't feeling in the least patient. He didn't want Irana Povak. He wanted Emily, dammit. But Emily could be reached by anyone she cared about, and she cared about Irana Povak.

You want another experience like the one with Joel Levy, Emily? Let's see if I can oblige you.

But now he had to throw a bone to Babin and do as the arrogant bastard commanded. He had to find someone else to do the job of going after Emily in Connecticut that he wanted to do himself. Who was efficient that he could control?

Sal Caprini. Sal was smart and lethal and would know that Staunton would come after him if he didn't do exactly as instructed. But there was the problem of finding Garrett and Emily. He frowned as he concentrated on the problem. Emily and Garrett had found Zelov and were digging deep. What would Garrett's next move be? In his position, what would he do?

Then it came to him.

He started to dial Sal Caprini in New Jersey.

Dardon knocked on the door at six forty-five the next morning, and when Garrett answered, Dardon said, "Got him. He was down in Miami doing a job for IBM."

"Hello, Pauley," Garrett said to the man standing beside Dardon. "Thanks for coming."

"Dardon said it was going to be profitable," Pauley said. "I've decided I have to retire like you. Keeping up with all this new technology is making an old man of me."

"Emily, this is Mark Pauley. Emily Hudson." Dardon gestured to the man who entered the room with him. "He's going to break into a phone-company database that everyone says is unbreakable and get us the information we need. Or so he says." He headed for the room service table where Emily was sitting. "Breakfast. I'm starved. At the rate you're charging us, we can only afford to give you a cup of coffee, Pauley."

"I'll survive." He came forward and shook Emily's hand. "I'm very glad to meet you. I understand that if I reveal I've seen you, I'll die a slow and horrible death. Titillating, isn't it?"

He had a faint British accent, but there was nothing of British reserve in his smile.

It was warm, intimate, and chock-full of charm. He was brown-haired, blue-eyed, in his late twenties, and stunningly good-looking. Emily couldn't remember even seeing a movie star that attractive. "If you can call death titillating. How do you do, Mr. Pauley."

"Oh, not actually experiencing the dire fate. I violently oppose death. But it's always interesting to skirt on the edge." He turned to Garrett. "How much time do I have?"

"Time to have a cup of coffee," Garrett said. "I'll even order you breakfast. I'm not as miserly as Dardon."

"I understand and forgive him. He's an amateur, and he resents a professional's expertise." He gave Dardon a sly glance. "I'll even let him come and watch a master at work. He may learn something."

"Bastard," Dardon muttered as he took a sip of coffee. "You're not so perfect. I will watch you, and I'll learn your bag of tricks."

"By all means." Pauley's smile faded. "Seriously, give me a time frame, Garrett."

"I want to be on a plane and heading out of the country by noon."

"Then you may have to take me with you. These days it's not easy hacking into a phone company and tracing past calls. There are all kinds of trip wires and firewalls. Even the NSA has trouble, and they're the snoopiest bastards on the planet."

"Do your best. Otherwise, you may have to take a short Russian vacation."

"It will have to be short. I don't like Russia." He shrugged. "Well, I don't mind it, but they don't like me. You'd think a country as into electronic snooping as the Kremlin would be a little more tolerant. I think they're jealous." He winked at Emily. "Like my friend, Dardon." He turned to leave. "I'll skip breakfast and go back to Dardon's room and see if I can make some headway. Maybe I'll even strike it lucky and meet your deadline."

Emily watched him leave. "Is he as good as he says he is?"

"Better." Dardon made a face. "He's a damn wonder. He doesn't look at things the way we do. He has a cyber connection."

"He looks like a movie star."

"And makes the most of it," Garrett said

dryly. "He makes the most of all his talents."

"I think I like him."

"You see? He's in the room five minutes, and you're on his cheering team." There was a faint edge to his voice. "Don't get too involved. I'll send him packing as soon as I get what I need from him." He sat down and started his breakfast. "Eat. We've got to get moving. I want to get to the courthouse as soon as they open." He turned to Dardon. "And you don't have time to stay with Pauley and play with the computers. You need to set up the flight, pick up documents, and arrange for a place for us to stay in Russia."

"Pauley, too? You were serious?"

"Pauley, too. Even after he gets us the address we need, we may be able to use him over there." He grimaced. "And it will give Emily something pretty to look at on the trip to Moscow."

That edge was in his voice again, and it was beginning to annoy her. "That would be nice," she said coolly. "I may learn something from him. I'm sure he's a good teacher."

Dardon chuckled. "He'll tell you he is."

"It depends on what he's teaching." Garrett met her gaze. "You could do better."

"Could I?" She finished her coffee. "But you never know unless you give someone a chance."

"My, my." Dardon's expression was suddenly wary as he looked from Emily to Garrett. "I believe it's time I made my exit. I have a lot of things to do."

"No, stay." Emily pushed back her chair. "I'm through. I'll go to my room and finish packing." She glanced at Garrett. "Ten minutes."

"Ten minutes." He was frowning as he got up, crossed the room, and stood gazing after her until she reached her door a few yards away. "I'll come and get you."

Lord, he was being careful, she thought. But she wasn't complaining. Even though this morning the sun was shining brightly, and Staunton seemed far away, she still was feeling that sense of threat just around the next corner.

"Do I detect a little tension between you?" Dardon asked, as Garrett closed the door and came back into the room. "Should I have gotten someone other than Pauley? I could have pulled Les Mobler in. He's not as good as Pauley, but he's real ugly."

"Very funny," Garrett said. "She's too smart to be taken in by sheer good looks." But he had been surprised that Emily had seemed to be drawn to Pauley. Surprised and irritated. It probably shouldn't have bothered him. Emily was a woman, and every day she was emerging more from that stunned, numb condition that had enveloped her since he had taken her away from Staunton. Women were attracted to Pauley, and he should probably be grateful that she was behaving normally.

He wasn't grateful. He had felt a flash of possessiveness and jealousy that had come out of nowhere and was primitive as hell.

And on some level Emily had recognized it and reacted with defiance. The mood between them in those last few minutes had been explosive.

"I've never seen you like this." Dardon was staring at him speculatively. "She's not your property, Garrett."

"I know that." But he felt as if she

belonged to him. Every minute they were growing closer, he was learning more about her, the bond was growing. "I wouldn't want to own any woman."

Not consciously but that primitive instinct was there.

Get over it. It was probably purely sexual, and as soon as they came together, it would fade.

And they would come together. To hell with patience.

And to hell with that pretty boy Mark Pauley.

TWELVE

"Did you get them? It took you long enough." Emily asked as she saw Garrett come across the marble lobby of the courthouse. "No problem?"

"No problem." He gestured to the file in his hand as he opened the door leading to the parking lot. "I copied everything I could get my hands on. They had to have everything Mikhail Zelov wrote translated into English for the court case. And there were all kinds of documents verifying the authenticity and accuracy of the translations."

"I still don't understand why the family

didn't lock the records down as confidential."

"I do. As long as the records didn't give out any information that they didn't want leaked, it was better for their image. It was a defensive move. They could prove to the world that Mikhail was nuts and that they weren't greedy bloodsuckers." He opened the passenger door of the car for her. "Which means we probably aren't going to find anything vitally important in the transcripts."

"It's a start. We'll get to know Mikhail Zelov and the way he thinks. It could become important later." She asked, "How long will it take us to get to the airport?"

"About fifteen minutes. It's not far from here." Garrett's phone rang as they pulled out of the parking lot. "Dardon." He listened, then said, "Okay, whatever it takes." He hung up. "Pauley hasn't completed the job. He's coming with us. He's at the airport with Dardon."

"He didn't think he would finish." She glanced at him. "And you said that he could be valuable, didn't you?"

"That's what I said." He looked straight ahead, negotiating the traffic. "It's amazing that, considering all the laws in the U.S., traffic still remains a major problem."

She didn't let him skate away from the issue. "Well, is Pauley valuable or not?"

"He's valuable," he said flatly.

"Then why don't you want him to go?"

He looked directly at her. "I'm jealous. I don't like to be jealous. It's childish and primitive. I'd rather avoid feeling either."

"Oh." She hadn't expected that degree of frankness. "Like Dardon? Because Pauley's so bright?"

"No," he said crisply. "Because I want to jump into bed with you, and I don't like the idea of his doing it. Or you even contemplating sex with our Adonis of the Internet."

She could feel the heat in her cheeks. "I wasn't contemplating any such—"

"Good. Then we won't talk about it. You wanted to probe about Pauley. I was honest and let you know the problem. Now we'll forget it until one of us decides to deal with it."

She was silent a moment. "Yes, we'll forget it." Then she burst out, "But you made me feel awkward as hell. How am I going to look at Pauley without remembering what you said?"

"Exactly." He was entering the freeway. "I might have had that in mind, too."

Clever. She felt that flash of irritation again. She smoldered for a moment, then shrugged. "I can handle it. Of course, it will make me much more aware of him." She saw his hands tighten on the steering wheel. Good. "And I've never slept with an Adonis of the Internet. You've made me wonder what it would—"

"You little devil." He was smiling faintly and shaking his head. "I think we'd better go back to talking about the traffic."

That would be safer, she thought. She had no idea why she had been tempted into goading him. She had never been a tease, and yet she had taken a sly enjoyment out of teasing Garrett. It might be because it held an element of danger. He was very sophisticated and had learned control in the trenches, but you were always aware that it was control and that darkness and violence lay waiting beneath.

But what was amazing was that she could even feel or think of anything besides Staunton and the search for the hammer. No, Irana had said she was coming back to life. Sex and emotion and all the other facets of living were gradually coming back to her. She should reach out to them. It was a way of proving to herself that Staunton had not permanently damaged her.

Reach out to Garrett? The cure might be worse than the sickness.

"Traffic," she repeated. "I don't think this traffic is so bad. At least we Americans respect the law. It's only occasional assholes that think they own the road."

"You still consider yourself an American? You've batted around so many countries, I wondered if you had lost your attachment."

She shook her head. "I'm not a citizen of the world. I'm a down-to-earth, flag-waving American. I always will be. I had to go to other countries for my job, but this is home. When I stop roaming, I want to get a nice house on the beach down in North Carolina."

"Why North Carolina?"

"My father grew up near the coast there and he loved it. Some of the best times of my childhood were the weeks we spent together there. I want to be near the ocean and the woods so that I can dig out my camera and take pictures of wildlife like my father. I'll go to football games and have cookouts and every Fourth of July I'll send up fireworks. I can understand Mikhail Zelov wanting to remind his family of their roots. It's important." She looked at him. "What about you? Irana said your father was an American."

His lips lifted in a sardonic smile. "He never inspired me to any sense of patriotism. If anything, I wondered what kind of country could produce a man like him. I never visited the U.S. until I was in my twenties, and by that time it was too late to put down roots."

"Where do you have roots?"

He shrugged. "Nowhere. I guess the closest I've come is Mykala Island."

"That's not good."

He smiled. "It's life, Emily. We all can't have everything you regard as important."

But she wanted Garrett to have it. It hurt her somehow that he hadn't had the solid start that her father had given her. She hadn't realized until after her father had died how important and valuable those years with him had been. "Then you should set out and make sure you put down roots yourself so that your children will have them."

He blinked. "Now we're talking about my children? How did we get so far from lousy traffic?"

"I don't know." She shook her head. "Sorry. I didn't mean to intrude on your privacy. Maybe you don't even want to have children."

"I do. I just never thought about it." He smiled. "I didn't realize I had to prepare the way for them. This is our exit." He got off the freeway. "I'll have to take my responsibilities in that direction under consideration." He glanced in his rearview mirror. "We may have a tail."

"What?" She glanced back over her shoulder. A tan Toyota was the only car behind them. "Why do you think that?"

"He exited behind us. He's been behind us on the freeway."

"Did you see him before that?"

"You mean at the courthouse?" He shook his head. "But I might not have noticed. I was a little distracted by the conversation."

As Emily had been. "If we're being followed, they must have been waiting at the courthouse. We wouldn't have picked them up on the freeway."

"I'm not sure it's a tail. I'm just naturally suspicious. Let's see." He sped up, glancing at the mirror. "They're speeding up, too. I don't think it's 'monkey see, monkey do.'" He slowed, then sped up again. "I'd say it's confirmed."

"They just want to see where we're going?"

"No, this isn't like one of Ferguson's guys tagging us and reporting back to him. I don't think this is a simple tail. They're waiting for something."

Her hands slowly clenched. "You can't lose them, can you?" The road they were traveling was a straight one, with only woods on both sides. "This isn't the city."

"It would be damn hard."

"Then what are they waiting for?"

"I don't know. A little more privacy? If so, they're going to get it soon. The turnoff for the airport is just ahead. There's a half-mile stretch that's virtually deserted."

"Maybe we should go straight ahead."

"No, I need to get rid of them. But as soon as we make the turn, I'm going to pull over, and I want you to get out and go into the brush before they see you."

"And leave you alone? Not likely."

"Emily, do what I say."

"Garrett, hell, no."

He gave her an exasperated glance as he made the turn. "Dammit, this is no game."

"Staunton may be in that car."

"Oh shit." He sped up as the Toyota came around the corner. "Keep down."

The Toyota had sped up too, and was getting closer. Emily craned her head to see if she could recognize the driver or the man in the passenger seat. They weren't near enough yet.

"Emily."

"No." She was able to make out the two men now. The driver was dark-haired, swarthy. The man in the passenger seat was fair-haired and thin. "It's not Staunton."

"Then will you please get down," Garrett said through clenched teeth. "They're right on top of us."

"They're trying to pull alongside," Emily said.

"Great surprise." Garrett said.

And the fair-haired man in the passenger seat was aiming a gun at Garrett!

"Down, dammit!" Garrett swerved sideways and hit the Toyota.

A bullet shattered the back window as the gunman was jarred by the impact.

Before the man in the Toyota could recover, Garrett hit the car again, sending it spinning toward the edge of the road.

Another bullet, this time burying itself in the metal holding the windshield.

Garrett went after the car, giving it another swipe that sent it off the road and bouncing down an incline and into a ditch.

"Get over into the driver's seat." Garrett was out of the car in an instant. "Get to the airport and bring Dardon and Pauley. It should only take you a few minutes. Don't argue. I'm going to need help."

Then why isn't he coming with me, she thought desperately as she stomped on the accelerator. He had darted to the side of the road and disappeared into the brush. She wanted to go after him. If he needed help, she wanted to be the one to give it to him.

But Dardon was better equipped to deal with a situation like this.

Hurry, get Dardon and Pauley.

And get back here before Garrett is killed.

"Stay here, Emily." Dardon jumped out of the car and started slipping and sliding down the slope toward the ditch. "Pauley!"

Emily ignored him and was right behind them as they reached the car. The driver was crumpled against the wheel. There was no sign of Garrett or the fair-haired man who had been shooting at them.

Pauley checked the driver. "Dead. Broken neck."

The impact of the car or Garrett? Emily had a memory of Garrett's arm around Shafir Ali's neck in that tent in the mountains.

Dardon was already moving toward the brush, examining the way the leaves were lying and the broken branches. "This way, I think."

"No." Pauley was moving toward the north. "I think I heard something . . ."

"Dammit, Pauley."

"I heard something."

Emily had heard it too. Low, scarcely audible. A groan? A scream? She started at a run after Pauley.

But they had gotten only a few yards into the woods when they saw Garrett moving toward them.

Dizzying relief surged through her. "You're not hurt?"

He shook his head. "But we'd better get out of here before anyone comes. Someone might have heard those shots. Two dead bodies are hard to explain."

Dardon's gaze went to the direction from which Garrett had come. "Do you know who he was?"

"The shooter was Sal Caprini. I don't know the name of the other man. The address on Caprini's driver's license was in New Jersey." He turned to Emily. "Staunton sent him. Orders were to kill me, take you."

"He told you that?"

"Yes." He smiled faintly. "It was sort of a deathbed confession." He tossed a phone to Pauley. "See if you can retrieve Staunton's number from Caprini's phone, in case we need it. It won't be easy. Staunton would be very careful."

"A challenge," Pauley said. "You do like to keep me stimulated."

"Yes. That's the only stimulation I want you to indulge in while you're on my payroll." He took Emily's elbow. "Come on. We have to get out of here. Dardon, is the plane ready?"

"Almost. Fifteen minutes after we get to the airport."

Emily looked back at the Toyota crashed in the ditch as they reached the road.

"Forget it," Garrett said. "Caprini and his friend would have served you up to Staunton and not given a damn what he did with you."

"I know that. It just happened so . . . quickly." And with brutal efficiency. She realized that Garrett hadn't really needed Dardon. He'd only wanted to get rid of her. Then he'd gone down and taken care of those men, those murderers, himself. There were moments that she forgot how lethal he was, but then it could be brought back to her with jarring suddenness. Had he killed the driver, too? She wouldn't ask him. Nor would she talk to him about Caprini. He had probably saved her and certainly his own life. She had no right to question how he did it. "Will the police be after us about this?"

"They will unless I can get in touch with Ferguson and use him to run interference. He has contacts. We'll see if he can get a cleanup crew out here."

She looked at him in surprise. "Again?"

"He won't like it, but he might as well make himself useful. It shouldn't be as hard as the one in Kabul. They both died of broken necks that could have happened in the accident. I'd bet Caprini has a record as long as my arm." He shrugged. "I can only try."

And Garrett would probably be successful if he tried, she thought. He seemed to be a master manipulator. She would never have guessed that Ferguson would have agreed to the deal in Kabul. Garrett seemed to know how to press just the right buttons.

"What are you thinking?" His gaze was narrowed on her face as he opened the car door for her.

"I was thinking that you're a very talented man."

"Oh, yes." He glanced back at the ditch. "And you particularly admire one of my talents." He slammed the door, ran around, and got into the driver's seat. "I've validated your opinion again, haven't I?"

"I'm not saying—" She stopped as Dardon and Pauley reached the car. It was just as well. She was too emotional right now to think, much less speak clearly. But she had to say one thing. "You saved my life. I'm not about to judge you." She looked straight ahead. "Now, can we please get out of here?"

Tangiers, Morocco

Borg straightened away from the curved archway as he saw Irana Povak come out of the Roman Catholic church across the street. She slipped her scarf off her head and started down the winding street toward the clinic. Watch and wait, Staunton had said. Find an opportunity. Any repeat routine activity might be the ticket that would let him get his hands on her.

The Povak woman had only been inside the church for forty-five minutes, but that might be an opportunity. The bitch had once been a nun, and she might make regular visits to the church for prayer and confession.

That could be his chance. God knows, he didn't see any other way. As he'd told Staunton, she was never out of the sight of one of Dardon's guards. Even now he could see a security guard who was strolling after her at a discreet distance but still staying close.

It might be better to be inside the church when she got there tomorrow. He'd managed to bug her cell phone, but that might not help get the information he needed. He'd ask some discreet questions at the clinic or bribe someone to tell him when she left the clinic to go to the church.

And, if he was prepared, there might be no more waiting and watching. He'd swoop down and take her before she knew what was happening and give her to Staunton. He smiled at the thought. Borg knew Staunton, and if he was frustrated about Emily Hudson, he wouldn't hesitate to play games with Irana Povak. Borg was beginning to look forward to those games.

By all means, go to church and say your prayers, bitch. You'll need them.

Emily looked down at the Atlantic as their jet took off over the water. "So easy," she murmured. "No customs. No Homeland Security . . ."

"Not easy at all. It takes a great deal of money and knowing the right people," Garrett said. "Bribes for this kind of thing are very expensive in this day and age."

"But all it takes is money." She looked up at him. "It scares me. All these terrorists' threats, and all it takes is money to skirt around the tightest security measures."

"What can I say?"

"Nothing. I'm abusing the system, and I have no right to complain. But I *am* complaining. I resent the fact that it can be done. I resent the fact that my country is at risk."

"Not from me, Emily."

"No." She leaned back in her seat. "Not from you. In your way, you're one of the good guys."

He chuckled. "Whatever gave you that idea?"

"Irana told me."

"Then of course it must be true." He shook his head. "And after what happened before we got on this plane, your faith in her judgment isn't shaken?"

"No." Emily reached for the envelope containing the court records. "Because it's not entirely her judgment. Now, I'm going to read these translations and see if I can get a handle on Mikhail Zelov."

"Do you want me to take some of that testimony and work on it?"

"No, I want to do it myself. Why don't you go see if Pauley has managed to hack into that phone company database?"

"I'm obviously being sent on my way." He stood up. "By all means let me run along. I wouldn't want to disturb you." He glanced back at her. "Actually, that's a lie. I do want to disturb you. But not that way, Emily."

Damn him.

She watched him walk away toward the seats near the cockpit, where Dardon and Pauley were sitting. He did disturb her. Just noticing the way he walked bothered her. Springy, catlike, athletic. What the hell was wrong with her?

She knew what was wrong. She had become too aware of him as her emotions had come back to life. That sexual magnetism was growing stronger the longer she was with him.

Ignore it.

Work.

Read about Mikhail Zelov.

Garrett didn't come back until they were over Sweden. "You've been working for hours. Am I permitted to talk to you now?" He dropped down in the chair beside her. "And, no, Pauley hasn't gotten through yet. He says he's getting closer."

"Good," she said absently as she looked up from the transcript. She was glad to see him, glad to see anyone who would bring her out of Zelov's world. She moved her shoulders as if shrugging off a burden. That's what she felt like, she thought. Heavy and carrying a crushing weight of evil and hatred. "There wasn't much in his letters except arrogance and demands on his family. It's in his journal that he let's you see him as he is."

"Was he as nuts as his family claimed?"

"Maybe. Like Hitler was nuts. He wanted to take over the world. He hated everything and everyone. He wanted to be emperor or the Pope. I can't tell you the contempt he felt for Tsar Nicholas. It's incredible that he managed to hide it from him. He worked there in the royal household and saw him almost every day."

"What about his relationship with Rasputin?"

"He regarded him as a puppet, as we thought. They were both of peasant birth, and Zelov was able to feed Rasputin's ambition and push him toward being the figurehead he wanted him to be."

"Why did he want a figurehead? If he had that kind of ego, I'd think he'd be willing to risk trying to take the power himself."

"He would have risked it. There was nothing wrong with his nerve." She flipped through the pages until she came to the one that she wanted. "Here, read this. It's one of the passages from when he and Rasputin were at the height of their power. It may give you an insight into Zelov." She leaned back, watching as he read the passage.

I had to sternly chastise Rasputin today. His arrogance and womanizing are beginning to make the Tsarina suspicious of him. She is a fool, but she has eyes to see and ears to hear the gossip. How can I convince her that he is a holy man when he fornicates with half the women of the city? Holy man? He is a joke. He has a few meager talents, but I am the one who could shake their souls if I decided to unleash my powers. I am the holy one. I could heal that woman's puny young son if I decided to do it. Instead, I had to stop only one of his bleeding fits and give credit to Rasputin. Now she believes he is a god.

I am the god.

I was tempted to come forward on that day and tell them all what fools they were, how little they were in comparison to me. And then I thought of doing what Rasputin is doing and mesmerizing all this court with my power and personality.

I could do it. I can do anything.

No, I must subdue this anger. I chose this role, and I must live with it. I set Rasputin to play the sorcerer and holy man of God for a reason. These fools are uneasy around me. I smile. I keep my hatred close to my heart. Still, they distance themselves from me. I believe they sense that they have a god in their midst.

Yet the women of the town spread their legs for that fool, Rasputin. There are rumors that he may be sleeping with the Tsarina and I cannot tolerate that stupidity. I have the Tsar within my sights, and I will soon have everything I wish from him.

I believe I will take Rasputin back to Jerusalem on a pilgrimage and get him away from the Tsarina. Then when he comes back with 'supposed' new holy powers, I can start fresh. If he's good and obeys me, perhaps I'll give Rasputin one of the grand duchesses to play with. They're pretty enough, and I can make them think coupling with Rasputin will get them closer to God. Much safer for me and Rasputin than his bedding the Tsarina. Though she's so enamored with the idea of his being holy that she probably thinks the Church would bless their fornication.

I think it's time I took aim at the Church. It has too much influence with the Tsar. I will have to break its hold on him even if it means destroying or discrediting those greedy bastards. Churches can fall even as monarchies can fall. Priests can be burned at the stake even as Tsars can be shot and bludgeoned.

I can do it. I can do anything. As long as I'm able to control that idiot Rasputin.

"Not exactly a sterling character," Garrett said. "Let's see, he had it in for the monarchy, the Tsar, the Tsarina, the Church, and Rasputin. Have I left out anyone?"

"Not in this passage. You should read the rest. He's quite a piece of work. He did go back to Jerusalem, and I don't know if he arranged to give one of those pretty daughters of the Tsar to Rasputin for sex, but he was trying to choose which one was safest for seduction."

"Shades of Anastasia," Garrett murmured.

"No, she was too young. She might talk," Emily said. "Olga was in contention, but he was leaning toward Maria." She shook her head. "It nearly made me sick. All that evil. All that corruption. And those royal children caught in the middle of it."

"It's clear he truly believed he had psychic powers." Garrett said. "Maybe he did."

"Why do you say that?"

"This was written years before the Tsar's death, but that was how he died. He and his entire family were shot, then bludgeoned with rifle butts."

"Coincidence."

"Maybe." He gazed down at the transcript. "Zelov said he was near getting what he wanted from the Tsar. What did he want?"

She shrugged. "The throne? Money? Influence?"

"He was practical. He'd know that a throne would be out of the question for a peasant."

"But power wouldn't be impossible. The revolution was right around the corner. Maybe he was a Communist?"

"If he was, then it was an ideology of convenience. And he had influence through Rasputin. No, it had to be money."

"And judging by that castle he built in Connecticut, he must have gotten all he needed. How?"

"The Tsarina and her daughters were vulnerable. I've seen photos of their jewels. They're fantastic. More opulent than the crown jewels of England."

"But he specified something from the Tsar. The Tsarina and her daughters were merely an annoyance he had to tolerate. Does he mention anything specific later?"

"No. He talks a lot about Rasputin. He gets pretty vicious toward the end of this ledger. Evidently Rasputin could be charming, if a little mad. Zelov resented that side of him. I suppose he wanted him under his thumb. He goes off on diatribes about the Church and how he was going to usurp its power. The venom got worse as the Church increasingly turned on Rasputin and tried to influence the Tsarina to forbid him to come to court."

"And at what point does the ledger end?"

"A few months before Zelov left for

America. He makes some kind of enigmatic comment that the time had come for his words to be put forth surrounded by the light cast by his *Book of Living.* So he must have continued his ledger in the book itself."

"The *Book of Living* again. No threats toward Rasputin? No dire plans of murder?"

She shook her head. "Just the same contempt he always felt for him. No change at all."

"What about any of the other letters? Any connection?"

"He seems to have cut the ties to Russia entirely once he left."

"Yet he built a Russian castle and wanted his children to speak Russian."

"Arrogance. He was always right, remember? Including his language."

"And we're back to the question of where he got the money to build that castle." He gathered the pages and put them back in the envelope. "If you don't mind, I'll take a look at these."

"I don't mind. But you're not going to find anything."

"Probably not. But, like you, I want to get

a handle on Zelov. For instance, he hated the Russian Orthodox Church. Why?"

"They had too much influence on the royal family."

"Enough for him to try to bring them down? It seems a little extreme."

"He was extreme."

"You've got that right." He smiled. "And maybe it had something to do with his belief that he was supremely holy because of his psychic powers. Didn't you say he belonged to the Khlysty sect when he first met Rasputin?"

"Yes. That's where Rasputin read Zelov's book. We *need* that book. We didn't find out nearly enough from these transcripts."

"We knew we wouldn't. Don't be unreasonable."

"Shut up. I feel like being unreasonable."

"Then by all means continue." He looked out the window. "We should be arriving in Moscow soon."

"I suppose you've got a way to get into that country, too, that avoids their version of Homeland Security?"

"Yes, I wouldn't favor one country over

another. It should please you that other countries are also vulnerable."

"It doesn't please me," she said wearily. "I wish there was no need for security anywhere."

"I do believe you're an idealist."

"There's nothing wrong with that. I hate war. I've spent a good portion of my life trying to save beauty from the beasts. I saw how those monsters can savage what should be treasured."

"So have I," he said quietly, his gaze on her face. "And that's why we're going after Staunton."

She couldn't look away from him. She tried to smile. "I'm no national treasure."

"No." His hand closed around her own. "But a treasure all the same."

She stared down at their joined hands. She should move away. She was aware of an intimacy that was not intense, just warm, and comfortable. Yet it was probably a more dangerous closeness than a more sensual connection.

She didn't move away.

Instead, she glanced away and out the window at the clouds. "Where are we going to stay after we land?"

"Dardon has arranged for us to stay in a farmhouse outside Moscow."

"Why Moscow?"

"We don't know where we're going to have to go until Pauley tells us. It's as good a place as any," he said. "And it's a hub."

"I've never been to Moscow. I've been to other places in Russia and the Republic of Georgia on the job. Maybe I'll see the church that Zelov's house was built to resemble."

"We're not sightseeing." His hand tightened on hers. "But if you want to see anything in the whole damn world, I'll show it to you."

Intimacy, again.

She didn't care. She needed comfort and a feeling that she was in touch with something besides hatred and ugliness. She'd take this intimacy now and draw back later.

If she could.

THIRTEEN

The large stone farmhouse that Dardon had chosen was surrounded by flat barren fields that seemed to stretch on forever. It was all on one level, with a thatched roof and a rock-paved driveway leading up to the front door. "The farmer who owns it left to work in the city," Dardon said. "A lot of farmers don't think the work is worth the income these days." He jumped out of the car and ran up to the window box beside the front door. "The key should be here. "

"Pretty obvious," Garrett said.

"There's not much to steal out here in the boondocks." Dardon unlocked the door and turned to Emily. "It should be comfortable if not elegant."

"That's all that matters." Emily entered the spacious kitchen–living room. Dark oak beams arched across the ceiling, and a huge stone fireplace was centered between the two rooms. "It's cozy. We stayed in a farmhouse like this in Georgia, and Joel said he felt like he'd gone back in—" She broke off. That memory had popped up out of nowhere. So many of her memories were connected with Joel. She saw Garrett looking at her, and quickly said, "It's very nice, Dardon."

"Tell him that after we find out if this place has a coffeemaker," Pauley said as he headed across the room toward the cabinets. "This stove looks like it's vintage 1930." He was looking through the cabinets. "I don't see—for heaven's sake, a samovar." He took out the elaborate tea service. "Very fancy but it's not a coffeepot."

"Stop complaining." Dardon was going through the cabinets, too. He triumphantly pulled out an old-fashioned coffeepot. "And there should be supplies, including coffee, in here somewhere."

Garrett turned to Emily. "Pick a bedroom. There should be three. Which is pretty palatial for a farmer. And there's supposed to be a lean-to with a comfortable enough mattress and pallet outside the kitchen door. We'll have enough places to sleep."

"And I won't be here that long," Pauley said. "If I can down enough coffee, I'll work all night and see if I can get a breakthrough." He smiled at Emily. "Much as I like the company, this place in the country isn't my idea of resort living."

"I can understand that." Emily smiled back at him. "We appreciate your coming."

"He's being paid very well for coming," Garrett said. "And Pauley getting his work done and getting on his way will be good for all of us."

"That's telling me." Pauley raised his brows. "Little edgy, Garrett?" He didn't wait for an answer, but went to the sink and filled the pot. "That will cost you."

"The price is set."

"But that was before you hurt my feelings," Pauley said. "I charge extra for that."

"And so you should," Emily said as she headed for one of the doors leading off the kitchen. "I'm going to see if I can shower and change my clothes. Where's the bathroom?"

"One bathroom. We share." Dardon said. "It's the door on the other side of the kitchen."

"Not exactly convenient," Pauley said.

"Shut up, Pauley," Dardon said. "I did the best I could on short notice."

"And I get one of the bedrooms," Pauley said. "I'm working and I need privacy and a soft bed to rest my weary and exceptionally brilliant head."

Dardon frowned. "The hell you do."

"I'll sleep in the lean-to," Garrett said. "Just get your work done, Pauley."

Pauley smiled. "I may forgive you for being so curt with me." He turned on the stove and put the coffeepot on the flames. "And I may give you a cup of my coffee."

Emily shut the door of the bedroom behind her and leaned against it. She was glad to close them all out and grasp this moment of quiet. They had been going nonstop, sidestepping bullets and jetting across oceans for the last days, and it was catching up with her. There had been only a short period that she had felt safe and content during that time, and it had been linked to those moments on the plane with Garrett.

Intimacy.

But there had been no hint of intimacy in the Garrett who had been cold with Pauley. It had annoyed her again, and she had struck back. Jealousy was absurd in their relationship. Even though he'd admitted that it was childish, he seemed to be feeling it still.

Why? It wasn't as if she was some Angelina Jolie. She could see a woman like that attracting Garrett. Emily knew that she was a fairly attractive woman and that she had brains and drive. She would not underestimate herself, but she would not make the mistake of believing that Garrett could be involved with her on a more permanent basis. They were too different. It had to be the situation that was binding them together.

Yes, the situation. That was the answer.

She gazed around the room. Clean, a worn off-white quilt on the bed. Cheap painted nightstand and a bowl and pitcher on the chest by the door. Good enough.

The bed looked particularly good to her. She was in no mood to pass through the kitchen to go to the communal bathroom for a shower.

Later.

She curled up on the bed and pulled the ancient cream-colored quilt over her. Why did old things always seem more soft and comfortable . . . ?

Someone was knocking.

She opened her eyes. The room was dark.

"Emily."

Garrett. She swung her feet to the floor, crossed the room, and opened the door. "Is everything okay?"

"That's what I was going to ask you." He smiled. "You've been in here for almost four hours. But judging by the fact that you're a bit tousled, I'd guess you were taking a nap."

She nodded. "I only meant to—I suppose I was tired."

"I suppose." He stepped aside. "And you were a little tired of us. Me, particularly. But Dardon and Pauley have gone to their rooms, and you can have the house to yourself if you want to take that shower."

She did want a shower. She felt sticky, and her mouth was like cotton. "Is there hot water?"

He nodded. "I lit the water heater."

She went back into the bedroom, opened her duffel, and took out her toothbrush and shampoo. Then she grabbed underclothes, shirt, and pants. "Good. I hate cold showers."

"Me too." He turned and headed back toward the kitchen. "Take your time. I'll make you coffee. You didn't get any from the first pot."

She could smell the coffee as she opened the bathroom door almost an hour later. Lord, she loved the smell of fresh coffee.

He smiled as she came toward the table. "Feel better?"

"Yes."

"Want something to eat?"

"No, I had that sandwich on the plane. I'm not hungry."

"That was a long time ago." He poured her coffee. "Maybe later."

"Maybe."

He sat down across from her. "Pauley said he's close."

"He said that on the plane, too."

"There are a lot of false starts and doubling back in his line of work."

"You sound as if you're familiar with it."

"Familiar, not perfect. That's why I moved on to other endeavors."

"Do you have to be perfect in everything you do?"

"Only in some things. But I have to be damn good, or it drives me crazy until I am."

"I was never that ambitious. I just wanted to accomplish what I set out to do and do it well."

"You grew up with a loving father and a secure home life. I had to be better than anyone else on the street or end up in the gutter. It trained me to be competitive."

"I can see that." She looked at him over the rim of the cup. Even now when he was sitting here, relaxed, she was aware of the vibrancy and wariness that was such an integral part of him. In those first days with Garrett, she had not dreamed she could become so accustomed to being with him. She was wary, too, and she was out of her element with him.

He had stopped smiling, and his gaze was suddenly intent.

He was still out of her element.

She could feel her chest tighten, and the heat move through her. She wanted to reach out and touch him.

Get a grip.

"I'm still competitive," he said. "You didn't like it when I wasn't all sweetness and light to Pauley. Sorry. It's my nature. I have to protect what's—" He broke off. "No, you wouldn't like that either. I seem to be saying all the wrong things tonight." He looked down at the coffee in his cup. "But I think it's the time to say them. I think you're ready. God, I hope you're ready."

"Ready for what? Sex?"

"Yes." He looked up at her. "Oh, yes."

She caught her breath. He wasn't even touching her, and she felt as if something inside her was melting.

"You knew it was coming," he said thickly. "You want it to come."

She did want it, and she'd be lying if she denied it. She wouldn't lie. "We have a certain chemistry." She moistened her lips. "But it's the situation. We've been thrown together, and we react. That doesn't mean we should—" She broke off and pushed her chair back. "I'm hot." Oh, shit, that had just tumbled out. "I need some air. I'm going outside."

He smiled. "I'm hot, too, Emily." But he remained in his chair as she left the house.

The night was chilly, but it didn't cool her. She leaned back against the house, gazing out at the barren fields. She was burning up, her body readying. For heaven's sake, she felt the way she had the first time she'd had sex. It was her first year in college, and she'd been mindless, uncontrolled, dizzy with lust. She hadn't run away from it then. She'd run toward it.

Because it was safe, just a new experience, a passage of life.

Sex with Garrett would not be safe, and the passage could take her down paths that would be new and strange.

And exciting. Yes, everything about Garrett was exciting and different. The way he thought, the experiences that had made him who he was, his body that drew her and made her want to—

The door opened, and Garret came outside.

She tensed, straightening against the wall.

He was also tense. She could see the tautness of his face and the contained violence in the bunched muscles of his shoulders.

"Don't worry. I'm not going to jump you," he said. "I'm not even going to try to seduce you. Though God knows I want to do it. I might be able to pull it off. That's one of the skills I studied until I got pretty good at it."

"I'm sure you did." Emily tried to keep her voice even. "It's one of the most necessary talents in a man's repertoire, isn't it?"

"You're damn right." His gaze narrowed on her face. "And it's frustrating the hell out of me that I can't use it now. My hands are tied. That son of a bitch, Staunton, tied them, and I can't do anything about it."

"I don't know what—"

"I'm telling you," he interrupted harshly. "You've been one of the walking wounded ever since we came together. How the hell am I going to get you into bed when I'm afraid you're going to shatter if I put a finger on you?" He reached out his hand and brushed her throat. "Your pulse jumped when I touched you." He rubbed his thumb in the hollow. "And it's going crazy now."

More than crazy. She couldn't breathe. Her heart was pounding so hard she thought it would jump from her breast.

"And I can't do a damn thing about it," he said between his teeth. "You're the only one who can make the move." His hand dropped away from her throat. "Just know that I want you more than I've wanted any woman in my life. I'm wild for you. I'd never hurt you, and I'd make it good for you. That's all I wanted to say." He turned on his heel and walked across the farmyard toward the road.

She stared after him, her head whirling with the words he'd just spoken.

Walking wounded.

You'd shatter if I put a finger on you.

Staunton tied my hands.

She slowly turned and went back into the house.

She should have worn her shoes. Her bare feet were cold on the rough ground as she moved toward the lean-to.

Cold feet. That was almost funny. But she wouldn't be nervous or afraid. She had gone through all that in the hours since she'd left Garrett. Now the time for nerves was over. Then why did she still feel them, dammit?

She opened the door of the lean-to. "Garrett."

"Come in." He was half-lying, half-sitting, propped up against the wall. "Quick." He lifted the quilt covering him. "Let me get you warm. I didn't expect you to be running around in a tee shirt."

She dove forward and under the covers. "I didn't really think about it. I just decided to come." She stiffened as she realized he was naked. "And you have less on than I do. You were expecting me?"

"I was hoping." His lips brushed her ear. "But I always sleep naked."

Dear God, she was trembling. His body was hard, hot, ready against her.

"You're shaking." He turned her over to look down at her. "It's so dark in here, I can't see you. Are you afraid?"

"For Pete's sake, I've never been afraid of you." She reached down and pulled her tee shirt over her head and threw it aside. "And I won't shatter. And, if I was among the walking wounded, it was never sexually." She pulled him down and then arched upward with a little cry as her breasts touched his chest. "And I won't allow Staunton to tie your hands. I want them moving over me. Get busy."

He chuckled. "Right. Whatever you say." His hand moved between her legs. "Like this?"

She inhaled sharply. "Yes."

"Maybe we should go to your room. I made sure this pallet was clean, but that's all it is." He was rubbing, manipulating. "You'd be more comfortable."

"No." She arched as he went deep. "This is fine."

"You're not cold?"

"Are you crazy?" No, the bastard was teasing, physically and verbally. "I'm not wounded. I'm not cold. I'm in lust, and you're not doing anything about it." She pushed him back and moved over him. "So I guess I'll have to do it myself."

"I can see why you didn't want to go to your bedroom," Garrett whispered. "Dardon would have run into your room gun drawn at the first scream."

"It wasn't a scream." But it had come close, Emily thought as she tried to get her breath. "It was a prolonged, loud, exclamation."

"I liked it. Call it anything you please." He was curved spoonlike against her back, and his hand was rubbing her belly. "I made you do it. You liked what I did to you."

Liked? She had been out of her mind every time they had come together. She was still out of her mind. Just his hand rubbing her flesh was causing it to start all over again. "You're not bad, Garrett."

"Not bad? I'm obviously going to have to up my efforts a notch. I want to impress you."

Oh, he had impressed her. She had tried to protect herself by making light of it, but she had to be honest. He had given her more than she had expected, more than she had thought she needed. She was silent a moment, trying to find the words. "You made me feel . . . alive again, Garrett," she whispered. "Thank you."

"You're welcome," he murmured. "But I didn't do anything much in that direction. You're the most beautifully alive person I've ever known. It was what I saw when I first saw your picture in the newspaper. Full of life and character and a sort of luminous joy." He kissed the tip of her ear. "I think that's why I got so pissed that you'd been taken and I had to go after you."

"There are so many little things that make us what we are. The memories, the way we face sorrow and disasters, the people we reach out to. I thought I was back, but there was still a numbness there. I couldn't make contact. I guess I haven't felt really alive since—" She stopped. "I hadn't even realized what I'd lost. But to-night I felt alive. My body felt beautiful and clean, and you made me feel as if I was very special."

"And so you are."

He didn't understand. She wasn't sure she could make it clear what he'd given her. It was more than likely it had just been a great roll in the hay to him. She was probably embarrassing him. She'd had to put it into words but it would be better to back away. "Of course, I am," she said lightly. "I'm glad you recognize it."

"I couldn't help it." He moved his hand to her throat and began lightly rubbing the hollow of her throat. "For instance, your flesh is very sensitive. Particularly here." He smiled as he felt the pulse leap beneath his touch. "Extraordinarily sensitive. It's good to know that no matter where we are, what we're doing, all I have to do is slip my hand under your blouse and you'll be ready for me in a heartbeat."

"Don't count on it." But it didn't sound very sincere when she could hardly get her breath.

"I am counting on it." He turned her over on her back. "Because you're going to back away. You're going to be afraid you'll lose your focus. I'll just have to bring you back. I know all the ways now. You know how good we are together. Every chance I get, I'll remind you."

"What about your focus?"

"I can keep my focus. There's no need denying ourselves this. That would give Staunton a victory." He moved over her. "You said you didn't want him to tie my hands." His fingers were moving, brushing, pressing. "I promise he's not going to do that, Emily. . . ."

"I've got it!"

The door of the lean-to was thrown open, letting in bright daylight and Pauley.

He stopped short, his gaze on Emily. "Oops."

"Oops, indeed." Garrett drew the blanket over Emily and raised himself on one elbow. "You could have knocked."

"I was excited. And I didn't know you weren't alone." Pauley made a face. "Sorry, Emily."

"It's okay." She was looking around for the tee shirt she had discarded all those hours ago. "Why are you excited?"

"Not for the same reason Garrett was excited," he said ruefully. "Lucky man. I wish I'd spent the night here instead of staring at that computer."

"What have you got?" Garrett reached over and retrieved Emily's tee shirt and handed it to her. "Why don't you go start the coffee and give us a couple minutes?"

"Right." Pauley moved out of the doorway and headed for the house. "And it's almost eight in the morning. It's time you got up anyway."

"You can go straight to your bedroom and get some clothes on, Emily." Garrett was pulling the tee shirt over her head. "I'll talk to Pauley."

"No. Give me your shirt. You get another one out of your suitcase." She slipped the shirt over her tee shirt and buttoned it. "That's good enough until I can hit the shower. It should only take a few minutes to hear what Pauley has to say." She got up and headed for the door. "Coming?"

"Could you wait until I get some clothes on?" He was already dressing. "I'll be just a minute." He smiled faintly. "You're already in strike mode. It's going to be a harder battle than I thought. It only took Pauley with his computer wizardry to jar you away."

"What are you talking about? Only? Why else are we here in Russia?"

"You're right, of course. Time to focus."

He was passing her as he headed for the door. "What could I be thinking?" He gave her a glance as he passed her. "But remember when I said I'd have it all? That didn't only apply to Staunton and his employer. I *will* have it all, Emily." He didn't wait for an answer but strode toward the house.

She had to run to keep up with him. The rocks were cold and biting into her bare feet. It was the same as last night. No, not the same. Last night she wouldn't have cared if she were walking on hot coals.

He glanced back at her, then stopped to wait. "Much as I like every part of you bare, I suggest you wear shoes from now on." There was a faint edge to his tone. "You may not be able to keep up with me. I intend to move very fast from now on. I'm beginning to want Staunton out of our lives very badly."

"I've never wanted anything else."

"Yes, you did." He opened the door for her. "Last night you forgot all about Staunton. I made you forget him. I can do it again, but it's not a good idea. You'd end up resenting me. So it's best if I just eliminate the bastard as soon as possible." He followed her into the room. "But I'd appreciate it if you'd put some clothes on as soon as possible. I don't like Pauley gawking at you, and it distracts me."

"Pauley isn't—" She stopped as she saw that Dardon and Pauley were both standing by the stove, and they were staring at her bare legs and feet. "That's not my problem. You all can deal with it. I'm decent." She strode over to the stove and took the cup of coffee Pauley handed her. "Thank you."

"Talk, Pauley," Garrett said curtly.

"I broke through to the database about two this morning." Pauley made a face. "Damn it was hard. I was tempted to go to bed, but I was zinging by that time, so I decided to plow through the records and come up with a name and address."

"And did you?"

"Sure. I told you, I got it." He took a notebook out of his back pocket. "Charles Vorstov-Babin. He used Babin in London but his full name in Russia."

Emily stiffened. "Babin?"

Pauley glanced up. "You've heard of him?"

"Only once."

On that hideous day that had so traumatized her, she hadn't even been able to remember it.

Pauley looked back at his notes. "He's an attorney who moved from London to Moscow at the end of the Cold War. There were a lot of Western industrialists who decided to come to the Soviet Union to do business and make a killing. Babin decided that he'd make a killing of his own by representing them and getting a cut of the gravy train. He's illegitimate, but his mother was Russian and he speaks the language. It came in handy when he moved back to Russia. He fit in with both the Russian government and his new clients from Great Britain and the U.S. He's very successful and not above skidding very close to the edge when it comes to honest business practices."

"And his address?"

"Got that, too. His office is in a little town north of Moscow. Dalbaz. His home is an estate that was confiscated by the Bolsheviks after they killed the royal family. It once belonged to Grand Duke Igor."

"How far north of Moscow?"

"About fifty miles."

"Not very convenient for doing business," Emily said. "And he must have done very well if he could afford to buy that estate."

He shrugged. "Maybe he has a select clientele that can afford to keep him in the style to which he'd like to be accustomed."

"How well is he doing?" Emily asked. She remembered the term Garrett had used when he'd spoken about Staunton's cash flow. "Unlimited funds?"

"I haven't had time to do an in-depth study, but I don't think so."

Dardon shook his head. "I'm sorry, I should have been able to locate Babin before this, Emily. Hell, I've been checking since before you went after Nemid. It was that damn double name that threw me off."

"It doesn't matter. We have him now. I just don't understand why his profile doesn't agree with what Garrett was told about Staunton. Staunton doesn't have unlimited funds, and now neither does Babin?"

"We'll find out, Emily," Garrett said quietly. He turned to Dardon. "Now you have a full name and address. Call Ferguson and get him to tap every source he has and see if he can find out anything more. See if he has a client named Staunton."

"You're using Ferguson again?" Emily asked.

"Hell yes, I want to see what dirt he can dig up on Babin. Ferguson has contacts, and we might as well use them. Let him earn his payoff. Tell him to get the information as fast as he can."

"Then you won't need me any longer," Pauley said. "Do I get to go home?"

Garrett stared at him for a moment. "It's tempting. But I think I'll keep you here for a little while. Something may come up." He turned to Emily. "Shower and get dressed. We'll go visit Babin and see if we can get a few answers ourselves."

Babin's office was located in a brick building on a street with other professional offices. The street was clean and well maintained, and the town of Dalbaz appeared prosperous.

"Very nice," Garrett said as he held the door open for Emily. "How are you doing? Are you okay?"

"Yes. Why shouldn't I be?"

"No reason. You can never tell how anything is going to hit someone. We're getting closer."

And she was feeling nervous. How had he known? Lord, he was perceptive. "Let's get even closer." She moved to the desk, where a blond receptionist was sitting. "We'd like to see Mr. Babin, please."

"You have an appointment?" Her English was faintly accented, and her smile was flashing white in her pretty face.

"No. But we need to see him. My name is Emily Hudson and this is—"

"I'm sorry, but Mr. Babin never sees anyone without an appointment. Perhaps you can—"

"Perhaps we can see him right now." Garrett took Emily's elbow and whisked her toward the inner door. "It will be fine. Trust me."

"It will not be fine." The receptionist's smile was gone as she jumped to her feet and ran after them. "I told you that—" She stopped and said to the man who had gotten to his feet as they walked into the room. "I'm sorry, Mr. Babin. I told them that you never saw—"

"John Garrett and this is Emily Hudson," Garrett said. "We need to talk to you, Babin."

"It seems to be somewhat important, Nadia," Babin said to the receptionist. "Perhaps we should make an exception. It will be all right."

"If you're sure?"

"I'm not sure, but I'm willing to be open." He smiled at Emily as the receptionist left the room. He was a heavyset man in his fifties, with smoothly barbered black hair and a toothy smile as glossy and slick as his hair. "Now what is this all about?"

She drew a deep breath, trying to smother the anger that was beginning to kindle. "Suppose you tell us. Nicholas Zelov called you two nights ago. He was frightened." She paused. "And he mentioned Mikhail Zelov's *Book of Living.*"

"I don't remember such a call. You must be mistaken. Did Mr. Zelov tell you that he'd called me?"

"No."

"Oh, my, then you must have tapped this call by illegal means." He shook his head reprovingly. "And I really can't discuss it with you."

"Discuss it," Emily repeated. "Illegal?" He was so smooth, so confident that she suddenly lost control. "How can you say that? My God, you couldn't be more dirty."

"Nonsense. You're the one who committed an illegal act. I wouldn't want to be an accomplice by even talking about your misdemeanor. Besides, you're mistaken; I know nothing about Zelov or this book."

"Nor Staunton?" she asked through clenched teeth. "Where is Staunton?"

"All of this is a complete mystery to me." He glanced at Garrett. "You're being very quiet, Mr. Garrett. You must have been forced to come here with this woman. I'm sure you realize that a man of my professional reputation would not be involved in anything in the least crooked."

"The lady said it all. She didn't need my help." Garrett stared him in the eye. "You don't know anything. You never heard of Staunton. We're mistaken. If you did know anything, you wouldn't tell us. Have I got it right?"

Babin nodded. "In a nutshell." He smiled. "Now I believe it's time you left."

"I believe you're right," Garrett took Emily's arm. "We've struck out here,

Emily. Let's leave before Mr. Babin has us arrested for illegal wiretapping. Gee, he has me scared."

Babin's smile remained firmly in place. "I'd never do that. It's clearly a case of mistaken identity, if there was such a call." He turned to Emily. "And I'd never cause this lady additional grief after all she's been through. Naturally, I recognize her from her photos in the newspapers. Perhaps she's a little distraught from her experience in the mountains?"

"You mean she's nuts?" Garrett asked. "No, I don't believe so. Are you unbalanced, Emily?"

"Stop it, Garrett. I've had enough." Emily took a step closer to Babin. "Yes, I'm distraught." Her voice was shaking with rage. "And who should know better than you about my experience in those mountains. You were *there.* Did you hear him screaming, Babin?"

Babin didn't change expression. "I beg your pardon?"

"No one begged Joel's pardon. No one stopped hurting him when he begged." The words kept tumbling out. "And then he couldn't beg any longer. Why would you—"

"Emily." Garrett's hand tightened on her arm. "Not now. It's not going to do any good."

"He's got to tell me where Staunton—" She drew a deep, harsh breath. She felt as if she was going to explode. He was right. Babin wasn't going to say anything. She could see nothing in his expression but bland satisfaction. She wanted to slap him, tear out that smooth hair by the roots. She jerked away from Garrett and turned on her heel. "I'm out of here." She strode out of the office.

Garrett caught up with her as she reached the front door. "Take it easy. This isn't the end. It's just the first round. We knew that he probably wouldn't cave. We just have to go at it another way."

"I lost my temper." She looked straight ahead as she walked toward the car. "I fell apart. I didn't mean to do that." Her hands clenched into fists. "But he kept smiling, Garrett. He was so smug. I was wondering if he was smiling like that while he was talking to Staunton that day. Joel was screaming, and no one cared but me. He kept smiling. . . ."

"Shh." He stopped in the street and

drew her into his arms. "I know. I know. You did fine."

"No I didn't." She buried her face in his chest. "I fell apart. I shouldn't have done that. I think he liked it."

"We'll just have to make sure he pays for it, won't we?" His arms tightened around her. "And I would have probably exploded myself under the same circumstances."

She felt warm and safe in his arms. A moment ago, she'd been crumbling away with fury and frustration, but, incredibly, it was beginning to be okay now. "Let's get out of here." She pushed away from him. "It's the middle of the street in broad daylight. If Babin saw us, he'd be very happy that he'd upset me this much."

"It would be short-lived." He pushed her hair away from her face. "I promise you everything about Babin will be short-lived."

She felt a chill. It was strange when she'd been in such a fury only moments before and wanted to strike out at Babin herself. "Not before we find Staunton and Zelov's book." She turned away and moved toward the car. "He didn't even change expressions when I mentioned Staunton's name."

"He's very slick, very smooth." Garrett got into the driver's seat. He glanced back at Dardon in the backseat. "Anything?"

"No." Dardon looked up from his computer keyboard. "Too bad. He's neither drunk, nor stupid. If he knew we traced him through Zelov, he wouldn't be caught in the same trap. He'd find another way to make contact."

"You think he'd be contacting Staunton?" Emily asked.

Garrett nodded. "Or someone else."

"You don't believe he's Staunton's employer?"

"I didn't say that. But he could be the middleman. From what you told me, Staunton's reaction toward Babin was annoyance, and there should probably be more intimidation and respect if it was Babin pulling the strings. And the bankroll Staunton had at his disposal couldn't be furnished by Babin."

"But Nicholas Zelov called Babin, and it seemed as if Babin was in control."

"We'll have to see. When I talk to Ferguson again, we may know more. Did you talk to Ferguson yet, Dardon?"

"Yeah, he was pretty sour, but he said he'd get back to you."

"I hope he has something for us. We didn't accomplish anything with Babin," Emily said.

"Actually, we did." Garrett started the car. "At least now we've taken his measure."

"And he's taken ours?"

He shook his head. "Hell no, he's not even gotten close."

FOURTEEN

Ferguson called Garrett two hours after they reached the farmhouse. "What? Just information?" he asked sarcastically. "No crime scenes to clean up? No dead bodies?"

"Dardon said you were a tad bad-tempered about this."

"I don't like being used."

"Neither do I. But you didn't hesitate when you came knocking on my door to get Emily out of those mountains. What did you find out about Babin?"

"Dardon said you knew the basics."

"The phrase I'm interested in is 'unlimited funds.' Does Babin have them?"

"No, he does well. But he's nowhere near that class."

"He has that estate in the country."

"He gambles a lot. He came back from Monte Carlo one day with a potload of money. Paid his taxes and still had enough to buy the estate."

"A lucky windfall," Garrett murmured, remembering the castle built by Mikhail Zelov. "It seems to be the preferred way of acquiring choice real estate. Did anyone check with the casinos?"

"Sure. It checked out." He continued, "Of course, who's to say that the casino didn't get a nice fee to say what Babin wanted them to say?"

"What a cynic you are," Garrett said. "You said he does very well. Who are Babin's principal clients?"

"He has several English manufacturers who moved here after the Cold War and have done even better than Babin."

"Names."

"His principal clients are John Broderick, Peter Joslyn, William Smythe. Now, any of those men would qualify for 'unlimited funds.' Babin also does some work for the Russian government and the Russian Orthodox Church. He often has meetings with Bishop Dimitri Pushkal."

"What?"

"Bishop Dimitri is one of the most powerful men in the Church. Both the Church and the government have tremendous influence in their different areas. Babin has to deal with both of them to protect his clients. You can never tell when a small bribe or deal in either camp might free up a piece of real estate or smooth the way toward licensing."

"Does Babin have any family? A mistress?"

"Not at present."

"He has a blond bombshell at the reception desk in his office."

"Nadia Vladar. She's not his mistress. Though he's been known to lend her out to his clients on occasion. She's very accommodating, and he pays her very well."

"She seemed pretty eager to please him."

"Anything else?"

"I'll need in-depth reports on Smythe, Broderick, and Joslyn."

"I'm ahead of you. It's already in the works." He paused. "You know I'm not going to let you make me go at this blind indefinitely?"

"No, but I think you will until you begin to doubt I can give you what you want."

Ferguson didn't speak for a moment, but Garrett could feel the frustration behind that silence. "You son of a bitch. What else do you need?"

"I'll let you know."

"I'm sure you will." Ferguson hung up.

"You heard him, Emily." Garrett turned down the volume on his phone before he hung up. "Any thoughts?"

"Babin is a middleman."

He nodded. "But for whom?"

"Maybe we'll know that when Ferguson gets back to us with his reports." She shook her head. "But I don't want to wait, dammit."

"You may not have to wait for everything. There's a good possibility that Babin got in touch with Staunton after Zelov called him. It's almost sure he'll manage to contact him now that he knows we're on his turf."

"And Staunton will come to us." The realization hit home with chilling impact. That was what she had wanted. Yet it didn't stop her from feeling vulnerable. "He still wants to get his hands on me. We can use that to set a trap for him."

"Not yet. We want to gather everyone in at the same time. We just have to sit tight until we're ready."

"And will Staunton let us just sit tight? What if he comes after us?"

"We're safe here for a little while. Dardon buried the paperwork for the rental of the farmhouse. And I made sure we weren't followed from Babin's office."

"I don't want to sit tight," she said. "We can gather everyone else in later. I want Staunton."

"I know you do." He leaned back in his chair. "But you also want to find the cause of all the misery he's caused. You want to find the hammer. You told me once you dreamed about it. Do you want some big-time industrialist to find it and get the treasure Joel paid for with his life?"

"Don't be stupid. Of course, I don't."

The hammer was like a Medusa's head with serpents stretching out and strangling everything around it. It had struck down Joel. Sometimes she felt as if it were still striking at her. "But I don't want you to be right either."

"I *am* right, Emily."

She gazed at him in helpless frustration. Dammit, she realized he was right. She knew he was being reasonable and setting goals that would take them to where they had to be, but that didn't stop her from wanting to move faster, reach out for Staunton before he could slip away. "Okay. For now." She turned on her heel. "But if the chance comes to get Staunton, I'm not going to wait." She strode to her bedroom and swung the door closed behind her with a firm click.

Garrett stared thoughtfully at the door.

Emily had temporarily given in, but it wouldn't last long. Ever since she had arrived here and confronted Babin, she had been in an emotional tailspin. Who could blame her? Every time she turned around, she was faced with a memory of that horror in the mountains. It was a wonder that she was doing as well as she was.

But that tension and horror were going to increase the longer they kept on the trail. He could only help her so far. In fact, he could be part of the problem. She had said he had made her feel alive. Dammit, he had never thought he would want her emotions to be dulled.

Okay, not dulled, just soothed.

But nothing about their relationship was soothing. It was hot and sexual, and they were still learning each other physically and emotionally. Yes, he wasn't what she needed right now.

He slowly took out his phone and dialed the number.

"Is Emily all right?" Irana asked immediately when she picked up the phone. "I had a dream about her last night, Garrett."

"She's fine. Just a little tense. How are you, Irana?"

"Fine. Busy. But Dr. Kaidu has so many assistants that they're tripping over each other." She paused. "He wouldn't really miss me if I moved on. When do you want me?"

He chuckled. "How do you know I do?"

"You called me. Your voice is a little hesitant. You probably don't want to ask a favor of me. You never do."

"It's a big favor. Can you come to Moscow right away?"

"Why?"

"As I said, Emily is tense. I'm trying to find a way to keep her from exploding and doing something that could be dangerous for her. You'd be good for her." He added, "But the situation isn't what I'd like it to be here. Things may get very ugly, and you could be in the middle of it."

"That wouldn't bother me. I didn't like the fact that Staunton blew up my hospital."

"He's capable of far worse than that."

"I assumed that the devil had a firm hand on him. He gave Emily nightmares, and she's very tough. She's the only reason that you wish me to come?"

"She's the main reason. You could help with something else if you would. We may have to deal with the Russian Orthodox Church. One of the paths is leading in that direction. You might be able to communicate with them on a higher plane."

She laughed. "Where did you get that

idea? A Roman Catholic nun who renounced her vows? They would probably toss me out."

"You'd know how they thought. You're well versed in the historical side."

"History?"

"It's only a thread, but it occurred to me that it was strange that the Church was involved in this at all. It may have something to do with Rasputin and his battles with the Church."

"You've lost me."

"Dardon will explain it all to you." He paused. "If you choose to become involved. I didn't want to ask it of you, Irana. I had you safely tucked away where I didn't have to worry about you."

"Only because I allowed it." She was silent a moment. "I will help you as far as my conscience will permit. There are many things we don't agree upon, Garrett. But we do agree that Emily should be loved and protected. I'll come as soon as you want me. I'll make reservations for a plane to Moscow right after I go to church tonight."

"No reservations. Is it necessary that you go to church today? I wonder if you'd mind skipping attending church and head for the airport within a few hours? Dardon usually uses a pilot, Chad Nalley, in that area. He's in and out of Morocco frequently. He'll contact him, and you can be on your way later tonight. I won't risk Staunton's knowing you're in the country." He added soberly. "I promise I'll keep you safe, Irana."

"Church is never a necessity, it's a solace. I wasn't able to get away from the clinic yesterday, so I thought I'd go today. But instead I'll go to the airport after I finish at the clinic and be ready for your Mr. Nalley." She paused. "I told you I had a dream about Emily last night. You didn't ask me what it was about."

"Threat? Danger?"

"No. Emily was happy, very happy. She was like a butterfly soaring in the sunlight. I woke up smiling. Was Emily happy last night, Garrett?"

I feel alive.

"I hope she was, Irana."

"So do I. I'll see you soon." She hung up.

A butterfly soaring in the sunlight . . .

He had never seen that side of Emily.

No, he had seen it but never been included in the world of that woman who loved Bruce Springsteen and *Casablanca.* He had come close last night, but sex had a way of overshadowing everything.

A butterfly soaring . . .

Dammit, at last.

Babin had waited all day until he could get on the road in his car and away from any possible electronic wiretaps. He dialed Staunton with frantic speed. "Where the hell are you?"

"Moscow. I arrived last night. You told me that you didn't want me to contact you directly." There was a faint mockery in his tone as he continued. "And you know I always obey you, Babin."

"You didn't obey me when I told you to get someone good to take down Garrett and collect the woman." Babin cursed long and fluently before he continued, "They're here. They came to my office today. They know about me."

"Really? I sent a good man, but you should have let me go myself. If you remember, it's what I wanted to do."

"Don't give me any I-told-you-so bullshit. You had orders to get the job done, and you failed me."

"I don't fail, Babin. You failed. You'll get the blame."

Staunton was usually not respectful, but there was a note of arrogance in his voice that Babin had never heard. "Blame?"

"Did you really think I didn't know about Joslyn? I'd never let myself go into any deal without being in control. I was very amused when you dribbled out your little bits of information to me. I knew everything you knew and more."

Shock made Babin go rigid. "You son of a bitch."

"But I can be generous. I won't even tell Joslyn how you've blundered."

"You're the one who blundered. Now what are you going to do about it?"

"What do you want me to do about it?"

"I want you to find Garrett and the woman and take them out of the equation. I want you to protect me and make sure that he doesn't find out anything he shouldn't."

"I don't believe our agreement included me protecting you, Babin. You have guards to do that. I have other fish to fry. Did you find out where Garrett and Emily are staying?"

"No, I was caught by surprise. I thought you'd taken care of them. I didn't have time to arrange—"

"Then it was doubly your failure. I'll have to work all the harder to locate them because you fouled up."

"I did not—" But Staunton had hung up.

Bastard. Babin punched the disconnect button. He had not expected this degree of rebellion from Staunton, and he'd never suspected he knew that it was really Joslyn who was in control of the money. It made him uneasy that Staunton was trying to blame him for everything that had gone wrong. After all, it was Staunton who had failed to get the information from the woman, then let her be rescued.

Is Staunton trying to avoid a possible dismissal by trying to frame me?

For the first time, Babin felt a jolt of fear. His instincts were usually sound, and they were screaming that Staunton was about to knife him in the back. Mistakes and failure that could not be corrected would not be tolerated. Not in Staunton. Not in Babin.

Staunton would have to be eliminated.

He had found Staunton, and he would find another killer to rid him of the son of a bitch.

He was driving up to his impressive front gates and could see the towers of the castle through the trees. He felt the familiar flush of pleasure the sight always brought him. No grand dukes, no Tsars, no Tsarina. This world belonged to Babin now. He had worked for it. He had lied and cheated and trampled over anyone who got in his way.

Just as he would trample over Garrett and that bitch.

Just as he would trample over Staunton.

There had been no sound from Emily's room for hours, and it was close to midnight. Is she asleep or just avoiding me? Garrett wondered. It could be either. She had been upset when she had left him, and their coming together last night might represent an emotional overload to her.

He would have to deal with that possibility later. Tonight he was just as glad that he didn't have to find a way to avoid her. That would have been extremely delicate.

He listened. Definitely no sound. *I hope you sleep well, Emily.*

Time to make the move.

He glided across the room and opened the front door. The car was parked down the driveway, and Pauley was leaning against it.

He straightened as Garrett came toward him. "What the hell is happening? Dardon just told me to meet you out here."

"We're going hunting. Get in the car. You drive."

"Hunting?" he repeated warily. "I'm not really the outdoor type. I thought you might have noticed."

"I don't think it will require outdoor activity." He got into the passenger seat. "But then again, it might."

"Look, you're not going to drop me somewhere by the wayside, are you?" He started the car. "I know you've been pissed at me, but just tell me, and I'll go."

"How could I drop you? You're the one driving."

"Well, it makes more sense than taking me hunting. I can't help it, you know. I'm irresistible to women. It's nothing I do."

"Pauley, shut up."

He was silent for a moment. "Where are we going?"

"We're going to pay a visit to Babin."

"Oh." Pauley thought about it. "Violence and mayhem? I'm not good at that either. Wouldn't you prefer to have Dardon?"

"With my whole being."

Pauley sighed with relief. "Then I'll turn around and go back."

"I need someone I can trust to watch over Emily. That's more important than having him back me up. Dardon has his orders."

"And what am I supposed to do?"

"Nothing that will get me in trouble. You may act as lookout or just as driver. I'll do the rest."

"Good," Pauley said. "That sounds relatively bloodless. Babin lives in a fancy estate. How do we get in?"

"We leave the car at the gate and climb the fence." He added straight-faced, "Hopefully, it's not electrified."

"Hopefully," Pauley said. "Look, I know that you probably know everything you could know about that estate. After all, it's a historical palace. I'd appreciate it if you'd get off my back. I'll do what you want me to do. I may not be good at it, but I won't say no."

Garrett studied him, then slowly nodded. "That's all I ask." He shrugged. "Dardon gave me a map of the place he got off the Internet, complete with security system. There's an alarm at the gate, but the fence isn't alarmed in any way. No electricity. The rest of the house has alarms, but it's a system that's twenty years old. It was installed by the former owner. I can get around it."

"I'm sure you can. You're sure you don't want to go back for Dardon?"

"I'm sure. I think you need a new challenge. It's good to stretch yourself occasionally." His smile was crooked. "You told me it was no effort at all being irresistible."

"Stay here, Pauley." Garrett checked his infrared detector. "Three people in the downstairs service quarters. One occupied bedroom on the second floor. Two guards at two o'clock. They're not moving. Just stay here in the shadows and come and warn me if there's anything that—"

"Come where?"

Garrett did a pass with the detector to make certain. "Bedroom. Second floor. I'll disable the side-door alarm and motion monitor." He moved toward the huge door at the side of the palace. "Don't move."

"Not a muscle." He tilted his head. "Do you know, I'm beginning to get a kind of zing from this. I'll be watching like a hawk. Trust me."

He wished he could trust Pauley, Garrett thought as he worked on disabling the security alarm. His response had surprised Garrett once he'd realized that he was going to have to go along with him. He might be able to trust his mind-set and willingness to help, but Pauley didn't have Dardon's experience. Well, he would have to do. Garrett needed to move forward quickly. Not only because Emily was on the edge and might go out on her own if he didn't show progress, but now that they'd exposed themselves to Babin, he might rush to cover his tracks before Garrett could convince him otherwise.

He made the final adjustment and swung the heavy door open.

No alarm.

It was strange that Babin hadn't updated the security. But maybe he had been so wrapped up in the past glories of the place that he'd assumed that everything was top-notch. Or maybe Garrett would get an unpleasant shock when he tried to get into the master bedroom.

He opened the door a tiny crack. He didn't get a surprise.

Okay. Move fast before Babin woke and could get his hands on a weapon.

He threw open the door and darted across the room toward the bed.

Babin wasn't there.

He'd rolled off the bed as the door opened and was clawing frantically at the drawer of the nightstand.

Garrett encircled his neck with his arm and jerked him backward. The next moment Babin was on his back, Garrett on top of him, his knife pressed against Babin's throat. "I thought it over, and I decided that we needed to talk a little longer." He reached up and turned on the lamp on the nightstand. He wanted to see expressions. Babin's face was flushed and full of venom. No fear. That wasn't good. He pressed the tip of the knife a tiny bit harder, and a rivulet of blood ran down Babin's throat. That was better. A trace of fear flickered. "Of course, if you choose not to tell me what you know, I could just kill you. That would be good, too. Emily would like that."

"That bitch."

He pressed a little harder. "I wouldn't talk about Emily in those terms if I were you. It annoys me."

Babin's dark eyes were blazing with rage. "You can't do this to me. This palace is full of guards. Any minute one of them will find out you're here."

"You have four guards on the ground. Two near the gates. Two on the west side of the palace. My men will take care of them." Yeah, sure. That was the bluff of the century. "You have servants, but I doubt if they'd come to your rescue. No, it's just you and me, Babin." He added softly, "And soon it will be just me if you don't talk. These are such grand, majestic halls. Do you want your spirit to be haunting them with the Grand Duke Igor's? No, somehow I think you won't be allowed any earthly territory. Straight to hell, Babin."

His expression changed, hardened. "I don't know anything. I told you the truth."

"Emily knows you were at that hut in the mountains. Staunton made a slip."

Babin's lip curled. "That son of a bitch. I knew he was out to get me."

"So you do know him. Now we're getting somewhere." He leaned forward. "Listen closely, Babin. Emily wants revenge, but I may be able to convince her that she doesn't need your head as well as Staunton's." He added, "If you give me something that I can work with."

"You're not going to kill me," Babin said. "That would be stupid. You'd still end up in the dark, knowing nothing."

"True. But there are always more ways than one to find out anything. You only appear to be the most convenient at the moment."

Babin shook his head, then yelped as the knife cut across his neck with the motion. "Look, take that knife away. And when my guards come, I'll tell them to let you go. I won't be vindictive."

Hell's bells, Babin was so full of his own pomposity and agenda that Garrett wasn't getting through to him. "But I'll be vindictive. Listen carefully, Babin. I want to know everything, but there are a few things that could save your life. I want to know who pays you and Staunton. I want to know why Nicholas Zelov came to Russia and why he went away with money to burn. I want to know where to find Mikhail Zelov's *Book of Living.* I want to know what's hidden in Zelov's hammer. And I want to know about the Rasputin amulet that Nemid had hidden away. If I find out all of those things, then I'll give you a reprieve." He held Babin's gaze, and said softly, "I want very badly to kill you. I'm getting impatient. Can you see it?"

Fear at last. Stark fear. Babin swallowed hard. "Why should I believe you?"

"Maybe you shouldn't. That's up to you. On the other hand, it might not be smart for me to kill you now in case there was a little detail I might need to know later." He said softly, "But it would have to be a very small detail, Babin. You'd better not hold back."

He moistened his lips. "I'll have to think about it. Will you let me sit in that chair?"

He was stalling.

In spite of his panic, the bastard was still hoping for a rescue. And the more time that passed, the better the chance that the guards would find Pauley and raise an alarm. "I like you where you are. By all means, think about it. I'll give you two minutes."

It's no use, Emily thought. She couldn't sleep. She had been lying here for hours, and her mind wouldn't shut down. Not only her mind, her emotions were so charged that she couldn't sort one from another.

Garrett.

The thought of him was a beacon in the darkness. In all this confusion and depression all around her, she could trust Garrett. They were working together, and though she didn't agree with everything he said or did, she knew that she could rely on him.

And she knew that when he held her, she felt safe and alive.

She needed that feeling after staring into that pig Babin's face and knowing that he was oblivious to anything but his own selfish greed.

She shouldn't go to Garrett and use him just because she wanted to push away the darkness and feel that same sense of beauty and rightness that she had last night. That would be selfish, too.

To hell with it. She needed him, she wanted him, and she'd make sure that he'd use her as much as she used him.

She swung her legs to the floor, got out of bed, and moved toward the door. Bare feet again. She didn't want to stop and put on shoes. She wanted to get to Garrett. Oh well, it was only a few yards to the lean-to, and it wouldn't hurt her to—

She stopped in surprise as she left her room. Dardon was sitting at the kitchen table, working at his computer. He quickly looked up and smiled. "Can't sleep? Neither can I. How about a cup of coffee?"

"Coffee? The caffeine would keep you awake."

"I'm not going to sleep anyway. Might as well enjoy a nice jolt of java. Did you know Garrett likes his with vodka?"

"He told me."

"Sit down." He got to his feet. "I'll make it."

She shook her head as she moved toward the front door. "I'm going to see Garrett."

"Emily." She looked over her shoulder

to see Dardon standing there and shaking his head. "I knew that something would go wrong. Nothing is ever easy."

She froze with her hand on the doorknob. "What's wrong? Has something happened to Garrett?"

"No." He made a face. "But he's not here right now."

She turned around and stared at him. "And where is he, Dardon?"

"Come back and sit down. I'll make that coffee."

"Where is he, Dardon?"

"He decided that he needed to get Babin to talk before the bastard could marshal his defenses and maybe pull in any big guns."

She wasn't even shocked. She'd known when she'd seen Dardon's expression where Garrett had gone. God, she'd hoped she was wrong.

"I'm sure that scum has big guns on his payroll anyway. He hired Staunton, didn't he?" She felt a sickening panic at the thought. "Maybe Staunton will be—"

"I imagine Garrett will be glad if he does run into him, but he's not expecting it," Dardon said quickly. "He can't see Staunton acting as watchdog for that slimeball."

Neither could she, and it was the only good thing she could see in the situation. "Why didn't you go with him?"

"He didn't want me." He turned away and ran water into the coffeepot. "He said that Pauley would do."

"Pauley?"

"Pauley's a good enough guy." Dardon still wasn't looking at her. "And anyway, Garrett likes to work alone on a job like this. He says it's safer not to have to trust anyone. You can react faster if something—" He added immediately, "But nothing is going to go wrong."

Anything could go wrong. For all she knew Garrett could be dead now. "How long has he been gone?"

"About four hours."

"And he hasn't called you?"

"I didn't expect it." He put the coffeepot on the burner. "He told me to call him if there was something that went wrong, but he—"

"Look at me, Dardon."

He sighed as he turned to face her. "I

told him that I'd be the one who'd take all the heat. Okay, shoot."

"He made you stay here because he wanted you to take care of me, didn't he?" Her hands clenched into fists. "And he didn't tell me. He just walked off and left me here without a word."

"As I said, Garrett likes to work alone."

"He took Pauley."

"He'd worry about you. Pauley wasn't going to do much, and he won't have to watch over him nonstop."

"He didn't say a word." She couldn't get over it. She felt as if he had betrayed her. Babin had been her enemy as well as Garrett's, and he had closed her out. He had gone to face Babin by himself.

And he might never come back.

"Sit down." Dardon was suddenly across the room, urging her toward the kitchen chair. "You don't look so good."

She didn't feel so good. Her knees were shaking and she felt sick. "Stop coddling me. I'll be fine." She dropped down in the chair. When Garrett walked through that door, she'd be fine.

And then she'd kill him herself.

FIFTEEN

It was almost dawn when she heard the car stop. It was barely audible, and she knew he had parked far away from the house.

A few minutes later he was quietly opening the front door.

"Too late," Dardon said. "I did my best, Garrett."

Garrett stood in the doorway, his gaze on Emily. "Good morning."

She wanted to run across the room and hold him. No, she wanted to hit him.

"You should put more clothes on," Garrett said. "It's a little chilly in here. "

She glanced down at the long tee shirt,

which reached her thighs. "I have enough on. And I don't feel chilly. I feel decidedly warm."

Dardon gave a low whistle. "I just remembered that I should be on my way to meet that plane bringing Irana." He got to his feet and headed for the door. "I'm out of here."

"Irana?" Emily repeated. "Irana's coming here? Why?"

"I thought we might need her. We were told Babin has some dealings with the Church, remember?"

"And you'd run that risk on 'might'?" she asked. "When were you going to tell me she was coming?"

"It was no secret. You were a little upset earlier, and I didn't want to disturb you."

"You're damn right. I *am* disturbed." She drew a deep breath. "But we'll go into that later. What about Babin?"

"Oh, he's still alive. Pauley is driving him to the airport in Moscow even as we speak. I drove Babin's car back here. He's going to stay at his house in Monte Carlo for a while. He told me he'd feel safer from Staunton if he was as far away from Russia as he could get. Though I think he was more eager to get away from me. He was a little worried that I refused to give him my word that I wouldn't go after him later." His lips tightened. "Which I will. He's just unfinished business. I only let him scoot out of here in case I found I needed more information from him later."

"He'll probably disappear anyway."

"Maybe. But I'll know where he is. I called Ferguson and asked him to have an agent trail him from the time he got off the plane in Paris. Could I have a cup of that coffee?"

"It's cold. Dardon and I have been sitting here for hours."

"I'll heat it up." He moved across the room and put the pot back on the burner. "And I'm sorry you've been worried. I hoped you'd sleep through the night."

"You could always have given me knockout drops," she said sarcastically.

"That wouldn't have been honorable. I took advantage of the situation. I didn't create it." He gazed at her. "And I knew I'd eventually have to face you over this. I had to decide if it was worth it."

"Babin," she prompted.

"He was reluctant, but I eventually convinced him that he'd talk to me or never talk again."

"Is he a middleman?"

"Yes, for Peter Joslyn, the big plastics industrialist." He took the pot off the burner and poured coffee into a cup. "Joslyn hired him when Nicholas Zelov came to Moscow with old Mikhail Zelov's book and three amulets and wanted to turn them into gold. Nicholas Zelov first went to Bishop Dimitri and offered them to him, but somehow Joslyn was pulled into the mix. Joslyn didn't want Zelov to know that he was involved so he used Babin as a go-between. He told Babin that he was to get the *Book of Living* and the amulets, and in return Zelov was to receive a huge lump sum that would get him out of financial trouble and quarterly allowances from then on."

"The amulets were that important?"

"Very important."

"And there *was* a treasure hidden in the hammer?"

"According to Babin. He said it was all in the *Book of Living*. As well as where the hammer was hidden away."

She shook her head. "What difference would that make when all that happened almost a hundred years ago? Why wouldn't he have gone back and retrieved it himself? Or why wouldn't the Communist government have discovered it in all that time?"

"Evidently they didn't."

"It's hard to believe that it could be safely hidden for nearly a century. Where?"

"In plain sight. With a collection of other farm equipment in a museum in Siberia. What could be safer?"

"Artifacts in museums aren't safe. I'd be out of a job if they were."

"This museum was different. It was called the People's Museum. The exhibit was a symbol of the workers' revolution. It was several tools artfully arranged, and over it flew the flag that had the hammer and sickle of the new Communist state. For decades it would have been considered close to treason to disturb such a patriotic showcase. Babin said that Joslyn must have believed that it had remained undiscovered, or he wouldn't have been willing to put out the kind of money he did to buy the *Book of Living* and the amulets.

Or to authorize him to hire Staunton to go after the hammer when they found out that the farm equipment exhibit had been sent on loan to that museum in Afghanistan. He told Babin to keep the amulets in the safe in his office. He didn't want to have them in his possession since they were stolen historical artifacts." He patted his jacket pocket. "We have them now. That makes three."

"Are they any different from the one we got from Nemid's safe?"

"Only minor differences in the scrolling of the gold around the picture."

"But did Joslyn take the *Book of Living*?"

He nodded. "Joslyn has one book."

"One?"

"Babin is a crook. Do you think he wouldn't make a photocopy of the book for himself before he let it out of his hands?" He reached into his jacket pocket. "By the way, he said that there was a map dated 1913 tucked in that *Book of Living* that he gave to Joslyn. He made a copy of that, too. That means Nemid's map was probably a very well done fake. Babin was very disappointed in most of the content of the book. He was only interested in the treasure that was in the hammer. He was likely thinking of doing a double cross, but when he found out that all the farm equipment had been sent on loan to the museum in Afghanistan, it complicated everything, and he felt out of his league." He pulled out a loose-leaf volume. "But he kept this copy in his office safe anyway. So we dropped in there and retrieved it before I sent him off to the airport."

She reached out and took the volume. "Russian."

"Yes, you'll have to trust me to translate." He gazed at her over the rim of his cup. "If you can."

"I think I can trust you in some areas," she said coolly. "But the hammer wasn't with the other farm equipment in that museum cellar in Afghanistan. So it has to be somewhere else, doesn't it?"

"So it would seem."

"And what was that amulet we found in Nemid's library?"

"A bribe. Babin said he left it up to Staunton how to get the hammer from the museum in the fastest manner possible. The U.N. was to be the first to go into that area after the fighting. So Nemid commandeered your team to go in so that Staunton could raid your truck on the way back."

Blood running from beneath the overturned truck.

"And that amulet with Rasputin's picture was Nemid's bribe money? Why? What's it supposed to be?"

He shrugged. "I didn't go into more than the bare facts with Babin. Staunton must have convinced him that it had some value. Probably it was supposed to seal the partnership. Maybe after we read the book, we'll know more."

"I want to see the amulet again."

"It's in my suitcase. I'll get it for you." He got to his feet and went outside to the lean-to. He was back in minutes and handed her the box. "Anything else?"

"You can translate Mikhail Zelov's book double quick." She opened the box and gazed down at the amulet of Rasputin. "Payment for all that blood and misery . . . Look at him. Those burning eyes. He looks like the holy man he pretended to be. The holy man Zelov created." Her gaze shifted to the words below the amulet. "You're sure this is just a blessing?"

He nodded. "And I looked for any secret compartments or other writing. Nothing. I checked out the map, too. No invisible ink or anything similar. Though if it was a copy, it probably wouldn't show any indications. That doesn't mean that under sophisticated tests something might not show up. But you have to consider that this amulet was created in the early twentieth century."

She closed the box again. "Did Babin tell you what was supposed to be in the hammer?"

"Oh, yes." He smiled faintly. "And it's quite a treasure. Not Anastasia's jewels or the Tsarina's favorite pearl pendent. It's precise directions to the location of the treasure the Tsar had sent out of the country in case the royal family had to flee the revolutionaries." He paused. "Billions, Emily. Billions."

"It didn't do him any good, did it? His whole family was butchered before he could get them out of Russia."

"But you can see how it would be a lure that would attract Babin and Joslyn . . . and perhaps Bishop Dimitri."

She nodded. "I can see it." She got to

her feet. "I'm going to try to get some sleep. Why don't you take a nap, then start working on that translation."

His brows rose. "That was more an order than a request."

She stared him in the eye. "Neither would really do me any good, would it? I know you'll do whatever you want to do. You proved that tonight."

"Is this where you tell me what a bastard I am for leaving you here while I went after Babin?"

"You like to work alone. Dardon was very definite on that subject." She paused. "So that leaves me no choice but to work alone, too."

Garrett muttered a curse. "That's exactly what I didn't want to happen. I didn't want you to get impatient and go out on your own because you thought I was dragging my feet."

"So you left me and went off and risked your neck. Was it to prove you weren't dragging your feet?"

He shook his head. "I won't lie. I was planning on doing it before we even went to Babin's office."

"And you didn't tell me."

"Dammit, I saw how you were at Babin's office. Just seeing him and knowing he was at the hut made you go into a tailspin."

"Okay, I was upset. But I worked my way through it. You didn't give me a chance. You just patted my back and said, there, there, little girl. Then you went off to do my job."

"It was my job, too, Emily."

"I thought it was *our* job. Last night I was going to come to you because I trusted you. I was feeling alone and uncertain, but I thought that we were partners, that we were working together. I wanted to be close to you." She added fiercely, "But I couldn't trust you. You were gone. You'd lied to me."

"Not exactly."

"Don't quibble. If I'd walked out of that room before you left, would you have told me the truth?"

He was silent. "Probably not."

"I rest my case." She turned away from him. "How can I trust you again, Garrett?"

"You can trust me to get the job done,"

he said. "You can trust me to keep you alive. You can't trust me to let you risk your life. I can't let that happen."

"It's my choice."

"No, it's my choice," he said roughly. "I can stop it. I can step in the way. I did that tonight."

"Why, dammit? We were working together."

"How the hell do I know? It just hurts me to think about it." He smiled without mirth. "And it's not because you're a great lay. Though you are. But I've had great lays before, and I didn't get torn up. You should have known it would come down to this. It's been hovering there since that first night at Shafir Ali's tent."

She shook her head in disbelief. "Is it because you pity me?"

"Lord, no."

"I think it is. Why else would you send for Irana? You'd risk her because you think that I'm not competent enough to do what needs to be done. You wanted to put me in one of those hideous *burquas* and throw me behind closed doors." Her hands clenched into fists at her sides. "Don't you *dare* pity me. Don't you dare discount me. I could do this alone. It would be hard. It would take me more time. But I could do it. You don't want me to go off by myself? Then you straighten up and keep the promise that you gave me. I asked you to help me, not take over." Her voice was shaking with anger, and she tried to keep it even. "And I didn't ask you to let me sit here and wonder if you were going to be killed at Babin's place tonight. You might deserve it for being so stupid and male and domineering, but that wasn't our agreement, and if you ever do it again, I'll—" She whirled and strode toward her bedroom. "Now you translate that book, dammit."

Staunton watched as Pauley and Babin got out of the car at the airport parking lot and entered the main terminal.

Yes. He'd hoped that Garrett's man would go in with Babin when he'd followed them from Babin's house. He got out of his own car and moved down the two rows separating them. He'd go in and check Babin's destination later, but this came first. . . .

He carefully slipped a bug under the

back bumper. It might not even be necessary. The man Garrett had designated to deliver Babin to the airport didn't appear any too sharp, and Staunton might be able to follow him back to Emily. But Staunton always prided himself on being thorough.

Ah, Emily. How he missed the bitch. They had been so close, they had almost become one when he was working on Levy. She would be an exquisite pleasure.

Soon, Emily. Bugging the car might not be needed at all. After receiving that call from Borg earlier in the evening, he was almost sure of it. If everything went as planned, Emily might be coming to him on her knees. What a pleasant thought.

He returned to his own car and slipped into the driver's seat. He would wait here and make sure that Babin was just being put on a plane and not accompanied.

In the meantime, he had other business to conduct. Garrett was proving to be difficult. It might be time to change tactics. Staunton had hoped to buy a little more time, but it could be that he'd have to be satisfied with what he'd already gouged out of Babin.

But he might still be able to tap the prime source. It was time Joslyn was brought into the real world and got his hands a little dirty. He couldn't hide behind Babin any longer. Staunton would know as soon as he told Joslyn what he'd done to get that hammer whether he'd go along or if Staunton would have to go in another direction.

A new day was dawning, things were changing, and he had to meet the challenge.

He dialed his phone, his gaze on the front entrance of the airport.

"Joslyn, this is Staunton. We have to talk."

It had been a long time since she'd been to Russia, Irana thought as she gazed out of the window as the jet came in for the landing at the small private field outside Moscow. She had been only a young girl, full of enthusiasm, thirsting for knowledge, ready to explore the entire world.

She supposed she hadn't really changed that much. She was older, more experienced, a little sadder, but she hoped that she had kept that enthusiasm and boundless curiosity.

But Russia had changed in those years, and she was eager to see those changes.

"We're here, Dr. Povak." The pilot, Chad Nalley, came out of the cockpit after taxiing to a stop. His smile lit his wholesome, boyish face with warmth as he said to Irana, "And if I'm not mistaken, that's Dardon parked by the hangar. Evidently he wants to make sure you're whisked back to Garrett with the speed of light."

"I got that impression." Irana smiled as she released her seat belt. "Thank you. You've been very kind."

"My pleasure. You're a very nice woman, Dr. Povak." He turned the switch that let down the automatic stairs. "You take care of yourself." He went down the steps ahead of her and turned to help her. "Garrett isn't the safest man to—"

Pain!

She was lifted, thrown like a paper doll down the rest of the stairs.

Fire. Heat.

Blast. There had been a blast. . . .

She rolled over on the ground and saw Dardon trying to get out of the car. But the windows had been blown out, and the doors were twisted.

The pilot was groaning a few yards away from her, blood dripping from a deep cut on his forehead.

She had to get to him. She had to help him.

She couldn't move. What was wrong with her? She struggled to her knees. If she could get to her medical bag in the plane, she could—

What was left of the Gulfstream jet was in flames.

"Welcome to Moscow."

She looked up at the man who was coming toward her. Sandy hair, broad fair eyebrows, carrying an AK-47. He was smiling. . . .

Who would smile at a moment like this?

"Come along, I've been waiting for you." He jerked her to her feet. "Emily must have told you about me. I'm Staunton." He was pulling her toward a car on the other side of the burning aircraft. "Now be a good girl. I'm in a hurry. You can either accommodate me, or I'll send a few bullets toward Dardon in that car and a few more at that pilot lying on the ground."

He would do it.

"Please, just give me a minute. The pilot is hurt. I need to help—"

"How kind you are. But he really doesn't deserve it. All Borg had to do was offer him enough money, and he gave him your flight plan."

She still held back. "Just let me stop his bleeding."

"You're wasting time. You want the bleeding stopped?" He sprayed a barrage of bullets into the wounded pilot. "It will stop soon. Now do you want me to aim at Dardon's gas tank and blow his car up?"

She couldn't take her gaze from the torn and bloody remains of the pilot. "No, I'll come." Her legs were working now, but she was still dazed. Just get him away from Dardon. Just stop the killing.

"Borg thought you wouldn't cause me any trouble, but the idiot almost blew you up. I wouldn't have liked that one bit. He should know how to set the proper charge by now." He smiled. "But here you are, and here I am. Won't that be fun?"

"Emily." Garrett was standing at her open bedroom door.

She scrambled up in bed. "Did you finish the translation?"

"No." He paused. "I just got a call from Dardon."

She tensed. Something was wrong. "Irana. Did something happen to her plane?"

"Oh, yes, something happened to it." He lifted his hand. "She's alive. She may not even be hurt. Dardon couldn't tell."

"What do you mean he couldn't tell? A plane crash is—"

"It wasn't a plane crash. Dardon had just pulled up to the hangar after Irana's plane came in. She was coming down the steps when the plane blew up. "

"What?"

"An explosion," he said. "An explosion timed to go off a few minutes after the stairs were lowered. At least that's what Dardon's thinking right now."

"Staunton," she whispered.

"He didn't set it. But he was there to shoot the pilot and pick Irana up and take her away after the explosion."

"Staunton has Irana?" She couldn't take it in. It was her worst nightmare. "You're sure?"

"Dardon saw him pulling her toward a car on the other side of the plane."

"Then, dammit, why didn't he stop him."

"His car was damaged by the blast, the doors were sealed. He couldn't get the door open until it was too late. The pilot was dead. Staunton was gone."

"And he's got Irana," she said dully.

"We'll get her back."

"How?" She turned on him, and asked fiercely, "How are we going to do that, Garrett? What are we supposed to do now? He took her away as if we were helpless children."

"Do you think I don't know that?" His voice was hoarse. "I'm the one who promised her I'd keep her safe if she came here. I didn't do it. That son of a bitch—" He broke off and turned away. "Get dressed. Dardon should be back here anytime now."

"How, Garrett?"

"We find out where he is and go after

him. Dardon got the license-plate number and the make of his car."

"That's not enough information. Russia is a huge country."

"But Staunton will stay fairly close."

"Why?"

He looked back over his shoulder. "You, Emily."

She nodded as she saw where he was going. "He doesn't really want Irana. He wants me."

"That's my guess. He'll try for a trade."

"Thank God."

"Which we're not going to give him. We have to find him before that—"

"Don't tell me what we're going to do." Her fists were clenched at her sides. "Do you know what he'll do to her? I do. I've seen it. You don't understand. He doesn't *care*. He likes it. I'm not going to let him hurt Irana. He wants me? He'll get me. Just find a way that I can keep a weapon to kill him."

"It may not come to that. Not if we can find a way to locate him before—"

"It will come down to that. I've always known that it might." She grabbed her clothes and headed for the bathroom. "So find Staunton if you can, but it doesn't really matter. One way or the other, we're going to get Irana away from him."

Garrett met Dardon as he drove up to the farmhouse thirty minutes later. The front bumper of his car was twisted, the paint blistered in places, and the glass in four of the windows was broken.

"God, I'm sorry, Garrett." He opened the car door with difficulty and got out. "I tried to—I managed to get the door open but then I—Hell, I was afraid he'd kill her like he did that pilot."

"I wasn't there. I can't judge," Garrett said. "I know you like Irana. You would have done everything you could."

"How is Emily taking it?"

"How do you think? I have to find that bastard before she puts her head on the chopping block."

"How?"

"That's what she asked." His lips twisted. "The big question. But I'll find the answer." He had to find it. First Karif, and now Irana. Staunton had taken too much from him. He couldn't let Irana die as Karif had died. He looked down the road. "In fact, the answer may be coming toward me right now."

Dardon's gaze followed Garrett's to the approaching car. "Pauley?"

"Pauley."

They watched as Pauley drove into the farmyard and parked the BMW next to the car Dardon had just gotten out of. He stuck his head out the window and gave a low whistle as his gaze wandered over the scorched and shattered body of the Mercedes. "Garrett, I have to talk with you about taking better care of your automobiles. That Mercedes was a fine car. As you can see, I'm delivering this car back to you in tip-top shape."

"Did you put Babin on the plane?" Garrett asked.

Pauley nodded. "And I waited until the plane took off. But I think he would have left anyway. He was very nervous. You're very good at intimidation, Garrett. Can I learn that, or is it a natural gift?"

"You wouldn't want to put in the time involved to develop it. Stick to your own talents."

"But I want to expand my horizons. You opened a whole new world to me last night."

"You want to expand your horizons? Then hit the computer. I have a problem that should give you enough of a challenge to satisfy you."

"That's not the challenge I—" He stopped, studying Garrett's expression. "You're pretty grim. Something's not so good."

"How perceptive," Garrett said. "Something's pretty damn lousy."

"And you want me to be Superman and set the world right for you," Pauley said. "Would you like to tell me how?"

"We have the make and model of a car. We even have the license-plate number. We just don't know exactly where it is."

"Call the Russian version of the highway patrol?"

"No."

"I was afraid that was going to be your answer. What am I supposed to do?"

"Hijack one of the military satellites that we still have focused on Russia and zoom into the area and locate that car."

"Hell, no."

Garrett ignored him. "And it has to be quick and not detectable. We can't have a SEAL team parachuting down and trying to take us out."

"Impossible."

"Not for Superman."

"If I got caught, I'd not only be thrown into prison for the rest of my life, but I'd probably have to do slave labor at my computer for the government. That's a fate worse than death."

"Can you do it?"

He didn't speak for a moment, then said reluctantly, "Yes, there are a few satellites that were sent up in the eighties that didn't have sophisticated security apparatus. I've played around with them a little. But I won't do it."

"Name your price. You want to retire and live like a king? No problem."

Pauley shook his head. "It's too hot, Garrett."

"Please, Pauley." Emily was standing in the doorway. "My friend, Irana, will be hurt," she said unevenly. "We have to find her."

Pauley gazed at her in frustration. "I don't want to do it, Emily. It's going to be difficult as hell and not worth—"

"He'll hurt her, Pauley."

And Emily was hurting right now, Garrett thought. She looked almost as pale and fragile as she had the night that Garrett had taken her away from Staunton. He desperately wanted to reach out, help her, comfort her.

Evidently Pauley was having the same reaction.

"Oh, shit." He got out of the car. "Give me the information you have, Garrett. How much time do I have?"

"As little as you can get by with. Emily's right, it's a nasty situation."

"Life or death? I don't like that kind of responsibility." He headed for the door. "It won't be hard finding a satellite that can do the job but I have to get in and get out fast. Do we have any general idea where the car is located?"

Garrett shook his head. "Maybe a hundred miles in any direction from Moscow."

"Great."

"Thank you, Pauley," Emily said.

"Thank me when I find the damn car." Pauley added gloomily, "Or when they tote me away to Leavenworth." He disappeared into the house.

"Will he be able to do it?" Emily asked Garrett.

"Yes."

"Will it be in time?"

"Maybe. I won't lie to you. It's going to be hard." He turned to Dardon. "Go in and give him a description of that car down to the size of the hubcaps."

Dardon nodded. "Hell, I'll even make his coffee for him."

Emily sat down on the doorstep and linked her arms around her knees. Garrett could see the tension that locked every muscle of her upper body. Again, he felt that urge to do anything he could to comfort her. But she wouldn't accept comfort. Not now, not from him. The only comfort he could offer either one of them would be to get Irana away from that bastard.

"I'll let you know as soon as Pauley makes some progress."

She nodded jerkily. "Please. I won't go inside. I don't want to disturb him."

"You won't disturb him."

"I can't take the chance."

"Then I'll bring you a jacket. It's chilly."

"I'm not cold. I'll just wait here."

Wait. It wasn't only results from Pauley

for which she was waiting, he knew. She was waiting for a call from Staunton.

He hoped to God Pauley came through before Staunton did.

"You're being very intelligent, Sister Irana," Staunton said as he pushed Irana into the small room at the very end of the warehouse. "I always appreciate a guest who causes me so little trouble."

"I'm not a sister," Irana said. "I gave up the right to be called that a long time ago." She gazed down at the ropes binding her wrists. "And I'd be foolish to try to escape unless I had a chance to be successful."

"That's right, you would." He smiled. "But I expected . . . fear. Emily was afraid. She fought it like a tiger, but the fear was there."

"It's more courageous to fight if you're afraid. Emily is very brave."

His smile faded. "But not you. You're helpless, but I don't see—I don't believe I like you, Sister Irana."

She gazed at him steadily. "I can see that you don't. It doesn't disturb me."

"I believe it would take a good deal to disturb you," he said softly. "What a challenge."

"Why would you want to bother? I'm not important to you. This isn't about me, is it? It's about Emily."

"But I don't want to cheat you of your share of attention. After all, you're the woman who is going to give me what I want."

"Why don't you leave Emily alone? She doesn't know anything. She would have told me if she did."

"Not necessarily. Maybe she doesn't like religious do-gooders any more than I do, Sister Irana."

She gazed at him without expression.

"No answer. No defense?"

"No, I was just wondering why you're prejudiced against people of faith. Did one of us hurt you?"

"They couldn't hurt me. I have nothing to do with any of you."

"I see."

"You don't see anything." He muttered a curse and reached for his phone. "I'm the one who does the hurting. I'm the one who gives the commands."

She tensed. "You're calling Emily?"

"Oh, that stirred you." He smiled maliciously. "Not yet. I want her to worry a little longer. Anticipation." He dialed. "No, I'm calling my old friend, Borg. It was Borg who arranged for your delivery here to me. He was planning on taking you in Morocco, but when he heard your call from Garrett, he had to adjust to the situation. He hurried out to the airport ahead of you and set the charge in the plane, then had a chat with your pilot. But it all worked out, didn't it?"

"Are you calling to congratulate him?"

"No, it's come to my attention that there has to be a change of agenda. I'll use Borg to accomplish it." He spoke into the phone. "Yes, everything is going splendidly here, Borg. Just checking to see if you're in Paris yet. That's good. Yes, go ahead with it. I look forward to hearing from you." He hung up and looked at Irana. "You see, I'm the one in control. I pull the strings. I give the orders. If I'd ordered Borg to kill you in Morocco, he would have done it. I *own* him."

"Poor man. He must be truly tormented."

Staunton's lips tightened. "And you're a stupid bitch. You can't see anything but what you want to see." He drew a deep breath, then smiled brilliantly. "But there are ways to open your eyes. I look forward to showing them all to you, Sister Irana."

"My God," Garrett whispered, his gaze on Pauley's computer monitor. The screen was filled with figures, equations that were constantly changing as Pauley's fingers were flying over the keys. "Is he as close as I think he is?" he murmured to Dardon. "It's only been six or seven hours."

"You told him to hurry," Dardon said. "He said he'd be quicker, but he has to build walls as he goes to keep anyone on another computer from seeing what he's doing. He should be able to zoom in any minute."

"It can't come too soon. Firepower? Did you have any problem getting the heavy stuff we may need?"

"In Moscow? There are black-market munitions dealers all over the place. I picked it up a couple hours ago."

"Good." Garrett leaned back against the wall and crossed his arms across his chest, his gaze on that constantly changing computer monitor. "Let it rip, Pauley. . . ."

SIXTEEN

"Get up." Garrett lifted Emily to her feet. "You're stiff as a board. I told you to come in out of the cold."

"Pauley? It seems like it's been a long time." She was stiff, she realized. She had been sitting huddled here for hours.

"For what he was doing it was only the blink of an eye. I'll believe him from now on when he says he's Superman." He was leading her into the house. "Come on. I want you to see this before Pauley has to release that satellite."

Pauley looked up impatiently. "This isn't

show-and-tell, Garrett. I can't keep this up indefinitely. One minute."

"Be quiet. She needs this." He pushed Emily forward and put his hands on her shoulders. "Look at the monitor."

There wasn't much to see. A flat aerial view of buildings and the surrounding fields.

"Zoom, Pauley," Garrett said.

The view narrowed as it plunged toward the earth.

To a dark blue Volvo parked beside the loading ramp of one of the buildings.

"Same license number, same description," Garrett said. "We've got him, Emily."

The relief was so intense it almost made her dizzy. "Do we know where that is?"

"A warehouse in the town of Sakvar, about sixty miles northeast."

"What if he abandoned the car?"

"It's possible. But the Volvo is parked off the road and hidden by the building. It appears more likely that Staunton is still using it."

"That's it. You've got what you need. I'm getting out." Pauley's fingers were flying across the keyboard. "And hope like hell I didn't leave any trace of evidence behind."

Emily turned to Garrett. "You have an address. Then we can go after her?"

He nodded. "Very carefully. If Staunton is with her, there's a good chance he'd kill her if he thought he had a chance of losing her to us."

She whirled and headed for the door. "We'll be careful. We just have to get her away from him quickly. Dear God, I wasn't sure that Pauley would be able to do it."

"I told you I could," Pauley said. "And followed through with my usual brilliant efficiency."

She smiled exuberantly at him over her shoulder. "Thank you, thank you, thank you, Pauley."

He returned her smile. "Since it looks like I was able to do this without endangering my life and liberty, I'll say that you're welcome."

"Emily, don't be too excited," Garrett said. "We've only located Irana. We haven't freed her."

Emily's smile faded. "She's alive, Garrett. I know it. He wouldn't kill her if he could use her. All we have to do is go get her." She was sounding simplistic. "Okay, it's not that easy, but we have hope now."

"Yes, we have hope." He headed for the door. "And we'll do like Pauley and follow through with brilliant efficiency. Let's go and see what—"

Garrett broke off as Emily's cell phone rang.

She went rigid as she reached in the pocket of her jacket.

It had to be Staunton. It had to be the call she had been waiting for most of the day.

And Garrett knew it, too. She could tell by his alert, watchful expression.

She punched the button and turned up the volume. She took a deep breath. "It took you long enough, Staunton. I was expecting to hear from you much earlier."

"I was busy. And I wanted to give you time to think about all the possibilities."

"I've thought about them. Is Irana still alive?"

"Yes, do you want to talk to her?"

"Of course, I do."

Staunton was gone from the phone for a moment, then returned. "The bitch won't talk to you. I think she wants you to think that I've killed her, and there's no reason to bargain." His tone had an edge. "I'm finding her very annoying. I can't wait to get rid of her and take you instead."

Her hand tightened on the phone. "Just don't hurt her."

"That's entirely up to you. I don't think you believe that I'd kill her until you and I could get together."

"No, you wouldn't do that. Tell me your terms."

"There's a deserted red-roofed silo about forty miles from Moscow, off of M-10. You'll meet me there, alone, and I'll take you to sweet Sister Irana. I have a pair of very powerful infrared binoculars. I'll be able to view the surrounding countryside for miles from that silo. If I see any signs of Garrett or any of his friends, then I'll phone and tell the man guarding her to dispose of the bitch."

"No, you bring her with you. You release her, and we watch her drive away."

"You're being demanding. I'm in control here, Emily."

"Then let's compromise. I come to the silo, but I won't get out of the car. When you see me, you tell your guard to release her. Have her call me and tell me she's been released, and I'll turn myself over to you."

He was silent a moment. "I did want to have both of you. I was so entertained by your response to Levy."

"I know you were. I won't go through that again, Staunton. Let her go."

Another silence. "Very well. Have it your way. Four hours, Emily. That will be about eleven tonight." He hung up.

Eleven tonight.

She turned to Garrett. "It seems we have to wait again."

"You're not going to meet him," he said flatly.

"The hell I'm not." She stared him in the eye. "There's no way you could keep me from going. This isn't Babin. This is Irana. It's a way to get him away from that warehouse and for you to be able to surprise whoever is holding Irana. You said that you thought he'd kill Irana rather than give her up if we surprised them. I think so, too. And I don't believe she has a chance of living long after he gets his hands on me." She moistened her lips. "So you have to free her before that happens. I won't get out of the car, and you can figure a way to keep me safe. But he can't know you're anywhere near. I won't have Irana put in danger."

"And do you have any suggestions as to how the hell we'll do all that?"

"That's up to you." She turned away. "Pauley rose to the occasion. You've got the experience at this kind of thing. Use it."

"Oh, I will. But experience doesn't mean shit when it's someone you care about. This is Irana." He paused. "This is you." He whirled on his heel. "And I know right now that I'm going to have to let you have a big part in this, and its damn well killing me. But I'll be like our friend Pauley and find a way to get the job done." He added grimly, "And hope that it doesn't kill you."

9:55 P.M.

"Ready?" Garrett asked, as Emily got into the driver's seat.

She wasn't ready. She was scared and a little sick to her stomach. "Sure. I'm okay."

"I'll be at the warehouse in Sakvar by eleven, and I should be able to get Irana out by eleven-fifteen. Keep Staunton busy talking so that he won't call and check on Irana before that time."

"That shouldn't be hard. Staunton likes to talk." She remembered all the hours he'd stayed with her—taunting her, questioning her.

"Don't get out of the car," Garrett said. "And don't let him leave the silo." He handed her the black box he'd demonstrated to her earlier. "When I have Irana free, I'll ring you twice on your cell."

"You've already told me all that," she said. "Eleven-fifteen, two rings." She started the car. "And don't get out of the car."

"I guess I have." He stepped back. "It bears repeating. Be careful."

"You be careful," she said. "And take care of Irana."

She glanced at her rearview mirror and could see him standing there, hands clenched at his sides as she drove out of the farmyard.

Then he whirled and strode toward the BMW, where Dardon was waiting.

11:02 P.M.

Emily couldn't tell whether the roof of the silo was red or not. It only appeared to be dark rust in the moonlight. But Garrett had said this was the right silo, and she had to trust him. She slowed the car to a crawl, then stopped a short distance from the silo.

The palms of her hands on the steering wheel were moist with perspiration. Her heart was beating fast, hard, as she gazed at the silo.

He was there. He was probably looking at her through the high-powered binoculars he'd mentioned. Keep her face without expression. Don't let him see his effect on her.

Her phone rang.

"My, my, you're right on time," Staunton said. "A little anxious, my Emily?"

"I'm not your Emily. Give the order to release Irana."

"Presently. I'm looking the terrain over to make sure that you haven't got any unwelcome visitors trailing behind you."

"You know better. I wouldn't take the chance."

"No, you're very concerned about your

friend. That's your greatest weakness, Emily. I'll always be able to come out on top because I don't have that weakness."

"I'm aware you don't give a damn about anyone. You've proved it time and time again. Let her go, Staunton."

"Get out of the car and come to me."

Don't get out of the car.

She looked at her watch—11:05. Keep talking. "I won't risk myself without being sure that it's worth it. Who is watching her? Borg?"

"No, Borg is busy attending to some other business for me in Paris. I had to call in a local. Fasrov is lethal, but not nearly as talented as Borg. I missed him this afternoon."

She stiffened. Block out the part that was causing panic to ice through her. "What kind of business?"

"Partly damage control. Partly long-term insurance." He was silent. "I do believe you've been a good girl. I don't see any signs of Garrett or his friends. Now get out of the car, put down the gun I'm sure you have, and walk toward the silo."

"I won't get out of the car."

"Then I'll call Fasrov and tell him to kill

our Sister Irana. Then I'll shoot out your tires, and we'll go from there."

She looked at her watch—11:12.

"I don't want to kill your friend," Staunton said. "It will be much more amusing if I can keep her alive . . . for a while."

"Like Joel."

"Exactly like Joel Levy."

"I told you that I wouldn't let you—"

"Your choice. I kill her now, or you take the chance you can free her later."

It was eleven thirteen.

"I'm going to hang up and call Fasrov now," Staunton said.

"Don't make the call. I'm getting out of the car."

"Very good. I told you that softness would beat you every time."

She got out of the car. "I'm putting down my gun." She set the Glock on the ground. "I'm going to walk toward you. Where are you?"

"I'm on scaffolding inside the silo. I'll come down to meet you."

Don't let him leave the silo.

"No," she said quickly. "I'm on my way to you."

"Now why do you want me to—"

"I'm hanging up the phone now." Emily clicked the button and moved slowly toward the silo.

Eleven fifteen, Garrett had said.

Two rings, Garrett had said.

But it was only eleven fourteen, and she was already out in the open and struggling to keep Staunton in that damn silo.

Where the hell are you, Garrett?

11:14 P.M.
Sakvar Warehouse

Only one guard and he were standing in front of the loading dock of the warehouse.

Garrett moved silently across the dock.

One yard.

Two yards.

Three.

Now!

His arm went around the guard's neck from behind. He pulled back, twisted, and snapped it.

"Dardon." He moved toward the heavy freight door. "Bring the car around."

He ran down the hall. It was eleven-fifteen. His infrared detector had indicated one person at the far end of the warehouse. He was praying it was Irana. He was praying she was alive. He couldn't call Emily until he was sure.

The door was locked. Dammit, he should have gotten the key from the guard.

He aimed downward at the lock. "Irana, stand back."

No answer.

The lock exploded as he blasted it. He threw open the door.

"Irana?"

Emily's phone in her pocket rang. Once. Twice.

Two rings. At last.

She heard Staunton's voice just inside the silo. "Just what are you—"

She pressed the remote control on the box Garrett had given her.

And Staunton was framed in the doorway as the silo blew.

Emily was running back to get the gun she'd laid on the ground, but the force of the blast threw her to the ground.

"Bitch," Staunton was cursing as he tried to pick himself up off the ground. "Whore."

A bullet whistled by Emily's ear as she crawled the final few feet to the Glock. She grabbed it and rolled behind the car. "But you like explosives, Staunton." She aimed carefully. "You blew up Irana's hospital. You blew up her plane. Garrett thought it only fitting that he come here and do some advance work so that he could return the favor."

"I'll kill her. I warned you, Emily." He was struggling to reach his phone. "You've signed her death—" He cried out as her bullet entered his shoulder.

Dammit, she had meant the bullet to hit his chest. If he hadn't moved for the phone, he would have been dead, and this would have been over. She took aim again.

But Staunton was up and running around the burning silo, blood pouring from the wound in his shoulder. An instant later she heard the sound of a car being started.

"No!"

She started to get to her knees as she saw Staunton's Volvo tearing out from behind the silo.

Was he coming toward her?

No, he'd passed her and was barreling down the road.

Shoot out his tires. She leveled the gun.

But he was zigzagging all over the tarmac.

And the next moment he was out of range.

Disappointment as sharp as it was deep tore through her. She'd failed. He was still alive. He'd been bleeding profusely, but if he stopped the flow, there was a good chance he'd live.

She could still see the taillights of Staunton's car.

It was all to do again, she realized in despair. Staunton was still out there. She would have to find him and kill him before he managed to hurt anyone else.

It wasn't over.

Bitch. Bitch. Bitch.

Staunton could feel the blood pouring down his arm as he stomped on the accelerator.

She had come close to killing him, he thought incredulously. She had tried to blow him up, then she had shot him. He might still die if he didn't get this damn blood stopped. He would have taken care of the bitch if he hadn't realized that he couldn't afford to take the chance of bleeding to death while he did it.

He would pull off the road, make a compress, and find a doctor somewhere in a nearby town to get out the bullet.

Then I'll be ready for you, Emily.

Emily dialed Garrett as she got back in the car. "Two rings. Tell me it wasn't a mistake. Irana is safe?"

"Irana is safe."

Relief soared through her. "Thank God."

"How are you? Did you blow that son of a bitch to kingdom come?"

"No. It didn't go as you hoped it would. I blew the silo, but he wasn't inside. I only managed to wound him."

"But you're okay?"

"Yes. He was bleeding badly and got away. I thought we had a chance to end it, Garrett. He was moving, and I only got his shoulder. Now we have to start over."

"No, we've made progress. We just have to keep going. I'm on my way back to the farm with Dardon and Irana. I'll meet you there." He hung up.

Garrett had already arrived at the farm-house when Emily pulled into the yard.

She jumped out of the car and ran into the house.

"Irana!"

"She's here." Garrett turned away from the stove. "She's in the bathroom. She said to tell you that she'd be out in a few min-utes." He poured coffee into a cup. "The bastard didn't feed her all day. I asked her if she wanted something to eat, but she said all she wanted was coffee."

"But she's not hurt?"

"She said she wasn't hurt."

"Is Dardon okay?"

"Yes. I sent Pauley to bed and Dardon out to do guard duty."

Garrett wasn't looking at her. "What's wrong? You're sure Irana's not hurt?"

"That's what she said." He still didn't look away from the coffee. "But she was very quiet on the trip back here."

"Quiet?" Emily's stomach clenched, and her gaze flew to the bathroom door. "What do you think that means?" Dear God, don't let anything be—

"You've scared her, Garrett." The door had opened, and Irana came out of the bathroom, drying her wet hair with a towel. "You shouldn't have done that." She threw her wet towel on the back of a chair. "She's had a bad enough time tonight from what you've told me."

Emily's gaze was raking Irana's face. "Irana . . . ?"

"Here's your coffee." Garrett held out the cup to Irana. His voice was hoarse, and when Emily glanced at his face, she was shocked to see the pain in his expression.

Irana shook her head. "I don't really want it now. I just knew that you'd feel better if you could do something for me. All I wanted was a bath and to wash my hair. I'm okay now." She turned to Emily. "Come on, Emily. Let's go outside and get some air. I hope you don't mind that I borrowed your clothes and one of your jackets. I can't seem to get warm."

"Am I invited to come along?" Garrett asked.

"No." Irana headed for the door. "I'll talk to you later. Emily needs me now."

"What do you mean I need you?" Emily asked when she'd closed the door behind them and followed Irana a few yards into the farmyard. "What about you? What do you need, Irana?" She gazed searchingly at the other woman. Irana was half-turned away from her, but her face appeared pale and strained in the light cast by the bare bulb over the door. "Did he hurt you?"

"It doesn't matter, Emily. It's gone. Soon it will only be a distant memory."

"Oh, God, he *did* hurt you," she said, agonized. "How?"

Irana turned to look at her. "I asked you to come out here because I knew that this was going to be bad for you. I wanted it over for both of us as quickly as possible."

"Garrett should never have asked you to come here. It's my fault. I think he did it because he wanted to keep me from—"

"Garrett gave me a choice. It's not your fault. It's not Garrett's. Though you'll both probably blame yourselves." Her voice was a little uneven. "You'll be doing me a great favor if you try not to do that. It's very difficult for me to try to heal both of you and myself at the same time."

"What did he do to you?"

"Nothing that I can't overcome."

I only wanted a bath and to wash my hair.

Torture of a woman usually starts with rape, Staunton had told Emily all those weeks ago.

"Don't look at me like that," Irana said. "I won't have him hurt you again, through me." Her hands grasped Emily's shoulders. "Listen, I'm going to say this once, then I'm not ever going to talk about it again." Her voice vibrated with passionate sincerity. "He didn't hurt my mind, or my spirit, or my soul. Anything else he did doesn't matter at all. Do you understand?"

Emily's throat was so tight, she couldn't speak for a moment. "I understand." She understood that Irana was probably even more special than she had dreamed. She stepped closer and enfolded her in her arms. "But I can't say it won't matter to me," she said unevenly. "You told me once I was one of the soldiers. I can't take the higher view."

Irana's arms tightened around her for

a brief moment. "I'm having a little trouble doing that, too," she whispered. "I'm working my way through it." She stepped back. "And now I think it's time we both tried to sleep. Tomorrow, everything will be clearer. Garrett said I could share your room."

Emily nodded. "Or you could have it by yourself if you prefer."

"I do not prefer. No guilt. No sacrifices." She turned toward the door. "And if you wish to do me a service, you can make sure Garrett understands and complies. He's a great one for guilt and taking the blame. I've tried for years to rid him of one guilt complex, and I don't want to contend with another."

Emily remembered Garrett's expression when he'd offered Irana that cup of coffee in the kitchen. "He knows, Irana."

Irana nodded. "I was . . . not myself when he came to the warehouse. And it's very hard for him. He cares for me. That's why you must make it easier for all of us to get through this."

"I'll do my best." She'd do anything to make the situation easier for Irana. Lord knows Irana was trying to make it easier for them. "No guilt. No blame."

Except for Staunton.

May you burn in hell, Staunton.

Irana was still sleeping when Emily crept out of the bedroom at seven the next morning. She was glad that Irana had finally dropped off a few hours ago. She had been curled up and silent most of the night, but Emily had been aware of her tension. She had wanted to reach out and touch her, but had given her space.

Garrett was sitting at the table, papers spread out before him. He looked up when she came into the room. "There's coffee on the stove."

"What are you doing?"

"You told me to translate Zelov's book. I'm obliging."

She went over to the stove and poured a cup of coffee. "That seems a long time ago."

He nodded. "A decade at least. A lot has happened."

Ugliness. Blood. Pain.

He turned back to Zelov's book. "But it

still needs doing if we want to move forward. And you wanted to read it."

"Have you been working all night?"

"Yes, I would have had trouble sleeping anyway."

"I didn't have a great night either." She leaned against the counter. "But I made a promise to Irana, and I have to make sure I keep it." She paused. "That you keep it."

He looked up at her. "You're making promises on my behalf?"

"This one. No blame. No guilt. She doesn't want to deal with it from either one of us."

He closed his eyes. "I can't keep your promise, Emily. You were right, I should never have brought her here."

"You *will* keep it. Or make her think you are. And you'd better do a good job of it. I won't have this made any worse for her than it is already. She's incredibly strong, but she's hurting. If she looks at us and sees that we're remembering, it will bring it back to her. That's not going to happen. I won't let it."

His eyes opened, and Emily could see the glitter of moisture. "No, that's not going to happen. I was thinking that I'd like to send her back to Mykala for a while. Dardon could go with her to keep her safe."

"Great. If she'll do it." The idea of Irana away from this hellish situation was wonderfully welcome. She took a sip of coffee. "Maybe we can persuade her." She glanced at the papers on the table. "How far along are you?"

"Not far enough. It's slow going. I'll probably turn it over to Pauley to finish. He can try to tap into one of the Russian language sites and see what he can do."

"Then why don't you try to take a nap? You look exhausted."

He smiled faintly. "Are you concerned about me, Emily? You weren't when you gave me this assignment."

"I was angry. I'm probably still angry." But that indignation and anger seemed remote and curiously unimportant right now. "Oh, just go to bed."

He shook his head. "I'll finish up this entry, then go and wake Pauley and call Dardon to come in from the perimeter. We have to get out of here."

"Why? Aren't we safe?"

"I don't know. I always move locations every few days just to make sure."

"I shot Staunton. It wasn't a fatal wound, but it will take a little while for him to bounce back."

"We still move. I'm not taking chances. As soon as Irana gets up, we'll decide if we have to get her on a plane to Mykala to send—

"Irana is up." Irana came into the room and headed for the bathroom. "I'm going to wash and get dressed, and Emily is going for a walk with me. Yes, Emily?"

Emily nodded. "But it's not like your island. It's all flat barrenness and vast spaces."

"That can have a splendor, too." Irana stopped at the bathroom door and spoke to Garrett. "And we're not getting me on a plane, so make your arrangements around that fact."

Irana and Emily were walking out the front door twenty minutes later.

Garrett looked up from straightening the pile of papers in front of him. "Can I talk you out of staying here, Irana?"

"No, Garrett." She smiled at him. It was a shadow of her usual smile, but it was still luminous. "I'm staying here with my friends. I wouldn't be happy on Mykala right now."

Garrett opened his lips, then closed them. He nodded. "Whatever you want, Irana."

Irana didn't speak for a few moments as she and Emily strode across the frozen ground. "He was very . . . accepting." She suddenly chuckled. "You must have been stern with him."

Lord, it was good to hear Irana laugh. "We had a talk." She shook her head. "Though *I* hoped you'd go, too."

"I know." She looked straight ahead. "It would have been good to go home for a while. But it's not right for me. Not now. Last night I thought about it. I prayed about it." She shook her head. "And I still came out with the same answer." She glanced at Emily with the faintest hint of mischief. "Now you should say, 'Whatever you want, Irana.'"

"No way."

"That's what I like to hear." Her smile faded. "Don't feel sad for me. I'm healing, Emily. Every minute, every hour, I'm healing and becoming the stronger for it."

"Considering who you are, that doesn't

surprise me." She hesitated, then said with a touch of awkwardness, "I . . . care about you. No, I guess I love you, Irana. I've always been afraid to make friends because I was always traveling, always having to leave them, and that hurt. It was okay with Joel because he was in the same job, and I could keep him with me." She shook her head. "I think you know how I feel, but I was cursing myself yesterday because I'd never said the words. You're my friend and my sister, and I thank God that Garrett pushed me into your life." She cleared her throat. "Even though I've caused you a world of trouble." She held up her hand. "Sorry. No guilt. No blame."

"Right. And it's never trouble when you care about someone as I care for you, Emily. Because I think God may have wanted to bring us together for a reason. Or maybe just to comfort and protect each other as friends do. That's sometimes reason enough." Irana looked away from her. They had reached the center of the field, and she jammed her hands into the pockets of her jacket, her gaze on the gray clouds hanging low over the flat, barren fields. "Yes, this land has a kind of somber splendor. And you can feel the storms that have passed through here. My island of Mykala is very ancient, but you don't feel the same sense of disturbance and turmoil. It's more serene."

Irana clearly wanted to ease the subject away from the personal and Emily followed her lead. "Russia has had a very turbulent history."

She nodded. "And the years that Mikhail Zelov was trying to manipulate the Tsar and Tsarina were some of the most violent. It wasn't the time to have a weak Tsar like Nicholas II. He sat on his throne surrounded by his beautiful wife and family and couldn't believe that revolution was right around the corner. For centuries the Tsars had been all-powerful, living in magnificence almost beyond comprehension. Why should they think that they would be deposed by those rabid Bolsheviks? Communism was everywhere, but the Tsar thought he had history on his side." She grimaced. "Until history was blown to bits when they took the royal family prisoner and executed them."

"But what did the Church have to do with all that turmoil?"

"Nicholas was very religious and trying to keep the Church afloat. Everyone was trying to climb over each other and gain power, and the Church was just attempting to keep the power it had."

"You sound as if you've studied it."

"When I was young, I studied all the religions of the world, including the Russian Orthodox Church. The Church was woven into the history of Russia. As I said, the power of the Church was being chipped away by all kinds of factions. It was a time of change. That was how Rasputin gained influence in the Church. They were looking for someone who could bolster its popularity. Enter Rasputin, who claimed to be a miracle worker and holy man and had a lot of people believing him." She shook her head. "But I never ran across any stories of Zelov."

"Evidently that was how he liked it," Emily said. "He was an evil man, and the evil he did is still present and continuing." She looked at Irana. "How could that happen? How could Mikhail Zelov not have been punished for his sins? He ended up in America with a fortune. Why didn't God do something?"

"Maybe he did. How do you know Zelov was happy with all his riches? You don't know the torment of the soul."

Emily was silent. "That wouldn't be good enough for me. And what about Staunton? Don't you want to go after him and punish him for what he did to you?"

"I was thinking about that last night. I'm terribly angry, and it's difficult for me to—" She shook her head. "But I won't let him twist what I am. He's evil, Emily. Perhaps the most evil man I've ever known. As long as he's free, he'll be a danger to everyone around him. That's why I have to stay, why I have to help you. I have to make sure that he can't hurt anyone else. But it can't be just for my sake. I have to trust that it's also God's will, and he will help me."

Emily shook her head. "I'm not like you. I can't wait for fate or God to give their okay. I want to make sure that evil is punished."

"You mean you want to do it yourself." Irana smiled. "That's a soldier's philosophy. Sometimes you have to leave things to God."

"Suppose I help him a little."

Irana smiled. "That sounds like Garrett. You're very alike, you know."

"No, I don't know." She started walking across the field toward the farmhouse. "And he doesn't think I'm a soldier. He wants me to sit with my hands crossed while he goes out and does—" She shrugged. "I don't want to talk about it."

"He let you go out and risk your life last night. It wasn't easy for him."

"That was different. That was for you, Irana."

"Yes, that was for me."

And Emily could see the faintest shadow returning to her expression, and she said quickly, "I don't want to talk about Garrett. Besides everything else, I'm very angry with him for bringing you here."

"He gave me a choice. I told you once, he always gives me a choice," she added, "And he said something about me being helpful in dealing with the Russian Orthodox Church if needed."

"Nicholas Zelov went to Bishop Dimitri first and offered to sell him the amulets and the *Book of Living* before Joslyn started negotiations. Garrett wanted to know why. I do, too, but it's not something we couldn't have handled." Emily made a face. "I know, I said I didn't want to talk about him, but here I am doing it."

"Because you can think of nothing else."

"I can think that I'm very glad to have my friend here. Though you should never have come."

"And I believe I should be here," Irana said quietly. "I knew when Garrett asked me to come that there was something waiting for me here. I don't know what it is, but maybe God had a purpose."

"Staunton was waiting for you. I don't think much of that purpose."

"No, Staunton is just a hurdle to over-come. It's something else that's waiting." She gazed once more at the gray clouds that didn't seem to move in the still sky. "And none of it will be your fault or your doing, Emily."

Emily felt a chill. "That's a good way to lighten my day."

Irana smiled. "Stop fretting. It may be a happy purpose. Most of God's plans are full of joy." She took Emily's hand. "Now we will go back so that we won't upset Garrett's plans. He seems to want us out of here and on the road."

"He wants to protect us."

"And there's nothing really wrong with that in spite of your resentment at his interference in your independence. It's his nature." Her pace increased as she dropped Emily's hand. "We have no lighthouse, but the farmhouse will do. Race me?"

"Why not?" It was a surprise that she welcomed, a return to the routine of Mykala, and perhaps a sign of that healing Irana had spoken about.

Emily took off running. She could feel the cool wind in her hair, and Irana was beside her. For this single moment, everything was good and right. Not perfect. But she would take it.

SEVENTEEN

Pauley was coming out of the farmhouse when they reached it. "Are you being chased? Should I come to your rescue?"

Emily skidded to a stop and tried to get her breath. "No. Just a little morning constitutional."

"What a disappointment." He smiled. "I'm really getting into this James Bond stuff. Though Garrett said that he'd strangle me if I didn't quit making cracks." He looked at Irana. "I'll introduce myself, since Emily is having trouble with breath control. I'm Mark Pauley, computer genius extraordinary and part-time lookout man. Not so extraordinary."

"Irana Povak." She shook her head. "And I'm not extraordinary at all. But I'm a very good doctor."

"They must think you're extraordinary. Garrett paid me a fortune to find you." He studied her and slowly nodded. "You know, I think they may be right."

"Have you loaded the suitcases in the car, Pauley?" Garrett had come out of the house.

"Yes, I was just coming back in to tell you when I stopped to see if I was needed to rescue Emily." He gazed at Garrett accusingly. "You didn't let me go along last night. You just used my brilliant brain and expertise and sent me off to bed. That wasn't fair, Garrett."

"Fair? Good God, have I created a monster?"

"It serves you right. I didn't want to go with you to Babin's house. But I didn't realize what a rush it could be taking a risk like that. I have a curious nature. I want to explore it again."

Garrett sighed. "It's not a computer game, Pauley."

"No, it's different, but it may be more fun." He nodded. "Now I think I'll go inside and get Dardon stirring. He's feeling a little too superior at the moment. I want to tell him not only that I'm a mental giant, but what a superb help I was to you at Babin's the other night. Better than he could do."

Emily looked after him in surprise. The venture with Garrett had evidently formed a bond between them that had overcome Garrett's annoyance with him. Not only that, but it had opened a door for Pauley she had not expected.

"Dardon may just crush his head," Garrett murmured. "Oh, well, Pauley's got to learn."

"You sound almost paternal," Emily said.

"I'm nobody's father. Not Pauley. Not you." He turned to Irana. "Am I, Irana?"

"You'd make a very good father," Irana said. "It would just take practice and opportunity."

Emily changed the subject. "What did Pauley say about the translation?"

"He'll do it . . . reluctantly."

"But it's not as much fun as being

James Bond." Emily added, deadpan. "However, I'm sure he agreed after you had a fatherly talk with him."

Garrett gave her a glance. "I'll get you for that." He went on, "Ferguson called and gave me a report on the three industrialists who dealt with Babin. I told him the only one we're interested in now is Joslyn." He paused. "He told me that I was barking up the wrong tree."

"Why?"

"Joslyn is an absolutely sterling character. Squeaky-clean. He has a wife and two college-age kids who are also squeaky-clean. His business transactions are aboveboard and fair. He's extremely religious, a pillar of his church. He donates a good portion of his income to the church and to charity. He took a sabbatical two years ago and went to Ethiopia with a mission group for four months. He worked so hard there that his immune system failed, and he became ill with fever. They had to ship him home."

Emily shook her head. "Then Babin didn't tell you the truth. It must be one of the other men."

"Perhaps," Garrett said. "But I don't

think so. I worked hard to make sure Babin was very scared indeed. I don't believe he would have lied to me. And I have enough experience to tell the difference if he tried."

"Joslyn seems unlikely," Irana said. "It's one thing to give money to the unfortunate, it's another to actually go and minister to them."

"Or someone very clever," Garrett said. "And willing to go to the final length to keep up his image. I'm going to bank on what Babin told me. If I get shot down, then I'll go down another path."

Shot down. Emily didn't like that phrase. It brought back all the worry and imagery that had plagued her during the last forty-eight hours. Garrett shot. Garrett dead. Staunton hovering over all of them like a hideous gargoyle. "Perhaps he didn't know what Babin was doing?"

"He's evidently a smart man, or he wouldn't be so successful. He'd be hard to fool unless he deliberately closed his eyes. He was the one who authorized Babin to make the deal with Nicholas Zelov for the book and the amulets." He added, "And the *Book of Living* led them to the hammer. Or at least the place where the hammer was supposed to be."

"But if he's a very rich man, why would he go after more?"

"Nicholas's escape fund was worth billions, remember? Billions equal power. Some men can never have enough money. Are you ready to leave?"

"As soon as I throw my clothes into my suitcase."

"I've already done that. I thought we'd buy some clothes for Irana somewhere on the road." He glanced at Irana. "You won't change your mind?"

She shook her head, and said quietly, "I'm coming with you all the way, Garrett."

"That's what I was afraid of." He shrugged. "Then I'll go rescue Pauley . . . or Dardon, and we'll get out of here."

"So we're going to see Joslyn?" Irana asked.

"Not now. I want to try to see if we can get something out of that *Book of Living* that we can use to make him want to talk to us. And I want to know how Bishop Dimitri figures in this."

Emily frowned. "Joslyn already has

the original book. He must already know everything in it."

"But he may not want us to know what was in it that made him want the book so badly."

"It's over a hundred years old. There's nothing in it that could affect Joslyn now. It has to be the Tsar's treasure drawing him."

"Does it? I never take anything for granted."

"So where are we going?"

"I think we should be close to Joslyn. His factories and main offices are in Ekaterinaburg. We'll find a house or inn near there."

"Ekaterinaburg," Irana repeated.

He glanced at her. "You know about it?"

She nodded. "I was there years ago. I thought it my duty. I never wanted to go back."

"Why not?" Emily asked. "What's in Ekaterinaburg besides Joslyn's factories?"

"For one thing, the museum where the hammer and the rest of the farm equipment were on exhibit for all those decades," Garrett said. "And it's also the place where

Nicholas II and his entire family were massacred."

Her eyes widened. "Dear God."

"Rather a curious coincidence that Joslyn is located there, isn't it?" Garrett asked. "Would it interest you to know that Bishop Dimitri also has his residency and jurisdiction in the same city?"

"Yes."

"That's what I thought," Garrett said as he turned to go back into the house. "And that's another reason why Ferguson may be wrong about Mr. Squeaky-Clean."

They reached Ekaterinaburg just before dark that evening.

Emily didn't know what she had expected, but it wasn't a large, bustling city. It might be totally unreasonable, but it seemed as if there should be a pall hanging over the town.

Irana nodded as she read her expression. "I know what you're feeling. It was the same for me the first time I came here. I'd read what happened, and all I could think of was Nicholas, Alexandra, and their children. Ekaterinaburg is actually the third-largest city in Russia. It came as a shock that the royal family was even brought here. You'd expect them to be held in some remote spot where there wasn't any potential for them to be rescued."

"Evidently not much potential," Emily said.

"Talk about potential." Garrett pointed at a huge factory with steam pouring out of the smokestacks. "That's Joslyn Plastics."

"It's enormous," Dardon said.

Garrett nodded. "And it would never have reached this level of success without the help of the Russian government. Joslyn's factories are clean, and the workers are treated well. He tries not to damage the environment. The Russians aren't that hot on keeping the environment green, but they don't mind that Joslyn makes the effort."

Emily leaned back, her gaze on the passing streets of Ekaterinaburg. Her first impression might have been of any large industrial city in the world, but now she could see sights that were pure Russia. Men and women dressed in drab gray and black, an occasional older woman in a *babushka*, a rare glimpse of a grand church that was almost oriental in splendor amid the practical Soviet-style architecture.

Ten minutes later, Garrett turned into the driveway of a large inn, a neat stone building with evergreens bordering the façade. "Here we are. It's not five-star, but Dardon says the businessmen stay here. That should make it at least tolerable." He parked the car and got out. "Emily, you and Irana go on in and register for all of us. Dardon, Pauley, and I will start unpacking the luggage from the trunk."

"Irana can register. I'll help you." Emily got out of the car. "There don't seem to be any bellmen running out to help."

"Garrett said low profile," Dardon said. "I didn't think you'd want to be in one of the bigger inns close to the site of the massacre. Some of them are tourist traps."

"No, I definitely wouldn't want that." She made a face. "The idea of making money out of tragedy is pretty repulsive."

Dardon nodded. "And the town sure does a good business out of the killing of the Romanovs. Boris Yeltsin tore down the Ipatiev House, where the family was butchered in the cellar. There's a memorial there now. A monastery has been built on the mineshaft where all the bodies were thrown."

Emily shook her head. "Museums and monasteries and memorials. Everyone trying to make up for that atrocity."

"Wait long enough, and people eventually come to their senses and abandon evil," Irana said. "But it took a long time for it to happen in this place. It was like the death camps at Auschwitz and Bergen-Belsen. Everyone denying that they had anything to do with it or even that it happened at all. Everyone was afraid of the Communist government and didn't even want to talk about the Romanovs."

"But that ended back in the 1980s."

"And then the death scenes became a carnival. When I was here before, couples were getting married and having their pictures taken at the memorial."

"Morbid."

"That was what I thought. I tried to understand, but I didn't have enough compassion." She smiled. "I'm better now, but that came with age and experience." She headed for the entrance of the inn. "I'll go take care of checking in."

Garrett turned to Pauley, who was absorbed in his computer and hadn't moved from the backseat. "What's your progress?"

Pauley looked up from the computer. "Good. I had plenty of time to work. It was a hell of a long trip. I've linked to a language site at a university in Tokyo. They have some amazing technology. If this inn has a printer, I may have something for you by later this evening." He closed up the laptop and got out of the car. "Okay, load me up with suitcases. Though a man of my caliber is wasted on physical labor."

"Live with it." Garrett gave him three suitcases. "Explore a new horizon."

"Whatever." Pauley sounded distracted as he followed Dardon into the inn.

"He's amazing," Emily said. "You dictate what you want, and he pulls it out of that computer."

"The wonder of the Internet." Garrett started the car. "But he is pretty amazing, and he just takes it as a matter of course."

It was a grudging admission, but it demonstrated how far Garrett's attitude toward Pauley had changed.

"We might not have been able to save Irana without him."

"That's true."

"And he was helpful at Babin's place?"

"Yes."

"Could I have done what he did?"

He nodded.

"Then why the hell wasn't I there instead?"

"We've discussed this."

"Yes, and the fact that you're unreasonable and chauvinistic." She glanced away from him at the inn. "And this is the last time I intend to mention it. I do *not* forgive you for it. But you did treat me as a partner and not a helpless doll when it was Irana at stake."

"And it may have been the most difficult thing I've ever had to do in my life."

"But you did it, and that's the only way you're going to keep from driving me away and doing exactly what you said you wanted to avoid. Understand?"

"Oh, yes, you couldn't be clearer. We'll have to see how it goes."

He wasn't going to commit, she realized. "Yes, we will." She grabbed her duffel. "And

I can't say that I can—" She broke off as Garrett's phone rang.

He glanced at the ID. "Ferguson."

He answered and turned up the volume. "Anything more on Joslyn?"

"No, I told you that there was nothing to find out. He's an Eagle Scout." Ferguson paused. "I'm calling about Babin. Did you change your mind about taking him down?"

"What?"

"You heard me. Did you think it might be more convenient to get rid of him permanently? I don't appreciate you making me go to the trouble of assigning a man to watch him if you're—"

"What are you talking about?"

"Babin is dead. Massive heart failure. My agent said he had the attack right before he boarded his flight for Monte Carlo."

Emily inhaled sharply.

"I didn't change my mind," Garrett said. "If someone put Babin down, it wasn't me. Have you got the results of the autopsy?"

"No. But we both know how easy it is to induce heart failure if you know what you're doing. A pinprick from a tiny hypodermic needle, and it's all over."

"I didn't do it, Ferguson. I wanted to keep him alive in case I needed him. Did your man spot anyone suspicious?"

"A possible encounter at the escalator. I've got my agent looking at mug shots."

"Let me know if you find out anything."

"Oh, I will. Count on it." Ferguson hung up.

"Could it have been a natural death?" Emily asked.

"It could be. Anything is possible," Garrett said. "I doubt it. Too coincidental." He took the last of the suitcases and closed the trunk. "But we may not know for a while. Some drugs are so hard to detect that even if the forensic team knows about it, they have to make a zillion tests to confirm."

"You think Joslyn ordered him murdered?"

"As I said, anything is possible."

"Maybe even probable. Staunton told me he sent Borg away to do a job." She remembered something else. "He even mentioned Paris." She shook her head. "Why? Revenge for talking to you?"

"Or to keep him from telling me something else. Or to try to implicate me in his murder. You heard Ferguson. He wasn't pleased with me."

"Yes, I heard him." She thought about it. "But did he believe you? Will he cause you any trouble?"

"He probably believed me. He knows I don't lie. If he thinks he can cause me trouble, he'll do it just because he's pissed at me right now. But he won't do anything that will cause him to lose the pot of gold at the end of the rainbow." He opened the front door for her. "Don't worry about it, Emily. I can handle Ferguson."

"I'm sure you can. There aren't many people you can't handle, are there?" Her lips tightened. "But I will worry. We're in this together. It's my job to worry and you're not going to push me into a corner and tell me to be a good girl and not bother you."

He smiled faintly. "My apologies. By all means worry all you please." He glanced around the lobby. "It appears everyone has scattered. I guess we should pick up our keys and go to our rooms." He paused. "Could I convince you to have dinner with Irana and me? I want to spend some time with her, and she seems not to want any intimate time with me yet. It may be a long time before Pauley comes through for us."

He acted as if Ferguson's call had never taken place, that Babin had not been murdered. Well, what else was he supposed to do? It had happened, and there wasn't anything that Garrett could do about it right now. It was just another ugly piece in this macabre puzzle.

"It's okay if you'd rather be alone." Garrett's gaze was on her face. "But sometimes it's better to be with other people. Even people you're not very pleased with."

And she didn't want to be alone, she realized. She had been feeling a sort of weird heaviness since they had arrived in Ekaterinaburg. She remembered she had thought a pall should be lying over the city, and maybe that was right. She had been in many places where tragic past events seemed to linger. Why should she stay in her room because she wanted to make a statement? That would be immature, and she had already said what she needed to say to Garrett. She wasn't about to remain closeted away and let memory and depression gnaw at her. "Where?"

He glanced at the restaurant across the

lobby. "We can try there. It's better than room service."

"We hope." She sniffed. "I smell cabbage. Even in the good restaurants in Russia, you get cabbage and more cabbage. But maybe they'll have *bliny*. Those little pancakes make up for a lot." She moved toward the reception desk. "I want to take a shower. It will be good to have a bathroom to myself again. In an hour?"

"Whatever you want. Anything you want."

She glanced back over her shoulder at the curious note in his voice to see that his face was without expression. But it was what she sensed behind it that made her catch her breath. "It's only going to be dinner, Garrett."

"I know. It's too soon." He held her gaze as he came toward the reception desk. "Isn't that what I said?" He repeated softly, "Anything you want."

Sheer hot sensuality.

He had given her anything she wanted that night in the lean-to. Anything, everything, and she'd still been hungry. The heat burned her cheeks as she remembered how many times she had satisfied that hunger.

He glanced away from her as the desk clerk came up to them. He began speaking to the woman in Russian.

Anything she wanted . . .

"These are quite nice rooms," Irana said when she phoned Emily almost an hour later. "Sort of a combination of Russian exotic and American Hilton. Dardon did better than I thought."

"He seems to have the knack. I'm almost ready to go down to the restaurant. What's your room number? I'll stop by for you."

"Four-thirteen, but I'm not going to dinner with you. I've decided to get some rest. I didn't sleep much last night." She paused. "And I wanted to give you a chance to be with Garrett without me acting as a buffer. Either for him or for you."

Wise Irana. "I wanted you to come."

"And you wanted your buffer."

Admit it. "Yes."

"Well, you'll have to do without me. You're both my friends, and I want peace between you. Work it out." She added, "And now I'll hang up and order room service. I'll talk to you later."

Emily slowly hung up the phone. Peace? There wasn't anything resembling peace between her and Garrett. That moment at the reception desk had been as charged and volatile as the moments before a tornado.

Irana had meant the anger that Emily had felt toward Garrett should be healed. The anger was still there, but it was constantly being overshadowed by other emotions. Her fear for him, her sympathy and empathy with the agony of his feelings for Irana, the flash of pure sensuality she had felt downstairs. Did she want that to happen? That night with Garrett had been incredible, but she would be safer not becoming involved with him. She had only taken small steps, but he was already having a massive impact on her. She was too vulnerable.

She could call Garrett and cancel.

And she was going right back to being Staunton's victim. Hiding away because she was afraid of being hurt.

Screw it. All this self-analysis and soul-searching was bull. She would go on instinct and let the cards fall where they may.

She grabbed her handbag from the nightstand and headed for the door.

"Anton Borg," Ferguson said, when Garrett picked up his call just as he was leaving his room. "Positive identification from the mug shot. He was the one who bumped into Babin on the escalator. He's a known cohort of Staunton."

"Did he fly in from Moscow?"

"No, from Tangiers. His flight got in an hour before Babin arrived in Paris." He paused. "And he took off on a Delta flight to New York within an hour of Babin's death."

"New York?"

"That surprised you."

"I was expecting him to come to Moscow."

"Maybe Staunton is in New York."

"No, that's not possible."

"Why else would Borg be going to New York?"

Garrett had a sudden thought. "Maybe not New York. Maybe Connecticut. Look, send someone to Connecticut to keep an eye on Nicholas Zelov."

"You think he's Borg's next target?"

"I don't know. I'm guessing. I'll try to call him. You send someone to check on him at his house." He hung up and called up his phone list. All he had was Zelov's home number, no cell. He could only hope he was at home and not too drunk to answer.

The phone rang six times before voice mail picked up.

Dammit.

"Zelov if you're there, answer me." He waited. No response. "If you get this, don't answer the door to anyone but the man I've sent up there to protect you. He should have CIA identification." Still there was no pickup. He hung up.

He could be wrong. Zelov might not be a target. Garrett had done what he could. He'd try to phone Zelov again later. Should he tell Emily and let her fret over something he wasn't even sure was threatening?

Hell, yes. He wasn't about to alienate her permanently because he wanted to protect her. She would take a hatchet to him.

But it wasn't the kind of conversation he'd wanted to have over dinner. He'd seen signs of softening, and he hoped to capitalize.

Face it; he hoped to do more than capitalize. That was too cold a word, and he wasn't feeling cold. He got hot and ready every time he looked at Emily. He hadn't had enough of her that night in the lean-to.

He was beginning to wonder if he'd ever get enough.

Okay, stop thinking about getting her into bed. That would have to wait. He'd have to tell her that it was Borg who had killed Babin and might be after Zelov. After that, there wasn't any question that she wouldn't focus on what was most important to her.

"Call him again," Emily said after dinner. "He's got to answer sometime."

"I called him before dinner and left another message." Garrett said as he poured a little vodka into his coffee. "I could be wrong. Why would Zelov suddenly be a target when he's been safe all this time?"

"Maybe Joslyn found out about Babin betraying him and decided that he had to give orders to eliminate both of them." She shook her head in frustration. "Oh, I don't know. I can see why he'd want Babin killed. Revenge is a pretty good motive."

"Excellent."

Yes, both she and Garrett were being driven by revenge. It was logical to her that Joslyn might want to punish Babin. Lord knows, Emily had wanted the same thing that day in Babin's office.

"Call him," she repeated.

Garrett took out his phone and dialed. "Still no answer. I should be hearing from Ferguson soon about the agent he sent up to the house." He poured her more coffee. "You didn't eat much. At least drink your coffee."

"I was distracted. I am distracted." She took a sip of her coffee. "It's frustrating, dammit."

"Yes, I knew it would be. I was tempted not to tell you at all." He held up his hand as she opened her lips. "I overcame it. It wasn't easy for me, but at least it wasn't a question of risking your neck. You know as much as I do."

She gazed at him for a moment. He

was being honest with her. For some reason it was tremendously hard for him to keep from protecting her. "Thank you."

"You're welcome. I make mistakes, but I do learn." He lifted his coffee cup in a half toast. "To progress." His phone rang, then he shook his head as she tensed. "It's not Ferguson. It's Dardon." He listened for a few minutes and said, "Let me know." He said to Emily, "Pauley's almost got it. Dardon says the room looks like a whirlwind of papers hit it. He'll call me when he's finished."

"Good. At least one thing is going right." She finished her coffee. "I don't want to stay here any longer. I'm tired of sitting and waiting for a phone call or something to happen."

He nodded and signaled for the waiter. "I'll take you to your room."

"That's not necessary."

"Yes, it is. I don't want you alone. You should have called me when you knew Irana wasn't coming down with you." He saw her expression and shrugged ruefully. "Okay, I just said progress, not perfection."

Five minutes later they were walking

down the corridor to her room. "Why?" she asked suddenly.

He glanced down at her as they reached her door. "Why what?"

"Why are you so protective? Have you always been this way?"

"By nature. Not in practice. I've trained myself to stand back and let people live their own lives. It took a long time. I've led a pretty violent life, and I've lost people I cared about. It's my instinct to step in and build walls and keep them inside." He made a face. "Most people are like you and don't like my walls. I had to adjust. At least, I thought I'd adjusted. It doesn't seem to work where you're concerned."

"Is it because you found me in a situation where I—"

"It's because you're you, and I'm selfish. That's it. End of story," he interrupted. "I don't pity you. I admire your guts and endurance. I want to keep on talking to you. I want to look at you and see you smile. I want to go to bed with you again. Oh yes, I want that. If you get killed, then I lose everything." He reached out and touched her cheek. "Irana would say that I should think of you and forget about myself. Maybe someday I'll learn to do that, but that's not now. All I can think about is what you mean to me." He leaned forward and brushed his lips across her nose. "Selfish."

His fingers were gossamer-light on her cheek, but she felt as if the flesh beneath his touch was burning. She couldn't breathe. He was so close that she could feel the heat of his body.

He stepped back and turned away. "I'll call you as soon as I hear anything from Ferguson or Pauley." He was moving away from her. "Good night, Emily."

No!

"You come back here, Garrett."

He stopped and then turned to look at her. "Why?"

"I don't want you to call me."

He smiled and moved back toward her. "That's promising. Go on."

"You want me to say it? I want you to lean across the bed and tell me anything you have to tell me." She took a step closer and put her hand on his chest. She could feel the pulse leap beneath her touch. "Because I'm selfish, too, Garrett. I don't want to be alone tonight."

"Then you won't be. Whatever you want, remember?"

"Yes." She remembered, and the memory was making her body meltingly ready. "That's good. And I'll try to give you whatever you want, too." She put her cheek on his chest, and whispered, "I won't mind your building walls. Not tonight, Garrett. I want to close everyone else out."

"Then by all means, let's start doing it." He reached behind her and opened the door. "Because there are all kinds of walls." He was leading her toward the bed. "And they don't have to be a prison." He pushed her gently down on the bed and started to undress. "There can be doors and windows and passageways that can lead anywhere."

Her hands were shaking as she took off her blouse. "I know where I want this passageway to lead. Hurry."

"You hurry." He was naked. "I'm already there."

Lord, he was beautiful, she thought hazily; lean hips, tight butt, and that air of leashed sensuality. In the lean-to at the farm, there had only been heated darkness, and she had not been able to see as

well as feel. The sight of him was sending a tingling electricity coursing through her. She could feel it in her breasts, her wrists, her belly. Her chest felt tight, and she was having trouble breathing.

"We'll get there." He was coming down to her. He didn't touch her skin as he rid her of the rest of her clothes. "But let's explore a few of those doors and windows."

"Not now." She tried to move toward him. "I'm done with that."

"Shh." He held her still with one hand on her shoulder. "Just a little." His fingers moved with teasing gossamer gentleness over her breasts. "Here's a window."

The muscles of her stomach clenched as heat moved through her.

"Oh, yes." He smiled as he moved down to her belly and started to rub. "There's another one. So many wonderful doors and windows."

She was burning up, she thought desperately.

She *needed* it.

And so did he, dammit. She could feel the heat emanating from him, and his body couldn't have been more ready for her. Seeing that readiness was almost as much a tease as his hand on her flesh.

Almost. Every stroke of his fingers was bringing her closer to—

"I love to see you like this," he whispered. "And know that I can do it to you."

"Now, Garrett. I can't take any more."

"Yes, you can." He leaned forward and kissed her belly. "But maybe not right now. Later." He moved between her legs. "I think it's time to open another door. . . ."

She cried out as he plunged deep and started to move.

"Were the walls high enough?" Garrett asked as he moved off her and rolled with her to his side of the bed. "Enough doors and windows? We can try again."

She laughed as she tried to get her breath. "No, we can't. Not yet. Give me a chance to—" She shuddered as Garrett's hand moved again over her belly. "Or maybe not."

He chuckled. "No, I've been rejected. I think I'll make you wait a while." He cuddled her closer. "Maybe another five minutes. This is good, too."

Yes, it is good, she thought. She felt

safe and wonderfully at home being held by him. It had been different tonight, after that first explosive beginning. Sexual, intense, mind-blowing, but there had also been a sort of joyous energy and fun that had surprised her. Was it because he had sensed that was what she needed?

"What are you thinking about?" he asked.

"That you're very intuitive." Her lips brushed his shoulder. "I believe you're a remarkable man, Garrett."

"This isn't the moment to admire that particular ability." He said. "I'd rather you concentrate on my sexual talents and the size of my—" His cell phone on the nightstand rang. He sighed as he checked it. "Dardon." He punched the button. "Has Pauley got it finished?" He listened. "No, we'll be down to pick it up." He hung up and gazed at Emily. "You heard me. Is that what you want?"

It wasn't what she wanted. She wanted to stay here with Garrett and not get out of bed for a week. But she knew what she should do, what she had to do. She nodded. "As soon as I shower and get dressed."

He tilted his head. "That sounded satisfyingly reluctant." He bent over and brushed his lips over first one nipple, then the other. "So I think we'll compromise." He got out of bed and pulled her to her feet.

"By all means, we'll tend to business as soon as we get dressed." His palm stroked her bottom as he nudged her toward the bathroom. "But we have to shower. It might as well be together. . . ."

EIGHTEEN

"Here it is." Pauley handed them two neatly bound blue books as soon as they entered his room. "Not only accurate content, but a fine presentation. Aren't I wonderful?"

"Exceptional," Garrett said. He flipped through it and gave a low whistle. "Really exceptional, Pauley."

"I'm the one who had to compile all those pages," Dardon said sourly. "Lord, he's nitpicking."

"No use being sloppy," Pauley said. "It reflects on the essential work. But I read bits and pieces of this book, and it's damn ugly. It doesn't deserve my effort, but I had to do my best anyway." He turned to Emily. "See? I'm not just a pretty face."

"I never thought you were."

"A woman of judgment. Will you marry me?"

"No."

"Will you go to bed with me?"

"No," Garrett said.

"I wasn't asking you to—" Pauley glanced warily at Garrett. "I don't believe I'll pursue that subject." He waved his hand. "You've got what you want. All of you. Get out of my room so that I can get some sleep."

"Delighted," Dardon said. "See you in the morning." He looked at his watch as he moved toward the door. "Which isn't that far away."

"He's right," Garrett said, as he and Emily stopped outside in the hall. "Do you want to do this in the morning?"

"No." But she didn't want to be alone either while she read what even Pauley termed ugly. "Can we go to your room and work on them? I thought we'd split it up. We'll scan through the first part that has the philosophy that so appealed to Rasputin. That shouldn't take long. Then we hit the notes that he said he wanted only in his *Book of Living*."

He nodded. "That sounds like a plan. I'll order coffee, and we'll see what Mikhail Zelov has to say for himself."

What Zelov had to say for himself was twisted enough to make Emily feel ill. After scanning his doctrines for the best part of an hour, she looked up at Garrett, who was sitting across the room. "No wonder Rasputin embraced him as a brother. This allows every debauchery known to man. It recommends everything from sexual abuse of children, to rape, to destroying the icons of the Church. There's even a section describing the methods of torture and murder of the enemies who oppose Zelov that's worse than anything I've read about the Inquisition."

Garrett nodded. "He wanted to start his own church, with himself as high priest. He spent fifteen years in Jerusalem and tried to establish his own temple there, but he gave up and came back to Russia to write this book. But there's so much venom in this doctrine that I can't even tell who he'd worship, God or the devil."

"Himself." Emily shivered. "If he could have taken the throne away from the Tsar, he would have done it. Now let's see how he applied that doctrine to the royal court."

She flipped to the last section of the book that was merely labeled *Notes.*

September 15, 1916

Rasputin is becoming uncontrollable. I have given him everything, but he is beginning to think he is all that I have made the world believe he is. I am losing my influence over him.

October 1, 1916

Rasputin tells me that he no longer believes my doctrines. He thinks I lied about the temple in Jerusalem. He thinks I lied about the sorcery of the hammer. He loves his position as the Tsarina's advisor and is going to cling to her skirts and that of her Church. I think he fears me too much to betray me, but I cannot be certain.

October 10, 1916

I stand alone. Rasputin shunned me when I called on him today. I must destroy him. What a fool he is.

November 19, 1916

Rasputin may be influencing the Tsar against me through the Tsarina. The Tsar and I have talked many times about the hammer, and I thought we were in agreement. Lately he avoids the subject, and I sense coolness. Does he not realize that chaos surrounds him? I could hold out my hand and save him as I did his son when the boy was bleeding to death. But he must first give me what I want.

December 5, 1916

I board my ship for America tomorrow evening. I have long thought of America. It is a country where a peasant could become a king if he has the money to buy the throne. I will have the money. I thought that I might stay here to gain my destiny, but it isn't wise. What I have to sell has no value for those Communist vultures who are soon going to devour the court and everything else around them. I can see it coming. Even the Tsar should see it coming.

I left a fond message of farewell for Rasputin.

He ignored it.

Good-bye, Rasputin.

January 12, 1918

I am back in St. Petersburg. I got off the ship in Liverpool as I planned, crossed to Marseilles, and made my way back to St. Petersburg by land. I traveled slowly, and more than a year has gone by since I left Russia. I had to make sure no suspicion fell on me, and the passage of time makes everyone forget what I want them to forget. Rasputin's murder was not as clean as I would have done it. Felix Yusupov and those other conspirators tried everything from poison, to shooting, to drowning before he managed to get the deed done. Perhaps

Rasputin acquired some of my power over the years that made him resistant to death. Not enough. He is dead and no longer a problem for me. I understand the royal family grieves bitterly for him. That is good. But they should grieve for themselves. The Tsar has been forced to abdicate, but he still has hopes that all will be well. What will it take to show him he should flee the country? I will wait a while longer in this small hamlet and not approach the Tsar at all for a time so that my appearance does not seem too suspicious. Then I'll go to them and tell them I heard of Rasputin's death and came back to comfort them in their sorrow. Then when the Tsar is convinced of my sincerity, we will once again talk of the hammer. I dare not move too fast, but he may have little time.

May 15, 1918

I waited too long! The Tsar and his family have been moved from St. Petersburg to Ekaterinaburg under house arrest. I must follow them. I will have no trouble blending in with the people holding him. They are peasants, and I am also a peasant. Though a thousand times more clever than they will ever be. I can still get what I need. The Tsar may be more inclined to listen to me now that he knows his only hope is escape.

June 18, 1918

The Tsar is a fool. He says he has no need of my hammer or its sorcery. He has coded the directions to the map in the four amulets worn around the necks of his daughters and his wife. He said that the amulets will be placed on a map according to the ages of his daughters. Olga will be the first, her amulet covering St. Petersburg and the scrollwork showing the first route out of the city, Maria's and Anastasia's will follow. The last amulet, the one worn by the Tsarina, shows the final route to the destination and also has the final directions to the treasure engraved on the gold beneath the painting. It is ironic that the amulets are paintings of Rasputin and the messages hidden in the wrought-gold framing of one of his prayers. Put them together, and they can lead a man to paradise or at least to the map that points the way.

I tried to persuade him to tell me a few details as to the place he found to store such a vast treasure. He would only say that it was in Austria and hidden so well that it would not be found for a thousand years without the amulets. When he escapes, he will use the amulets to guide him to the cave in the Alps where the treasure was placed years ago. I must be with him every step of the way if I cannot get him to cooperate.

The Tsar said he would have no trouble getting the girls to wear the amulets to show their love for Rasputin, but his wife wished to make sure her pearls were safe and had asked him to have their son carry the final amulet. That was my opportunity! I told him that it would endanger his heir and offered him the hammer to hide the final amulet. I was very eloquent, and told him that Rasputin had blessed the hammer, and it was sure to bring him additional good fortune. He said he would think about it.

June 21, 1918

The Tsar sent for me and told me he would accept the hammer to hide the final amulet.

Accept? Arrogant bastard. I wanted to bludgeon him with it. But I smiled and bowed and told him how grateful I was that he would let me help.

July 5, 1918

I think the Tsar is planning his escape. He is being very cooperative with all of his captors and is even planning on visiting the new People's Museum that was built across the street from the residence. He must be trying to avert suspicion for he loathes those Communists who hold his life in their hands.

July 13, 1918

I gave the Tsar the hammer tonight. How I hated to let it out of my hands. The bastard would not even tell me where he intended to hide the hammer until they escaped the country. Never mind. I will find it. Sometimes I feel as if the hammer knows me, calls to me.

The amulets on the necks of the grand duchesses are a more difficult matter. How to get them away from them? How to do it . . .

July 17, 1918

It is so simple.

I have been working on influencing Yurovsky, the head of the Tsar's captors, and it will happen tonight. I will not let the Tsar see my face until the last minute. He must know who is responsible after all the annoyance he has caused me.

July 18, 1918

They are dead. The Tsar and all his family shot to death and bludgeoned in the cellar of Ipatiev House. I convinced Yurovsky they all had to die. He was only going to kill the Tsar and his son. I stayed in the background as I planned and only stepped forward as they were killing the Tsar. But I had to help with the killing of the grand duchesses. No matter how many bullets we sprayed them with, they would not die. I found out why once we stripped them down. They had sewn diamonds into their corsets, and the bullets were bouncing off! I started to laugh, but then I realized everyone was grabbing at the amulets as well as the diamonds. No! They were mine.

They tossed all the jewels into a sack and onto the wagon with the bodies. I had to go with them. It was most annoying. I was going to slip away, but I have to get my hands on those amulets.

They threw the bodies down into a mineshaft, but I had no opportunity to grab the sack with the amulets. Some bastard had already taken it. I will find them. I must find them.

"Had enough?" Garrett asked.

Emily looked up and saw that Garrett was studying her face. "I'll finish it and tell you about it," he said. "You look as if you're about to throw up."

She did feel sick. It was as if all of Zelov's evil was reaching out to her, smothering her. She smiled faintly. "You're being protective again."

"Yeah. I guess I am."

"He reminds me of Staunton." She moistened her lips. "Did you get to the part where he laughed because the diamonds in the corsets were deflecting the bullets?"

"Yes."

"Those poor young girls. What a nightmare for them. What a horror he was. Like Staunton." She added, "But now at least we know why that map was with the amulets. The Tsar had to have a particular map that he could fashion to work with the scroll on the amulets. It's not as if you could place the amulets over just any map and expect it to lead anywhere."

"You didn't answer me. Do you want me to finish it and tell you the rest? I'll make it brief."

She shook her head. "I just needed a break for a few moments. There doesn't seem to be much more. And it can't be any more terrible than—"

Garrett's cell phone rang. He glanced down at it. "Ferguson." He answered it.

"What's the story?" He listened for a few moments, then said, "Let me know."

As he hung up, he said, "Nicholas Zelov was not at his house in Connecticut. The servants don't know where he is. He drove off about noon to go to his tailor, then to a cocktail party in Manhattan. He was a little drunk, but they said he was always at least a little drunk."

"Then he could have had an accident," Emily said. She wished she could believe that was true. But she had read about too much blood and murder tonight.

"Yes, Ferguson is checking to see if he can get the state police to try to spot his car. It shouldn't be difficult. It's a red Lamborghini."

What a shame to destroy a sweet car like that, Borg thought. It was almost a crime.

Borg smiled at the thought as he watched the tail end of the Lamborghini slowly sink into the marsh. Actually, the crime was not the killing of the car. With any luck, Zelov would not be found for a very long time.

And Borg felt lucky. Everything had been

going off very well. He dialed Staunton. "I've earned my bonus. What next?"

"Come to Moscow. It's time we finished the job."

"Garrett and Hudson?"

"Not Hudson. Emily Hudson is mine."

July 17, 1918

I have three of the amulets. I found out which of the peasants who had been at the mine had taken the sack and waited until they took the jewels to the flea market and sold them. The stupid oafs got a pittance for the diamonds, but they only wanted to get rid of them. I followed behind them, and when the amulets were sold, I bought them back.

But dammit, there are only three. Where is the hammer that has the fourth? It is the most important of all of them, for it has the engraved directions beneath the painting. I went back to Ipatiev House, but I couldn't find it. Maybe the Tsar persuaded his wife to wear the amulet after all. No, the Tsarina had been stripped and robbed like the girls.

But a worthless amulet might not have been noticed. It could have still been around her neck when she was thrown into the mine.

Worthless? The fools. The stupid, careless fools.

I'll have to go back to the mine tonight.

July 17, 1918
11:40 P.M.

I went back to the mine, but it was guarded. Yurovsky does not want anyone to know where the bodies were thrown. I had to wait until later to kill the guard and go down into the mine. The water was icy cold and the bodies starting to stink. There was no amulet around that royal bitch's neck. It has to be in the hammer.

I climbed out of the mine, and my anger was so hot I did not feel the cold. Think, I told myself. Where had the Tsar hidden the hammer? If it wasn't at the house, where could he have—

Then it came to me. The People's Museum. What better place to hide the hammer? Across the street from Ipatiev House and easy to retrieve. He had visited the museum to pay his respects the day after I gave him the hammer. I had thought he was trying to pacify his captors and save his neck. It had even amused me.

It did not amuse me now. It filled me with exhilaration.

I tried to break into the museum that night, but there were guards all over the street. The next day I went into the museum with a crowd of peasants who wanted to gawk at the few exhibits the new government had set up to glorify themselves.

The hammer is there! I saw it.

But I cannot touch it! I can tell they suspect me of the murder of the guard at the mine. And someone might have seen me at the flea market when I bought the amulets. I'm sure I was followed today.

I must not panic. I must control myself. I cannot stay here any longer. My position is too dangerous. And too many people may remember I was at court with the royal family. This country is in turmoil, and I will not let myself be swept away in the bloodbath. I will go to America as I planned. But I will not go as a pauper. I do not have all the keys to the Tsar's fortune, but I can come back for the hammer later. I can still be a king.

I will go to Nartova. The political situation may be just what I need to pressure him. The Bolsheviks are howling for blood, but it will not be mine.

Emily thought it was the last entry, but she flipped the pages and found two more. Both were decades from the time of the massacre.

July 25, 1932

It is no use. I've gone back many times, but I cannot find a way to get that hammer out of the museum. I've tried everything from bribery to hiring thugs to help me attack the guards who watch over the museum. No one will take my bribes, and it's ridiculous how heavily the museum is guarded. I've been foiled twice when I made the attempt to kill them and get into the exhibition hall. It's just a poor, unimportant historical museum. Why should it be so well guarded? I suspect Nartova. He is clever enough to find ways to manipulate the government even if he has little power. He is standing guard over the hammer like a giant gargoyle.

It is of no matter. I still have my grand palace and I'm almost as rich as if I'd found the Tsar's billions. Nartova still pays into my coffers regularly. I may up the payments to punish him for thwarting me.

May 24, 1942

I have started to dream of Rasputin. Are they death dreams? I will not permit it. I will live a long time, and if I meet Rasputin in hell, I will still be his master. I will hold the hammer over his head, and he will cringe and kneel before me.

Emily closed the book. "He died in 1943. Maybe he was being haunted by Rasputin during those last years." Her lips twisted. "I won't believe it was conscience. I don't think he had one."

"Neither do I." Garrett got up and poured a cup of coffee. "But he died a rich man and years after the massacre, this Nartova was still funneling money to him." He brought the cup to her. "The question is who was Nartova? And how did Zelov convince him that he'd managed to hide the amulet in the hammer? Or was it blackmail that Nartova was paying Zelov?"

Emily rubbed her temple, then took the cup. "I have no clue. I was hoping that we'd be able to put a period to Zelov's part in this. Lord, I want to get away from Mikhail Zelov."

He shook his head. "We're not going to do it. He's the center, like the eye of the hurricane."

"And Nicholas Zelov must have known who this Nartova was before he came to Russia. That has to be why Joslyn paid him off." She shook her head. "But why in hell would hush money still be paid in this day and age for something that happened in 1918?"

He shrugged. "Why don't we ask Mr. Joslyn?"

"But Nicholas Zelov went to see Bishop

Dimitri first. We might get more information by going to him." She shook her head. "We'll talk to Irana in the morning and see what she thinks."

"Mikhail Zelov was truly from Satan." Irana finished reading the notes and looked up at Emily and Garrett, who were sitting at breakfast at the room-service table across the room. "And I'm sure he's with him now. Is there anything else?"

"Just a translation of his *Book of Living*," Emily said. "I scanned it, but then went right to the notes." She grimaced. "I don't think you'll want to read it. Total debauchery. Total permissiveness. Whatever you want, you take. Sexual intercourse with small children and any woman who crosses your path. It's no wonder that Rasputin was drawn to it."

"But Rasputin tried to pull away from Zelov toward the end," Irana said. "I think I do want to read it."

"Be my guest," Emily said. "Keep my copy. Garrett has one if we need it."

"By all means," Garrett said. "But what we wanted from you were any ideas you might have as to why Nicholas Zelov went first to a revered bishop of the Church before he went to Joslyn?"

Irana stared down at the book. "I have a few thoughts on the subject. Let me go over what we know so that I can get it clear in my head. I'm not as familiar with this as you are." She tapped one finger on the book. "Mikhail Zelov was instrumental in the assassination of the royal family for the purpose of stealing the three amulets from the grand duchesses. The fourth amulet was supposedly hidden in the hammer he provided to the Tsar. The Tsar hid the hammer in a Soviet museum near the execution house. Zelov was unable to retrieve it." She frowned. "But Zelov felt confident that he could get money from Nartova and that the hammer would stay safely in that museum so that he might be able to get it later. He was right. In all those years, Nartova didn't try to get the hammer for himself. He obviously wanted that hammer to stay in the museum."

"But why?" Emily asked. "And who the hell is Nartova?"

"I don't know why," Irana said. "But I believe you'll find that the man who was supporting Mikhail Zelov all those years was Bishop Sergai Nartova. The time frame is right."

"Another bishop?" Garrett asked. "Mikhail Zelov hated the Church."

"That doesn't mean that he wouldn't try to use it," Irana said. "In fact, it's more likely that he'd do it."

"You're sure that this Bishop Nartova could be the same man?"

"No," Irana said. "But I've studied the period, and the Russian Church and Sergai Nartova definitely had the power to siphon off enough money to keep Zelov happy. He was regarded with great respect and at one time was in line to be the Patriarch of all Russia. He refused, and said he was not worthy and would prefer to serve in a humbler position." She paused. "And after the Bolsheviks took over, he requested that he serve God and the Church here in Ekaterinaburg. It didn't please the new government since they were trying to make everyone forget what happened here."

"But steal from the Church to make that bastard rich?" Emily asked. "That would make him as bad as Zelov."

"It's definitely criminal. It must have been a very strong motive to keep him paying Zelov all those years. You say the payments stopped in 1943?" When Emily nodded, Irana said, "I'd have to check to be sure, but I think that's about the time that Nartova died. And since Zelov died shortly after the payments ended, no one learned anything about it."

"Until Nicholas Zelov got money hungry over sixty years later and resurrected it," Garrett murmured. "So he went to Bishop Dimitri and either tried to stir up some mud about past criminal practices of the Church or offered the three amulets to him so that the bishop could complete the set with the one in the hammer."

"It's guesswork," Irana said. "And I'd think that Nicholas Zelov might try to get the hammer for himself to try for the Tsar's billions."

"Too difficult," Emily said. "He's an alcoholic, and he obviously likes the easy way. That was why the steady flow of money appealed to him. He gave Babin the *Book of Living* and the amulets and went his way with his pockets lined." She glanced at Garrett. "But Babin was hired by Joslyn, not this Bishop Dimitri. Joslyn's got to be up to his ears in all this mess."

"Because you'd rather he be the bad guy than Bishop Dimitri," Garrett said. "They both may be scum. Money does corrupt, Emily."

"I know that." It was true that she didn't want a man of the cloth to be involved in this ugliness. There were so few holy or pure things to cling to in this world. "You believe that Bishop Dimitri contacted Joslyn and they became partners?"

"It's reasonable," Garrett said. "Joslyn had the money, and I don't see how the Bishop could provide Nicholas Zelov with the cash he wanted. Nartova was able to do it with old Mikhail Zelov because it was a different world, and he wielded power in the Church. These days accountants scrutinize everything." He shook his head. "No, Joslyn had to be involved."

"I'm more interested in what the Church had to do with this." Irana was already glancing through the book. "I think I should get to know more about Zelov and his relationship with it."

"I know all I want to know about him."

Emily shuddered. "I keep thinking how much like Staunton Zelov is. It seems strange that two such evil men born in different generations would both be drawn by the same lure."

"Maybe not so strange." Irana didn't look up from the book. "Sometimes I think that if the evil is strong enough, it takes on a life of its own."

"Reincarnation?"

She shrugged. "I think anything is possible in God's world. But that wasn't what I meant."

"Good. I'd hate to think there could be a constant string of Stauntons emerging in every generation." She turned to Garrett. "When are we phoning Joslyn?"

He shook his head. "Soon. But maybe we should do as you suggested and go to see Bishop Dimitri first."

"No, let me," Irana said suddenly. "Isn't that why you brought me here?"

"But I didn't think the bishop was actually a conspirator then," Garrett said.

"It doesn't change anything. I speak the language and I have the background. I want to do it."

Garrett shook his head.

"Stop protecting me, Garrett. I will do it," Irana said. "I *should* do it."

Her tone was totally, almost passionately, determined. Emily remembered the chill she had felt when Irana had told her that it was meant that she come here.

Irana glanced at Emily as if she had read her mind. "Stop worrying." She smiled. "After all, isn't it true that I'm the best qualified? I will meet him at his residency in full daylight. Nothing will happen." She got to her feet. "Now I will finish getting dressed and call Bishop Dimitri."

"He may not see you," Emily said.

"I believe he will see me." She headed for the bathroom. "In fact, I'm quite sure he will see me."

"I suppose God told you he would?" Emily asked.

"Heavens no. It's just a feeling. We all have these feelings occasionally."

"Why don't I go with you?"

She chuckled. "My feelings say no. It will be fine, Emily." She disappeared into the bathroom.

"I don't want her to go alone," Emily said. "Why won't she listen?"

"Maybe she objects to you trying to

protect her. I've heard independent women have a tendency to violently resent it."

"That's not amusing."

"I know. It's a big problem." He reached out and took her hand. "I'm not going to let her go see the bishop without protection. She'd object to me going, but I'll have Dardon drive her and stay close."

Relief rushed through her. "I know she's right, and visiting the bishop shouldn't be— I just don't like the idea."

"You have a 'feeling'?"

She nodded. "Dardon won't let her out of his sight?"

He nodded. "And I know that won't be enough for you, so we'll be parked in a car two blocks away, just in case."

She didn't speak for a moment. "Irana won't like it."

"Will that stop you?"

"Hell, no," Emily said.

"Great." He grinned. "It will give me fuel for future discussions on the subject of protective interference." He got up and moved toward the door. "I'll go talk to Dardon."

Bishop Dimitri leaned back in his leather chair after he had hung up the phone. Why had he consented to see Irana Povak? She had given him a brief description of herself and her background, but just because she had mentioned Emily Hudson should not have made him halt his objection and agree. Perhaps he should have refused and let his housekeeper turn her away if she appeared on his doorstep. It would have been prudent. It would have been safer.

But he didn't want to be safe any longer, he thought wearily. His soul was sick to death of protecting himself when he was not important. Who knew what was right or wrong? All his life he had been certain of his judgment and his creed. Where had that certainty gone? Why had he stepped beyond those borders?

He slowly reached out and dialed Peter Joslyn. "I've agreed to see Irana Povak. She says she is a friend of Emily Hudson."

"I know who she is," Joslyn said. "Staunton told me. It's a mistake to see her, Dimitri."

"I wanted you to tell me that. I wanted an excuse to turn her away." He looked out the window at the red roses blooming in the garden. It was too late for roses, but

Joslyn had given him a hardy variety that bloomed several times a year. "And when a man looks for excuses, it usually means he's wrong." He paused. "Are we wrong, Peter?"

Silence. "I don't know. We probably are wrong. But we can't go back."

"No, we can't go back." It was too late. Too much had happened. Too many lives had been lost. "But perhaps we can make peace."

"I don't like the sound of that. Look, I'm on my way over. Don't talk to anyone until I get there."

"Only Irana Povak. I've been sitting here and gazing out at the beautiful roses that you gave me and wondering why I gave her permission to come. Do you know what I decided? Sometimes God sends a messenger, and if we're wise, we don't shut him out. Perhaps I felt that this woman was my messenger."

"Dimitri, you're just tired and discouraged. Let's talk, and we can come—"

"You're right, I'm tired. And I'm feeling very old today." He rose to his feet. "I'm going out to my rose garden and sit in the sunshine and wait for Irana Povak."

"Don't see her," Joslyn said quickly. "I'll be there as soon as I can. Put her off. Don't do anything that—"

"Good-bye, Peter." He hung up, then turned off his phone. He moved toward the French doors that led to the garden. The sun was beckoning and he knew that the heady scent of the roses would surround that bench near the fountain. His housekeeper would show Irana Povak to the garden when she arrived.

Come, messenger. Cleanse my soul.

The residency was a large brick building on the outskirts of Ekaterinaburg surrounded by several equally-prestigious-appearing buildings. Irana gazed out the window at the wide arched windows and heavy mahogany door as Dardon pulled over to the curb in front of it. "Very impressive," she murmured as she opened the passenger door. "Okay, Dardon, go away."

"Nope. I have to stay with you. Orders."

"And my orders are for you to either go away or wait here." She moved toward the door. "I don't want you getting in my way."

"What difference does it make if I come with you? I'll keep my mouth shut."

She didn't know why she was being insistent. She was operating on instinct alone. "It will make a difference. Stay here." She climbed the three steps to the front door alcove. "I'm sure that Garrett and Emily will consider that close enough."

"You're wrong, Irana," Emily said as she came around the corner. She held up her hand as Irana opened her lips. "Garrett said that we should wait a block away so that you wouldn't be annoyed with us. I thought about it and decided that I don't care if you're annoyed. You and Garrett have done whatever you thought best for me since the moment we met. Why shouldn't I do the same? I'll give you your space. I'll sit in the anteroom while you have your talk with Bishop Dimitri, but I'm going to be a hell of a lot closer than a block away."

Irana gazed at her a moment, then smiled. "I'd have to knock you out to keep you from coming with me, wouldn't I?"

"If you think you're tough enough."

"I'm tough enough, but it's hard to overcome the power of affection with force. It gets too complicated." She reached out to ring the doorbell. "And it warms my heart that you care for me. But I truly think that I'll get more information if I'm alone with the bishop. When I spoke to him on the phone, I got the vague impression that he wants to—" She shrugged. She wasn't sure she could describe what she had felt in that moment when she had heard Bishop Dimitri's voice on the phone. "So you may guard me from a very respectable distance. Understand?"

"I didn't expect anything else. I just didn't want you to be alone."

"I'm not alone." She pressed the doorbell. "Ever since I decided to come here, I knew I wasn't alone." Her face lit with her warm smile. "And now I have you, too."

NINETEEN

Bishop Dimitri was older than he had sounded on the phone, Irana thought as she walked down the path toward him. His hair was snow-white, and his brown eyes indented with deep lines. He was staring thoughtfully, almost dreamily, into the waters of the fountain.

He looked up and smiled. "I've been waiting for you." He studied her face and nodded. "Yes, it's you I've been waiting for. Sit down, child."

"I'm not a child, Bishop Dimitri."

"You are to me. I've reached my eightieth year. Not that age matters. The soul is eternal." His smiled faded. "But if the soul is weighed down, it can't seem to see eternity. You understand that, don't you?"

"Yes, I understand that."

"I thought so. A messenger would sense many things."

"Messenger?" Irana shook her head. "I'm not a child, I'm not a messenger. I've only come to ask you a few questions."

"I know." He gazed at the roses across the path. "And I will answer. Do you know there are millions of children in this world that live in garbage and dung and never see a flower? How sad that is."

"I wish to ask you about Nicholas Zelov and what he said to you when he came to visit you."

"I believe you probably know a good deal, or you wouldn't be here."

"We think he offered you three amulets and Mikhail Zelov's book . . . for a price."

"That's true. But I didn't have his price."

"So you involved Peter Joslyn?"

He nodded. "To my infinite regret. I saw no other way. Nicholas Zelov was not a good man. Greed would have goaded him to go to someone else, perhaps even the government. I couldn't allow that."

"And when you couldn't retrieve the hammer that contained the final amulet, Joslyn turned Staunton loose to get it back."

He flinched. "It wasn't Peter's fault. He didn't know what kind of man Babin had hired until recently. He only did as I asked. I had to get the hammer. I thought it my duty."

"Duty?"

"To my friend, to the man whom I respected more than anyone in my life. I didn't want all his work and sacrifice to go for nothing."

She studied his face. "Bishop Sergai Nartova?"

He nodded. "He was my idol. He was the reason I entered the church. He was as close to being a saint as man can be."

"Saint? You knew he stole from the Church?"

"He had to make a choice. As long as he paid off Mikhail Zelov, then Zelov would be satisfied to stay away and not try for the hammer. If he didn't have the final amulet, then he couldn't go after the Tsar's treasure." He shook his head. "He couldn't be permitted to have that kind of power. He would have been Satan on earth."

"He came very close without the treasure."

"But imagine if he had billions to call upon. My friend, Sergai Nartova, kept him leashed." He smiled faintly. "And all the while Zelov thought he was in control. He told Sergai that unless he gave him money, he would turn the amulets and hammer over to the new Communist government. It was a formidable threat at the time. The Communists were draining us, forming a godless nation, and Nartova didn't want them to gain more influence by finding the fortune of the Tsar they'd murdered. But that was not the reason he risked his soul to keep Zelov at bay."

"Evil," Irana said. "He thought Zelov was close to being an archdemon?"

"You do understand. I thought you would." He nodded. "He told me once that he knew from the moment he met Zelov that he realized what he was or could be. He read his book and even visited Jerusalem to try to find out more about him. When Zelov came to him, it was his chance to harness him and keep him from becoming what he was destined to be."

"He went to all those lengths?"

"Yes. He should have been Patriarch of all Russia. He gave up everything to come here to Ekaterinaburg and watch over the hammer. For God's sake. For mankind's sake."

"And you didn't tell anyone all these years? Even after Nartova died? You knew that the hammer was in that museum, and you didn't try to get it out?"

"Why should I? Nothing really changed in the government until the eighties. The Communists would have snatched the Tsar's treasure and used it to keep the nation under their thumb. After Nartova died, I wanted only to follow in his footsteps. He made the decision; I just kept to his guidelines." He made a face. "Though I nearly failed him. Two years ago, the Patriarch summoned me to Moscow for a month. When I came back, I found the curator of the museum had sent the exhibit on loan to the museum in Afghanistan. I couldn't get it back. The area had been put out of bounds because of heavy fighting in the area. All I could do was wait and watch."

"Until Nicholas Zelov came to see you."

He nodded. "It was as if Mikhail Zelov had reached out from the grave and tried to destroy everything Sergai Nartova had tried to do."

"The Communists' power was tremendously lessened."

"But they wouldn't have permitted the Tsar's fortune to leave the country. They would have absorbed it, devoured it. And, if they had not done it, the Romanov heirs would have been fighting for the next fifty years to get a share."

"And you weren't going to let that happen."

"If anyone was going to get the Tsar's billions, it should be the people who needed it. There are charities all over the world that need help. Children have always touched me. Special children, starving children, children who have been abused. Jesus said let the little children come unto me. I thought that my friend Nartova would have liked that I might be able to help them. He had guarded the hammer for all those years to keep the treasure from being used by those who wanted only to corrupt. He told me once that the only way to win the treasure was to leave it alone. I had to protect the hammer, protect the children. But now I had the amulets, and I could reach out and give back to the world. Isn't it better that I take the hammer into my keeping than let it go to someone who would not care for it as I would?"

Irana shook her head in amazement. For a man of his years and education, his view in this matter was incredibly simplistic. He obviously looked upon the treasure as belonging to Sergai Nartova rather than the Tsar or any other entity. His friend had cared for it, guarded it, and therefore had more right to it than anyone else. "I don't believe that the government would agree with you."

"Exactly. That's what I've been telling you." His eyes were narrowed shrewdly on her face. "But you agree with me, don't you? I thought you would."

"I agree that those in need would better profit than bureaucrats, but that doesn't mean you have the right to take what doesn't belong to you." She smiled. "Good

Samaritans should dole out their own alms, Bishop Dimitri. Not borrow from others."

"I appreciate the fact that you didn't say steal." He chuckled. "But I admit that I committed that sin. It's a sin I could live with if I could see thousands of hungry children fed because of my transgression." His smile faded. "But I cannot live with the horror that has come of all this. When Joslyn told me of what Staunton has done, it made me—I was stunned. I never thought it would happen. But I still must accept the blame for it."

"Joslyn paid out the money."

"Are you trying to give me an excuse? Peter is a good man. I was the one who drew him into my scheme." He shook his head and corrected, "No, into my dream. Such a good man . . . Even now he's rushing here to try to protect me."

"And what do you want to do now?"

He leaned back on the bench. "I want to sit here in the sun. Later I will pray and let God decide what is best." He smiled. "I believe he is already at work. After all, he sent me a messenger."

She shook her head.

"I've made you uncomfortable," he said.

"Don't be. Messengers sometimes don't recognize their mission." He searched her face. "But I think you were sensitive to . . . something. But I sense pain within you. Tell me, have I hurt you, child?"

"No, you haven't hurt me, Bishop Dimitri."

"Then I pray your pain will leave you." He closed his eyes. "We won't talk about it anymore. But I want you to know you've brought me comfort."

"I don't know why. I can't keep what you've done a secret."

"You'll do what you have to do. But will you stay with me for a little while? It's not every day a messenger comes to visit. There's a blessed . . . peace about you."

She felt a sudden rush of sympathy. He had been wrong, but his motives had been right. He had wanted to save children and been willing to sacrifice himself to do it. How many other people could say as much? "I'll stay with you." She leaned back. "As long as you like, Bishop Dimitri."

"Everything okay?" Garrett asked, when Dardon answered the phone.

"As far as I know," Dardon said.

"They've been inside the residency for the last twenty minutes." He added, "I tried to go in with them, but Irana wouldn't let me. I didn't think she'd let Emily go either for a few minutes."

"I didn't have any doubt." When Emily had suddenly jumped out of the car and told him that she was going with Irana, he'd known there would be no way to stop her. "But I don't like it that they're not out yet."

"Do you want me to go after them?"

Yes. But he knew better. It would only antagonize both of them, and the time wasn't unreasonable yet. But he wanted to be closer, not sitting here on pins and needles. "No." He opened his car door. "I'm coming to you. I should be there in five minutes."

Emily got up from her chair and strolled over to the French doors through which Irana had disappeared. She shook her head in wonder as she saw the bishop and Irana sitting together on the bench by the fountain. The old man was sitting with his eyes closed and looked as if he was about to drift off to sleep, and Irana had taken his hand and was sitting in silence. Emily couldn't have imagined a more comfortable or tranquil scene. Irana might have been the old man's granddaughter and certainly wasn't interrogating him with any degree of urgency. In fact, Emily could almost feel the bond that was drawing the old man and the young woman together. Strange, but no stranger than Irana's insistence on coming here.

Her phone rang, and she didn't check the ID. It had to be Garrett wondering why—

"Hello, Emily, beautiful day, isn't it?"

She felt as if she had been kicked in the stomach. "Staunton?"

"You're always surprised when I call you. I don't know why. You should know I want to keep in touch. I've made sure that I know where you are, where you go. It seems a long time since our chat at the silo."

"I was hoping you'd bled to death."

"Yes, I was very angry with you about that. But I wasn't seriously hurt, and I'm back in fine form."

"That's unfortunate. I'll try to do better next time."

"I'm sure you will. I gained a new respect for you, Emily. At first, I only wanted to kill you at the earliest possible opportunity, but then I realized that nothing had really changed. In fact, my admiration will be like a savory flavor added to our experience."

"Babin is dead. You killed him, didn't you?"

"Did I?"

"You murdered Nemid and Babin. Did you kill Nicholas Zelov?"

"Not personally."

"Borg?"

"I really shouldn't incriminate Borg. He's been very helpful."

"Why? Why are you doing it?"

"Can't you guess? But you're such a smart woman."

"Tell me."

"Old Mikhail Zelov had the right idea. You have to clear the way if you're going to become a god. Witnesses are awkward. It's better that no one is left alive to tell the tale."

"A god?"

"That much money can make a man into a god. That's why Mikhail Zelov kept coming back here and trying to get his hammer. I understand him perfectly. He was a rich man, but he didn't have enough to become what he thought was his destiny."

"He was a monster. He was responsible for the deaths of the royal family and Rasputin."

"And that left no one who could get in his way. Very smart. I admire his efficiency. From the moment I read that *Book of Living* that wimp Nicholas Zelov had sold to Babin, I knew that Mikhail Zelov and I were so much alike, we could have been mirror images. Except I'm much smarter. I can do it better. That's why I made out my list. I wonder if Mikhail Zelov had a list."

"Nemid, Zelov, and Babin were on this . . . list?"

"Of course."

She moistened her lips. "And who else?"

"You and your friends." He paused. "I have a special plan for Garrett. I've decided I'm going to take a long, long time killing him. It will be worse than what Levy suffered."

Shock and panic rippled through her.

"You're not speaking. Does the thought

upset you? I believe I'll let you watch again."

No, not again. Not to Garrett.

Don't let Staunton know what his words had done to her. She kept her voice steady. "Who else?"

"So that you can run to the rescue?" His tone turned malicious. "As you did with Sister Irana? You were a little late. Did she tell you what I—"

"Shut up. Don't talk about her."

"Oh, I did hurt you there, didn't I? If I'd had more time, I would have—"

"I said shut up."

"You can't stop me. Not with her. Not with Garrett. That's the way to hurt you, Emily. I remember you were so terribly upset that you couldn't save your friend, Levy."

"Who else is on your list?"

"I don't believe I'll tell you. You should really worry about yourself. That's what I want you to do. I want you to sweat. I want you to panic. I want your heart to start pounding when you hear my voice. Terror is a bit like sex if it's done right. Same moist palms, same tightening of the muscles. Is your heart pounding now, Emily?"

"No."

"It will. I've neglected you far too long. Your Garrett was too savvy. I had to work around him and do damage control. But don't worry; I can give you the majority of my attention now."

"By all means. Stop hiding and come out in the open. Maybe you're afraid that I'll manage to kill you. I'm really a very good shot. You would have been dead if you hadn't moved at the last second. Let's see if you can do anything but make threatening phone calls."

He chuckled. "You're taunting me. How very brave . . . and foolish. For you see, it's all at what location I make those threatening phone calls."

She stiffened. "What location?"

"It's a beautiful day and the rose garden is particularly lovely, isn't it?"

She forgot to breathe. She couldn't speak.

"And I believe that our Bishop Dimitri is taking a little snooze. Your friend, Irana, must not be a good conversationalist."

"*Where* are you?"

"At a point where I can see everything

you can see. I was disappointed when you didn't follow Irana Povak out to join the bishop. But then I realized it was all to the good. I want you to be last, and now I'll be able to let you witness, as you did with Levy. You must like Irana Povak very much to go through all you did for her. You took her away from me, but now I can take her back in the most final way possible."

"Where are you?" she repeated hoarsely.

"Close enough. I'm very good with a rifle. I'm sighting now . . ."

"No!" She jammed the phone in her pocket as she tore open the door. "Irana! Get down!" She was running down the path. "You've got to get down!"

She could see Irana's startled face. The bishop was opening his eyes, straightening on the bench. "It's Staunton. Get down. He's going to—"

"You get down, Emily." Irana had thrown herself on the bishop and was pulling him to the ground.

A low pop came from somewhere above and behind Emily.

Irana!

Irana and Bishop Dimitri were both crumpled on the ground.

Blood . . .

And Staunton must still be up there with his rifle.

Emily instinctively dove sideways and rolled behind a bank of rosebushes lining the path.

No shot.

She had to help Irana. She began to crawl toward them.

No shot.

"Emily!"

Garrett! "Get down. Staunton—"

"I know." Garrett was beside her. "Are you okay?"

She nodded jerkily, as she tried to pull him down to the ground. "Staunton—"

"Are you sure it was Staunton? We caught sight of a shooter on the rooftop next door when we ran into the garden, but we couldn't identify him. Dardon is chasing him."

"I'm sure. He called me. He wanted me to know." She got to her feet. "He wanted me to know he was going to kill Irana."

"Irana?"

Emily wasn't listening. She was running toward the two people lying by the bench. "She was hit. There was blood. . . ."

"Not my blood." Irana was slowly sitting up, her gaze fixed on the face of the bishop. "I tried to drag him down. I tried . . ."

Emily was staring down at Bishop Dimitri. A bloody hole had blossomed in the exact center of the bishop's forehead. "Very precise," she said dully. "Staunton told me he was a good shot. It wasn't you he meant to kill at all. He just wanted to see me panic."

Irana reached out and gently touched the bishop's cheek. "He didn't get a chance to pray. He told me he wanted to pray."

"We've got to get out of here." Garrett was pulling Irana to her feet. "The house-keeper knew you were with him, and she must have seen Emily, too. Staunton was using a silencer, or she would probably have run out here when she heard the shot."

"So I'm now a murder suspect?" Irana's eyes were glittering with moisture. "He said I was a messenger, but I don't think that's what he meant. I don't believe he expected—" She broke off, then said wearily, "Or maybe he did. I don't know. . . ."

"I know we should get out of this garden," Garrett said. "We'll go out the garden gate and—"

"My God." A heavyset, red-haired man in his late forties stood in the doorway. "What have you done?"

Garrett stiffened warily, his hand moved to his jacket pocket. "Who are you?"

"Wait," Irana said. "Joslyn. The bishop said he was on his way."

"You've murdered him," Joslyn said dully. He moved toward the fallen man. "I warned him that he shouldn't see—"

"You're the one who murdered him," Emily said coldly. "Staunton pulled the trigger, but you hired him."

"Staunton did this? Yes, I can see him—" He fell to his knees beside the bishop. "Dimitri . . ."

There were tears in his eyes, Emily noticed. For a moment she felt a flicker of sympathy, then pushed it away. "What did you think he'd do? You hire a cobra, and you don't expect him to strike as many people as he can reach? How much extra did you give him for killing Joel Levy?"

"I didn't know." He looked down at the bishop. "Neither of us knew. I told Babin to get someone who could do the job. I didn't think he'd—"

Emily couldn't stand any more. "Let's get out of here." She turned toward the gate. "I don't want Irana to get in trouble because his pet killer decided to—"

"Wait." Joslyn got to his feet. "I'll go in and talk to his housekeeper and tell her that you've left the residency. Then I'll send her home for the weekend. She shouldn't be back until nine or ten Monday morning."

"You can do that?" Garrett asked.

Joslyn nodded. "She knows Dimitri and I are very good friends. I've had dinner here at least once a week for the last ten years."

Garrett gazed at him without expression. "And then what?"

"And then I'll carry my friend to his room and say a prayer and leave him there." He gazed down at the bishop. "He told me he wanted to make peace. I knew that meant he wanted to confess his sin, our sin. I ran here to stop him. I wanted to protect him. I didn't do it, did I? I was protecting him from the wrong people. I didn't know Staunton would—" He shook his head. "But that doesn't mean that I wasn't at fault."

"You're right," Emily said. "You've been like Pilate, washing his hands of blame."

He shook his head. "Not anymore. Not since I found out the ugliness I unleashed." He met her gaze. "You're angry. I'm sorry. I hurt you."

"Yes, you did," Emily said. "You hurt a lot of people." She glanced down at the bishop. "And so did he."

"Attack me," Joslyn said. "Not Dimitri. He only wanted to save the hammer, save the children. I could have said no. But I'd spent too much time in Ethiopia, seeing the devastation hunger could do to children. He trusted me. I could have paid more attention to what Babin was doing. I could have been more careful."

"That's not what Bishop Dimitri told me," Irana said. "He said that he took full responsibility." She added quietly, "And I believe he did make peace before he died."

"This isn't the time for shuffling blame," Garrett said. "If you're going to talk to the housekeeper, go do it." He took Irana's arm and nudged her toward Emily, who was standing by the gate. "You go on to the car. I'll stay and help him move Bishop Dimitri to his room."

"The car?" Emily repeated. She was remembering something else Staunton had said. "Staunton knew where we were. He told me so. It's not logical that he would have been waiting for us here. Could he have bugged the car?"

"It's possible," Garrett said grimly. "No, it's damn probable. We just rented the car that Dardon used to drive Irana here this morning, so it's more than likely the car we've been using since we arrived here in Russia was bugged. Dammit to hell, I wasn't *careful* enough. I told Dardon before I left the farmhouse that night that he had to be sure to check the car out after we came back from Babin's, but it didn't happen. All any of us could think about was getting Pauley to find Irana. We knew we had to move fast and—" He stopped and shook his head. "That's water under the bridge. Damage control. Go get in the car that Dardon rented today. We'll abandon the other one." He turned back to Joslyn. "Hurry, let's get this taken care of."

Joslyn nodded and moved toward the house.

Dardon was hurrying down the street when Emily and Irana arrived at the car. His hair was mussed, and his breath was coming in short pants. "I didn't get him. He had a car parked in the next block and was driving off when I got around the house." He looked behind her. "Where's Garrett?"

"In the garden," Irana said. "Bishop Dimitri is dead."

"Shit." Dardon headed for the gate. "Garrett may need help." He disappeared into the garden.

Irana opened the rear car door. "Get in. I don't like the idea of your being out on the street. Staunton may be on the run, but there might be someone else who—"

Emily got into the car. "You're right, but I imagine his man, Borg, hasn't had time to get here from New York. That was probably why Staunton did the killing himself." She shuddered. "Though I'm sure he enjoyed it. You should have heard him on the phone. He was—" She stopped and steadied her voice. "And actually I'm not his target right now. He wants me to be last. He made me think it was you he was going to shoot. And he has a list."

"And who is on it?"

"Everyone who knows about the treasure. He admires Mikhail Zelov very much. He says he was very efficient. Kill everyone and leave no witnesses."

"And that's why he killed the bishop."

"Yes." Where was Garrett? She was still caught up in the panic caused by Staunton's words. Perhaps she should go back and see what—

She breathed a sigh of relief as she saw Garrett coming out the gate, followed by Joslyn and Dardon.

"Dardon, you drive." Garrett got into the passenger seat. "Joslyn, where's your car?"

"Around the corner." He stood watching as Dardon got into the driver's seat. "Thank you for your help. It bought me a little time. I'll have to make arrangements for my family before I go to the police."

"Don't be in a hurry," Garrett said. "Maybe we can work something out. The Russian government isn't going to be very lenient about this. That billion dollars is going to look very good to them. They need money, and they like to set examples."

He shook his head. "Make peace, Dimitri said. I don't know how else to do it." He stepped back. "Again, I'm very sorry. I wish I could make amends, but I know that—"

"Don't let him go," Emily said. She leaned forward, glaring at Joslyn. "This isn't over for you. You can't walk away and bribe your way out of a Russian jail. I won't let you."

"I have no intention of—"

She turned to Garrett. "He's on Staunton's list. He has to be. Staunton's not going to let him go to the police. He's going to kill him."

"I'll take my chances," Joslyn said. "Though I'm surprised you'd care."

"I don't care. You'd deserve it," she said fiercely. "But I'm not going to let Staunton kill anyone else. That's what he wants to do. Kill and kill and kill again." She whirled on Garrett. "We're not going to let him do it. Do you hear me? Not one more death. Not one more person in pain. This is where we draw the line. This is where we stop him. Joslyn wants to make peace? Then let him help get rid of that killer. That's the only way to make peace."

"Joslyn?" Garrett asked.

"Don't ask him, tell him," Emily turned back to Joslyn. "Staunton has a list. I'm sure you're on it. I'm not sure if your wife and children are on his kill list. I'd bet they are because Staunton is very thorough, and he couldn't be sure that you hadn't talked to them. If I were you, I'd send them somewhere safe, then help eliminate the threat."

Joslyn was silent a moment. "My family?"

"Do you think he'd stop because they were innocent? He's like Mikhail Zelov, who killed those poor young royal children just because it was convenient. Staunton wouldn't think twice."

Joslyn turned to Garrett. "It seems that I won't be talking to the police anytime soon. I have to protect my family."

"Good," Garrett said. "Will you come with us now?"

"No, I've got to get home as quickly as possible. My family may need me."

Garrett said to Dardon, "Follow him to his car, and we'll check it out."

Joslyn's brows lifted. "For explosives?"

"For explosives, for bugs. Whatever. It won't take long. Dardon is an expert. But you have to be safe." Garrett shrugged. "We have our orders. Emily wants you kept alive."

"I don't want it," Emily said. "That's the way it has to be. And we may be able to use him."

"I'll do anything I can for you," Joslyn said quietly. "After I take care of my family." He turned and strode down the street.

Emily leaned back in the seat as Dardon started the car and cruised slowly after him.

"He's not a wicked man." Irana's gaze was on Emily's face. "I believe him when he said that he didn't know what Staunton was doing. I think he and the bishop were both trying to do what they thought was right."

"It doesn't matter. He paid out the money. He made it possible for Staunton to do what he did to Joel," Emily said. "And even if he honestly wanted me to forgive him, I wouldn't do it. I may have to work with him, but that's all."

"It's more than I expected," Garrett

said. "You're angry enough to cut him loose for Staunton to take down."

"Yes. You're the one who said you wouldn't be satisfied until you found the man who funded Staunton."

"And we have him. I'm just not sure exactly what we have." Garrett turned around to look at Emily. "Now tell me exactly what Staunton said on the phone. Every word."

She wouldn't tell him every word. She wouldn't tell him the part that had frightened her almost more than the threat to Irana. The terror was still hanging over her like a dark cloud.

"I'll make sure it's worse for him than it was for Levy."

Don't think about it. It won't happen. I'll make sure it can't happen.

"I got the call after I'd been in the study for about thirty minutes. Staunton was . . ."

Pauley was waiting in the lobby when they walked into the inn an hour later. "You should never have left me here alone," he said reproachfully. "It was very cold of you after all I've done. I was wondering if I was going to have to come and

rescue you. That might have been a disaster, since I'm not exactly experienced
at search and rescue. It would have been
much better just to have let me come—"

"Pauley, be quiet," Garrett said. "We
have enough problems without you yam-
mering."

"I don't yammer. I speak with great—"
He broke off as he met Garrett's eye.
"Problems? What can I do to help?"

"I'm not sure. But you can bet I'll let you
do whatever you can." He headed for the
elevator. "You can start by getting the desk
clerk to change all our rooms to the same
floor. I don't want anyone more than hailing
distance away."

"That may be difficult," Pauley said.
"The inn is full now. No one is going to
want to move."

"Can you do it, or not?"

Pauley glanced at the desk clerk, who
was frowning as she studied her computer. "It's not the kind of work I really
like."

"It's what I need from you."

He sighed as he turned back toward
the desk. "Give me an hour."

The last thing that Emily saw as the elevator doors closed was Pauley leaning his elbows on the desk. He was smiling with a voltage that was stunning in intensity as he spoke to the desk clerk. Good heavens, he was mesmerizing. Emily had never seen Pauley operating with more than a casual charm. This was not casual, this was pure charisma, and it was meant to captivate and sway. "I believe we may have found something that Pauley handles better than computers," she murmured.

"Just so he gets it done," Garrett said.

"I thought you'd want me to change hotels," Dardon said. "Since Staunton evidently knows where we are."

"This is as good a place as any," Garrett said. "And we're not running anymore." He smiled as he looked down at Emily and quoted her words. "'We've drawn a line.' Isn't that how it goes?"

"That's how it goes." Emily turned to Irana. "Are you all right? All of this was pretty rough on you."

"It was pretty rough on you, too. You were faced with your bogeyman again. I just had to deal with an old man who wanted to do good and did evil instead." She got off the elevator as it stopped on her floor. "And now I'm going to my room and pray for that old man's soul. I'll call you later."

"Stay where you are. I'll send Pauley and Dardon to move you as soon as Pauley arranges it." Garrett punched the HOLD button on the elevator and watched until she reached her room and unlocked the door.

Emily was glad to see his caution. That moment in the garden when she'd thought Irana was the target was still with her. She was trying to maintain her composure, but she kept seeing Irana shot, Irana dead. "She should pray for herself. If that bullet had been six inches to the left, she'd be dead."

"She won't pray for herself," Garrett said. "She told me once that prayers should be for those who can't help themselves. She's not sure if she wasted them on herself that God would pay attention when she prayed for someone else."

"That sounds like her," Dardon said. "You can't say that she's not an original." He got off the elevator at his floor. "Do you want me to go down and try to help Pauley?"

"I think he's got it under control," Garrett said dryly. "Just pack up and get ready for the move." He added, "And be careful."

Dardon tilted his head. "You're really worried about this Staunton. I don't think I've ever seen you this uneasy."

"Because I can't figure out what he's doing," Garrett said. "It doesn't make sense to me. And I don't like not knowing which way he may jump. Just take care of yourself."

Emily didn't speak until after they'd entered her room a few minutes later. "I've told you which way he's going to jump," she said curtly. "He told me. He's killing witnesses and anyone who knows about the Tsar's treasure."

"But why now? It seems a little unreasonable. Think about it."

"I don't want to think about it." She was barely maintaining control. "Maybe later." She threw her purse on the bed. "All I want to think about is how we're going to trap Staunton before he kills you and Irana and—" She stopped and had to fight to keep her voice steady. "No more, Garrett."

"Shh." He took her in his arms. "No more. I promise."

"You can't promise. You can only promise to do your best." Her arms slid around him, and she buried her face in his chest. "And sometimes best doesn't do the job."

"It will this time."

"How do we trap him?" she repeated. "He's like a phantom."

"We start with his phone call."

She took a step back. "What?"

"We have Pauley dig out Staunton's number as he did Babin's. It will be harder, since you can bet Staunton has been even more careful than Babin. When we're ready, you call Staunton back, and we put a trace on his location. Then we move in for the kill."

"What do you mean 'ready'?"

"It has to be in a place that we can get to him." He added, "And he can't get away as he did today."

"Won't that be hard?"

"Extremely. But that's why we have Pauley. Maybe he can do a little satellite magic again."

"It took him a long time to get Babin's location. We may not have a long time."

"He appears to rise to the occasion. Let's see if we can give him a little encouragement."

"Money?"

"I'm not sure. Pauley has been surprising me lately." He smiled. "Maybe I'll use an incentive. I'll tell him that James Bond could do it in a heartbeat." He paused. "I'm going to make sure I have a room only a few doors down the hall. I'll probably be spending a lot of time with Pauley until he comes through for us. I'm no wunderkind like he is at manipulating the Internet, but I'm pretty good. I may be able to offer a suggestion here and there. I'll at least be there to apply pressure. Do you want me to go to my own room tonight? It's your call."

She didn't have to think about it. She was still hearing Staunton's words over and over in her mind. She didn't want Garrett only a few doors down the hall. She wanted him close enough to touch, close enough to protect. "Stay."

He nodded. "Good. I got what I wanted,

and I didn't have to bypass the freedom-of-choice issue. Second question. Do you need me to be with you this evening?"

"I don't need you." But she wanted him here. She wanted to be able to reach out and assure herself that Staunton hadn't taken him away from her. "Don't be ridiculous. Go on to Pauley. I want to have dinner with Irana. She may be more upset than she's letting us know." She turned toward the bathroom. "I'll take a shower and give her an hour or two, then I'll call her." She looked at him over her shoulder. "Staunton will phone me again. He enjoyed himself too much not to want to get that rush again. I could almost feel the pleasure he had taunting me. It just may not be convenient for us."

"Then we have to rely on Pauley doing his magic." He added, "In the meantime, Joslyn may be able to help with information. We'll have to see."

"If we see him again. He may decide to go with his family to safety."

"I don't think he will."

Neither did Emily. She wanted to believe that he was as bad as Staunton, but she couldn't forget his expression as he stared down at his friend, the bishop. Agony, pity, horror, regret, and other emotions that she couldn't decipher. Was guilt one of them? "I hope you're right. We need all the help we can get." She closed the bathroom door behind her.

TWENTY

Irana knocked on Emily's door two hours later. "I'm right across the hall now. Dardon is next door, and Pauley is three doors down. I wasn't sure that Pauley would be able to negotiate that extensive a switch."

"I was." Emily remembered that last glimpse she'd had of Pauley leaning on the counter of the reception desk. "I didn't have one doubt." She closed the door and nodded at the covered tray on the small table across the room. "I was going to order room service for us, but Dardon went down and got us takeout from the kitchen. Garrett said it would be safer."

She smiled faintly. "Garrett's protective instincts are flying high right now."

"And you're not objecting." Irana's gaze was fixed on her face. "Why is that?"

Because she was feeling just as protective of Garrett. More. For the first time, she was experiencing an urgency that was frantically intense. "It won't hurt to let him have his way in the little things. Perhaps my confidence was shaken today."

"Or perhaps you just slid away from my question. But I should warn you, Garrett's not ever going to back off from protecting you now. And it won't only be in the little things. I believe he tried, but it's not going to happen. I saw that in the garden today." Irana lifted the metal lid off the plates. "It smells good. What is it?"

"Some kind of stew or borscht, I think. And potato pancakes." She sat down. "Sturdy fare. Dardon's choice. I wasn't sure you'd be this hungry."

"I usually have a good appetite." Irana sat down opposite her and lifted her fork. "And though I appreciate your respecting my sensitivity, I'm pretty tough. I'm a doctor, and I'm used to God taking unexpectedly."

"Not like that."

"No, not like that," she said quietly. Irana didn't look at Emily as she took a bite of the potato pancake. "Violence is ugly."

"I thought it was going to be you."

"I know. You were worried from the moment I told you that I felt that I was meant to come here." She took a sip of water. "It's hard for you to look on anything but the darkest side right now."

"Then why did you tell me that?"

"I wanted to prepare you. Just in case." She raised her eyes. "I knew God had a purpose. I just didn't know what it was. You like me. I didn't want it to come as a shock."

"Irana . . ." She swallowed hard. "Well, it didn't happen. So maybe he didn't have a purpose this time."

"I believe he did. But it was for the bishop, not me. He wanted me there to help ease his way. Dimitri had spent all his life serving God. He took one wrong path, but God wouldn't have wanted him to die alone, with no one to understand his pain." She smiled. "So he sent a messenger. Not a very wise messenger, but I did understand, and I think Bishop Dimitri did die more peacefully than if I hadn't been there."

"I believe he did, too."

"But you still can't forgive him."

"Maybe I will someday. I can only think about Joel. I'm not like you. It will take a long time."

Irana nodded. "When you're away from all this. It's difficult to see beyond the hurt and the anger." She paused. "After I prayed for the bishop, I sat down and read some of Mikhail Zelov's *Book of Living*. I remembered what you said about Staunton and Zelov being so much alike. You're right, perhaps history does repeat itself. Zelov was trying to take over his world, and now Staunton is doing the same thing. And both were using the hammer to do it. It's curious. . . ."

"It's horrible."

"That, too." Irana nodded at Emily's plate. "Stop talking and eat something. Garrett will not be pleased if I don't see that you stay healthy."

"Now who's being protective?" She

picked up her fork. "I told him that I wanted to make sure you were okay, and you immediately set about taking care of me."

"It's my job. It's what I am." She smiled. "And my pleasure. Eat your dinner."

Garrett was standing naked beside her bed. "Awake?"

"Yes." She shifted a few inches and curled up against him when he slid under the covers. "It's almost three. Did you get anything done?"

"Enough. It was interesting. I think that Pauley could probably hack into the CIA if he set his mind to it."

"Don't let him do it. I don't want Ferguson becoming irritated. You seem to have to call on him too often." She was silent a moment. "The bishop?"

He knew what she was asking. "Ferguson wouldn't touch a cleanup here. Bishop Dimitri is a revered institution in this city, this country. We have three days before he'll be found. We'll have to think of something else."

"We can find his murderer."

"That's why I'm pushing Pauley to work at top speed. We'll get there."

"Yes." She paused. "I should never have brought you into this. It's been a domino effect. If I'd died in that hut with Joel, none of you would have been on Staunton's list."

"Shut up," he said roughly, his arms tightening around her. "That's crazy talk."

"Yes, it is. It just tumbled out. I've never had a death wish, and I'd never give Staunton that satisfaction. But I should have found my own way out of that camp. And I should find a way now to—" His lips on hers stopped the words.

"Be quiet," he said fiercely as he lifted his head. "You're not going to do anything. You're out of it. I'll figure a way to get Staunton. I won't have you—" He broke off, holding her close. "Not you. Nothing is going to happen to you, Emily."

"You're hurting me."

His grasp loosened. "That's the last thing I want, dammit. I just want you to be safe."

Garrett's not ever going to back off from protecting you now, Irana had said.

I believe he tried, but it's not going to happen.

And Irana was right. He'd put his life on the line and try to keep her from being at risk.

And he could be killed doing it. Killed and tortured as Joel had been those two weeks.

Panic soared through her. No, she wouldn't allow it.

"You're too quiet. I don't like that." He pushed her away again. "What are you thinking?"

How had it happened? Sex she could accept. But this wasn't mindless pleasure; it was deeper and completely terrifying in its intensity. What was she thinking? *I'm thinking that it would kill me if Staunton hurt you. I'm thinking that somehow I have to keep that from happening.*

"Nothing." She buried her head in his chest. "I guess I was more shaken than I thought. Forget it."

He didn't move. "I won't forget it. I never forget anything about you."

Distract him. Blur the edginess. Mask the desperation.

"Then I'd better make sure the memories are pleasant," she said as she moved over him. "Let's see how unforgettable I can be tonight."

He was asleep.

Emily nestled her head into the hollow of Garrett's shoulder, feeling the steady rise and fall of his chest. She wanted to lie here and feel, not think. Tonight their emotions had contained an element as desperate and explosive as the physical togetherness. She might have distracted Garrett by sex, but nothing had been blurred for either one of them.

Which meant that he would be on guard to make sure that there had been no lingering substance in the words she'd spoken before they had come together.

It would be three days until Bishop Dimitri's body was found and the police came after her and Irana.

Less than that now. It was almost morning. Two days. She had to move fast.

But how was she to know the right direction?

The same direction that Garrett was

following. The phone calls. That was the only lead they had, and it could work if Pauley came through.

Or maybe even if he didn't.

Pauley . . .

Irana was having breakfast in Emily's room when there was a knock on the door. "It's Dardon, Emily," he called. "You have a visitor. Peter Joslyn."

Emily instinctively stiffened.

Irana shook her head as she saw Emily's reaction. "You're the one who said we should work with him, Emily."

"I know." She got up, crossed the room, and opened the door. "Why come to see me, Joslyn?"

"You're the one to whom I owe the most penance," Joslyn said quietly. "May I come in?"

She shrugged. "If you like." She stepped aside. "But it's Irana who Staunton almost shot. I'd say you owe quite a bit to her."

"Is it okay?" Dardon asked Emily. "I didn't want to bother Garrett. He's been with Pauley since dawn, and he's very edgy."

Garrett hadn't been edgy toward Emily

when he'd left early this morning, but he'd been quiet. Very quiet. "It's okay, Dardon."

"Good." He turned away. "Call me if you need me."

Joslyn entered the room, and Emily closed the door. "Yes, I do owe Dr. Povak a great debt," he said as he crossed the room to stand before Irana. "But when the sin is as deep as mine, one doesn't know where to start. I hope you'll let me try to make amends even if you can't forgive me."

Irana studied him, then slowly nodded. "Staunton didn't hurt me, and I believe your friend's death hurt you very much. I'm sorry for your pain. Did you get your wife and children away safely?"

He nodded. "I sent them back to London with an army of guards around them." He paused. "I had to tell them why. They wanted me to come with them. I told them I had reparations to make and that our lives might have to change."

"Really? In what way?" Emily asked coolly.

"I decided that unless we can get Staunton, I'll confess to Dimitri's killing."

"What?" Irana said. "As far as reparations go, that's a little extreme."

"I won't have either of you suffer for it," Joslyn said. "That's what I came to tell you."

"That's very generous, but let's hope it won't be necessary," Irana said. "We have two days to find a solution."

"It's not generous," Joslyn said. "I've always tried to do my duty to God and my family. I failed both in this. I have to do what Dimitri said we should do. I have to make peace." He turned to Emily and said, "You understand. You don't want to let me off easily. I don't want that either."

There was no doubting his sincerity, Emily thought. But sincere or not, he was right. There was no way she would say that he should get off easily. "I've no wish for you to be executed for the bishop's murder. I want Staunton to pay. Yes, you deserve to be punished. But I won't give up Staunton just to see you hurting. You want to help, then let me use the hell out of you."

He nodded. "That goes without saying. Whatever I can do. Babin handled all the dealings with Staunton, so I can't help you locate him." His lips tightened. "I can't tell you how I wish I hadn't trusted Babin. He worked for me since the early days, when I first came to Russia, and never gave me any reason to doubt him. I'd promised Dimitri, and I just wanted the hammer found." He added bitterly, "But I admit to blinding myself until Staunton called me a few days ago. He told me everything that had happened and left me in no doubt that I was to blame for all of it. He said he expected me to continue to fund his search for the hammer."

"And what did you say?"

"I told him to go to hell."

"A little late."

He nodded. "And it probably sparked everything that's been happening since that night. But if we're all targets, perhaps you could stake me out, then—"

"Don't tempt me," Emily said. "But I don't think Staunton would consider you a big enough drawing card. You're not high enough on his list."

"Who is?" Joslyn asked.

She didn't answer. "But you may be able to help in some other way."

"Just let me know. It seems I'm staying here at the hotel. On this floor, actually. Garrett's orders."

She nodded. "Garrett likes to keep us all close. He wants to protect the whole world."

A shadow crossed over Joslyn's face. "Dimitri was like that. It was one of the things I respected most in him." He turned and moved toward the door. "Let me know. I won't refuse you, no matter what it is."

"You didn't answer him," Irana said when the door had closed behind him. "But I could do it for you. You're at the top of Staunton's list."

Emily nodded. "But there's a problem. He wants to take his time with me, and that puts me last in order."

"I don't see that as a problem." She stiffened. "Unless we're talking about drawing Staunton to you. What are you planning, Emily?"

"I don't have a plan."

"Are you telling me the truth?"

"Yes." She looked Irana squarely in the eye. It was the truth. She had nothing as well-defined as a plan. There was only a kernel of an idea that could become one.

"I have no plan. Do you think I don't know that Garrett would never let me do anything like that?"

"I know that you're a determined woman when your mind is made up." Irana said. "Trust me, Emily. I know you think that Garrett and I were a little arbitrary when we teamed up to do what we thought best for you. You're right. But our intentions were good, and if you decide to make a move, don't close me out."

And let Irana put her life on the line again for her? She would never forget that moment in the garden when she had been sure Irana was going to die. "I don't have a plan," she repeated. She poured herself a cup of coffee. "We have to wait for Pauley to come up with something. Then I'm sure Garrett will pull one together. I hope it's soon. I'm getting restless, aren't you?"

Irana nodded, her gaze still fixed on Emily's face. "It's pretty obvious."

"I've always been clear as glass to you," Emily said with affection. "And I've never minded because I knew that whatever you saw, you'd never condemn. That's pretty wonderful, Irana."

"The glass is a little cloudy right now,"

Irana said. "I think that I'll stick around and see if it clears up. If you don't mind?"

"Don't be silly. You're always good company, Irana."

Irana gazed at her for a moment, then said flatly, "I was going to be patient and go along with you until you got around to confiding in me, but that isn't going to happen." She stood up and faced her. "And this is too important to worry about being diplomatic. You're scared about risking Garrett. I can understand that because you care about him. Maybe more than you even realize. You're scared about risking me. You think that you'll be responsible if Staunton hurts me. So that leaves you alone." She shook her head. "I won't let you be alone, Emily. I won't argue with you about keeping Garrett out of it, but I'm going with you. Staunton is an evil man; He hurt you, he hurt me, and he killed the bishop, Nemid, Kafir, your friend, Joel. I'm sure there were many others. I can't let him kill anyone else. Now tell me what we're going to do to get Staunton."

Emily stared at her in despair. She had tried to deceive Irana, but she would not lie. "You don't want to be involved in this, Irana. I've never meant to catch Staunton and put him in a jail somewhere. I wouldn't take the chance of his escaping or getting off on a technicality. I'm going to kill him." She smiled crookedly. "Just as he's going to try to kill me if he gets the chance. He'd rather toy with me for a month or two, but he will kill me if he has no other option."

"Yes, I know." Irana moistened her lips. "He described what he'd do to you in some detail while he was . . . hurting me. I think he thought it would add to the—" She stopped and drew a deep breath. "I don't know if I could kill Staunton. It would be against who and what I am. But I know that I can, in all good conscience, hunt him down and protect you or any other of his victims." She added, "So I repeat, how are we going to get Staunton?"

Emily gazed at her in frustration. She was not going to dissuade her, and there was nothing she could do but accept her help and try to keep them both alive. "I have a chance if I can get him to meet me in the open somewhere. Fields, swamps, or woods with plenty of cover."

"What good would that do?"

"I'm very good in the woods. I used to go on photo expeditions with my father, and we'd spend weeks tracking and setting up for shots." Her lips tightened. "I'd stack my woods savvy against Staunton's any day. Plus, I'm an excellent shot, and my motivation alone should carry the day."

"I can see that it would."

"I'd take two weapons. I'll hide one weapon when I enter the forest in case I might be forced to give up the other." She looked at Irana. "After that, I'll play it by ear. One thing my father taught me was that you could never be sure which way the prey was going to jump."

"Providing you can persuade Staunton to meet you where you want him to meet you."

Emily nodded. "I have a chance. He's hungry. He's arrogant. He thinks of me as the prey. Those are all factors I can manipulate."

"We can manipulate," Irana said. "And I take it that's not the only factor you're hoping to manipulate."

She nodded. "I'll need a car, someone

who knows the city, and someone to watch my back."

"I'll watch your back." Irana tilted her head. "You're going to bring Joslyn into this, aren't you?"

"He has his own car. He's lived in this city for years."

"And you're not opposed to letting him run a little risk."

"Not if it will help me keep Garrett out of it." She paused. "Do you have a problem with that?"

She slowly shook her head. "Joslyn wants to help you. He needs to make amends, and driving a car shouldn't be too dangerous. I'll talk to him."

"Be my guest. But having Joslyn cooperate won't mean a thing unless I find a way to contact Staunton."

"Pauley?" Irana asked.

The key to unlock all doors. "Pauley."

Pauley's hair was rumpled, and his expression was abstracted as he opened his door. "Garrett's not here, Emily. I think he went to see Joslyn."

"I know he did. Irana asked Joslyn to

keep him with him for thirty minutes or so." She came into the room. "How is the work going?"

"Good. It would be better without interruptions," he said pointedly. "I could concentrate."

"I'll just be a moment. How soon before you get Staunton's number?"

"Five, six hours. But it's going to take me a hell of a lot longer to get that satellite fix."

"When you get the number, don't tell Garrett. Give it to me."

The abstraction in his expression became wariness. "Don't tell Garrett? Why not? He pays my salary."

"I just want you to delay telling him for a few hours. You'll still be earning your money." She met his gaze. "And there's no reason for you to do as I ask. I'm not offering you anything. I'm just asking you to do me a favor. I promise it won't hurt Garrett, and it will mean a great deal to me."

"I don't like it," Pauley's expression was skeptical as he gazed at Emily. "And Garrett isn't going to like it either."

"I know," Emily said. "I can't worry about that. I won't let Garrett take any more chances for me. I have to do this myself."

He was silent, studying her. "You're going to go after this Staunton. Garrett would strangle me if I did what you asked. You could get killed."

"I won't get killed. I like life too much. I'll make sure this isn't a suicide mission."

"You'd go alone?"

"No, I'm taking Irana. She won't have it any other way. And Joslyn says he wants to make amends." She smiled crookedly. "I'm going to let him prove it. He's the one person that I won't mind risking."

His brows rose. "You're more ruthless than I thought."

"Where Joslyn is concerned. It will be safer if I have someone who knows the area. Will you help me?"

He tilted his head. "Why do you think I would? As you said, you're not offering me anything."

"I'm taking a chance that there's something that would tip the scales and make you give me what I want. You're an unusual man and wouldn't do it for the usual reasons. You're brilliant, and you can always get money." She grimaced.

"Sex? Not a chance. You like to play at the game, but it's just a game. I saw you with that desk clerk downstairs. It's like the money; you don't have any problem getting it."

"Were you considering it?" He smiled. "Don't give up on that. Maybe I'm just discriminating."

"I did consider it. I'd do anything to keep Garrett safe. Sex? Garrett's life? No contest." She met his gaze. "But that wouldn't tip the balance. You tell me what would."

"I'm a loyal employee. I like Garrett."

"Tell me."

His eyes were suddenly twinkling. "You're a persistent woman. Get thee behind me, Satan."

"There's only one Satan you have to worry about."

"But Garrett won't let me worry about Staunton. He closes me up in this room and makes me delve into boring cyberspace."

Her eyes narrowed on his face. Pauley's expression was now radiating an excitement and vibrancy that was mesmerizing. "I don't believe you find it boring."

"Not generally. But I've been exposed to

something more interesting lately." He dropped down in a chair and spread his legs casually out before him. His shirt was open at the throat, and he reminded Emily vaguely of one of those Regency rakes on the cover of a Pseudo–Georgette Heyer novel; lazy, elegant, slightly wicked. "You see, from the time I was a kid and everyone found out what a whizbang I was at all the mental hijinks I was herded in that direction. I guess I went along with it because I liked to be a star. I don't have the smallest ego in the world."

"Really? I didn't notice."

"You noticed." He grinned. "But you also noticed what a kick I got when Garrett took me hunting. I'm addicted. I liked that rush I felt. It made me want more."

"Is all this going somewhere?"

"Eventually. I liked it, but I'm not good at it." He made a rueful face. "Garrett said he didn't know how Staunton managed to bug that car, but I imagine he's making a good guess. It had to be me that screwed up. I don't even know how I did it. That's a real amateur."

"This isn't a sport, Pauley."

"It felt like one that night. It was like

winning a marathon and going on a king-size drunk at the same time." He shook his head. "But I made a mistake, and I don't like to make mistakes. Particularly ones that put other people in danger. I'm a perfectionist."

"This *is* going somewhere."

"I have to correct my mistake and come out looking like a rock star." He smiled. "Garrett's not going to let me go onstage so the only way I can do it is to go hunting with you and Joslyn."

She frowned. "This isn't what I wanted from you."

"It's what you're getting. You get the information, and you get me with it." He chuckled. "Though I can see you don't want to endanger my valuable hide. I can understand your hesitation. It's like risking damage to a Rembrandt."

"Not quite."

His smile faded. "I won't make another mistake, Emily. You don't have to worry about my being a hindrance."

"I'm not worrying about you making a mistake, dammit."

His smile returned with a radiance that

lit his face with dazzling warmth. "Then I was right. You do like me."

Of course she liked him. He was part Peter Pan and part Pied Piper. Who could help it?

He got to his feet and one finger traced the two frown lines indenting her forehead. "Stop frowning. This is the way it should be. We'll take care of each other. Okay?"

It wasn't okay, but it was the only way she was going to get his help. She sighed. "Okay."

He turned her around and pushed her toward the door. "Now out with you. I'm getting excited about finishing this so that we can hit the road."

She wasn't excited, she was distinctly on edge, she thought as she went down the hall. Now she had to worry about not only Staunton, but Irana and keeping Pauley from trying to push his limits so that he could reach his idiotic goal of perfection.

But at least it would be Pauley she was worrying about and not Garrett.

———

What the hell had that been about? Garrett wondered, as he left Joslyn's room. He had thought when Joslyn called him that he might be able to tell him something more about Staunton, but he had come up with zilch.

Joslyn had just repeated his apologies and asked him innumerable questions about Pauley's work and how Garrett intended to use it. He'd had trouble breaking away from him.

"You're frowning." Dardon was coming down the hall toward him. "Isn't Pauley doing well?"

"When doesn't he do well? It's only a question of time." He jerked his head toward Joslyn's room. "No, it's Joslyn. I felt as if I was being interrogated. In the politest possible way, of course. But he doesn't impress me as being the nervous type who needs reassuring."

"You think he may be striking a deal with Staunton?"

"I don't think so." But thinking didn't cut it, he had to be sure. "We'll have to keep a close eye on Joslyn."

"How close?"

"Use your own judgment. He may be a weak link."

Dardon grimaced. "And that means I'm responsible if that weak link breaks."

"Exactly."

"Great," Dardon said sourly as he turned and headed for the elevator.

Garrett was passing Emily's door, and he hesitated. He hadn't been back to her room since he'd left early this morning, and he wanted to see her, touch her.

More, he wanted to break through that barrier that he'd sensed she was building.

No, he had tried to do that last night and had not succeeded. There was no time to waste on a futile effort. He needed to get back to Pauley and push him to his limits. Once they got Staunton, everything else would fall into place.

Providing he could manage to do that in time.

Pauley knocked on Emily's door at just before seven-thirty that evening. "Here it is." He handed her a piece of paper. "I've got to get back to my room. I told Garrett that I needed to take a walk around the hotel to get away from the work for a while." He grimaced. "He wanted to send someone along in case I ran into trouble. Does that tell you how little he trusts me?" He glanced at the paper. "Well, I guess he can't trust me. But not in that way. I can take care of myself." He turned. "I'll keep Garrett working with me until I hear from you. Call me when you're ready to move."

She looked down at the numbers on the paper as she slowly closed the door. She was feeling suddenly cold with dread. She could change her mind. She didn't have to contact Staunton right now. She could go on with Garrett's plan.

No, she couldn't. She couldn't risk Garrett ever again.

She sat down and reached for her phone. Okay, get it clear before she talked to him. How was she going to handle him? The principal goal was to set it up for tonight, and in her choice of location.

What was she thinking? There was no way she could plan anything. Just hearing Staunton's voice blasted her emotions. Just go by instinct. Her hand was shaking, and she steadied it before she dialed the number.

It rang four times before the phone was answered.

"Emily?" Staunton sounded startled.

"Yes."

"What an unexpected pleasure. You must have enlisted exceptional help to have located my number. Of course, I was tempted not to answer, but I couldn't resist. However, I'm going to call you back so that you can't trace me. I'll feel safer on my line." The call was abruptly cut off.

But he called back almost immediately. "Now we can talk. What little scheme have you concocted to try to sting me? Is Garrett there at your elbow?"

"No," she said. "I'm alone."

He was silent a moment. "I believe you're telling the truth. I know you'd lie to me if you could, but I'd know. I learned too much about you during our weeks together. I studied every tone of your voice, every expression of your face."

"Because you wanted to know where that damn hammer was."

He was silent. "Yes, of course, that was it. It was necessary. But it became an intense kind of pleasure."

"You're sick."

"That's been brought to my attention. But those who accused me of crossing that line are fools, and I'm the one who will have the power to crush them all."

"You sound like Mikhail Zelov."

"He knew about power. Even blocked by historical events, he still managed to come out on top. Not an emperor, but a very rich man." He chuckled. "And I may be able to go even higher. There are places in this world where a man can become whatever he wants to be. A new face, a new identity, and a billion dollars. What could be sweeter?"

"But you don't have the hammer that has that final amulet. And we have both Nemid's amulet and the two that were in Babin's safe."

"Before I bargained with Nemid, I had that amulet photographed and had a complete 3-D facsimile made of it. Do you think I'd let it out of my hands if I wasn't sure I wasn't losing anything? I promised Babin I'd steal it back, but I wouldn't have had to do it. And I did the same with the other two amulets Babin was holding. He never knew that I was as familiar with the contents of his safe as he was. I knew everything he knew, had everything in my possession that he had. As for the hammer . . ." His voice lowered to softness. "Zelov swore that it had magic properties for him, that it would bring him good fortune. Well, I'm like Zelov. I think the hammer is only waiting for me to find it. It will come to me."

"And you want me to help."

"I want *you*."

"Then I'll come to you and let you try to get me."

"A trap."

"No, but I've realized that this can't go on. I can't stand looking over my shoulder any longer. You're like a nightmare, and I have to get rid of you. I'll choose an open place where you'll feel safe."

"No, I'll choose. . . . If I decide that I'm going to let you lure me into your clutches. The idea is . . . interesting."

"I don't care where it is, but I want it to be in the country or the woods, a place for me to run, not be caught like a mouse in a trap. I want my chance at you."

"Now you're being demanding."

"You said that you wanted me to be last. Well, that's too bad. You can work on everyone else on your list later. I came first. You kept me in that hut and nearly drove me insane. Everything else came afterward. One way or the other, I'm coming after you tonight."

"Tonight? You are eager. I'll have to think about it." He was silent. "No Garrett?"

"No. Joslyn will be coming with me."

"Joslyn," he repeated. "Actually, he was next on my list. He came before you, Emily. You might say he led the way to you. I'd think that you'd feel a bit uncomfortable hobnobbing with him."

"On the contrary, I feel very comfortable under these circumstances. He's expendable."

"Expendable? What a delight you are. You're the most interesting combination of ruthlessness and softness on the face of the earth. You'd sacrifice poor Joslyn on Garrett's altar?"

She didn't deny it. "He offered. I don't think you'll be alone."

"Oh, no. I'll have Borg, who is much more talented than Joslyn at this kind of thing. I don't regard that bleeding heart Joslyn as a threat. No one else?"

She hesitated. If she wasn't honest with

him, it might blow everything. "Irana. Mark Pauley."

"Dear Sister Irana? I must have made a great impression on her to make her want more. Pauley . . . Oh, yes, I'm familiar with him. I investigated him after I found he was part of your little group. By all means, let's see if he's improved since he let me plant that bug on your car." His tone was amused. "You must have wanted to make me feel very safe. You've surrounded your-self with useless ineffectuals."

"You won't find me ineffectual, Staunton."

"I hope not. I always knew you'd be a challenge if you were ever in a position to make your presence felt."

"Then you agree?"

"Perhaps. I'll let you know tomorrow."

"It has to be tonight or not at all." She *had* to persuade him. "It's your best bet, dammit. You may consider Joslyn and Pauley ineffectual, but you know that Gar-rett or Dardon will cause you big trouble. I can't hold Garrett off after tonight."

"And you don't want him involved." Staunton's tone was malicious. "I knew that you'd react that way when I told you what I was planning on doing to him when I got my chance. It was bound to torture you and set you in a panic. I know you so well, Emily. Tell me, do you fuck him?"

"You don't know me at all. The only passion Garrett and I share is the desire to rid you from the face of the earth."

"I think there's more than that. I can't tell you how that will add to my pleasure."

"Wouldn't it be strange if I actually managed to take you down before you got the chance to hurt him? Think about it. I put a bullet in you at the silo, and you haven't managed to touch me since that hut in the mountains."

"I could have touched you." A hint of annoyance edged his voice. "It wasn't my choice.

"Then why are you hesitating now? I think you're lying."

He didn't speak for an instant, and Emily could almost sense his rage. "I didn't want to hurry. I wanted at least a week with you. But I can make a day seem like a week. Come and play, Emily."

Move quickly. Don't let him change his mind. "Where?"

"Tell that do-gooder Joslyn to bring you

to his favorite monastery. I'll be in the woods in the mountains behind it." He hung up.

It was done.

Emily drew a deep, shaky breath as she hung up the phone. She felt limp with relief. She hadn't been sure until the last minute that he'd agree to meet with her in a place where she had a chance. She would bet she could function in that forest better than Staunton. It might be her main advantage.

Monastery?

He'd seemed sure that Joslyn would know the place. She hoped he was right. She had no time for puzzles. She had no time for anything if she was going to get out of the hotel before Garrett came back to the room. She called Joslyn. "Go down to your car in the parking lot. I'll be there in five minutes." She phoned Irana. "Now, Irana." She hung up and went to the small duffel she'd packed earlier in the evening. It contained her Glock, the Magnum she'd taken from Garrett's case, and the infrared detector she'd seen Garrett use at Nemid's.

She hesitated as she reached the door. She didn't really want to call Pauley.

She had made a deal, dammit. She had to keep her part of the bargain.

She phoned Pauley's number. "Joslyn and I are on our way. Come if you can make it."

She hung up the phone.

Dear Lord, she hoped he couldn't make it, that he was so tied up with Garrett that he couldn't break free.

He would be another target, and Staunton would go after him with the same viciousness he'd shown any prey.

TWENTY-ONE

"Monitor that program for me, will you? I'll be back in fifteen minutes," Pauley told Garrett as he headed for the door. "I just need to go downstairs and get a snack. I haven't had anything since breakfast. Do you want anything?"

"No, why didn't you get something when you went for your walk?"

But Pauley was gone.

Garrett checked the computer. There was a program running as Pauley had said. That was a little weird. It wasn't like him to let anyone else monitor his work.

That wasn't all that was weird. Garrett

had been aware of restlessness, a sort of suppressed excitement brewing just below the surface all day.

No, not all day. Just since Garrett had returned from talking to Joslyn this afternoon.

A connection?

Perhaps. The possibility was enough to make him uneasy.

Screw Pauley's program. Garrett headed for the door to go after him.

His phone rang as he reached the elevator.

Dardon.

"Look, I may be out of line, but I thought you should know. I'm down in the lobby and I just saw Emily going out the front entrance."

"What?"

"You didn't know? I didn't think you'd let her go out without having me trail behind to protect her."

"Hell, no. Catch up with her. See if you can stop her. I'll be right down." He whirled and ran down the corridor and threw open the door to Emily's room. He called Irana's room as he checked for Emily's duffel.

Irana wasn't answering.

Emily's duffel, where she kept her gun, was missing.

Shit. He whirled and headed back toward the elevator.

He was going over the sequence of events of the afternoon. Joslyn's calling Garrett and asking to see him. The visit that had yielded nothing important except Joslyn's repeated apologies, which had struck Garrett as a little out of character.

Pauley's odd attitude and his leaving the room twice within a three-hour period.

Irana's not answering her phone.

Why the hell hadn't Emily waited? Yes, he'd done the wrong things, said the wrong things. He hadn't been able to help himself. He'd been almost as scared then as he was now.

Because that bastard Staunton had put her through hell and watched her writhe in pain.

And he wanted to do it all over again.

Keep calm. Keep cool. He wouldn't be able to think if he let emotion riot through him.

Now the only thing that was important was to find Emily before that son of a bitch killed her.

"Monastery?" Emily asked Joslyn as he drove the car around the corner. "Do you know what he meant?"

"Yes," Joslyn said. "The monastery Ganina Yama. It's the monastery that was built over the mineshaft where the bodies of the royal family were thrown after they were assassinated."

"Why did he say it was one of your favorite places?"

"I contribute to their charities. Dimitri always felt that the Church should have done more to protect Nicholas and his family. I didn't know that Staunton was even aware that I did it."

"It doesn't surprise me," Irana said. "Staunton seems to have developed a fascination for everything connected with Zelov and his history. He has a voracious appetite for gore and death."

"And where do we go after we reach this monastery?" Pauley asked. "I assume we're not attacking the monks."

"He said the woods in the mountains in back of the monastery," Emily said. "That's the Ural Mountains, Joslyn?"

"Yes," Joslyn said. "I'll go with you no matter what you decide. I owe it to you. But I can see that this isn't going to be simple. How do you intend to do it?"

"He wants me. But he doesn't want me dead. Not yet. I'm counting on using that." She showed them the infrared detector. "And I may be able to find them before they find Irana and me."

"I know that gadget," Pauley said. "Garrett used it at Babin's place. I found it very comforting."

"I'm sure you did."

"Irana and you?" Joslyn asked.

"Your part ends when you drop us off at the monastery. I'll use either of you if I have to do it, but you may be more of a hindrance than a help." Pauley was looking at her, and she said, "This isn't some kind of lark. I don't want you dead, Pauley. I don't want anyone dead but Staunton."

"That's very kind," Pauley said. "But I really think I can make a contribution. "

"Irana is the only one who goes in the woods with me. Staunton won't look upon her as a threat. If I show up with you and Joslyn, it will be the quickest way to have

Staunton on offense. He wants to take me alive, and he'll think I'm vulnerable if Irana and I are alone in the forest."

"He'll be right," Joslyn said. "The woods at night . . ." He shook his head. "It can be very intimidating."

"I'm not as vulnerable as he thinks," Emily said. "I practically grew up in the woods. It's an advantage, and the fact that Staunton doesn't know I have it makes it more valuable."

"You intend to track Staunton?" Pauley asked skeptically.

"Yes. But it may end up with letting him track us. There's not a chance he won't know when we enter those woods. I'll just make sure I lose him right away so that I have a chance once he pounces." She turned to Joslyn. "How long until we get there?"

"Another twenty minutes."

"Park on the road at least five minutes' walk from the monastery." Her palms were moist with sweat as she clutched the duffel holding the guns.

It was coming closer. Staunton was coming closer.

Irana reached out and took Emily's hand. "It will be okay, Emily. I feel it."

"Yes." Her hand tightened on Irana's. She mustn't be afraid. This was the moment she had been working toward.

Staunton . . .

Dardon was waiting for Garrett when he reached the lobby. "She was gone when I ran outside. And Joslyn's car is gone from the parking lot. How bad is it? Is Joslyn working with Staunton?"

"No, I think he's only doing what Emily asked him to do. He told me that he wanted to make amends. So he decides to take Emily right into the lion's mouth," Garrett said. "That's not what I call amends. Emily is calling the shots with all of them. Irana, Pauley, Joslyn . . ." He glanced at Dardon as he headed for the front entrance. "Tell me that we've got a chance of tailing them."

Dardon nodded. "You said you didn't trust Joslyn. I knew my ass was on the line. I bugged his car right after you talked to me." He pulled out a black monitor and checked the red light. "About two miles north of here."

Relief poured through Garrett. At least something was going right. "Good man. Let's get going."

"She's coming, Zelov," Staunton murmured. "I can feel it." He peered into the shadowy darkness of the forest around him. Shadows. Yes, this forest, these mountains, even that monastery built to whitewash the massacre, were full of shadows. Mikhail Zelov had cast those giant shadows, and the fools didn't even realize it. Staunton realized it, and it made him feel closer to Zelov. Not that Staunton wouldn't cast even greater shadows than Rasputin's master when he hit his stride.

"A car is parked down the road." Borg was hurrying back toward him. "Emily Hudson and Irana Povak got out and are heading toward the woods. What do you want me to do?"

Pauley caught up with Emily and Irana as they reached the forest line. "I've decided I'm going with you."

"The hell you are," Emily said. "You have to be quiet in the woods. You'll tramp around and Staunton will be on us. Go back to Joslyn."

"I didn't come because I wanted to protect Joslyn." His expression was uncharacteristically sober in the moonlight. "After all, I have an investment here. You wouldn't have been able to save Irana if it hadn't been for me. I don't want all my work to go down the tubes. And I . . . like you, Emily. I want to help."

"And you want to experience something new and different."

"That, too. But I'm not altogether shallow." He suddenly smiled. "Just bits and pieces of me. What can you expect? I need to stretch myself. I think that being your sidekick might do the trick. I have a gun, and I'll use it." He made a face. "Though I'm not experienced at stuff like that. Tell me what to do, and I'll do it."

He really meant it, she thought in frustration. If she hadn't been so tense, she would have been touched. "I'm telling you to go back to Joslyn, Pauley. Take care of him and yourself. I don't want Staunton to take any more lives than he has already. I don't know what we're going to face. If

Staunton has more than a couple men, I'm not going to be stupid. We may need a way to get out of here fast. The best way you can help me is to make sure I have it."

"I don't want to—"

She stared him in the eye. "You said you wouldn't say no to anything."

He hesitated. "I don't like it." He turned back toward the road. "But you'll have your way out. You be careful, Emily."

She didn't watch him leave, but glided quickly into the forest. "Come on, Irana. Stay close."

"Oh, I will. I'm better on the beach than I am in the woods."

Emily stopped as soon as she reached the shelter of the trees. She could almost hear her father. *Listen. Watch the bushes for any movement.*

Was Staunton close?

She took out the infrared detector. Squirrels. Perhaps possums. No sign of any large life-forms.

"He's not anywhere near, Irana," she whispered. "We have to go deeper." She moved slowly forward.

Walk softly, her father had always told her. Most animals have better hearing than we could dream of having. Learn to walk on the balls of your feet and watch the path to make sure you don't break a branch or even brush against a shrub.

I'm trying, Daddy. It's been a long time. I'm trying.

And it was all coming back to her. She stood still again, using the infrared detector to scan the darkness. Nothing close except small animals.

"The gun," Irana reminded softly. "You said you wanted to hide one of the guns. Do you want me to do it?"

"That fir tree." Emily moved farther into the woods and found a path winding snakelike through the forest. She placed the Glock beside the fir tree and covered it with leaves. Then she checked the Magnum she'd taken from Garrett's suitcase. "I'm surprised Staunton hasn't made a move yet. I was expecting—"

A shot shattered the silence!

"Down." Emily instinctively fell to her knees before she realized that the shot had come from behind them, from the direction where they'd parked the car.

"Pauley?" Irana whispered. "Could Staunton have—

"I'm betting that Staunton's still here in the forest," Emily said. "And he sent someone to get rid of Pauley and Joslyn."

"Only one shot." Irana voice was tense. "Joslyn or Pauley?"

Emily's gaze flew to Irana's face. Irana was looking back, her expression as tense and concerned as her voice. She wanted to go to them, help them.

As it was right for her to do, Emily thought.

"Go and find out," Emily said. "Circle around and see if you can help either one of them."

"No," Irana's protest was startled. "I'm staying with you."

"Why? You're no good here, Irana." She smiled with an effort. "You're making too much noise. You'll give me away to Staunton."

Irana's gaze was searching Emily's face. "Is that the truth?"

"Yes. And you know if anything goes wrong, Staunton will use you against me. Just as he tried to do before." She added, "You've done your part. You've helped us, you found out what we needed from the bishop, you've persuaded Joslyn to bring

me here, you've watched my back just as
you said you would, but now it's time you
left me. We all have our skills, but you're
not a soldier, you're a caretaker. You told
me that yourself."

"I don't want you to be alone."

"I know, but you'd do better doing what
you do best. You're a doctor. Someone
may need you back there. Circle around
the clearing and make sure it's safe before
you go to them." She grimaced. "Safe? No
one's safe tonight. I may be wrong. I may
be sending you straight to Staunton."

"But I'm not helping you here." Irana
nodded slowly. "Yes, I can see that."

"Do what you do best," Emily repeated.
"And do it quickly." She got to her feet.
"Be careful, Irana."

"God bless, Emily."

Emily moved swiftly away from her
through the forest. She hoped that Irana
had turned and was going back toward the
clearing. There was danger all around
them, but Staunton was the primary threat,
and Emily had a gut instinct that he was
here in the woods.

She glanced over her shoulder. Irana
was nowhere in sight.

Keep safe, my friend.

She was a hundred yards deeper into the forest but there was still no sign of Staunton. Was he there, watching her, letting her come closer before he pounced?

No, she trusted her training and her instincts. She would have heard him, sensed him.

Another fifty yards, and she used the detector again.

She stiffened. That was no small animal. It was a single large figure straight ahead.

She drew her gun and moved slowly forward.

"Are you out there, Emily?" Staunton called. "I can't hear you, but I can feel you. I'll always be able to sense you near me. When two people are as close as we are, that's the way it will always be."

She froze. Was he taking a wild gamble or did he really know—

"I'll give you two minutes to give up, then I'll start spraying this entire area with bullets. I have my AK-47. It will take you down before you can get near me."

AK-47. Yes, she'd seen what that attack weapon could do at the scene of the ambush in Afghanistan. He might be lying, but she had seen him carry it frequently when he was moving around the compound. A handgun would be worse than useless against it. She had known that he might do something to weigh the odds to his side.

Unless she could take him by surprise.

And she had already set the surprise in motion when she had hidden the Glock by the fir tree.

"One minute," Staunton called. "I don't want to cut you in two with those bullets, Emily. It's messy and totally unsatisfying."

She strode quickly toward the sound of his voice.

"Emily."

She stopped. "I'm on the path."

"Good, you're being smart. Stay where you are. I'm going to take a look before I come out in the open. I want to make sure you're not being too smart."

She stood straight, staring straight ahead. She could feel him looking at her. He was right, that repulsive closeness was like a bond linking them.

"Hello, Emily." Staunton strolled out of the shrubs, cradling the AK-47 in his arm.

There was a thick bandage on his right shoulder, but it didn't seem to be hindering him. "Now stand very still while I search you. You've got to have a weapon."

"Of course, I do." She stood still, gritting her teeth as his hands moved over her. He found the gun in her jacket and stepped back. "How else could I hope to kill you?"

He chuckled. "But it's not doing you any good now, is it? Now where is Sister Irana? Borg saw her enter the forest with you. I'm not really worried that she may leap out and attack me. She's one of those do-gooders who will always be a victim."

"When we heard the shot, she went back to see if she could help."

"There won't be anyone left alive to help. Borg will see to that. All that will be left is for her to pray over their bodies." His lips curled viciously. "Stupid bitch."

"She's not stupid." She studied his expression. "And I don't believe you think she is. But you're very angry with her. Why would a 'do-gooder' manage to disturb you that much?"

"She didn't disturb me. I told her that I was the one who called the shots. I was the one who made people afraid.

"And did you make Irana afraid?"

"Of course, I did. She just pretended that she wasn't afraid. She had to be afraid. I hurt her, then I hurt her again. I kept hurting her, and all she did was look up at me with those big dark eyes as if she was seeing right through me. Stupid bitch."

"I think she probably was seeing through you, Staunton." She paused. "You might have hurt her, but she beat you."

"You're crazy."

"No, she saw you for what you are, and she didn't let what you are really touch her. She beat you."

"No, if I'd had time I'd have—" He stopped. "But I will have time if Borg doesn't kill her. I'll have both of you. It was kind of you to bring her with you. Of course, I'm disappointed you didn't bring Garrett. I didn't think you'd pull Garrett into the fray. Though he might come calling anyway. He appears to be quite devoted, by the extreme lengths he's taking to protect you."

"You killed his friend, Karif."

"That's true. Karif was very difficult to break. But Garrett was involved with you before I eliminated that Afghan. He's going to be very disappointed that I snatched you away from him. I half expect him to come swooping down to rescue you." He smiled. "But you chose not to bring in the big guns. I knew you would. That's why I took the opportunity when you offered it. It was too good a chance to pass up. I can always get Garrett later. You'll make excellent bait to lure him."

Bait. Yes, Garrett would come after her. He probably was trying to find her now. The idea sent panic racing through her.

She had to get this over before he found a way to do it.

"The blip stopped," Dardon said. "Joslyn must have reached his destination."

"How far?" Garrett asked.

"A few miles to the northwest—3.5 to be exact." He frowned. "It could be—"

"What?" Garrett said.

"I'm not certain. But it could be the monastery."

"Why here, Staunton?" Emily asked, her gaze going to the looming monastery barely visible in the distance through the trees. "Is it supposed to make me think of those poor victims who were thrown down that shaft? Some kind of mind game?"

"I do like mind games. But actually, I've been here a few times since I came back to Russia." He gazed up at the mountains. "It was the site of one of Zelov's biggest defeats. I can see him going down into the waters at the bottom of the mine shaft, searching for that last amulet. Maybe I wanted to prove that I could do better. A sort of encore performance. Yes, I do feel a deep sense of competitiveness with Zelov. In fact, before I take you to a cottage near here to commence our final relationship, we'll go to the museum where Zelov discovered that the Tsar had hidden his hammer. Another defeat for him. I want you to be there and see that place, too. I think you should know what a failure he was in comparison to me. Wouldn't that be amusing?"

"I know you're a sadistic bastard, but I didn't think that Mikhail Zelov had that deep an influence on you."

"Oh, he did. He inspired me with a strange mixture of admiration and jealousy. When I was reading his *Book of Living,* I felt as if I was the one who was pulling the strings of all those fancy people in that Imperial Court. At first, I was only going to be a man for hire for Babin. I was just curious about what was behind this entire search for a hammer. So I broke into Babin's safe and made my copies of Zelov's book and all three amulets. I saw what a man could accomplish if he was bold enough."

"Or evil enough."

"Evil is always subjective, according to Zelov's bible. And that was what his *Book of Living* was all about, you know. He set himself up to be a god. So he had to have a bible. He just didn't quite get there."

"Thanks to Bishop Nartova."

"Yes, it's very curious. Zelov and I seem to be traveling on the same path with similar obstacles. But I'm stronger than Zelov. You saw that Bishop Dimitri didn't have a chance against me."

"I saw that you murdered a defenseless old man. Did it make you feel brave?"

"No, it made me feel like a god. Zelov had the right idea." He took a step closer to her. "But I didn't have time to really enjoy it. But I will with you, Emily." He reached out and touched her cheek. "So brave to come alone."

"I didn't come alone. Don't touch me."

His finger remained on her cheek. "You might as well have come alone. Joslyn, Pauley, and Sister Irana will be nothing for me to get rid of. Borg's probably taken one of them down already."

"I'm surprised you have someone as loyal to you as Borg. But then he has the same killer instincts, doesn't he?"

"Yes, he's been useful. I'll be sorry to have to dispose of him when this is over."

"Even Borg?"

"He's a witness. I kept as much as I could from him, but he still knows too much. But I don't want to talk about Borg. He'll do his job. I'm too absorbed with you, my Emily."

He was so certain that it sent a chill through her.

"And you're absorbed with me," he said softly. "I can feel your fear. It's making me hard. I don't really like to fuck women, but you've always been the exception. I'd finish with Levy for the day and come in and sit beside you and talk to you, watch you. It was the most exquisite sexual thrill I'd ever known. You've become quite the obsession to me."

Her stomach was churning. "Take your hand away."

"Presently." His head bent and his lips were hovering over hers. "Do you know what I'll do if you bite me this time? I've thought of many new things I could do to Garrett that I never tried on Levy."

"You won't be able to touch Garrett."

His tongue touched her lower lip. "Then bite me, Emily. Sink your teeth into me and show me that—

Another shot rang out!

She jerked away from him, her gaze flying in the direction from where the sound had come. The clearing again.

"It's just Borg," Staunton said. "That's number two. I wonder who he took down this time. Joslyn or Pauley? Or maybe it was your friend, Irana. Well, it doesn't matter who went down. Borg will keep on going until they're all dead. He has his orders. That's another two off my list. Soon you'll be truly alone, Emily."

Dear God, she hoped he wasn't right, that Borg hadn't killed them. "You can't be sure of that."

"Yes, I can. Borg is very good. I trained him."

"All these deaths, and for nothing. You can't even be sure you'll find that hammer."

He smiled. "I told you, it will come to me."

He was so damn positive. "Not from me. I never knew where it was, and I still don't."

"But it's so enjoyable to probe and dig." He nudged her down the path. "My car is on the road a few miles from where you parked. Now I think we'd better go and get to a more comfortable place to continue our discussion. I don't know if the good monks might have heard those shots."

It was almost time to make the break. The gun was by the fir tree several yards down the path. Try to be meek and cooperative. Or maybe not. Make him angry? Anything to distract him.

"Probe and dig? Is that what you call what you did to Joel?"

"It's as good a term as any for one of my favorite pastimes. Of course this time it lacked the icing on the cake."

"And what was that?"

"Purpose." His hand was beneath her elbow as he urged her forward. "That's why having you there made it more tolerable."

"I don't know what—" She stopped as his meaning hit home with massive force. Her body arched as if he'd struck her spine with a crowbar.

Oh, my God.

Why now? Garrett had said. *Why get rid of everyone now? It doesn't make sense.*

"I'm not worried; the hammer will come to me."

"It lacked the icing on the cake . . . purpose."

She whirled to face him. "You *have* it. You already have the hammer. That's why you think it's time to get rid of everyone who knows about it. You have what you want, and now you want to get rid of the witnesses to keep yourself safe."

"Do I?" His question was as faintly mocking as his expression.

"You know you do. And you want me to know it, or you wouldn't have been throwing out hints."

He inclined his head. "I admit I gave in to temptation. It's frustrating, no one knowing how clever I am. I was tempted to tell you when we were together before, but there was just the faintest chance someone would whisk you away from me."

"You have it." The monstrous truth was unfolding in horrible waves. Her throat was so tight that she could barely get the words out. "And you had the hammer for all those days when you were torturing Joel and asking me over and over where it was."

He nodded. "Oh yes, from the very first day. When I went back to the museum, I didn't find the hammer with the rest of the tools, but it was in a shack in the back."

"Why?" The ugliness was totally incomprehensible. "For God's sake, why?"

"I wasn't ready to make a move. I needed Babin's money to keep pouring into my bank account so that I could build up a reserve. Finding the Tsar's fortune would only be the start. I'd have to set up a system to protect it, launder it, and disappear until I was ready to make my move. As long as Babin thought I was still trying to locate the hammer, then he'd keep funding me. He didn't trust me worth a damn, so I knew I had to make it appear absolutely authentic. I was right; he even came to the mountains to check on me. But he went away convinced."

On the day that he'd tortured Joel so terribly that she'd had to block it out of her memory. She stared at him in disbelief. "You're a monster."

He nodded with satisfaction. "But monsters control the world. Haven't you noticed?"

The hatred was flaming through her veins. For an instant, she couldn't even see him through the red haze. "You did that to Joel just to—"

"I thought it would upset you to know. Though I don't know why it would make a difference. Why should you care why? It's the act, not the motive, that counts."

"Yes, it's the act that counts." She turned and strode down the path. A few more yards, and she'd be even with the fir tree. "But I believe that you may have reached your goal in besting Mikhail Zelov. I'm not sure anyone else could ever be that evil and corrupt." She was right next to the tree. She could see the pile of leaves under which she'd hidden the gun. "You're beyond belief."

"You'll believe. It will just take a little more effort on my part. I intend to—"

She dove sideways and grabbed the Glock as she hit the ground. She got off a shot as she rolled behind the tree.

She heard Staunton cursing, then a spray of bullets spiked against the bark of the tree. "Bitch."

Her shot hadn't struck him, dammit. She risked a glance.

He wasn't there.

Panic soared through her. Was he in the trees across the path, or had he dived into the brush on this side? She couldn't take a chance. She had to move.

"You're not going to get away," Staunton said. "You're foolish to even try."

He was to her left. She crawled into the shrubbery to her right, rose to a half crouch. "I don't want to get away. I'm going to kill you, Staunton."

Bullets plowed into the earth at her feet. Close. Very close.

Don't talk to him.

Don't give him a target.

She tossed a rock into the bushes across the path and watched the shrubbery torn away by a barrage of bullets.

Where had the shots come from? She looked at the angle of the torn-away bushes. To the north of her.

Maybe. It had been years since she had read those forest signs with her father.

She moved warily, with painstaking care.

A branch broke under her foot, and she dove forward and to the right.

Bullets tore into the spot where she'd stood only seconds before.

She scrambled backward and to the left.

Okay, this was taking too long, and Staunton was too good.

She had to put an end to it.

The oak tree two yards away. There was a branch about fifteen feet above the ground that had a decent leaf cover.

Now no sound at all. No mistakes as she moved toward the tree. Silence and smoothness so as not to disturb the prey. Help me, Daddy.

She paused two yards from the tree, reached down, and grabbed a branch. She took a deep breath and threw the branch at a shrub that was close but not too close to the tree she'd chosen.

Bullets plowed into the shrub seconds after the branch hit.

She cried out as if in pain even as she dove for the trunk of the oak tree. Her heart was pounding as she shinnied with frantic speed up the tree. Dear God, she hoped there weren't birds or squirrels that would be set off by her movements.

"Emily?"

Another few feet and she'd reach the branch.

"Emily? I do hope you're only wounded. I have such fine plans for you."

She wriggled beneath the leaf cover on the limb and drew her gun out of her jacket.

Come and get me, bastard. I'm waiting for you.

"I'll be most displeased if you've forced me to kill you. I've waited such a long time to be with you." He was moving, circling around through the trees to her left. "Though I can accept wounds if they're inflicted by me."

Take shallow breaths. He mustn't even hear me breathe.

She could see a faint trembling of the shrubs several yards away. He was being careful. Probably scanning the area where he'd heard her cry out. Should she take her shot now?

No, the brushes weren't shaking any longer.

Where was he?

"I hear you moving, you little whore." Staunton moved out of the brush, his gaze on the path. "How did you get across the path?"

Across the path? She thought in bewilderment.

Then she froze as she heard it, too. Footsteps in the brush across the way. Clumsy footsteps. Who . . .

A strangled cry.

Her gaze flew back to Staunton.

Garrett!

Garrett was behind Staunton his arm around his neck. Staunton's AK-47 had dropped to the ground. But even as she watched, Staunton was reaching for a knife in his belt.

No!

She raised her gun and aimed. Not the head, it was too close to Garrett. The heart or stomach. But what if the bullet went through his body and struck Garrett?

Staunton had the knife out and was plunging it into Garrett's arm.

Garrett flinched, but then ignored it as if he hadn't felt it, his arm tightening and jerking back, the blood pouring over Staunton's throat.

Blood.

Garrett's blood. Joel's blood.

No more blood, Staunton.

"Let him go, Garrett," she called. "Dammit, let him go."

Garrett's grasp loosened for an instant as his gaze rose to the branch where she was hidden.

Staunton tore away and his knife plunged toward Garrett again.

She pulled the trigger.

She watched Staunton arch as the bullet struck his body. She fired again, and he slumped to the ground. And then again. Was he dead? Please, let him be dead.

She had to be sure.

"Emily." Garrett was watching her slide down from the tree. "Are you okay?"

She ignored the question. "Watch him." It didn't seem possible that she had actually brought Staunton down. All the weeks, the searching, the agony . . .

She jumped the rest of the way to the ground and crossed to where Staunton lay. "I have to be sure." She turned Staunton over. His blood was bubbling from the two wounds in his chest and a faint line was trickling from the side of his mouth. At first, she thought he was dead, but he slowly opened his eyes. "Emily . . ." Then, incredibly he smiled. "I won't die, you know. Zelov never really died, and neither will I. You can't beat us. Zelov and I are invincible. I'll get well and come back, and I'll do whatever . . . I wish with you."

"You're dying now. You probably only have a few more minutes." She stared into his eyes. "And if I thought any differently, I'd put another bullet in your head. I may still do it."

"Would you?" For an instant he looked uncertain. "But that isn't how—" His expression became twisted, ugly. "No, I won't die. I'm going to live. I'm going to be so rich, I'll be a god. Like Zelov. Only better. Better . . ." He suddenly arched upward, his eyes glazing over. "No!"

"Give up, Staunton."

"I won't—I'm going to—"

He screamed and slumped backward.

He was dead.

Garrett's hand grasped her shoulder. "He's gone, Emily."

She knew that he was gone, but she couldn't stop staring at the ugliness still imprinted on his face, even in death.

"Let him go," Garrett said.

Something warm and liquid was dripping on her shoulder.

Blood. Garrett's blood.

The knowledge jarred her, and she shook her head to clear it. She jumped to her feet and took his arm in both her hands. "How bad, is it?"

"Flesh wound. But it hurts like hell."

"It's almost stopped bleeding. But it's going to have to be stitched."

"Be quiet." He took her in his arms. "Just be quiet for a minute. Okay? I need this."

She needed it, too. "You shouldn't have been here."

"You're wrong. I had the right to be here. I should have been here sooner, dammit."

"No, I was the one who—I could have handled it." But, Lord, it had been close. "I didn't want you—"

"Is she all right?" She looked up to see Pauley coming across the path. "I know you told me to stay over there, Garrett, but she's covered with blood. I'm damn good at first aid. I saw a whole series about it on the Learning Channel."

"It's Garrett's blood." She looked down at Staunton. "And maybe a little of his."

"I think it's too late for first aid on him," Pauley said, staring at Staunton. "He's the bad guy?"

"Yes," she said. "And, yes, Staunton was definitely the bad guy." She wearily brushed the hair away from her face. "I'm glad to see you, Pauley. When I heard those shots, I thought Borg had killed both you and Joslyn."

"Was that his name? He shot Joslyn. He was there before I knew it. I was in the woods on guard when I heard the shot. I circled around and came back and shot Borg." He shook his head. "It gave me a very weird . . . feeling. I'll have to think about it."

"Is Joslyn dead?"

"No, but he's pretty bad. Irana showed up right after I killed Borg, and she's working on Joslyn, trying to keep him alive.

Dardon is helping her. Garrett told me to come with him when he took off after you. I was to be the decoy while he went in for the kill."

"Irana is safe?"

"Yes," Garrett said. "No more talk. It can wait until later." He took her arm. "Let's get back to Irana. I want to get you both out of here before someone gets curious about those shots."

"Do you want me to bandage that arm?" Pauley asked. "Or maybe a pressure bandage. Oh I guess not, the bleeding's almost stopped. Too bad. I was looking forward to practicing. How about my cleaning it instead?"

"I think I'll pass," Garrett said dryly. "I wouldn't want to run the risk of you having missed an episode in your TV course. I might get gangrene."

"I wouldn't do that. I told you, I'm a perfectionist."

"I'll still wait to have Irana look at it."

Emily stopped at the turn of the path and looked back at Staunton. The moonlight was full on his face, and that last, enraged, incredulous expression was frozen, his eyes wide open and staring up at the sky.

She almost expected him to stand up and come after—

"Emily?"

"Even in the end he didn't believe that he could be destroyed," she whispered. "He kept talking about his power, Zelov's power. He was mad, wasn't he?"

"I don't know," Garrett said. "You knew him better than I did."

"I'm not sure. I'd think anyone that evil would have to be insane." She moved her shoulders as if shaking off a burden. "It doesn't matter. He's dead. He can't hurt anyone else again." She turned her back on Staunton and grasped Garrett's arm. "But he hurt you, didn't he? Let's get you back to Irana."

TWENTY-TWO

When they arrived back at the road, Irana was kneeling on the ground beside Joslyn applying a pressure bandage. "Thank God," she said as she glanced up and saw Emily. "Are you hurt?"

"No, but Garrett is wounded. I don't think it's serious." She looked down at Joslyn. He was obviously unconscious and appeared stark pale in the light of the lantern sitting beside him. "Is he going to die?"

"Not if I can help it. He's lost a lot of blood, and I don't know if the bullet clipped an organ yet." She glanced at Garrett. "I told Dardon to phone for an ambulance. He went to the monastery to meet them and bring them here. I'm going with him to take care of him."

"I'm not arguing," Garrett said.

"You were angry with all of us when you got here." She looked at Emily. "And you blamed Joslyn enough to use him to bring us here. He may be dying because he wanted to make amends for what he did wrong."

"Are you trying to make me feel guilty?"

"No, I'm not judging you. I helped to make sure he'd come with us. Who knows? Maybe Joslyn was looking on you as his own messenger to help him make peace with himself." Her lips tightened. "I'm just saying that no matter how you feel about him, it's not going to stop me from helping him."

Emily stared at her for a moment. "I don't want him to die by Staunton's hand. Maybe I don't want him to die at all. But I can't forgive what he did. Don't expect me to pretend that I will."

Irana smiled. "No, I don't expect you to pretend anything. You're not at all good at it." Her gaze shifted to Pauley. "Come here and keep pressure on this bandage while I take care of Garrett's wound."

He moved forward with alacrity. "Right. That's really much more dramatic and worthwhile than cleaning up that knife scratch."

Garrett took out his telephone. "Give me five minutes, Irana."

"No. I'm going to do it now." Irana took his phone and handed it to Emily. "When that ambulance gets here, I want to be ready to go. Let her make your call or wait."

He frowned. "I have to move fast, dammit." He glanced at Irana's expression and then told Emily, "Call Ferguson's number. Tell him what happened here and that it's time for his payback. He's got to hop on a plane and get here right away. I'll meet him at the monastery." He turned to Irana. "Arrange to have Joslyn put in seclusion when you get to the hospital. I don't want him talking or any publicity."

"That's going to be hard to do," Irana said dryly. "He's been shot."

"A hunting accident."

"No one is going to believe that."

"But it will take them time to decide to go to investigate what really happened. As soon as Dardon gets back, I'll have him drag Borg's body into the woods. That will buy us time." He said to Emily, "Now, dammit, make that call."

"I admit I never expected to see you at a place like this, Garrett. I'd bet you're not planning on doing penance for all your past sins." Ferguson gazed at the two monks weeding the vegetable garden. He turned to Emily, who was sitting on a wooden bench beside the scullery door, and scowled. "You've caused me a hell of a lot of trouble."

"And, of course, I did it all on purpose." she said. "I planned it all to make your life inconvenient."

"Do you expect me to apologize? Okay, I'm sorry you had a bad time, but you made choices that gave me king-size headaches. You're still giving them to me. Bishop Dimitri's murder is going to be very delicate to handle." He turned back to Garrett. "You're sure it was Staunton who was responsible?"

"No question. You can probably scrounge up whatever proof you'll need." He shrugged. "Or plant what you can't find."

"You don't have much time. The bishop's housekeeper should be coming back to the residency within a few hours," Emily pointed out.

"She's already been diverted," Ferguson said absently. "I don't make mistakes like that."

Garrett smiled. "And I'd guess you sent someone into the forest to make sure the locals didn't find Borg's and Staunton's bodies until you were ready."

Ferguson didn't deny it. "You said that I was going to have my payoff. I wasn't going to be cheated."

"I've kept my promise. You're here, aren't you?"

"To get your ass out of hot water," Ferguson said. "And I'll do it. I just want to come out of this smelling like a rose and with enough prestige for a promotion, maybe even a political career."

"You're going to be the one who finally caught Emily's kidnapper and Levy's murderer. Added to that, you have the cachet of solving Bishop Dimitri's murder. It will be a major media circus."

"I want more."

Garrett tilted his head, waiting.

He nodded at Emily. "I want her."

"No," Garrett said sharply.

"Yes. She's the draw, the sun that will draw all that media to me. I want her to give interviews with me, to tell everyone how grateful she is that I managed to find Staunton."

"No way."

"I can make this cleanup the most pristine you've ever seen. No one gets hurt. I forget any illegal shenanigans you've pulled on the way to Staunton."

"You want the glory of catching Staunton. You'd do it anyway. Try again."

"Wait a minute, Garrett," Emily said. "I'm the one who's involved here. I'll make my own decision."

He swore beneath his breath. "They'll tear you apart, and he'll stand by watching and smiling like a Cheshire cat."

"I wouldn't allow anyone to tear me apart." She stared at Ferguson, considering the situation. "We might be able to work a deal. But it will be on my terms, under my control."

Ferguson gazed at her warily.

"I'll let you use me if you guarantee that Garrett won't ever suffer for either helping me or doing anything else even slightly irregular in the future. I can see you have rather an adversarial relationship. From now on Garrett will come up golden. You'll be the angel on his shoulder."

"Hell, no," Garrett said. "Emily, you're not going to—"

"Be quiet, Garrett. I know you probably may even enjoy battling with Ferguson, but that's too bad. I've got to set everything straight. I've got to pay you back for all you've done for me." She added soberly, "Though there's no way I can make up for the loss of your friend, Karif. But maybe I can make your future a little smoother." She glanced back at Ferguson. "And if you go back on your word later, you'll see a media blitz that will tear any career you might build to shreds. Don't ever doubt that, Ferguson."

Ferguson studied her before he nodded slowly. "Oh, I don't doubt it," he said. "Anything else?"

"Find a way to keep Garrett and Irana out of this."

"Anyone that's close to you will automatically be fodder for the paparazzi," Ferguson said.

"They won't be close to me." She didn't look at Garrett. "It will be just you and me, Ferguson." She could feel the storm of emotion building in Garrett. She had to get this over before he exploded. "One more thing. When you've milked this situation, I want you to ease me out of it. Find a way to make sure the media considers me a story that's run its course."

"That won't be easy."

"You can do it. I have faith in you. You appear to know every dirty trick in the book." She stood up. "Now I have to go to the hospital and see Irana. I'm sure you're going to be very busy in that forest, doing some intricate staging."

"Yes." Ferguson hesitated. "You'd better tell your friend that we're transferring Joslyn to a hospital outside London within the next few hours. I can control the situation better there."

Ferguson was obviously already in high gear, she thought. "You'll have to talk to

Irana about that. She may have something to say to you." She stared him in the eye. "Now, do we have a deal?"

"Yes." He smiled faintly. "Though you practically stole the shirt off my back. It's going to be a nightmare erasing Garrett and your doctor friend from the equation." He was silent a moment. "But I've been thinking that maybe I'll recast Staunton in this story."

"Recast?"

"Well, since the hammer has never shown up, it would be counterproductive to bring up this wild tale about Nicholas II's billions. It will complicate things enormously. It's probably a bunch of bull anyway."

"Really?"

He nodded. "So why don't we do a little background tinkering and make Staunton a terrorist. He kidnapped both you and Levy to make a statement and would have bargained your lives for a release of political prisoners if I hadn't tracked him down and freed you."

"Go on."

"The bishop's death could be attributed to revenge against the Church. We can find a way to ignore Babin's and Zelov's deaths. The attack on Mykala Island had a distinct terrorist profile."

"And?"

"That's all. I killed Staunton and his cohort, and we're working diligently on apprehending his cell group."

"Could you really stage a big lie like that?"

He smiled. "Watch me."

"I'm not going to lie," Emily said.

"You don't have to make a statement at all. I'll do all the talking." His brows rose. "Yes?"

She nodded slowly. "I don't care what you say about him as long as everyone knows what a bastard he was." She turned and walked away.

Garrett started to follow her, then whirled on Ferguson. "You take care of her," he said fiercely. "You treat her as if she was made of the finest crystal. If you don't, I'll know about it, and I'll come after you." He turned and caught up with Emily in three strides. "You know why he's concocting this bullshit about terrorists, don't you?"

She nodded. "It's starting all over again. He's going to try to find the Tsar's treasure for himself."

"Ferguson is going to go crazy sifting through Staunton's belongings, trying to find a clue that will lead him to the hammer."

"Good. I can't think of anyone I'd rather see go off his rocker."

"You don't think he'll find it." Garrett's gaze was narrowed on her face. "That's why you agreed."

"I agreed because enough people have died over that damn treasure. And it will never stop. Even if the Russian government took possession, the corruption would go on. Irana said that Nartova told Bishop Dimitri that the only way to win the treasure was to leave it alone. I believe he was right."

"And what about Bishop Dimitri's plan to give the money to needy children?"

"A wonderful scheme. Yet whom could you trust to make sure that all the money was protected and went to charity? You saw what happened when Joslyn and Bishop Dimitri tried to do it. No, let Ferguson beat his head against the wall, then start believing that the treasure was the myth he called it."

He said slowly, "As I said, you seem very sure he won't find it among Staunton's effects. Why?"

She looked at him. "Do you really want to know? Do you want to find Zelov's hammer?"

He shook his head. "I can't imagine anything I want less. I have plenty of money, and I don't need that kind of burden. It would smother me."

"I don't have plenty of money, but I feel the same way. It would be the only way that Zelov and Staunton could really destroy me." They had reached the car, and she turned to face him and braced herself. "I don't want you to come with me to the hospital to see Irana."

"This is good-bye?" His lips twisted. "You're cutting me loose?"

"I don't want anyone to see us together."

"And I don't give a damn."

"I know. But I have to wipe the slate clean. I don't want debts on either side." She paused. "And I want to put time and space between us. I want to know that it wasn't circumstance or pity that brought us this close."

"I've never pitied you. For God's sake, you should know that by—" he stopped. "I'm not going to change your mind, am I?"

"Time and space," she repeated. She would *not* cry. She was right. This was better for both of them.

But dear God, it was hard.

"Then get the hell out of here." He opened the car door for her. "Start chalking up your damn time. Because I'm going to be on your doorstep before you know it. Be ready for me."

She'd be ready for him. She was ready for him now.

Don't look at him; he'd see the tears.

Don't say the words. Just start the car and drive away.

Don't say the words. . . .

"What do you mean he's taking Joslyn away from here?" Irana demanded as she strode down the hospital corridor toward Emily. "I'm not sure he's ready to travel. He just regained consciousness an hour ago."

"If Ferguson has to wrap Joslyn in cotton

wool, I'd be willing to bet he'll be on a plane out of here before the end of the day," Emily said. "You'd better get him ready." She paused. "And you'd better go with him, Irana."

"That sounded loaded with significance. Am I going on the lam?"

She smiled faintly. "You didn't find that phrase in a Jane Austen book."

"Am I?"

"No, but Joslyn will be in seclusion until he recovers, and it will be more comfortable for you to share it."

"I don't usually do what's comfortable for me."

"I know. But you'll be doing me a favor this time if you do."

"Why?"

"Ferguson and I are going on the road. Lots of paparazzi and TV cameras. You don't want to be involved."

"I might."

"I don't want you involved. You'd be defeating the purpose."

"What is the purpose?"

"Going back to square one. If it had been Ferguson instead of Garrett who rescued me from Staunton in those mountains, it's what I would have done anyway. Ferguson would have seen to it. But now we can get something for my trouble."

"For heaven's sake, you're trying to protect all of us," Irana said in disgust. "And I thought Garrett was bad."

"Will you go with Joslyn?"

She didn't speak for a moment. "Is Garrett furious?"

"Among other things. Will you go?"

"Probably. I can't see how I can help you, and I somehow feel that there may be more I have to do with Joslyn. You'll keep in touch?"

"No, not until no one is interested in who my friends are."

"But you'll call when you need me."

"Oh, yes." She gave Irana a hug, then held her close for an instant longer before she released her. Her eyes were stinging again. "But then, I always need you, Irana." She smiled shakily. "Oh, by the way, Ferguson is going to be spinning a fairy tale about what went on with Staunton. There's no longer any Tsar's treasure. Don't be surprised when you see the story in the newspapers."

"How did that come about?"

"I think Ferguson has decided he wants to be a Tsar, too. He'll be disappointed. He won't find the hammer."

"You're sure? Did Staunton tell you where it is?"

Emily shook her head. "No, he didn't tell me." She gave Irana another hug and turned to go. "Good-bye, Irana. Keep safe and take care."

"Of course, I will." Irana's face lit with her luminous smile. "I told you, that's what I do. I'm one of the caretakers of the world."

The caretaker.

Whom could you trust to make sure all that money was protected and went to charity?

And did Emily have the right to take the responsibility of denying the caretakers of the world?

"What is it?" Irana was studying Emily's expression.

"You can forget this or remember it," Emily said. "Your choice. I choose to forget it. Staunton didn't tell me where he hid the hammer. But he was comparing himself constantly with Zelov while we were talking. He was jealous of him. And one of the things that he said was that he wanted to take me to the museum where the hammer had been on exhibit all those years, the one across from the execution house. He wanted me to visit another site of Zelov's failure."

Irana's eyes widened. "You actually think he put the hammer back there?"

"Mikhail Zelov wasn't able to find a way to get the hammer out of that museum. Too many guards. Staunton would have been delighted to prove that he could not only put the hammer back somewhere in that museum, but steal it away again whenever it suited him. It would prove he was better than Zelov." She turned away again. "Of course, it's just a guess. Do whatever you like with it. Except let it destroy you. That's not one of the choices."

She didn't look back as she walked toward the elevators.

Four months later
People's Museum
Ekaterinaburg, Russia

The hammer was lying beside two huge fake rocks in a display depicting the progress of man through the centuries. The central figures were a peasant farmer and his wife laboring in the field.

Irana had thought the hammer would have been hidden away somewhere on the premises, but Staunton, with his customary boldness, had chosen to place it on exhibit. Because it would have been harder to retrieve and another taunt at Mikhail Zelov if Staunton managed to do it?

Whatever his reason Irana was sure that the hammer lying on the ground as if carelessly tossed there was Zelov's hammer. It was crude and smaller than she would have thought, but it had a hefty ten-inch wooden handle and an iron head. It looked ancient and primitive but as if it could strike a sharp blow.

Why was she so certain it was Zelov's hammer? Irana wondered. Why had she felt as if she recognized that hammer from the moment she had seen it? Why couldn't she force herself to look away from it?

And why has she felt compelled to come back from England to see if Emily had been right about its being here?

Too many questions. But one of those

questions had been answered. The others might never be answered.

She finally managed to pull her gaze away, turned, and headed for the front entrance. Her flight to return to England and Peter Joslyn was due to leave in two hours. She needed to be on it.

Two days later
Chadwick Estate, England

"You're looking much better, Peter," Irana said as she walked across the terrace toward Joslyn. "Your color is good, and you appear more relaxed than I've ever seen you. Soon you'll have no need for me."

"I feel better." He smiled as he gestured for her to sit down in the chair opposite him. "Why not? The sun is shining, and it's a beautiful day. My daughter is down from university, and she keeps me young. But I'll always need you, Irana. My wife is convinced you saved my life."

"She's right; I'm a very good doctor." She amended, "Well, I helped. God gave me the skill, and your family gave you the reason to fight. You're very lucky, Peter."

"Yes, I am. Not only to have you as my doctor, but also as my friend. I missed you while you were gone. You must think I'm doing better if you thought I was well enough for you to leave me."

"I had some business that I had to take care of, and you were beginning to resent my hovering."

"I didn't resent you. As I said, I know I'm lucky." He looked down at the newspaper in front of him. "Luckier than Emily. Why don't they leave her alone?"

Irana glanced at the photo. "Ferguson is feeding the frenzy. But she'll be fine. She just has to get through it. She's very strong."

"Yes." His gaze went to the beautifully manicured lawns stretching out before them. "I wish she'd let me help her."

"I know you do," Irana said. "So do I. But friends sometimes have to step back."

"She doesn't regard me as a friend." His expression clouded. "Who can blame her after all I've done to her? She went through hell, and I'm going to get off scot-free. I wish Ferguson hadn't been quite so efficient in erasing my involvement. I should be punished."

"You are being punished," Irana said. "Your soul is scarred, and you're suffering. You've lost your friend, Dimitri. You live with regret and guilt. That's great punishment, Peter."

"Not enough."

"Then God will have to decide. I hear you're planning on going back to Ethiopia on a mission as soon as you're able."

He nodded. "To help the children. Dimitri would want me to do it."

"Yes, he wanted desperately to help the children, didn't he? One of the last things he said to me was that he had to protect the hammer and protect the children." She followed his gaze to the rolling green lawns. "It was a rather odd phrasing. I didn't think anything of it at the time. It was only later that I began to wonder. I had plenty of time, staying here in your lovely home for these months." She could sense the slight stiffening of his body. "There were so many things that puzzled me."

"Really? I thought everything had pretty well been explained."

"Yes, so many explanations about the

Tsar and Zelov and the great, grand fortune that everyone was after. All that was clear to me."

Joslyn's expression was distinctly wary. "And what was not?"

"The Tsar. He never trusted Zelov, but he accepted the hammer to hide that final amulet. Why?"

"Zelov convinced him that it was lucky, that it would bring him good fortune."

"And Zelov had been working for years, trying to use the hammer to cement his influence with the Tsar. That was only the last and most successful attempt. Why would he think that he could gain power in that way?"

"I have no idea." Joslyn looked away from her. "Why don't you tell me?"

"Nicholas II was extremely religious."

"That's no secret. Oh, yes, I remember that Zelov told the Tsar the hammer had been blessed by Rasputin."

"Yes, but that was almost an afterthought. Zelov had already prepared the way with the Tsar."

"You're talking a great deal about this hammer."

"Because it always seemed strange to

me that you and Bishop Dimitri would be so determined to get the hammer back." She paused. "Even for the money to help a world of children. "

His gaze shifted back to her. "What are you saying, Irana?"

"I'm saying the Tsar's fortune would lure most people. Not you, not Bishop Dimitri, not Bishop Nartova. So it had to be something else."

"Of course, it did. To keep Mikhail Zelov from getting the money, then to keep it away from other factions. Like Staunton."

Irana shook her head. "Plausible. Not enough."

"Then what?"

"The hammer itself," she said quietly. "I think that when Mikhail Zelov went to Bishop Nartova, he told him something that made it certain that he'd get his money to become a king in America."

"Really? What would that be?"

"Zelov was obsessed with the hammer. He'd brought it back from Jerusalem. He thought it gave him power. Add it all together. What hammer could he have unearthed in the Holy Land that would make him think that?"

She could see the pulse leap in Joslyn's temple. He didn't answer for a long moment. "You're talking about the Crucifix. Very far-fetched, Irana."

"Yes, it stunned me when I realized that's where it was leading. Far-fetched and probably completely impossible to prove. But I think Bishop Nartova must have believed Mikhail Zelov enough to try to do anything to keep it away from him. The hammer could represent the holiest of sacrifices, but Zelov was using it for greed and evil. Nartova couldn't bear the thought of risking the chance that the hammer in Zelov's possession was the one used on that day." She shook her head. "And neither could Bishop Dimitri. Nartova probably confided his suspicions to him, and your friend wanted only to protect it from the Zelovs of the world."

"If you're correct, it would seem that it all went wrong," Joslyn said.

"Bishop Dimitri was trying to make it right."

"You're saying that there's no amulet in that hammer, no Tsar's fortune?"

"No, I believe that the Tsar did use it for

that purpose. But it wasn't the treasure you and Dimitri and Nartova were protecting."

Joslyn stared her in the eye. "I'm not admitting anything to you, Irana."

"I know. Bishop Dimitri probably made you swear not to mention it to anyone," Irana said gently. "And you'd never break your word."

"No, if I gave my word, I'd never break it," Joslyn said. "And you're right, it could never be proved, but it could cause endless conflict and turmoil if even the possibility of its existence was mentioned."

"I agree. That's what has been troubling me." She smiled slightly. "And that's why I decided to talk to you about it."

"It shouldn't trouble you. The hammer has disappeared and may never be found again. That bastard Staunton must have hidden it very well."

Irana nodded. "Yes, I believe you're right about that. He did hide it well."

"Then what are you going to do?" Joslyn's voice was urgent. "Leave it alone, Irana. You know what an uproar you could start if you begin making statements that even hint at what you're saying."

"I'm not one to hint at anything, Peter. I have a tendency to say everything with deplorable frankness."

"Not so deplorable except in this case."

"You're still trying to protect the hammer, Peter. You don't have to protect it from me."

"I have to protect it for Dimitri. I have to do what he'd want me to do. *If* there was any truth in your supposition, Dimitri would have said that if the hammer is ever found, it would be better to use the Tsar's fortune for good and not address the question of the origin of the hammer at all. Leave it to God to decide."

"I try to do that, but sometimes God wants us to handle things ourselves."

"Not now," Joslyn said emphatically. "Don't do it, Irana."

Was he right? Her heart and soul were leaning toward helping those children just as Bishop Dimitri had wanted to do. But to throw the Christian world into conflict over the hammer would be a terrible thing to do. It was what Zelov and Staunton would have loved to have happen.

And there were so many questions, and some answers, Joslyn didn't even know about. He thought the hammer was still lost, and that would have postponed any decision. She had not really come to Joslyn for advice, she had just wanted confirmation and to share a heavy burden. It had probably not been fair to him. She had always shouldered her own burdens, and in the end this would be no exception.

Irana once more gazed out at the verdant lawns and brilliant blue sky. It was a day so beautiful that you wanted to tuck it into your memory to hold forever. She had many of those memories from Mykala. Each day was a gift and a blessing.

Why was she worrying when she had already been given so many gifts? She must only clear her mind of all selfishness, and the answers would come to her. To act now? To act later? To not act at all? It would come to her what her purpose was in this if she just accepted it as she did each sparkling day.

A blessing . . .

"Bishop Dimitri was a very wise man, Peter." Irana smiled as she leaned back in her chair. "Yes, I'm sure God can take care of it. Let's leave it to him for now."

EPILOGUE

Fourteen Months Later
Dylan Bay, North Carolina

Garrett was walking down the beach toward her.

Emily stiffened, then forced herself to relax. Don't let it mean too much.

Bull. How could she help letting it mean too much? She had missed him every minute of every day since she had left him at the monastery. Just seeing him smile at her was throwing her into a tailspin.

She stood up on the dune, her bare feet sinking into the warm sand as she faced him. "You're looking . . . well."

"Is that all you've got to say?" he asked. "I've been waiting for you to call me for over a year. I was wondering if you'd ever get around to it."

"It took a long time for the media to look on me as past history." She paused. "And I wanted to make sure that all the scars were on the way to healing. I wasn't going to be good for anyone else until I was good for myself."

"You had to do that alone?" His face was without expression. "You had to close me out?"

"I thought I did." And she hadn't been sure he would tolerate it. She still wasn't sure. He had come when she called him, but now that he was here, she couldn't read him. She turned and started down the dune. "Will you walk me back to my cottage?"

"Why not?" He fell into step beside her. "It's the first thing you've asked of me. I had to watch you going through that hell Ferguson set up for you, and I couldn't do a thing."

"It wasn't pleasant, but it wasn't hell. I just had to hold on to the knowledge that it would eventually be over." She smiled faintly. "And it lightened the load seeing Ferguson so frustrated when he couldn't find any trace of that hammer among Staunton's belongings. He came up with the three amulets facsimiles, a map, and a copy of the *Book of Living* but nothing else. No hammer. He traced Staunton's steps back six months just to be sure he wasn't missing something."

"Has he given up?"

"I have no idea. I think so. He's out of my life now. I want him to stay that way." She looked out at the sea. "I'm going back to work soon. I'm only here getting my head together. I rented this place because it was on the beach, and yet it had those ten acres of woods adjoining it." She nodded at the stretch of green in the distance. "Trees to climb, animals to photograph . . ."

"As you did with your father. Is it bringing back memories?"

"Yes. And they're all good. But you can't live on memories." She looked at him. "How is Irana?"

"You haven't talked to her?"

"No, you were the first person I called. She was going to be the second. What's she doing?"

"Her hospital on Mykala is rebuilt now.

She's fine-tuning the staff and equipment."

"That's all?"

"That's enough." He glanced at her curiously. "What did you expect?"

She didn't know what she had expected. Irana would have done nothing hurriedly or without the deepest consideration. She might be going to act later . . . or not at all. As Emily had said, it was her choice.

She answered his question with one of her own. "What about Pauley?"

"Pauley is working with Irana on the island. He's been doing everything from keeping her labor force in line to in-depth research into some of her projects."

Projects. What projects? Pauley and Irana? What an unusual and intriguing combination. What use could Irana have for—

She suddenly went rigid as the answer came to her. "Dear God."

"What's wrong?"

She smiled brilliantly. "Nothing. Not one thing on the face of the earth. It just occurred to me that if you wanted to secretly and safely launder or distribute a billion or so dollars to charities, who would be better able to do it than Pauley?"

"You think Irana has the treasure?"

She nodded. "Oh, yes. It will be interesting to find out—"

"I don't care about the treasure," he suddenly said roughly. "And I'm tired of your talking about Irana and Pauley and Ferguson." He stopped and turned to face her. "I want you to talk about me. I want you to talk about us. That's why I came here. Now cut to the chase. You've had your damn time and space. A hell of a lot too much of both for me. Now talk to me."

"What do you want me to say?" No, that was too passive, and she was not feeling in the least passive. "And just why did you come here? It could be because you wanted to tell me that I was right to take that time, and you decided that we couldn't make a relationship work. How do I know?" She stepped closer. "But here's what I do know. I've never met a man who I wanted or respected as much as I do you. Do I love you? I think I do, but I'm never going to be sure unless I live with you and share something besides threats and trauma. We deserve that chance to discover who we really are together. So that's what I'm going to do. If you don't want to do that, then I'll just have to follow you around and dog your footsteps until you give in. You'll have to have me arrested as a stalker to get rid of me. And when they let me out of jail, I'll come to you again." She drew a deep breath. "So why not save time and give in now? I promise I'll make it worth your while."

He smiled. "What an interesting offer."

"Is that all you've got to say?"

"Yes, I'd better accede graciously because I'm clearly not going to change your mind." He reached out and cupped her face in his hands, and said thickly, "Thank God."

For a moment she couldn't get her breath for the rush of sheer joy. Oh, yes, thank God. She said unsteadily, "I believe that means I'm not going to have to do any serious pursuit."

He kissed her lightly. "It means that I'm taking you up on your promise to make it worth my while." He kissed her again, not so lightly. "For the next fifty or sixty years. After that, we'll renegotiate." He pushed her away and took her hand. "But right now you're going to show me your cottage. It has a bed I assume?"

"Absolutely."

"Then we'll start there, and we may end there." He smiled down at her. "But maybe tomorrow we'll take time for you to take me to your woods, and you can show me a little of what your father taught you." His warm grasp tightened on her hand as they started down the beach. "If we're embarking on this journey of discovery, I think I want to know that side of you, too."